For Better

And

For Worse

An Israel Odyssey

Batya Kroopnick

For Better And For Worse
An Israel Odyssey
ISBN978-965-92480-0-1

Copyright © 2015 by Batya Kroopnick

In Memory of my Father

Ya'acov ben Mordechai

Jerry Snyder

תנצב"ה

CONTENTS

THANK YOU

My greatest thanks is to G-d for all He has given me, including a rich and meaningful life in the Land of Israel.

I especially want to thank my oldest friend, Elisheva Levin, to whom I am eternally grateful for being the beacon that led me to Israel and for pointing me in the direction that would ultimately keep me here forever.

With heartfelt appreciation, I would also like to acknowledge the following people for their help at various stages in producing this book:

- ❖ Michal Draizen, Sara Feld, Liora Silberstein, Judy Simon, Shira Victor and Hadassa Yates—for the time and effort they put into reviewing the manuscript and for their valuable feedback.
- ❖ Bracha Steinberg, Naomi Stiebel and Shifrah Devorah Witt—for editing.
- ❖ Gila Green and Bracha Steinberg—for copyediting and proofreading.
- ❖ Moshe Kaplan—for layout and typesetting.
- ❖ Chaya Sarah Ben Eitan—for cover design and graphics.
- ❖ My husband and children—for their support and patience.

I have enormous gratitude to all of you for your helpful advice and encouragement. Thank you!

TO THE READER

A few notes before you begin:

* The stories in this book are based on actual events and real people. I've changed names and some details, so any resemblance to people with the same names or descriptions is purely coincidental.

* While preserving the essence of each story, I've also enhanced certain elements. At the same time, I've done my best to reconstruct the historical events and personal experiences as accurately as possible, spending many hours jogging my memory and researching facts.

* Though the stories that take place in Or Tzion are genuine, the town itself is a fictitious place created to represent various Jewish communities in Judea and Samaria.

* To help readers who aren't familiar with the Hebrew words appearing intermittently throughout the book, I've defined them in footnotes. Please also note that in Hebrew transliterations, "ch" should be pronounced as a throaty/guttural h and not as these letters sound in English.

MAP OF ISRAEL

LEBANON

SECURITY ZONE

● Kiryat
Shemona

Nahariya ●   ● Mt. Meron

*GOLAN
HEIGHTS*

● Tzfat

SYRIA

Haifa ●   *GALILEE*

Tiberias ●

SEA OF
GALILEE

MEDITERRANEAN SEA

Kadim ●
Ganim ●

Sa Nur ●
Netanya ●   Homesh ●

SAMARIA

Herzliya ●

Tel Aviv ●   ● Shilo
Petah ●   *Or Tzion ●
Tikvah   Beit El ●   ● Ofra-
Ramallah ●   Amona

Ashdod ●

Jerusalem ●

DEAD SEA

Ashkelon ●

Gaza City ●

*GAZA STRIP
(GUSH KATIF)*   Sderot ●

Hevron ●

JORDAN

JUDEA

● Be'er Sheva

NEGEV

EGYPT

● Ramon Crater

SINAI DESERT

*Fictitious town

Eilat ●

For Better

And

For Worse

An Israel Odyssey

(October 2014)

"Oh my G-d!" I braced myself as we skidded off the highway and crashed right into the metal side barrier. The front of the car I was riding in now looked like an accordion. Miraculously, everybody in it walked away with only bruises or scrapes—except for me. I landed in the hospital with two broken ribs and a crushed leg.

The accident ruined my visit to the US. Now it would be extended for much longer than I'd planned and I'd be spending most of it in a rehabilitation facility.

My family in Chicago and my worried husband and children back in Israel were relieved that I would be all right. I was, of course, grateful to be alive and thankful that I'd taken out overseas medical insurance before traveling. Now, all I wanted was to recover quickly and get back home.

"So, how'd you end up living all the way in Israel, Shelly?" Fran, the Asian-American nurse at the rehabilitation center was checking my blood pressure. "It's so far away."

"And why'd you stay there?" Carol was standing on the other side of my bed waiting to begin our morning physical therapy session. "There always seems to be problems over there."

I looked at the two women in white and smiled. "It's kind of a long story." I couldn't explain in just a sentence or two how decades ago I'd left a comfortable secular American life to live halfway across the world in the troubled Middle East. It would take more than a few short breaths to describe the encounters with anti-Semitism I'd had in the US or to share the adventures, struggles and miracles I'd experienced in Israel. I would want to tell how I'd fallen in love with the Jewish country and formed a tight bond with the people and with my religion, and how I'd wrestled to cope with all the difficulties and conflicts that challenged me along the way.

Now, an observant Jew and a devoted Israeli in my early fifties, bedridden and far from my normally active life in the Holy Land, I had plenty of time to tell my tale. But I couldn't imagine that single, hard-working Fran or mother-of-two Carol with their busy schedules would be interested in hearing it.

I was wrong.

"I always work the morning shift and you're the last patient I check on," Fran told me, removing the blood pressure cuff from around my thin arm. "Maybe while you and Carol work on that leg of yours, you can tell us about it."

"That works," Carol said. "You can do two things at once, can't you?"

They both stared at me with smiles on their faces. "You want me to tell you about my life?" I asked, with surprise. "Why?" I looked from young, slim Fran with her long black hair pulled up in a high ponytail to older, heavier Carol whose short blond hair was tucked behind her ears.

"Well," Carol began, "I'm Jewish and my mother was a Holocaust survivor. After World War II ended, she had to decide whether to come to the United States or go to Israel. As you see, she came here. But if it had been different, I would have been born an Israeli." Carol shrugged her shoulders. "I've always wanted to know more about Israel."

Fran moved the blood pressure machine to the side and told me why she was interested. "I'm also a first generation American. My family is originally from Japan, but my younger sister and I were born in the US. My father was a businessman and before my parents moved here, they traveled a lot, mostly around Asia and the Middle East. When my sister and I were young they told us all kinds of stories about the different countries they'd visited. Even now, as an adult, I'm curious about those parts of the world."

"She was so excited when she found out that you live in Israel," Carol spoke for Fran.

"Israel is in the news a lot," Fran said. "But that was one place my parents didn't make it to on all their trips. So I never heard anything about that country from them." She pointed her pen at me. "You're the first person I've met who actually lives there."

"We'd love to hear a firsthand account of what life in Israel is really like." Carol's gleaming eyes revealed her eagerness.

I didn't have a problem opening up to others and I didn't want to dampen Fran and Carol's enthusiasm, but I wondered if I'd be able to give them all that they were looking for. "I can only tell you about my personal experiences," I answered truthfully.

"That's good enough for me." Fran said, pulling over a chair and sitting down. "I've got time before I have to be at the fitness center to teach my afternoon exercise class."

Carol put a pillow under my knee and positioned my foot. "Let's get started on that leg of yours. Try to lift a little higher than you did yesterday."

Sinking my teeth into my bottom lip, I carefully moved my injured limb in an upward motion and then slowly lowered it back down onto the bed.

"You're doing great," Carol praised. "So, how 'bout that story?"

"Okay." I was more than happy to oblige. "And now," I said with an exaggerated nod of my head. "Get ready for the life and times of the infamous American-Israeli celebrity... Shelly Kaplan."

Carol chuckled and Fran clapped her hands with fake excitement. I smiled at them again. Then turning more serious, I took a moment to think back in time. Where to start? As my mind flew over the years, my eyes brightened.

I knew *exactly* where to begin...

PART ONE

August 1972—August 1984

·✧· *CHAPTER 1* ·✧·

KEEPING THE PEACE

(August 1972)

It was the first berry fight of the summer. Heidi and I were whipping handfuls of the little red ammunition at our friends. Although I was nine and Heidi was eight, the youngest of the 'warriors,' we were determined to remain in the battle.

"We're gonna win this time!" I shouted to Heidi, as we chased after two kids from the opposing team. Screeching with excitement, my neighborhood friends and I were running in all directions, dodging in and out of backyards and alleyways and sprinting down walkways between the houses.

Summers on the block where I grew up in Chicago were always filled with fun and adventure. I spent much of the long hot days playing with my older brother and sister and some of our neighbors in our predominantly Jewish neighborhood. Our group of friends ranged from eight to fourteen years of age and consisted of a couple of churchgoing Christians and several non-observant Jews. That morning, after filling containers with inedible berries that we picked from bushes around the neighborhood, we all gathered at a pre-designated meeting place.

Then the fun began.

In the midst of all the racing around, laughing, yelling, and berry hurling, a woman's loud, angry voice suddenly pierced the air.

"Shut up, you lousy Jews, you no-good kids making so much noise!"

All nine of us froze in our tracks.

"Just shut up! Why do we need all you stupid Jews around here? Just shut up..." The shouting and cursing increased in volume with each word, assaulting anyone within hearing range.

It wasn't the first time we'd been subjected to verbal attacks by our elderly neighbor. Mrs. Mahoney, a big woman with pasty white skin, a large fleshy nose and a painful-looking limp, lived with her retired husband two houses away. Usually, she was very friendly to everyone. But occasionally she drank, and then the tirades began.

Our game was suddenly over. Fearfully, we each crept like little thieves towards our homes. I took the alley route behind my house, where I spotted my father inside our open garage. He was standing still with his head down, listening to our neighbor's offensive outbursts. Relieved to find him close by, I ducked inside.

As we waited together for the barrage of insults to end, I began to feel foolish hiding out in the garage. Young and scared, I wasn't going to respond to Mrs. Mahoney's ranting. But I wished my father and the other adults who heard the yelling through their open windows would stand up to her.

*Why was everyone so easily intimidated? Why didn't anyone tell **her** to be quiet? She was the one with the problem, not us.* I felt ashamed of myself and my friends for being so nervous and frightened, like cockroaches that scatter when the light is suddenly turned on. *How can we let ourselves be treated this way, especially in our own backyards?*

Seconds later the shouting ended. Slicking back thin

strands of hair that had fallen forward over his glasses, my father slowly lifted his bowed head. Then, without a word, he pushed the lawn mower out of the garage and began cutting the grass.

I went into the house. *It's not fair!* Sitting in the dark at the bottom of our basement steps, I took off my pointed cat-eye glasses and wiped my red, perspiring face with the back of my hand. *We were having such a great time before our fun was ruined.* My frown was so long, it felt like the edges of my mouth could touch the floor. I wanted someone to say something, someone to do something about the incident. But nobody did. Everyone just went back to their daily lives as if nothing had happened.

It was how we kept the peace.

"Being Jewish wasn't a problem for me," I told Fran and Carol, while Carol adjusted the pillow under my leg. "But as I grew older, I realized it *was* a problem for many other people. Usually it wasn't something personal. It was more like a disdain or irritation that people had about Jews existing in the world. I gradually came to understand something that Adolf Hitler had made very clear: no matter how hard one tries to cover up or disregard his Jewish identity, there's simply no erasing it."

NEO-NAZIS ON THE MARCH
(May 1978)

When the neo-Nazis announced their plan to hold a rally and march in front of the Skokie Village Hall, I was horrified. Skokie was home to tens of thousands of Jews, many of them Holocaust survivors. Northern Chicagoans frequently visited friends or family who lived in the nearby suburb, often stopping at one of its many Jewish shops, pharmacies, restaurants or bakeries. Nobody ever imagined that one day neo-Nazis in militant uniforms, complete with knee-high black boots and swastikas, would be threatening to parade around in one of Skokie's peaceful neighborhoods.

Jews for miles around were disturbed and outraged about the prospect of such a blatantly hateful and inciting event taking place in the primarily Jewish suburb. Skokie officials passed ordinances aimed at outlawing the Nazi demonstration, but the American Civil Liberties Union (ACLU) fought for the neo-Nazis' right to march. The case was brought all the way to the U.S. Supreme Court. Now, more than a year after the Nazi's plan had been announced, we were all waiting for the court's decision.

"How could anybody defend Nazis' rights to anything?" I chimed in at an unusually serious supper table conversation my family was having before the case was determined. "The Holocaust wasn't that long ago. How could they even think of ruling in their favor?"

"From what I've been reading, they'll probably be allowed to march," my seventeen-year-old bookworm sister predicted.

Passing the potatoes down to my mother at the other end of the table, my father explained why my sister might be right. "Unfortunately, the Constitution's First Amendment protects the neo-Nazis' freedom to assemble and freedom of speech, the same as anybody else."

I knew that rallies and demonstrations were a form of speech that needed to be protected. But I couldn't believe that the harm this type of gathering would cause to so many people could be considered less important than guarding the privileges of Nazis, neo or otherwise.

"Aren't they supposed to be allowed these rights only if what they're doing doesn't endanger or cause harm to other people?" A sophomore in high school, I was trying to remember what we'd learned in class about the Constitution.

My brother, who'd just come home from college for the summer, looked up from his plate. "If they actually do this thing, it will be the Nazis who will be in danger."

Jews from all across the country stood in solidarity with Skokie. Thousands of Jewish ACLU members resigned, while others communicated their support for the threatened suburb. For their part, many of the more local Jews in the Chicago area had no intention of standing by quietly if the neo-Nazis marched in Skokie. They would join in on counter-demonstrations and would hold protests of their own. They would come armed with baseball bats, rocks and any other head-splitting paraphernalia that could be acquired.

As it turned out, the Illinois Supreme Court issued a permit allowing the march to be held in Skokie.

"This will be the most painful freedom-of-speech experience ever," one of the Jewish boys in my history class announced after we'd heard the news.

"This time, we'll make sure that *they're* the ones who suffer, not us!" another classmate said, slamming his fist into the palm of his hand.

Being both short and slight in build, I was a little afraid of aggressively protesting against the marchers. I didn't believe in violent demonstrations, but I did believe in fighting for our right to live without fear or harassment. So I decided that if the event actually took place, I would do my best to support those who would be attempting to break it up.

Ironically, the neo-Nazis decided to move their rally to downtown Chicago. They'd held demonstrations there in the past, before they were banned from the area. Now they claimed they were willing to change location and forego Skokie because they'd just won the right to protest again in the city.

That's baloney. I'm sure the real reason they're not marching in Skokie is because they hadn't counted on us "weak" Jews flexing our muscles or making so much trouble for them. They're worried about all the threats against them if they did demonstrate there.

The change of venue didn't make me feel better about the whole thing. Although it was a relief to have the blatant anti-Semites far away from Skokie, I felt that the move back to Chicago was only a small victory for the Jews. For the Nazis, however, it was a great face-saving tactic.

"How has this really changed anything?" I asked my friends on the way home from school.

"Well, for one thing, I probably won't make it downtown to demonstrate against the march," one of my girlfriends said. "It's much farther away and not as easy to get there."

"I won't be going either," replied another. "I don't think Nazis marching in Chicago is as bad as marching in Skokie."

It seemed to me that many Jews had lost their ambition to thwart the whole affair. Furious crowds did show up to counter the neo-Nazis in Chicago, but not the hordes that were expected in Skokie. I thought the post-Holocaust slogan "Never again!" didn't seem to carry much weight after the fact; the Holocaust had actually returned to haunt many people. Like a poisonous germ it had reinfected many wounds.

Jews worldwide, especially those living in Skokie, would probably never forget this particular struggle against the unleashed hatred and evil that had once again threatened their people.

Neither would I.

·❧· CHAPTER 3 ·❧·

"I remember that whole Nazi incident," Carol said. "It put Skokie on the map for a lot of us who'd never even heard of the place. And thinking about it now, I can only imagine what an event like that would have done to my mother, as a Holocaust survivor, if she'd lived anywhere near there."

"It's wild that they were actually allowed to hold that march," Fran said, "and wherever they wanted!"

"Believe it or not, these kinds of rallies and demonstrations still happen," I told Fran, "and not just here in the US, but in lots of other countries too." I winced in pain, as Carol slowly lifted my leg off the pillow.

"That's pretty horrible," Fran's voice had an edge to it. "I'm not Jewish and I don't know very much about the Holocaust, but I've seen movies and read some novels that show how anti-Semitism has plagued the Jews over the centuries." Fran caught my eye. "Hopefully that was the last of it that *you* had to deal with."

"Well," I let out a sigh, as Carol set my leg back down, "not exactly."

WITH FRIENDS LIKE THESE...
(July 1979)

For years, Debby, Pam and I were inseparable friends. Debby was a soft-spoken brunette with pale skin and light blue eyes. Pam was strong-minded with dark, frizzy hair. And I was something in-between: outgoing and near-sighted with green eyes and light brown hair. Living within a few houses of each other, we had all played together as babies and had always been in the same class in school.

It wasn't easy for our threesome when Debby's family moved from the city to a cottage in the suburbs the summer before our senior year of high school. After her family was settled in, Pam and I made the trip to Debby's new home to spend the afternoon with her and to meet some of her new girlfriends. Everything was going well as the eight of us lounged around in Debby's living room, snacking on chips and drinking soda... until the Jewish jokes began.

"What's the difference between a Jew and a pizza? Pizzas don't scream when they're put in the oven!"

Debby's new friends snickered at the first joke and then came up with more.

"How do you get a Jew to start a marathon? Roll a penny down a hill."

"What's the object of Jewish football? To get the quarter back."

"How do you get a hundred Jews into a Volkswagen Beetle? Two in the back, two in the front and ninety-six in the ashtray!"

What's going on here? I tried to hide my shock and offense. Although I quickly grasped that none of Debby's friends were Jewish, I didn't feel confident enough to confront all of them with the information that some of us in the room actually were. I could see by their expressions that Pam and Debby were also taken aback by the jokes. But, unfortunately, they didn't have the nerve to speak up either.

Then, as if a light bulb suddenly turned on in her head, one of the girls asked, "Nobody here's Jewish are they?"

"I am," Pam answered after a second's hesitation.

"Me too," I admitted timidly. "And so is Debby."

Debby looked down at her feet in embarrassment. I was sure the girls already knew that she was Jewish.

Once it had been determined that there were three Jews present, the jokes abruptly came to an end. Debby's friends offered a few sheepish grins and one or two "sorrys" as a consolation. I thought the whole thing was in poor taste, but decided not to hold a grudge.

Later that afternoon something happened that changed my mind. We all walked over to the nearby shopping mall. Meg, one of Debby's new friends, wanted to go home first and get her jacket. Pam, Debby and I agreed to go with her. We'd meet the rest of the group afterwards.

Meg gave us a quick tour of her house. As we followed her from the kitchen into the master bedroom, I immediately felt unwelcome. Painted on the wall in her parents' room, in clear view for everyone to see, was a large black swastika. I couldn't believe it. But there it was. I tried not to stare at the thick spidery symbol that was "decorating" the room like a picture one would hang for its beauty. Nobody said anything, but Pam shot me a look, as if to ask "What are we doing here, Shelly?"

Meg didn't even seem to be aware of the awkward situation at hand. She just kept on with the tour, showing us one room after another, as if she didn't understand that her parents would probably disown her for allowing Jews to extend so much as a baby toe into their home.

"Let's hurry and catch up with the others," I suggested. I was feeling very uncomfortable and eager to leave that house.

As we trekked over to the mall, my thoughts raced around in my head. I was mulling over the afternoon's events. *How could it be that Debby was friends with these girls?* None of us were observant Jews, but I couldn't imagine being friends with anyone who made fun of me because of my religion. *Was Debby having a hard time finding real friends? Did she feel she had to pretend to them and to herself that none of this mattered?*

I wasn't able to come up with answers to my questions that day. But putting aside any confusion I had about my own commitment to Judaism, by the end of our visit, I had reached one solid conclusion: to me, it mattered.

·❧· CHAPTER 4 ·❧·

"As far as I knew, there weren't any swastikas painted on anyone's bedroom walls in the area where *I* lived," I said, watching Carol, who was now helping me move my leg sideways. "But I had seen some carved into desks or scratched onto lunchroom tables in my high school. A swastika or two had also been scribbled onto the bathroom stalls in the neighborhood movie theater where my Jewish friends and I collected tickets and sold popcorn."

"I guess being Japanese and not Jewish, I've always been pretty oblivious to swastikas and things like that," Fran said, tucking some loose hairs into the bobby pin under her ponytail. "But I remember my grandparents saying they'd been called Japs or Nips, which I know was upsetting to them."

"Well," Carol tilted her blond head to the side so she could look at my leg and see Fran at the same time, "my mother had seen so many swastikas and had been called so many derogatory names during World War II, she didn't want to have anything to do with Judaism afterwards. That's why she decided to come to Chicago and not go to Israel with some of the others who were liberated from the concentration camps. She married my father, who's Jewish, but she was adamant about not living in a Jewish neighborhood. In her new life in America, she only wanted to be known as a friendly, smart, hard-working person—not as a Jew."

"How'd that work out?" I asked Carol.

"It wasn't so great." Carol turned her focus back to my leg. "Even though my siblings and I are all fair-skinned with light colored eyes, and I have blond hair, everyone in school knew we were Jewish. We were practically the only Jews in the whole school, so we kids had our share of anti-Semitic remarks thrown our way. Then, my parents decided to move to a different part of the city where there was a mix of people, including many Jewish families. We became pretty close to some of them and my mother actually felt okay about joining a synagogue. By the time I went off to university, I was fine about being Jewish. I don't remember being bothered or ridiculed about it again."

"And you, Shelly?" Fran asked me.

"Unfortunately," I turned to Fran, "I can't say the same. Anti-Semitism kept finding me, especially when I went off to college."

THE COFFEE MAN
(December 1981)

"You're Jewish? But, you don't look Jewish!" One of my coworkers at the student newspaper was shocked when she discovered that I was planning to attend the university's Rosh Hashanah prayer services for the Jewish New Year.

Comments like that paled in comparison to what happened one evening at the off-campus family-style restaurant where I waitressed on weekends. A few nights before Christmas, a smartly dressed middle-aged man stopped in for coffee. While I was filling his cup, he thanked me politely and began to make small talk. The restaurant was fairly empty, so I didn't mind chatting with him for a few minutes. He commented on the approaching holiday and, obviously considering me to be of the "right" faith, asked me how I planned to celebrate that year. I informed him that I didn't celebrate Christmas.

"Well what *do* you celebrate then?" He asked, with an edge to his voice.

Not sure where the conversation was headed, I answered cautiously. "Well," I smoothed out the apron part of my uniform and cleared my throat, "I celebrate Jewish holidays."

"Oh." the man said, slowly stirring his coffee. "So I guess you'll just be going to hell, huh?"

I froze right there next to the table. Suddenly, I was anxious to return my coffee pot to its burner in the kitchen. Instead, I attempted to defend myself. I didn't really know what Judaism considered hell to be like, but I knew that it didn't involve a red, pointy-tailed devil and a lot of wild fire.

Feeling a bit nervous and unable to think of a good and quick reply, I told the man what I did know. "We don't believe in a hell like that," I answered honestly.

Clearly straining to control himself, the suddenly ill-tempered man pressed the palms of his hands down on the table top and stretched his neck and shoulders up closer to my face. Through gritted teeth he hissed angrily, "So then, where do all you *bad* little Jews go?"

That was it! Without a second glance, I turned my back on the red-faced man and made a swift escape into the kitchen. Once out of his sight, I let my guard down and allowed myself to feel the sting of his words. I was both shaken and furious. *What nerve! How obnoxious! How dare he talk to me like that!*

The only person at that moment with whom I felt I could share what had just happened was another student-waitress friend of mine. "The truth is," my friend said softly, bending her blond head close to mine, "I think he's right. I've wanted to tell you for a while: I feel really sorry for you and all the other Jews, because whoever's not saved and doesn't follow Jesus will go to hell." She looked up at me. "I like you a lot, and I don't want that to happen to you."

I wasn't prepared for the bomb that my Catholic waitress-friend was dropping on me. Too stunned to reply, I threw a weak smile in her direction and went to occupy myself in a different section of the kitchen. *How could it be that, within five minutes, I was twice caught off-guard and reduced to a worthless soul who would rot in hell?*

Using the time between customers, I collected my thoughts and sorted through my feelings. By the time my shift was over, I was feeling better again. I knew there were many others in the world like my friend and that Coffee Man who were convinced that I was doomed because of what they considered my bad luck to have been born a Jew. I was no scholar on Judaism, but I knew that Jews had been around almost from the beginning of man's history—*before Christianity even existed.* And I was sure that no Jew had ever been sent, or ever *would* be sent to hell because he chose to light up a Chanukah menorah instead of a Christmas tree.

CHAPTER 5

PROTESTING THE PROTEST

(April 1983)

"Hey, Shelly! Did you see the 'Zionism Is Racism' protest at the Quad?" One of my classmates caught me on my way out of the campus library.

"What are you talking about?" My interest was piqued.

"I heard some Palestinian and pro-Palestinian students are protesting there. They're against the whole idea of a State of Israel."

"I'm going to go see," I announced, turning around and immediately starting towards the University's outdoor grassy Quadrangle. Stopping a few yards away from the protest, I saw a small gathering of students standing in a line. They were proudly holding up huge posters with anti-Israel slogans. A crowd of pro-Palestinian students and teachers rallied around the demonstrating group, while the Jewish students and faculty members stood staring on the side.

I was taken aback by what I was seeing. I knew very well that the scene before me was permitted under the Constitution's First Amendment, which protects freedom of speech and the right to assemble. There was nothing anyone could do to stop it. But what affected me most was that none of the Jews made even the smallest attempt to speak up against the protesters.

In my mind, Jews and Israel went together. As I stood watching, my heart beating fast, my blood rushing to every part of my body, I couldn't just stand there and be intimidated. For one short moment, any insecurities I had disappeared. I walked indignantly over to a student in black jeans and a long-sleeved sweatshirt holding a giant "Zionism Is Nazism" poster over his head. Standing directly in front of him, I said, "What do you think you're doing?" I couldn't believe I was actually confronting him.

The student's somber expression quickly transformed to wide-eyed surprise. He hesitated for a second and then answered, "It's our land. It belongs to us."

I stood on the tips of my toes, looked up into the taller protester's eyes and shouted, "You're full of it!" Then I turned and stomped away in a fury, rushing past some of my Jewish friends who were still passively watching. I could feel their eyes on me, my face hot with anger, my arms vigorously flinging themselves forward and backward as I stormed towards my student apartment. I was feeling disgusted with the anti-Semites of the world. I was even more disappointed in the apathy of the Jews.

After a few blocks, I slowed my pace to a calmer stride and began rationalizing. *Maybe those Jewish students and teachers weren't sure how to respond to the event. Or maybe they were just too shocked to react. Maybe they didn't think anything they would do could make a difference.* Then I turned my thoughts to my own actions. *Could it be that I over-reacted and made a fool out of myself in front of everyone?*

No! I didn't believe that. In my heart I knew I was right and there was no apologizing this time. I knew enough Jewish history to justify my feelings and actions—exiles, pogroms, inquisitions, holocausts. *And now, we're being attacked over a teeny piece of land that rightfully belongs to us!*

When I arrived at the apartment, I found my room-mates in the kitchen and the good-looking non-Jewish boy I'd been dating waiting for me on the couch in the living room. Tossing my backpack onto the coffee table, I sat stiffly on the edge of the worn lounge chair across from him and rehashed the whole scene.

"It was so pathetic," I said, still fuming. "Nobody said or did anything to counter those anti-Israel protesters. It's bad enough that all those students were there, but what about the teachers and professors? They just stood there watching, as if they supported the whole thing!"

I didn't know why I was being so intense about the incident. I grew up in a non-religious home. Both sets of my grandparents had kept Jewish customs and traditions while in Europe, but that changed when they came to America. My parents, who were less connected to Judaism, joined a Reform temple. They enrolled my siblings and me in Sunday school to learn a bit about our religion and, as a family, we would celebrate some of the Jewish holidays, to a certain extent. We attended prayer services in the synagogue mainly on the two High Holidays—Rosh Hashanah and Yom Kippur. But Judaism had never been the central focus in any of our lives. *So why am I so upset now?*

"Zionism is racism—what's that supposed to mean?" I went on. "Zionism is Nazism—How stupid! What did we do to deserve such condemnation? Why should we be subjected to such... such stupidity?"

I crossed my legs and then uncrossed them. My boyfriend sat with a blank look on his face. "You seem a little stressed," he finally offered.

That's it? That's all he has to say? I felt the distance between us widening.

Although I had some doubts about religion and about an omnipresent Creator, I did at times catch myself praying here and there to my Sunday school High Holidays G-d, hoping that He really did exist. Now, this was another time I was feeling some kind of deeper connection to being Jewish. But as I sat across from my Protestant boyfriend, I realized he would never be able to relate to that. It was something we would never share. Though he was smart and fun and we did share many similar interests, I suddenly felt that we didn't really belong together.

Slowly getting up from the lounge chair, I left the living room. In my own room, I walked over to my bed and lay down on my side, my knees pulled up to my chest. Staring at the wall, I thought about how there were times I didn't feel like I fit in with people or the life around me. I wondered if there wasn't something more to it all. *There must be. Somehow... somewhere.*

I closed my eyes to the hatred and the apathy. Then, listening to the small plastic alarm clock ticking softly next to my bed, I slowly slipped into a lonesome sleep.

·ৡ· *CHAPTER* **6** ·ৡ·

WHY THERE?

(July—August 1984)

Fresh out of college, I was nervous about my first professional job. I was working as an intern at a daily newspaper. Despite my anxieties about starting out in the real world, I managed to settle into my new temporary life without too much difficulty. Although I was the only Jew in the entire newsroom, I appeared to be no different than the rest of the staff with whom I had a good working relationship.

With the last day of my internship drawing near, some of my coworkers asked me where I would be working next as a journalist. The question flustered me. For more than a year, I had been planning a backpacking trip, first to Israel and then on through Europe. I knew that the newspaper only hired college graduates who were serious about working in the field. I understood their reasoning and had fully planned on doing just that—after I returned from abroad.

Running through potential answers in my mind, I decided the best thing to do was to tell the truth. "I'll be looking for a job as a reporter after my three months of travel," I admitted. "Of course, I'll be collecting many exotic and unusual stories to report on while I'm away, especially from Israel," I added quickly.

Standing in medium-size heels, lightweight slacks and a pastel blouse, I waited, a bit uneasy, for some kind of response from the news staff all around me. I thought I might get "That sounds great!" or "Well, you'll have plenty to write about when you get back!" or "Why are you traveling around the world instead of immediately continuing on with your career?" I hoped for a good response, braced myself for a bad one, and was completely unprepared for what I actually received.

"Israel?" One of the editors blurted out in disgust. "Why would you take a vacation *there?*"

"Yeah, why *there?*" a female reporter echoed the question with matching revulsion.

Here we go again, I thought. I understood that none of them had any desire to spend their free time visiting a little Jewish country that was riddled with troubles and constantly fighting for its existence. I felt once more like the sore thumb sticking out. I was the out-of-place token Jew again. *That was the only part of the conversation that mattered? Nobody cared about anything else except that I would be going to Israel?* Suddenly, I didn't feel so comfortable standing, as if on trial, before those reporters and editors, who were staring at me like I was from Jupiter.

Drawing in my breath, I paused to think. I wanted to give a convincing answer that would reassure everyone that I wasn't crazy. But then, one of my fellow reporters spoke up for me.

"Why d'ya think she's going there?" His fat moustache rose and fell as he spoke. "She's Jewish. That's why."

Well, I let out my breath, *that pretty much sums it up!* I knew *I* wouldn't have said that. I wasn't even sure myself why I wanted to go to Israel. I thought I was just curious about the country. The idea that I was going there based on the pure and simple fact that I was Jewish hadn't even crossed my mind. I hadn't considered any concrete reason or particular desire to attach myself to Israel or the Israeli people. I didn't know much about the place, except that there were communal farms called kibbutzim and that Israelis exported juicy oranges and little chocolate Chanukah coins.

At that moment, I also realized that the non-Jewish newspaper reporter standing next to me understood better than I did why I would be traveling six thousand miles away from home to be in Israel, instead of pursuing my new career as a journalist. But as the days grew nearer to my long-awaited trip, it became increasingly more important for me to discover for myself what was so special about that little dot of a country in the middle of the map, in the center of the world.

PART TWO

September 1984—June 1989

·❦· CHAPTER 1 ·❦·

"I think we're finished for now." Carol lifted my leg with her creamy white hands and removed the pillow from underneath it.

"That's it?" Fran sounded disappointed. "We were just getting into Shelly's story."

Carol looked at me. "Can we do this again tomorrow? Pick up from where you left off?"

"I'm not going anywhere," I said. "If you can both make it again, it's fine with me."

"Don't worry. I'll be back for more tomorrow." Fran's brown Asian eyes were smiling as she turned to leave. "Just don't start without me!"

❧ ❧ ❧ ❧

"I'll begin from when I arrived in Israel," I told Fran and Carol the next day.

"Good. Just don't forget to work on your leg like I showed you while you're storytelling," Carol said, playfully wagging her finger at me.

"That's the idea," I nodded. "I'm doing okay here, but I want to get back home as soon as possible."

ISRAELI WELCOME
(September 1984)

The wheels of the El Al jumbo jet bounced once and then glided down the Ben Gurion Airport runway. Passengers cheered and applauded enthusiastically with the famous Hebrew song *"Haveinu Shalom Aleichem"* playing throughout the aircraft as it landed. Swept up by the unexpected excitement, I felt the sudden urge to lock arms with my two seatmates and dance the Hora in the aisle. But I settled for clapping my hands and humming to myself until we came to a complete stop. *What a great way to enter the country!* My fears of traveling to a foreign place on my own were pushed aside for those few energized moments when I felt connected to the rest of the travelers on the plane.

Waiting for my luggage at baggage claim, I couldn't believe I was actually halfway around the world... in Israel! I took a Nesher taxi from the airport to Jerusalem, where I'd be spending my first week with Esther, my childhood friend from Chicago.

Esther grew up in a family that was a bit more religious and a lot more Zionistic than mine. She and her four siblings had been brought up to keep some aspects of Shabbat[1] and her parents had always made it a point to support Israel in whatever way they could. Though Esther and I had been friends since kindergarten, it wasn't a surprise that we'd taken separate paths after high school. While I'd gone to a state university for college, Esther had made *aliyah*[2] and had come to live in Jerusalem. She spent

---

[1] The Sabbath.
[2] Immigration to Israel; lit., "ascent."

her first few years in Israel learning Hebrew, tutoring children in English and attending classes on Judaism, before applying to Hebrew University to study social work.

Now, wearing a peasant blouse, a long skirt and flat leather sandals, Esther cheerfully welcomed me into her home. As my hostess, she helped me change my dollars into shekels, taught me some useful Hebrew words to enrich my very basic vocabulary and acquainted me with the Jerusalem bus system. After a couple of days, I felt confident enough to travel on my own to the center of town to look around and do some souvenir shopping.

"Here's the key to the apartment," Esther said, flipping her long, sun-bleached braid over her shoulder and handing me a yellow plastic key chain. "I'll probably be home around supper time, so just let yourself in."

"What about your two roommates?" I asked, wondering if I'd be returning to an empty apartment or not.

"They usually get home after me," Esther explained. "Come back whenever you want and just make yourself at home."

We walked out to the street together and then parted for the day. I managed to get on the right bus to the center of town and return to Esther's place later that afternoon without any problems. But when I reached the apartment, the key Esther had given me didn't open the door.

I rested on the stairway inside the building while I waited for Esther or her roommates to return. Opening the *Jerusalem Post* I'd just bought, I tried to make myself comfortable on the hard, stone-tiled step halfway up the first landing. With Esther's apartment just below me, I would be able to see when someone arrived.

After only a few minutes, I heard the door to the apartment on the second floor open. I looked up and saw a group of feet emerge above me. An Israeli couple and their young teenage son came clomping rapidly down the stairs. Snatching up the newspaper, I quickly stood out of their way. The family glanced at me as they rushed by and then quickly disappeared out of the building.

An hour passed and still nobody returned to Esther's apartment. The sun was setting and the light in the stairwell was growing dim. I had already read nearly the entire newspaper and was having a hard time making out the back page. Just as I was wondering how much longer I would have to wait, the sound of footsteps echoed from the building's entranceway. The Israeli family was back from grocery shopping.

I stood up in anticipation of their ascent as they approached the stairs carrying their bulging grocery bags. They started up, but stopped on the step just before mine. The slender woman in beige slacks and open-backed shoes looked at me and said something in Hebrew that I didn't understand. Not used to conversing with strangers on shadowy narrow stairways, I just shrugged and prayed that they would hurry up and be on their way. When I didn't reply, the woman switched to simple English.

"You still here?" she asked me, wrinkling her nose.

Seeing that I wouldn't get away without revealing something about my predicament, I tried to explain.

"I'm waiting for my friend," I said, not even attempting to figure out the words in Hebrew.

The woman gestured for me to follow them up to their apartment. "You wait with us."

Unaccustomed to such an offer from people I didn't know, I shook my head. "No thanks. I'm fine," I managed to say this time in Hebrew with a sharp American accent.

The woman's husband, who had a stocky build and a pleasant face, apparently wasn't satisfied with my answer. Using hand motions and English mixed with Hebrew, he tried to persuade me to wait in their apartment, where the conditions were more comfortable. I wasn't sure about trusting these neighbors and I felt a little uneasy about getting so much attention from them. So I again politely refused their offer.

Resigned to the fact that I wasn't joining them, the family continued up the steps with their bags. I heard them open their door. When it clicked shut, I breathed a sigh of relief.

Sitting on the now dark and silent stairway, I wished that I was already inside Esther's apartment. I eyed the door half a floor below me then looked up to the neighbor's door once more. I was caught by surprise when it suddenly opened again, showering the stairway with light. *Oh no!* I groaned to myself, not interested in an encore of the previous scene. Quickly laying my forehead down on my knees, I pretended to be cat napping while hoping the encroaching pair of feet would hurry past me. They didn't. They stopped right on my step. Feeling I had no choice, I looked up.

What I saw amazed me, put me to shame and made me smile all at the same time. The tanned, athletic-looking teenage boy was standing over me, holding a cup of hot tea in one hand and a dish with a large piece of cake in the other. He set the tea and the cake down on the step above me and said, "*B'vakashah.* Please, enjoy."

"Thank you." My heart melted as I watched the boy run back up the stairs.

When he reached his apartment he turned around and motioned that he was leaving the door open. "So you will have light," he called down to me, his English better than his parents'.

"*Todah.*"[3] I called back to him. "*Todah rabbah.*"[4]

---

3 "Thank you."
4 "Thank you very much."

When Esther returned home, about fifteen minutes later, she apologized for the key mix-up. I relayed to her the events of my day, including my encounter with the upstairs neighbors.

"I couldn't believe how nice they were. At first, I was afraid to have anything to do with them because they were strangers. And then, the cake and tea, and the light... and everything! I never expected anything like that."

"Welcome to Israel," Esther said, pulling two apples out of the refrigerator. "You'll get used to things like that happening, if you stay in the country long enough." She washed the apples and held them out to me. "Want one?"

"Thanks." I nodded.

Taking a bite from my apple, I wondered how long I actually *would* stay in Israel. "I can't worry about this now," I said out loud.

"Worry about what?" Esther asked.

"I was just thinking about how much longer I'd be in the country," I replied.

"But you just got here. Don't think about that now." Esther sat down at the kitchen table and cut her apple with a small paring knife. "Just enjoy yourself, and get the most out of everything for as long as you *are* here."

Taking a seat next to Esther, I thought about how natural it seemed for her neighbors to help me. If many of the people really were like them, it would be easy to enjoy being in Israel. And, of course, I *would* do my best to get the most out of everything.

"Right," I said, with a nod. "That's *exactly* what I'm going to do."

CHAPTER 2

BUILDING AND REBUILDING

(September 1984)

The cover of the brochure read "Livnot U'Lehibanot—To Build and Be Built." Esther had given it to me a couple of days after I arrived.

"It's a three-month program in Tzfat that starts next week," Esther said, sitting next to me on the living room couch. "A friend of mine recommended it."

"Where's Tzfat?" I asked.

"It's a small city up north, in the Galilee."

I opened the colorful flap and took a minute to read the inside of the brochure. "It's a program for English-speaking Jews from age twenty to thirty with little or no formal background in Judaism. Yep, that sounds like me." I looked at the pictures of the smiling, suntanned past participants and then continued paraphrasing out loud. "Let's see, it's a community experience that involves volunteer work projects, learning about Judaism, experiencing Jewish life at its roots and going on hiking trips."

"*Tiyulim*," Esther said.

"What?"

"*Tiyulim*. It's the plural for *tiyul*. It means a hike or a trip. It's a word you should know. You'll be hearing it and probably using it a lot. Israelis love to go on *tiyulim*."

I fingered the brochure in my hand. "Hmmm. Helping, learning and... *tiyuling*." I looked at Esther. "Sounds interesting."

ᵒ§ᵒ ᵒ§ᵒ ᵒ§ᵒ ᵒ§ᵒ

"It *does* sound interesting." Carol said. She was helping me flex my ankle today.

"Remember, we don't have a lot of time," Fran smiled at Carol. "So maybe we should let Shelly continue."

"Okay. You're right," Carol said. "I'm all ears..."

ᵒ§ᵒ ᵒ§ᵒ ᵒ§ᵒ ᵒ§ᵒ

(October 1984)

Tiny droplets of rain fell gently from the blue-grey sky onto the mountain city of Tzfat. All eighteen of us Livnot U'Lehibanot particpants were frantically trying to complete our morning of volunteer community work before the expected downpour. For the past six weeks we'd been learning about Judaism and Israel, and working daily on reconstructing an old stone building that had collapsed in an earthquake many years before.

The group, or *chevreh*, as we fondly called ourselves, had spent days reinforcing and cementing the unstable roof. Arnon, Livnot's American-born founder and director, was determined to finish it by the end of the day.

"It's looking good," Arnon said, praising the part of our *chevreh* who'd been working with him up on the flat rooftop. Then, using his hand to hold down the crocheted yarmulke[5] that was resting on his brown curly hair, Arnon tilted his head back and looked at the dark, drizzling sky. "The rain's coming early this year," he said. "Looks like we're in for a real shower."

Walking over to the edge of the roof, Arnon called down to the ground crew. "C'mon, everyone! We're going to have to work faster. We gotta get the rest of those buckets of cement up here before it starts to pour!"

I was part of the team below passing buckets of gravel, sand and water in assembly line fashion over to Steve, our tall, energetic work manager. Steve was emptying each bucket into a big spinning cement mixer and filling them up again with fresh cement.

"Let's go, guys," he called over his shoulder, as he sent the buckets of cement, one at a time, up to the roof on a makeshift pulley rope.

"These pails are starting to get heavy," I grunted, taking a bucket of sand from Liz and running awkwardly with it over to Mitch who ran it over to Steve.

"I know," Liz agreed. The red highlights in her hair were shimmering in the sunlight as she shook her freckled arms melodramatically and shouted in Steve's direction, "My arms are about ready to fall off!"

"Hey, no moaning," Steve joked as he grabbed the sand bucket Mitch was handing him. "We're not just building a stone and cement structure. We're building muscles out here!" He threw the sand into the cement mixer along with buckets of gravel and water that had already been passed down to him.

"Hey, Arnon!" one of the workers operating the rope pulley called out. "We need more manpower over here

---

[5] Skullcap.

pulling up the cement."

Arnon wiped drops of rain off his glasses with the corner of his checkered flannel shirt and gave out more orders. "Okay, guys. It looks like you've done enough down there. We need you on the roof. Come on up!"

We dropped our buckets and enthusiastically clambered up the ladder and the old stone steps at the back of the building. Steve wiped his dusty hands on his faded work jeans and instructed Mitch, who was short but husky, to stay behind and attach the last few heavy buckets of cement onto the pulley hook before joining the rest of us on the roof.

"Today is our deadline for this part of the building project," Steve told everyone. "If we move quickly, we can do this!"

Excitement filled the air as twenty pairs of arms and legs worked in a unified effort to beat the rainstorm. Moving as fast as we could, we broke off into groups to haul up the rest of the buckets with the thick ropes, carry the cement over to the unfinished sections of the roof and quickly pour it out over its level surface.

Liz and I got busy filling in cracks where the cement had already dried from the day before. "You missed one over there," Liz pointed out to me with her usual knack for details.

"It's impossible to get all of them," I said. "I hope this roof doesn't fall in one day!"

"Talk. Talk. Talk." Steve walked over to us with a half-filled bucket of cement. "We don't have time for that, you two. Leave it to the females to gab while the rest of us are slaving away!"

"Ha!" I laughed. "You'd better be nice to us. Don't you know that we have the most important job?"

"Yeah," Liz jumped in. "We're the ones keeping this roof from a future cave-in."

"So watch out!" I shook my cement-covered hand spade at Steve.

Steve laughed as he knelt down to slap some of the mixture from his pail onto a small crevice that I had missed. He was about to give a witty reply when someone announced that the last bit of cement had just been poured and spread out. Loud whoops and wild cheers rang out from every part of the roof. Some of the group began dancing around. Despite the slightly heavier drizzle and the dark looming clouds, everyone was excited. We had worked hard all week and were now finally completing our mission.

"Let the rains come!" Mitch cried, throwing back his head and opening his muscular arms up to the sky. "We're ready for them!"

Steve gave Liz and me a thumbs-up and left to help the others quickly finish up their jobs. I felt a sense of satisfaction as we filled the last few cracks in our section of the roof.

While Arnon went around congratulating everyone on a job well done, I put down my spade and looked out across the hazy sky. I could just make out the shape of Mount Meron straight ahead in the distance. Below us, antiquated holy synagogues and quaint houses lined the stone pathways that wound in and out of Tzfat's Old City and through its famous Artist Colony. Great Torah scholars, prominent Jewish leaders and pious rabbis were buried in the sacred mountainside cemetery just beneath the Old City.

Jews from all over the world came to Tzfat to capture its spiritual essence and absorb its mystical atmosphere. I felt both Tzfat and Livnot U'Lehibanot were leaving their mark on me. Livnot classes and late night discussions about our Jewish heritage, religion, the people and the country opened me to new insights and ideals. Working together with the *chevreh* and giving to others in the community was rewarding. And with every *tiyul*,[6] I began to fall more in love with the Land and its beauty.

What I really hadn't expected to get from the program was my growing appreciation for the spirit of Shabbat.[7] Wearing the nicest outfits we had with us, we'd all gather together on Friday at sundown to light Shabbat candles. Then, silhouetted against the evening sky atop a wider flat rooftop across the way, our group would welcome the Sabbath with prayer and song. After conducting our own Shabbat service in the nearby centuries-old Abuhav Synagogue, we'd be one step closer to G-d, our Jewish souls, and the special delicious feast that was waiting for us back at Livnot U'lihebanot.

Spirited singing always highlighted the three festive meals we ate together throughout Shabbat. We often found ourselves enthusiastically pounding the white cloth-covered tabletops with our fists or drumming with our hands to the rhythm of the Shabbat songs. And in-between satisfying our appetites and exercising our vocal cords, we'd share with each other an idea or lesson we'd learned from one of our Torah classes. I was impressed with how the ancient writings had messages that were also relevant for our own modern lives.

The most beautiful sunsets I had ever seen were just as Shabbat was ending. Sitting up on the same rooftop where we had greeted the Sabbath the evening before, we would sometimes spend the last few minutes of the day watching the blazing sphere descend. Tinting the sky with assorted shades of orange, red and yellow, it would slip slowly behind the mountains until it finally disappeared.

---

[6] Hike, trip, excursion or outing.
[7] The Sabbath.

Liz nudged me with her elbow. "Isn't that awesome?"

I blinked away the images that had momentarily stolen me away and looked at Liz's cement speckled face. "What?" I asked innocently.

"Didn't you hear anything Arnon just said?"

I *had* heard Arnon congratulating us before I got lost in my thoughts. "We did great, didn't we?" I said, my focus returning to the roof.

"Arnon's promising us a special celebration supper tonight," Liz filled me in, "and he's adding an extra day to our Shabbat away."

"Yes!" I raised my arms over my head. "And tomorrow's Friday already."

Although we were all enjoying Tzfat and the program, we looked forward to every third weekend, when we were free to travel to other parts of the country. There was so much of Israel I wanted to see. I would be able to spend some of the extended "away Shabbat" with my newly-discovered Israeli relatives in Netanya.

"Whoa! It's really starting to come down!" Liz cried out excitedly as she jumped up from her place on the roof.

Like an explosion, the rain suddenly burst forth from the heavy clouds. Everyone began shouting and scrambling down from the roof for cover. Liz grabbed my arm and pulled me towards the stone steps that looked as if they might crumble under the barrage of pounding feet.

"Hey, *chevreh!*" Steve called out, cupping his hands around his mouth. "The rain is good for the cement, but not for the tools. Don't forget to bring all of them with you!"

Before hurrying down, I turned back to catch a quick glimpse of our completed work. Arnon was standing alone in the middle of the roof smiling, as the giant rain drops fell onto the fresh cement and spread like a sheet over its surface.

"Are you coming?" Liz called to me.

"Yeah, I'm coming." I turned away from Arnon and the rain-covered roof and hurried down the stairs after her.

Almost as suddenly as it had started, the rain stopped. By evening, the warm air had dried the outdoors. We enjoyed a special supper that Arnon's wife Meira had organized. Then we relaxed for a while in the Livnot courtyard.

At eleven o'clock the light was off in the room I was sharing with Marcy and Liz, my two roommates, who were both from Florida. It had been a long day, and we were nestled under our blankets, ready for sleep.

Marcy, wearing red and white striped pajamas, broke the silence. "The name Livnot U'Lehibanot is pretty appropriate for this program. Isn't it?"

"Uh huh," Liz sounded half asleep as she spoke into the darkness. "To build and to be built," she yawned. "We've definitely been doing the 'to build' part. Don't know about the 'to be built' though."

"If you ask Arnon, he'd say that the 'to be built' part is happening too." Marcy informed us. "Supposedly we, ourselves, are also being built, or maybe rebuilt, with everything we're learning and doing here."

I rolled onto my side. *Be built, rebuilt.* "Is it okay if we go to sleep now? I'm exhausted." I shoved my head under my pillow, but could still hear the girls' muffled talking.

"Yeah, let's go to sleep," one of them said.

"So we'll have energy to build ourselves and all of Tzfat again tomorrow," the other one laughed.

"Tomorrow's Friday. We're going away in the morning for three days, remember?"

"Of course I remember. How could I forget that?"

Under my pillow, I closed my eyes. Something was stirring inside me, but I was too tired to think about it. Even so, I had to agree, there was definitely a lot of building going on.

·❧· CHAPTER 3 ·❧·

NETANYA COUSINS

(October 1984)

"So, you came to Israel to cement roofs and paint old people's apartments," Gidon's jolly laughter filled the room.

Gidon was my mother's first cousin. He'd come to Israel from Lithuania with his parents and siblings when he was a teenager, just before the Holocaust. Now a grey-haired, rosy-cheeked math professor, he and his Israeli wife Aviva were hosting me in their modest home in the seaside town of Netanya.

Though I'd only arrived a few hours ago from Tzfat, I'd already become fairly acquainted with the middle-aged couple and their two sons, Tzvi and Yair. Tzvi, twenty-four, thin and fair-haired, was studying to be an accountant. Yair, twenty, brawnier and darker than his brother, was in the midst of his three-year army service. An officer in his unit, Yair had gotten permission to leave his base and come home for the weekend. I was happy I was finally meeting the Israeli cousins I'd heard about many times back in Chicago.

"In all my years living in this country I never heard of this Livnot U'Lihebanot program." Gidon was still chuckling. "You joined this group to do construction work?"

"It's a bit funny because you're so little," Tzvi teased me in his excellent English. "I really can't picture it."

"Actually I have some photos to show you." I pulled out some pictures I had recently taken. The family gathered around me in the living room. "See, here I am in my hard hat helping rebuild a ruin from the earthquake that shook up Tzfat in the 1800s."

"Why didn't you tell me?" Gidon grinned at me. "I would have had you build me a house here in Netanya too!"

"What are all these other photographs?" Yair, still in uniform, was flipping through a second set of photos I'd set down on the coffee table. "Looks like you're back in school in this one." He pointed to a photo of me and the rest of the Livnoters sitting at a long table with our notebooks open.

"Yeah, kinda," I replied. "We don't only help out with community projects. We also have classes where we learn about Israel and Judaism and stuff like that."

"Why don't you stay with us?" Aviva asked, happy to be able to practice her less-polished English on me. "It would be nice to have a girl around here," she said, with a toss of her auburn hair. "And then, you wouldn't have to work so much. Or do *that*," her deep brown eyes shifted to a photo of me, Liz and Mitch chopping vegetables while preparing supper for the *chevreh*. "You could just relax because, around here, I do all the cooking."

"Of course," Gidon agreed. "And you have the beach right here—only a few blocks away. You could go there whenever you wanted."

I was moved by their warm welcome. "Thanks," I said. "But I'm really enjoying this program."

Gidon stood up from his spot on the sofa and switched on the television. "It's time for the news," he said matter-of-factly. Then turning back to me, he added,

"Whatever you decide is fine. In any case, you're welcome to use our home as your base for as long as you're in the country."

Before I could properly thank Gidon and Aviva for their generous offers, the newscaster's sober voice filled the room. Everyone's attention turned to the TV screen.

I had already begun to understand how important the news was at all times for Israelis. The small, dynamic country was not only in a new and exciting stage of development, it was also dealing with endless difficulties and troubles. Everyone was affected in some way or another by the events of the day. Radios and TV sets were often turned up when the news came on. People riding in buses or cars usually sat quietly and listened as the hourly reports were broadcast. To Israelis, even minor incidents or discoveries were significant and worthy of their attention.

My basic Hebrew didn't help me understand the news. Gidon and Tzvi translated for me. After a while, Tzvi got up to make himself a hot drink. Yair and I joined him in the kitchen.

"What are you having, tea or coffee?" Tzvi asked me.

"Tea's good," I said.

We sat down at the kitchen table and waited for the water to boil. "In a couple of weeks I'm going on a three-day hike with Livnot from the Sea of Galilee to the Mediterranean Sea," I said. "It's supposed to be one of the highlights of the program. We'll be camping out in the mountains and hiking through the valleys."

"Do you have good walking shoes?" Yair asked.

"I've got my trusty sneakers," I tapped the white canvas soles on my feet.

"What you need is a good pair of hiking boots," Yair advised me.

"I think these will be okay," I replied, looking down at my shoes with confidence.

Yair exchanged a knowing smile with Tzvi and then got up to make tea. Gidon came into the kitchen with a pleased look on his face. "Nothing major happening in the country to report," he told us. "Except of course, all the action you're involved in up in Tzfat on that program," he chuckled again. "Do they take old men like me to help lift those boulders?"

"You'd have a great time on their three-day *tiyul* next week," Tzvi joked with his father.

"Three days? No thanks. I'll just keep to my daily neighborhood walks around our block."

"Don't worry," I told Gidon. "As a long time Israeli, I'm sure you've already experienced whatever exciting adventures we'll be having on our *tiyul*."

"Who's worried?" Gidon laughed. "In this country, we have plenty of excitement, whether we want it or not." He took a seat next to me. "But you're welcome to come back anytime and tell us all about your interesting experiences."

"Just be careful that you don't get eaten by any wild bears while you're out there," Tzvi warned.

"Bears?" I looked at him in surprise.

"Ha! Just kidding," Tzvi laughed. "There aren't any bears in Israel—only in the zoo." He pushed my cup closer towards me. "Maybe you should drink your tea," he said, grinning. "It's getting cold."

I rolled my eyes and sighed dramatically. "No wild bears in Israel. I knew that."

"Of course, you did." Now Yair was smiling too. "So since there's nothing for you to worry about, you should have a lot of fun."

"Right," I said with certainty. Hebrew or no Hebrew, hiking boots or no hiking boots—I was already having a great time in Israel and I was sure I'd enjoy every minute of the *tiyul* too.

Bears or no bears.

·❧· CHAPTER 4 ·❧·

NEVER JUST NATURE

(October 1984)

"Ouuch!" My painful cries of agony breached the peaceful mountain air. "I've got to stop. I can't walk anymore. My feet hurt me too much." I sat down in the middle of the rocky trail, realizing that I should have taken my cousin's advice and bought a good pair of hiking shoes for the three-day Livnot *tiyul*.

"Arnon!" one of the *chevreh* called up ahead, "Hold up a minute. We've got a problem here."

As the news spread, everyone stopped and began pulling off their backpacks and setting down their water jugs. Those who were near me walked over to see what they could do to help, while the others, further down the path, waited for more information about the "crisis" at hand.

"My feet are in so much pain," I moaned.

"Let me see. Take off your socks and shoes," demanded Liz, who had been walking beside me.

I took off my shoes and then carefully peeled off each sock. Both of my feet were red and blistered.

"Oh my G-d!" Marcy came from behind us. "Look at your feet! How're you going to make it through the rest of the *tiyul*?"

"I don't know," I groaned.

Steve came running from up ahead to find out what was holding everybody up. "What's the story here?" he bent down to check on my situation. "Wow! That doesn't look good," he admitted. "Are you sure you want to go on? You can go back to Tzfat when we reach the car that's bringing tonight's supplies a little further on."

"No. I can make it," I insisted. I had no intentions of leaving the group or missing the rest of the *tiyul*. It was too beautiful in the valleys and breathtaking up in the mountains. "I can make it." I started putting my socks back on.

"Wait!" Liz was out of breath from running. "I got some gauze bandages from Arnon."

"Thank G-d!" Relieved, I took the bandages from Liz.

Most of the *chevreh* started again on their way. A few stayed behind with me as I wrapped my feet and then replaced my socks and shoes.

"Let's go." I winced, taking baby steps to get started.

"Hurry up, you guys!" someone called from up ahead. "Wait till you see what's over here!"

I painstakingly picked up my pace. When I reached the others, I understood why I had to continue on, no matter what shape my feet were in. We had come to a lookout point with a panoramic view near the mountaintop. Mountains were spread out for miles around. Some were barren, while others were covered with trees, bushes and patches of wild flowers. The sun's bright rays flooded the deep blue sky and reflected onto the flowing riverbed in the valley below. Giant birds, soaring high above with their wings spread wide, occasionally stopped to glide over the proud peaks.

"Oh my G-d." I was mesmerized.

"That's right," Arnon was standing next to me. "He's responsible for all of this."

I folded my arms in front of me over my pink tie-dyed

T-shirt. "Actually, I'm not sure I believe in Him."

Arnon wiped his perspiring forehead with a red bandanna and stuffed it into the back pocket of his loose jeans. "Just look around," he said, sweeping his arm through the air. "Do you think that all of this exists just by chance?"

I didn't know how to respond. Although I wasn't completely comfortable with the concept of G-d the Omnipotent Creator, I had to agree that the complexities and beauty of the world probably couldn't have just happened on their own. I looked around with Arnon for another moment, and then with a little shrug, turned to join the others who were setting up a late lunch.

"We have views and nature like this in Colorado too," Mitch said, unloading food from his backpack.

"Like this?" I asked.

"Yeah, it's just like being back in Colorado."

"Not really," interjected Arnon's friend Yonah, who was studying to be a tour guide and had come along to help lead the *tiyul*. "In Israel, it's never just nature you're looking at," he said. "Here each place is full of significance and a long history."

"What do you mean?" Marcy was sitting on a thick log, scooping tuna out of a can for the sandwiches.

"Every event that happened in Israel throughout our Jewish history has affected our world and our own lives to some extent," Yonah explained. "Nothing here was created without a purpose. Take the mountains, for instance." Taking off his sunglasses, Yonah waved them towards the mountains in front of us. "They're not just majestic. A lot of important things happened on many of our mountains."

"Yeah, like what happened on Mount Sinai?" Mitch joked.

"Hey, I went to Masada!" Marcy called out. "That was a pretty wild thing that happened there: A thousand Jews living on the mountain and taking their own lives rather than being enslaved or massacred by the Romans."

"I've heard that something similar happened on Mount Gamla in the Golan Heights." Liz said, sitting down in the shade by a small tree.

"Similar, but not exactly the same," Yonah said.

"Mount Hermon." Arnon came over with a bag of small purple plums. "Who can tell me what's so important about Mount Hermon?"

"It's got great snow for skiing?" Mitch winked at Arnon.

Arnon's hazel eyes twinkled as he handed Mitch the plums to distribute among the others. "It separates us from Syria," he said. "It secures part of our border and gives us a military advantage from up high."

Nineteen-year-old Penina, who was helping out at the program as part of her army service, threw out another piece of trivia. "In case you don't know," she told those of us who were part of the *chevreh*, "Mount Moriah was where Isaac was almost sacrificed."

I sat down next to Penina with a sandwich and some carrot sticks. "I don't think I ever heard about Mount Moriah before. But I did actually pay attention in class last week," I announced proudly. "So I can tell you about the mountains during the time of the Chanukah story with the Maccabees."

"You guys already learned about the Maccabees in class?" Penina asked. "That's pretty good, since Chanukah's not for another month and a half."

"Ha!" Marcy laughed. "We didn't get to Chanukah yet. She doesn't remember *what* we learned," Marcy said, pointing her finger in my direction. "She always falls asleep during classes!"

Taking a swig of water from the large communal water jug, I pointed a carrot stick back at Marcy. "I can tell you that King Antiochus and the Greeks forbade the Jews to pray or to learn Torah. So they hid in mountain caves and did all of that in secret. After the Maccabees fought the Greeks and won, the Jews left the mountains, returned to their homes and cleaned up the Temple that the Greeks had defiled. And that's when they found that little jar of pure olive oil, which was only supposed to be enough to burn for one day."

"But," Liz jumped in, "it miraculously burned for eight days, giving the Maccabees enough time to make more oil so the menorah would always stay lit."

"Whoa!" Mitch shook his hand up and down in front of his chest. "I'm impressed."

"I didn't know all of that," Marcy said.

I smiled at her. "That's probably because you must have fallen asleep during the Chanukah class that we didn't have! And because we," I gestured towards Liz and myself, "read parts of that holiday book that's been sitting on the back table."

For a moment the *chevreh* sat quietly while eating. Mitch eyed Yonah, who was casually leaning against a big rock and biting into a plum. Then he turned to Arnon. "So you're saying that here in Israel there's something special about every place and every thing."

Arnon looked straight at Mitch and nodded. "That's right. Every tree, rock and flower; every stream and hill; every dirt path, paved road and Jewish home here is special because of its place in the history of the Land and the nation—and because of the important role it plays for us in Israel today."

Mitch picked up a stone from the dusty ground and began rubbing it between his fingers.

I stood up to get another look at the breathtaking view that surrounded us. "It's not at all like Colorado," I said, taking in the clear skies, the lofty mountains and the picturesque valleys.

"It's not like anywhere."

·❖· CHAPTER 5 ·❖·

EVERYDAY EVENT

(October 1984)

I was both happy and thankful that I had made it to the end of the three-day *tiyul*. The sun was setting as we relaxed on the shore and enjoyed the calm waters of the Mediterranean Sea near the northern coastal city of Nahariya. I immediately removed my bandages and hobbled over to immerse my feet in the cool water, which was a relief, despite its salty composition.

After a while, Arnon suggested that everyone begin walking by the roadside towards Nahariya. "If you split up into pairs or groups of threes, it will be easier to catch a *tremp*,"[8] he advised. "We'll meet in the city for a quick supper and then take the bus together back to Tzfat.

I wasn't used to hitchhiking. But my feet were sore and walking any distance now seemed like torture. I was hoping a ride would come along quickly for me and Penina, as we walked together along the side of the road.

"Let's talk to each other in Hebrew. I need to practice," I told Penina.

"But *I* need to practice my English." Penina said, flash-

---

8 Ride offered to hitchhikers.

ing me a wide smile and speaking in nearly perfect English.

"Fine," I laughed at Penina. "Even though I know your parents are originally from England and they speak to you in both Hebrew *and* English, I'll give in this time." It was easier for me to speak in my own mother tongue, anyway. "You know," I changed the topic, "in the States hitchhiking is illegal and dangerous. Are you sure it's okay to do this?"

"Positive," Penina said, nodding her head of long golden-brown curls. "Everyone *tremps* here. In Israel it's not only legal, it's normal. Everyone gives rides and everyone gets rides. That's the way it is."

"And there's nothing to worry about?" I persisted.

"Like what?" asked Penina.

"You know, like strangers doing who knows what, or of being stopped by the police, or something like that."

"Strangers aren't really strangers here," Penina pointed out. "If you don't know them, you meet them and you get to know them. Everyone helps each other out, like a family."

Penina quickly shifted the position of her backpack on her back and then went on, "I wouldn't suggest getting into the car if an Arab driver stops, but otherwise, it's usually fine," she reassured me. "It's a Jewish country. We're surrounded by our own people. Don't worry about it."

I had to admit to myself that I felt great being in a place where people actually felt proud to be Jewish. I loved that it was the Star of David, found literally everywhere, and not the swastika, that was always reminding me of who I was.

We turned to look as a car approached from behind. A police van was heading towards us. "Fast, put out your finger," Penina ordered, stretching her arm out and pointing towards the road with her index finger. "This could be our ride."

I followed Penina's example and extended my right arm and finger, Israeli hitchhiking style. The police slowed down. "*Yaish!*"[9] Penina clapped her hands together.

"I thought it was legal," I muttered to myself, not sure what to make of the police van that just stopped in front of us.

Penina didn't hesitate. "Let's go," she said, opening the two rear doors of the vehicle and climbing in.

I followed close behind her. After we settled ourselves and our backpacks on the narrow bench seats, the officer sitting on the front passenger's side got out and shut the doors behind us. I felt strange as our two police "escorts" drove us down the road towards Nahariya.

Holding on tightly in the bumping van, I leaned forward and whispered loudly to my friend, "We're in a police paddy wagon!"

"Yeah, the police like giving rides to soldiers," Penina said. "It's good I'm wearing my uniform," she patted her olive green army shirt.

A short time later, we arrived in downtown Nahariya. One of the policemen opened the door for us and we jumped out. *This is obviously an everyday event,* I thought as Penina called out our thanks to the two officers.

The driver stuck his head out the window and wished us, "Good luck," and "All the best."

I watched the police van drive away. "That was great," I said.

"Yeah," Penina agreed, slipping on her backpack. "Good thing we got a *tremp* fast. Now let's go find everyone. I'm hungry."

I felt lighthearted as we went to meet the rest of the Livnoters near the outdoor fast food stands and cafes. I was

---

[9] "All right!" "Yes!"

happy that I'd decided to postpone my backpacking trip to Europe next month. I couldn't imagine leaving Israel so soon.

Liz and I were planning on renting an apartment together in Jerusalem after the program ended. We'd hang out and maybe learn a little more about Judaism and the country. There was so much I wanted to see and do.

I ordered a slice of pizza and sat down to eat with the others. I was looking forward to living in Jerusalem—almost as much as I was looking forward to getting back to Tzfat to soak my blistered feet in a basin of warm water.

·☙· CHAPTER 6 ·☙·

"So you went to Jerusalem." Fran prompted me to continue after I took a short break to drink some water.

"Right," I said, taking a last sip.

Carol took my empty cup and set it down next to my bed. "Where'd you live?"

CHANUKAH APARTMENT
(December 1984)

I rented my first apartment in Jerusalem on Chanukah, the holiday of miracles and light. Liz and I looked at a few different places before we found our "Chanukah apartment." We checked the rental ads in the *Jerusalem Post*, making appointments to see the ones we'd circled. Ayelet was the first person we met for a tour of a vacant basement apartment in the neighborhood of Romema.

"It's my parents' place." The young Israeli woman spoke to us in English. Her accent was strong, but her voice was gentle.

We looked around the apartment for a few minutes before deciding it wasn't for us. "Thanks anyway," Liz told Ayelet, "but we're interested in something a little brighter and a little cheaper."

"That's okay," Ayelet replied, throwing one end of her

red knit scarf over her shoulder. "There will be others who will come to see it, and you will find some place good for you too." She led us back up to the street and continued walking for a few steps. Then she stopped. "I live right over there," she said, pointing ahead, "only a few doors down. "Why don't you come with me back to my apartment? I just baked cookies."

Liz and I happily accepted Ayelet's unexpected offer and followed her home. After being in the country for a few months, I already knew that the precautions about strangers that had been ingrained in me since my early childhood in the US were for the most part unnecessary in Israel. Most of the people I came into contact with were friendly, open and trusting. Here, being distant or wary of others actually seemed improper and even unfriendly.

Sitting on chairs in Ayelet's small living room, I was glad she had invited us to spend some time with her. We munched on freshly baked cinnamon cookies, drank tea and spoke about our different lives. I was amazed at how comfortable we all felt together. We might not ever see each other again, but that wasn't important. What mattered to all of us was the moment we were in.

An hour later, Liz and I thanked Ayelet and got up to leave.

"I'm glad you came for this visit," Ayelet said, walking us to the door. "Good luck in finding an apartment and have a good stay in Israel."

"We will," we both answered at the same time, before starting on our way again.

It took us a few more days of hunting before we found what we were looking for—a small two-bedroom apartment in Kiryat Moshe, the same neighborhood where my friend Esther lived. Eager and excited, we agreed to meet with the landlord the next evening at his home to review the rental contract. He'd translate the Hebrew for us.

The landlord, a short, clean-shaven man with scarcely any hair left on his head, reviewed the contract with us around a low coffee table in his family room. It was the first night of Chanukah and a large menorah was set up next to the window for all who passed by outside to see. Just as we finished signing all the papers, the landlord's wife entered the room with four young children who gathered around the menorah.

"That wraps things up," the landlord said, clipping his pen into his shirt pocket. "If you need anything, you know where we are." He handed Liz and me our copy of the contract and a set of keys to the apartment.

We were halfway out the front door when he spoke again. "We're about to light the Chanukah candles with some of our grandchildren. They're staying by us for the first night of the holiday," he said. "You're welcome to join us, if you're not in a rush."

I looked to Liz for an answer. Her eyes showed the hesitation I was feeling. We weren't in a rush, but neither of us knew how to respond to the unexpected invitation. I felt a little embarrassed. *Who lights Chanukah candles with their landlord and his family?* Not wanting to be rude, we accepted the offer to stay longer.

"Let's just light the candles with them and then leave right away," I whispered to Liz as we walked back to the family room behind our new landlord. Liz nodded in full agreement.

After the three traditional blessings were recited and the candles were lit, the landlord's smiling wife brought out a plateful of traditional Chanukah jelly doughnuts, called *sufganiyot*. The oldest boy passed them around, offering Liz and me first. His grandfather then put on a cassette of Chanukah songs. Soon the candle-lighting ceremony turned into a festive celebration. Our peppy landlord took two of his sticky-fingered grandchildren by their hands and danced with them around the room. His wife and the rest of the children clapped and sang along with the music. Liz and I ate our *sufganiyot* slowly and watched the action around us.

Despite my reluctance to let loose, I found myself laughing along with the others. Soon, Liz and I were also quietly singing the traditional tunes. I had a warm feeling inside me that was beginning to feel familiar.

"I'm glad we stayed," I leaned over and whispered in Liz's ear.

"So am I," Liz whispered back.

The celebrating gradually came to an end and we left with smiles on our faces. I knew that I had not only made a good choice about which apartment to rent, I had also made a good decision about staying in Israel, where remarkable people and uplifting experiences were everywhere. And where my soul felt at home.

"Sorry I'm late," Fran rushed into the room. "We had some difficulties with the patient before you, but everything's okay now." She checked my temperature while Carol instructed me on a new exercise. "I see that according to the most recent X-rays," Fran said, her nose in my charts, "your ribs are healing nicely."

"She's doing great," Carol agreed. "Bring your chair," she told Fran. "Shelly's got more stories for us."

"The ones I'm going to tell you today will be spread out over about a year."

"Sounds good." Fran was already seated.

Carol smiled in my direction. "I've been telling my husband some of your stories. My twin teenage sons also listened in on one or two of them. They're fifteen and usually not interested in our conversations, but I caught them actually paying attention."

"That's funny," Fran said, "yesterday I told my sister about us because I had to explain why I couldn't meet with her before my afternoon job at the fitness center. Then I told her a couple of Shelly's experiences. She said she wished she could join us."

"Whoa, now I'm starting to feel *quite* embarrassed," I said.

"Oh, don't worry," Carol reassured me. "Nobody's really focusing on you—just your stories!"

"That's right," Fran nodded. "So," poised at the edge of her chair, she looked at me, "whenever you're ready."

RIDING THE BUS
(February 1985)

I was sure that any minute I would lose my lunch. I still wasn't used to the way Israeli bus drivers sped through their routes.

Israel's elaborate bus system is the standard means of public transportation. When I wasn't learning about Israel and Judaism at the Machon Ora Seminary in Jerusalem, I traveled by bus to do errands, meet with friends or visit other parts of the country. Although I suffered from motion sickness, the bus rides were often experiences worth remembering. Sometimes, they were even worth feeling a little nauseous.

Today's memorable journey, and also the cause of my state of nausea, was a bumpy, twisting ride through the streets of Jerusalem. The screaming infant one seat ahead of me didn't help matters.

"Why's she crying?" asked the woman with burnt-orange dyed hair sitting next to the baby's mother.

"Is she hungry?" The plump woman across the aisle pulled her glasses down to the tip of her nose and leaned over her knitting to get a better look.

Before the young, anxious mother could open her mouth to reply, the elderly passenger sitting next to me stuck her long, thin face between the two seats in front of us and gave her opinion on the matter. "Could be she's got gas."

"Does she take a pacifier?" asked the knitting woman from across the aisle.

"Here, let me try to burp her." The orange-haired woman next to the mother stretched her arms out towards the tiny howling baby.

The bus came to a jerky stop. My stomach did summersaults as I watched the now desperate-looking mother pass her fitful child over to the inviting stranger at her side.

A soldier, an elderly man and two boys wearing white buttoned-down shirts and black yarmulkes got on the bus. They paid their fare, and walked down the aisle towards the back. The elderly man didn't get far before a girl stood up to give him her seat. Just as the door shut, a woman wearing a blue skirt and a silvery blue head scarf came rushing up the street pushing a baby carriage towards the bus.

"*Rega, nahag!*"[10] someone called out to the driver who hadn't seen the woman coming from behind.

"*Nahag!*"[11] Another man shouted for the driver to open the back door. "There's a carriage that needs to get on!"

The back door opened and the woman guided the bulky carriage up the metal steps. A young man on the bus helped pull it up as the door rattled shut and we continued on our way.

The woman in blue maneuvered her buggy to a corner of the open standing area near the back steps. Leaning against the buggy to prevent it from rolling, she pulled a thin, rectangular bus card out of her purse and handed it to the man standing next to her. The man passed the green and white card to the girl sitting ahead of him, who handed

---

[10] "Wait, driver!"
[11] "Driver!"

it up to the next passenger. Passed forward from person to person, the card finally reached the driver. After pulling away from the bus stop, the driver skillfully punched a small hole in one of the numbers on the card and sent it back over his shoulder.

Meanwhile, the first infant crying in front of me was still inconsolable. The plump woman from across the aisle had put the sweater she was knitting on the empty seat next to her and was now vigorously searching for a pacifier in her shoulder bag. "Aaah, I found it!" she exclaimed, waving the small, round silicone apparatus in the air. "I bought this the other day for my nephew." She removed the pacifier from its cellophane plastic wrapping and handed it over to the mother.

Reaching over her orange-haired neighbor who was rocking and patting the screeching baby in her arms, the hopeful mother popped the pacifier into her frantic daughter's open mouth. Everybody waited a moment to see what would happen next.

"It's working!" one of the women cried out, as the little one instantly quieted down.

"Finally, she's calm," sighed the plump woman who'd found the pacifier.

The thin-faced grandmother next to me peeked through the space between the seats again. "Just look at the sweetie."

"What a little doll she is." Caressing a soft, miniature cheek, the woman holding the now pacified baby smiled at the young mother next to her and then handed her the quieted bundle.

"*Todah*,"[12] the grateful mother said, cradling her peaceful child in her arms.

---

[12] Thank you.

I leaned my forehead on the seat in front of me, where both mother and baby were feeling more at ease. I was relieved that the "bus nannies" had succeeded.

"Are you okay?" A gentle hand lightly touched my shoulder. I lifted my head to find a woman in a caramel-colored pants suit standing next to me in the aisle. "My apartment is right around the corner, if you want to get off with me and come in for a rest or something to drink."

I thought that I must look pretty sick if someone was offering me help. I politely declined the offer in the best Hebrew I could conjure up. "*Todah,* but I get off soon," I said weakly. "I can wait another minute."

When the bus finally slowed down for my stop, I could hear whimpers coming from the area behind me, where the woman dressed in blue was standing with her baby carriage. As I made my way towards the back door, loud wails suddenly burst forth from the carriage.

"Why's he crying?" a woman sitting near the standing area asked the baby's mother.

"I don't know." The mother was gently rocking the carriage in an effort to calm her unhappy son.

The bus stopped. With one hand on my upset stomach, I slowly began walking down the back steps.

"Does he take a bottle?" another passenger inquired.

I was relieved when my feet touched the pavement. But, as I was thankfully breathing in the fresh air, the sound of shrill cries came from inside the bus. Then, just as the doors were slowly shutting behind me, I heared an anxious voice calling out above the commotion.

"Hey! Anybody here have a pacifier?"

·❖· *CHAPTER* *8* ·❖·

SHABBAT AT MALKA'S

(April 1985)

Shabbat[13] at Malka's was the best. Malka was director, teacher and house mother of the English department of Machon Ora girls' seminary in Jerusalem. A widow, she often invited her students to spend Shabbat with her in her comfortable apartment in the Old City. I never tired of sitting around Malka's table singing Shabbat songs, feasting on her homemade meals, learning about the weekly Torah portion and listening to her many stories. All the girls knew Shabbat with Malka not only promised to be restful, but also delicious and spiritually elevating.

"I've been having such a hard time making *aliyah*,"[14] complained a student from South Africa while we were eating Malka's famous chocolate cake. "The bureaucracy is crazy."

"I've also been having problems," the tall English girl on the other side of the table informed us in her proper British accent. "But mine are with the Student Loans offices."

---

[13] The Sabbath.
[14] Immigration to Israel; lit., "ascent."

"Well, you guys don't know what I've been through with my landlord!" joined in the excited New Yorker sitting next to me.

One by one, the different hardships or problems that we were each having in Israel circulated the Shabbat table.

Malka slowly and quietly savored the last bite of her cake as she listened to us. "It's true there are plenty of things that we are not used to here," she finally said, interrupting our chorus of complaints. "But think how far this country has come in such a short time. And we all know there is much, much more to Israel than these unpleasant experiences we all have at one time or another."

"That's true," agreed the student from New York who was upset about her landlord. "But like you said, we're not used to the way things are done, or for that matter, sometimes not done here," she admitted.

"I know," Malka said sympathetically. It can be difficult, especially when your families aren't here to help you deal with these things." Malka smoothed her hands over her pleated skirt and collected her thoughts. "Let me tell you a story."

We all loved Malka's stories. They had a way of making us feel good and positive, and they usually contained some words of wisdom. We waited as she paused to sip her tea.

Then, with grey and blond wisps of hair peeking out from under her elegant Shabbat hat, Malka began, "A few months ago, I was redoing my bathroom. You know how in Israel the faucets are usually high up over the basin and water can sometimes splash out when you're washing? Well, I didn't want that anymore. I wanted the faucet on the wall to be closer down to the new sink that had just been installed. So," Malka's blue eyes sparkled as she spoke, "I marked a big X on the spot where I wanted the plumber to put the faucet. I had to go out to the grocery store, so I showed him the X. He said he would be sure to put the faucet right there.

"Well..." Malka paused. Lowering her head, she shook it slowly from side to side. Then, with the palm of her hand she tried to stifle a laugh. "When I came back from shopping," she continued, "I saw that the plumber had done just as he had promised. He put the faucet right exactly on the X. But," she cried, "he made the sink lower!" Now Malka was laughing hard, her eyes squeezed tightly shut, her shoulders bouncing up and down. "He moved the basin of the sink down from its original place!" she gasped.

"Oh my G-d," the South African student groaned, shaking her head in disbelief.

"So what'd you do?" I was both curious and amused.

"Yeah, what'd you say to the guy?" My friend Liz, who'd also come to learn at Machon Ora after the Livnot program, was curious too.

Malka gradually stopped laughing. "I didn't say anything," she managed to reply with a straight face. "I just laughed—like I was laughing now. What else could I do? I figured that's probably the way Israeli plumbers are used to installing sinks and faucets. I'll just have to get used to it." She chuckled again.

"But you know," she continued more seriously, "we can't let these differences or little annoyances take away from the reason we're all here in the first place. We're lucky to be living through this part of Jewish history in our own country. After more than two thousand years of exile, we've finally returned, and now we have the chance to help make the State of Israel great like it once was." Malka wiped a bit of chocolate off her fingertip with a napkin and then looked at all of us sitting around her table. "It might take a while to do that. But that's why we're here."

We sat quietly for a moment, absorbing Malka's last words. We had all come to Israel from different parts of the world. Although we complained about our difficulties, each one of us had fallen in love with the country and the people, and some of us had already made it our new home. I knew Malka was right. The obstacles we had to overcome were small sacrifices to make for the privilege of being in Israel, even at that very moment.

When the meal was finished, we helped Malka clear the table. I carried some glasses into the kitchen. Liz was there stacking plates in the sink.

"I think I'm going to go for a walk down to the Kotel,"[15] I said, handing her the glasses. Malka's story and its message had gotten me in the mood to walk around the Old City and visit the Western Wall. "Want to go with me?" I asked Liz.

"Go to the Kotel, now?" Liz turned on the tap and let the water run over the dirty dishes. "Hmmm, no thanks. I'm getting tired. I think I'll go in the morning." She waved a hand in my direction. "You go. We'll talk when you get back, if I'm still awake," she promised.

A few minutes later, I was strolling in the crisp night air down the pathway that led from Malka's house to the long staircase overlooking the Western Wall. All was quiet around me, with the exception of an occasional Shabbat song flowing from the apartment windows I was passing. Skipping one by one down the many steps towards the Wall, I thought about the other times I had visited the Old City. This was the first time I'd be visiting the Western Wall at night.

As I neared the enormous ancient stones, I walked more slowly. Except for a few figures praying or walking nearby, the plaza area leading up to the dimly lit wall was empty

---

[15] Western Wall—remnant of the ancient wall that surrounded the Second Temple's courtyard.

and quiet. Anywhere else would have felt creepy or eerie to me. But the closer I drew to the Wall the more secure and peaceful I felt.

Only recently had I come to really believe that the world wasn't haphazard, that there was a guiding force. My faith had come without me trying to logically understand it. Gradually, I had come to feel that I was not alone—ever. G-d was always with me, watching over and guiding me. As I moved slowly in the dark, towards the faint light of the only remaining wall which had once surrounded the Second Holy Temple, I felt closer and more open to Him than ever.

Walking back to Malka's place after saying a short prayer at the Wall, a cold breeze brushed against me and I shivered. But on the inside, I felt warm and content. When I returned to the apartment, I found some of the girls talking in the living room.

"You should have been with me at the Kotel," I told them, unzipping my blue Israeli *dubon* jacket. "It's so different at night."

"That's what I've heard," said the red-headed Australian girl sitting on Malka's couch.

The South African pulled the reclining chair she was lounging on to a sitting position. "I like being there during the day when hundreds of people are milling about."

"We weren't even allowed to get *near* the Kotel before we won the Six Day War in '67," the tall English student stirring her cup of tea reminded us. "So I'm happy we can go there now whenever we want."

Continuing our discussion for a while longer, I was the first to say goodnight. I dragged myself wearily up Malka's carpeted stairs to the guest bedroom Liz and I were sharing.

"I'm exhausted," I announced, flopping myself onto the bed next to Liz's.

Liz was sitting up reading with her blanket pulled up to her waist. "Me too," she said, putting down her book. "I've been up late every night this week because of Passover vacation. I haven't caught up on my sleep yet from the Seder.[16] We didn't get to bed that night until two o'clock in the morning."

Stretched out on top of the yellow flowered blanket, I turned to face Liz. "Penina from Livnot got out of the army for Passover and invited me to her family's Seder in Petah Tikvah," I said. "We finished at about one o'clock."

I sat up on the bed and crossed my legs under me, Indian-style. "I didn't expect it to go on for so long. We did everything from the very beginning to the very end. We read the entire Haggadah,[17] sang all the songs and ate an amazing meal. We also discussed the different meanings of each part of the Seder as we went along. I don't remember ever doing that before. And at the end," my face lit up as I continued, "Penina's whole family jumped up from the table and started dancing and singing: *"Le'shanah ha'ba'ah be'Yerushalayim!"*[18]

"We also had a great time," Liz said. "Even the younger kids stayed up really late."

"Passover is special here."

"That's right. We were brought out of slavery in Egypt way back when, to live freely in the Land of Israel." Liz's eyes opened wider and a broad smile spread across her face. "And here we are!"

"And here we are!"

Suddenly, two voices outside calling out Shabbat greet-

---

[16] Celebratory meal held on Passover with narrations, rituals and prayers that commemorate the Jews' exodus from Egypt.

[17] Book with ceremonial narration of the Jews' exodus from Egypt read at the Passover Seder.

[18] Next year in Jerusalem!

ings to each other sailed into the bedroom through the slightly opened window.

"*Shabbat shalom!*"[19]

"*Shabbat shalom!*"

Opening the window wider, I stuck my head out and looked down onto the stone walkway that wound throughout the Jewish Quarter of the Old City and down to the Western Wall. "*Shabbat shalom*," I murmured quietly to the stones below before bringing my head back into the warmer room.

"You know who said '*Shabbat shalom*' to me last Shabbat?" I shut the window and pulled the yellow curtains over it.

"Who?" Liz yawned.

"Prime Minister Shamir."

"What?"

"It was so cool! Esther and I were walking through the Gan Sacher park on the way to her friend's apartment. And there he was with only one bodyguard, strolling through the park with his arms behind his back. He came straight towards us. At first I didn't know it was him. But then he got closer and it was obvious who he was. He nodded his head at us and said, '*Shabbat shalom*.'"

"What did you do?"

"We said '*Shabbat shalom*' back. We couldn't believe it was him. He's really short!"

"Look who's talking!" Liz laughed. "I would love to have been there with you." She yawned again. "Oh, man, I'm really tired. Can we go to sleep now?"

"Yep," I said. "If you can, that is. You know I snore, don't you?"

"Okay," swinging her legs around from under her

---

[19] Have a peaceful Sabbath.

blanket to the side of the bed, Liz threw her pillow at me. "You're not going to do that tonight, right?"

"Don't know," I laughed, throwing the pillow back at Liz. "But don't worry, I don't grind my teeth or sleepwalk," I teased.

"Thank G-d for that." Liz snuggled down under her blanket, putting her pillow under her head. "Goodnight, sweetie."

"Goodnight dear." I grabbed my toothbrush from my overnight bag and started across the narrow hallway towards the bathroom.

Malka's house was quiet. Everyone had gone to sleep. Silently, I closed the bathroom door behind me. The serenity of Shabbat, especially at Malka's in the Old City, was calming and peaceful. Setting my toothbrush down on the sink, I stood looking at my reflection in the bathroom mirror. Then, leaning closer to the glass, I smiled at myself.

"And here we are."

·❖· CHAPTER 9 ·❖·

RIGHT PLACE, RIGHT TIME

(October 1985)

"I don't think we're going the right way. Shelly, stop!" my pint-size Israeli friend Penina called from a short distance behind me. We were hiking down the mountainside to Wadi Amud, the valley that connects Tzfat to the Meron Mountain range.

"What do you mean we're going the wrong way?" I stopped walking and turned around on the dusty trail to face Penina. "We're going down. That's what we want to do."

Penina caught up to me. "Yeah, but there's no real path here. And look over there!" She pointed ahead. The mountainside ended where a cliff with a short, but steep drop took its place.

"Oh my G-d, we did come the wrong way!" Moving closer, I peered over the edge of the mountain. "This is bad."

Arnon and Meira had asked me to join the Livnot U'Lehibanot staff and help run the upcoming fall program. After spending the summer visiting family and friends in Chicago, I returned to Israel and to Tzfat. The new *chevreh* had the day off, so I went on a *tiyul* with Penina, who had just recently finished her army service.

We stood for another moment in our hiking shoes and sun hats, staring at the cliff ahead of us, contemplating what to do next. "We can't go back up and start coming down somewhere else," I said. "It will take us too long. We'd be tired out before we even started our hike down in the valley."

"Plus," Penina added, "if we start from a different point, we might not have enough time before the sun sets to go through the valley and get back up one of the mountains on the other side near Meron."

We took a minute to consider our predicament. "Let's check if there's another way to get down from somewhere around here," I suggested.

Penina was reluctant, but agreed to walk along the side of the cliff and look for a path that might lead down the mountain. The morning sun had not yet warmed the cool mountain air, and the ground was still moist with dew. With the exception of an occasional croak from a hidden toad and the snap of a twig underfoot, all was quiet as we began our search.

Suddenly, Penina stopped. "I think we could go down from here," she indicated a narrow, rocky path that looked like it might lead to the bottom of the mountain.

"It's pretty steep." Now I was reluctant.

"Yeah, you're right. So let's head back up to where we started from and find the real way down," Penina said decisively.

"Really? We're giving up, just like that?" I stared hard at the unconventional, twisting path that plunged downward before us and considered what the odds were of making it to the valley in one piece. Then, I looked up the mountain, my eyes sweeping the area above from where we had just come. "*Ooof!* I really don't want to go back up and start over," I admitted.

"Okay," Penina said. She pulled the wide rim of her

sunhat further down over her eyes and shifted the weight of her backpack to a more comfortable position on her back. "Let's go for it."

I let Penina take the lead. As a Sabra,[20] she'd been going on *tiyulim* since she was a little girl, and had been on many more mountain hikes than I had. We both hoped that her past hiking experiences would come in handy now.

Slowly, we started down the steep, jagged pathway, immediately discovering that it was too difficult and too dangerous to continue in an upright position. Sitting on the ground, we began inching our way down, stretching out one leg at a time and then cautiously pulling the rest of our body forward. We grabbed onto rocks and shrubs to help prevent us from slipping. Neither of us spoke, as dirt and small stones fell away from under our feet, silently landing far below.

Afraid to look down, I kept my focus on each step. "This is crazy!" I gasped in a strained voice through my clenched jaw.

"Just concentrate," Penina advised. I could tell by the tenseness in my friend's voice that Penina was more nervous than she was letting on.

After a few stressful minutes, our feet finally touched down on a solid plateau. We both sighed in relief.

"Whoa," I said, catching my breath. "I wasn't sure we were going to make it."

"I don't think I can really talk about it right now," Penina said quietly. I noticed that her normally bright pink cheeks had gone pale.

We rested for a few minutes before continuing on with the much easier descent to the bottom that was ahead of us. The walk through the beautiful valley proved to be

---

[20] Native Israeli.

worth the trouble it took us to reach it. The sun was now shining brightly. We were enjoying the warm autumn day and the tranquility of being in nature. Wild flowers, butterflies and open-mouthed caves on the side of the trails accompanied us along the way. Occasionally, we heard the gurgling water of the nearby Amud Riverbed.

We stopped to picnic in the shade by a stream and discussed the route we would take for the rest of the hike. Penina was fairly certain that after we climbed up the mountain on the other side of the valley, we would arrive at a bus stop on the road at the top.

"We could catch the first bus that comes and hopefully be back in Tzfat by suppertime," she said.

The day passed quickly. The sun was lowering in the sky. We had only stopped one more time to eat and rest, but according to Penina, we were now behind schedule.

"If we don't speed up, it will be night before we manage to get up to the road," she said looking at her watch.

"How long do you think it will take us to reach the mountain and then hike up to the top?" I asked.

"At the rate we've been going, it will probably take us about an hour and a half. But it looks like the sun will be going down before then." Penina wasn't optimistic.

We were worried. We didn't want to be stranded in the valley or halfway up the mountainside in the dark. It wasn't a steep climb, but it wouldn't be as easy in the dark and I was sure it would be pretty scary.

"Let's get going," I urged Penina.

We picked up our pace to a swift gait, half running over stones and weeds lining the coarse path, until we reached the mountain base. Dusk had arrived. Hurrying, we strained to pull ourselves up, clutching at whatever brush or branches we could find growing out of the rocks. With just a short distance left, the mountain plunged into darkness. Only the crescent moon and the glittering stars provided relief from the black that enveloped us. Unable to make out the designated course in the dark, we took any trace of a pathway that led upwards.

I struggled to keep up with Penina, who seemed to be moving with the speed and stride of an experienced mountain goat. Nervous and out of breath, I worked even harder to haul myself up over the rocks, determined not to lose sight of my friend.

I hope we don't run into any wild animals. I prayed we'd find our way without any problems.

At last, we saw lights and heard the sound of a passing car not far above us. I wanted to stop and rest, relieved to see signs of civilization. But I didn't dare stray from Penina, who was already much further ahead.

When we reached the road at the top of the mountain, I breathlessly plopped myself down on the nearest bolder. Every muscle in my body ached. Looking around, I realized right away that something wasn't right.

"Where's the bus stop?" I asked.

Penina had arrived before me and had already checked out the premises. "It looks like we veered pretty far off the regular trail and came up at a different point," she answered.

"How are we going to get back to Tzfat?" I was drained.

"We could walk," Penina offered halfheartedly.

"No way!"

"You're right. I don't think I could do that right now either," she agreed. "So let's *tremp*."

Hitchhike. I loved the idea. Being chauffeured back to Tzfat by car sounded heavenly. Although there weren't many vehicles on the road, we were confident that someone driving by would stop for us. Within a few minutes, a solemn-looking young man in a little red car pulled over. He was headed for Tzfat! We could hardly believe how quickly we were being rescued from our marooned state.

"He came right on time," Penina said cheerfully.

"Thank G-d," I moaned, dragging myself and my backpack towards the car.

Though we didn't know our young "savior," Penina and I listened sympathetically throughout most of the short ride back to Tzfat as he told us about the tragedy his family had recently experienced. "My cousin was just killed in a terrorist attack a few weeks ago," he lost no time informing us. "He was supposed to get married next month. We should be reacting with more force to terrorism. I don't understand why we give in to outside pressures."

I listened to the grieving man, understanding a good amount of his Hebrew. His openness was drawing me in, as his frustration and pain continued to gush out of him like an exploding geyser. I was feeling sympathy and sadness for him, his family and all who'd suffered losses throughout the years.

Then, pushing his thin black hair off his forehead, the young man suddenly changed the subject. "Where are you coming from?" he asked, glancing sideways at Penina in the passenger's seat, his expression brightening.

"We were on a *tiyul* in Wadi Amud," Penina answered.

"That's a great hike. And what are you doing in Tzfat?" He guessed we didn't live there.

"We're helping out at a program in the Old City. It's called Livnot U'Lehibanot."

"And you took the day off to be out in the fresh air and sunshine?" It seemed that a calmness of some kind had taken hold of our driver. The change in his manner lightened the atmosphere in the car. We spoke about more trivial and mundane things for the last few minutes of our ride.

"*Todah,*" Penina and I both said when we reached Tzfat.

The man gave a slight nod of his head. "No problem."

"We should only hear good things," Penina added, as we got out of his car.

"Amen." Smiling, he raised the palm of his hand as if to say goodbye. Then he drove away.

A mixture of feelings were swirling around inside me—from the scary beginning of our *tiyul,* through the relaxing, fun and beautiful hike in the valley, to the worrisome climb up the mountain and the somewhat unsettling, but helpful ride back to Tzfat.

"I'm sure we were meant to meet up with that man and his little red car," I told Penina, as we walked through the stone pathways of the Old City of Tzfat. "Everything about today caused us to be at the exact place at the exact moment for us to meet him. And he wasn't just there because we needed him to help us out. I think he really needed us right then too, to vent and to let out some of his sadness and frustration."

"I think so too," Penina agreed. "Everything happens for a reason."

As we walked down the steps towards Livnot U'Lehibanot, I thought about how in just ten hours, we'd experienced danger, fear and worry, a closeness to nature and an appreciation for the environment, satisfaction and relief, sorrow and pain, compassion and sympathy. It had definitely been more than just a regular *tiyul.* It had been an extraordinary day. But then, I was beginning to feel that just about every day that I spent in Israel was extraordinary.

I hoped that would never change.

·❧· CHAPTER 10 ·❧·

"I'm guessing there must be something extra-ordinary or special about the holidays in Israel too." Carol shifted her attention away from my leg to look at me.

"Uh huh," I nodded. "Even the minor ones that I never really knew much about, like Tu B'Shvat."

"That's a Jewish holiday that celebrates trees and their fruits," Carol told Fran, pleased with herself that she actually knew what it was.

"How does one celebrate Tube Shvot?" Fran asked.

"Shelly's going to tell us, right Shelly?" Carol smiled at me.

"If you say so, I guess I am." I rested my leg for a moment as I looked out the window and tried to jog my memory. "Okay, I'll tell you about one of my first Tu B'Shvats in Israel. I remember telling my friend Esther about it too. It was after she got married."

"We didn't even know your Esther was engaged," Carol said.

"Right, I can't tell you everything about everyone."

"Did she marry an Israeli?" Fran asked.

"Yep, she did." I started my exercises again. "But I'm not going to tell you about all that now."

Carol and Fran were quiet, waiting to hear what I *was* going to tell them.

TREES, FRUIT & PERFECT BLESSING
(January 1986)

"I really enjoyed Tu B'Shvat this year," I told Esther, as I peeled a large Jaffa orange. Esther and her new husband had invited me and some of their friends for a Shabbat meal a couple of days after the holiday of Tu B'Shvat. I had recently moved back to Jerusalem and was glad to steal some time alone with Esther in the kitchen while we made a fruit salad with the holiday leftovers.

"My family never paid much attention to Tu B'Shvat," I told Esther, cutting up the orange and adding it to the apple slices in the large glass bowl on the counter. "But I remember our Sunday school used to collect money for the Jewish National Fund to buy trees for planting in Israel. Each kid got a thick sheet of white shiny paper with a picture of a big tree on it to take home to his parents. There were little blank squares that we were supposed to stick stamps on—one for each tree that our families bought."

"I remember those." Esther nodded as she opened a ripe melon. "So what did you enjoy so much about the holiday?"

"I went with Malka and the girls and teachers from Machon Ora to plant trees on a hillside somewhere outside of Jerusalem. We spread out over the hill and took turns digging with our shovels and spades. We must have planted about a hundred trees!"

"I've also planted trees here," Esther said, adding chunks of melon to the bowl. "It's really a good feeling."

"Right," I agreed. "Once our parents paid to have others do the planting, and now *we're* the ones doing it."

I felt proud of my small contribution to the country. I knew how important and valuable each tree in Israel was, not only ecologically and environmentally, but also because it played a part in reclaiming our Land.

"And that wasn't all we did," I went on. "Later that afternoon, we walked over to one of our teachers' houses for a Tu B'Shvat Seder." I began removing the brown fuzzy skins from two large kiwis. "I had never heard of a Tu B'Shvat Seder before."

Esther smiled and pointed her knife towards me. "I bet you were expecting matzah again, like on Pesach. Weren't you?" she teased.

"Ha ha! Nope, I wasn't," I answered good-humoredly. "Actually, I didn't know *what* to expect. None of us did." I cut the emerald green kiwis into small pieces. "I figured we'd learn a little bit more about the holiday—talk about trees or something like that, probably have a drink, some snacks and then leave. "But when we saw what the teacher had set up for us, I knew we were in for something special.

"The long dining room table was covered with a white tablecloth and beautifully arranged platters and trays with every type of fruit you could imagine. There were dried wrinkly fruits like figs, dates, apricots and even dried pineapples and cherries. All the different kinds of citrus and regular everyday fruits were laid out in-between the rarer exotic ones. There was papaya, lychee and passion fruit. Some had unusual shapes and colors, like the yellow star fruit."

"And obviously, everyone sat down and tasted everything," Esther prompted me along.

"Nope. First the teacher gave an explanation about each and every one of the different fruits—the part of the country they came from, the type of tree they grow on, the season they grow in, and all kinds of other stuff."

"And *then* you had a fruit feast."

"No. Then we learned a song about trees taken from a verse in the Talmud.

"I know that one," Esther said, throwing some raisins into the bowl. "It's about a traveler who wanted to bless a tree that had given him a place to rest, kept the hot sun off of him and provided him with something to eat and drink while on his journey. But the tree was already blessed with everything—sweet fruit, nice shade and a stream of flowing water beneath it. So the man gave it a blessing that all the saplings that came from it would be just like the tree."

"Yeah, that's it!" I was impressed with Esther's ability to recall the verse so easily. "I really like that. It's the perfect blessing, isn't it?"

"Esther, *mah koreh*?"[21] Esther's husband was calling from the dining room. "Did you forget about us poor creatures out here?"

He and the guests around the table had been waiting patiently for us to return with dessert. We *had* been talking for quite a while.

"Here, you can take this in," Esther handed me a platter filled with bite-size assorted cakes. Picking up the large bowl of fruit salad we had just prepared, she started out of the kitchen ahead of me. Then she stopped and turned around. "So, *nu*? Did you eat all those fruits or not?"

"Of course. We all did," I said. We tasted every single one of them, more than once! And" I smiled sheepishly, "don't ask. I loved celebrating the holiday, but I felt *so* sick to my stomach afterwards!"

Esther tossed her head back and let out a hearty laugh. Then, as we entered the dining room, she held the glass bowl up high like a waitress and cheerfully called out in Hebrew to all who had been waiting, "Fruit salad, anyone?"

---

21 What's happening?

❖ *CHAPTER 11* ❖

"Anybody want some grapes?" I gestured to the bowl of green clusters next to my bed that my mother had brought earlier when she came to visit me. I suddenly felt like eating something juicy and sweet.

"No thanks," Carol and Fran both shook their heads.

"Any other holidays you didn't know much about?" Carol was trying to get me back on track.

"Hmmm," I went through the calendar year in my mind. "Have you ever heard of Jerusalem Day?"

"No," both women shook their heads again.

"I assume it has something to do with Jerusalem," Fran said.

"That's right. It's a holiday celebrating the reunification of Jerusalem."

"What do mean by reunification?" Fran looked puzzled. "When was Jerusalem ever separated?"

"About the same time the surrounding Arab countries rejected the reality of Israel becoming a Jewish state," I said. "Right after the United Nations accepted the Partition Plan in 1948 and granted Israel its independence, five Arab countries started a war to prevent Israel from existing." I looked at Fran. "That's when the Jordanians took control of major parts of Jerusalem. For nineteen years the city was split into Arab sections and Jewish sections. Jews weren't allowed to go to the Hadassah Hospital on Mount Scopus, the Western Wall in the Old City or any other holy Jewish sites located in Arab sections."

"So Israel officially becomes a state and right away parts of its capital city get taken over. How does that work?" Fran looked confused.

"It doesn't," I laughed. "So when the Arab countries, who still hoped to wipe Israel off the map, lost the Six Day War in 1967, Israel took back the parts of the city that the Jordanians had seized in 1948. That's when Jerusalem became reunified."

"And thus," Carol tilted her head towards me, "Jerusalem Day."

I nodded. "And thus, Jerusalem Day."

EVERY YEAR IN JERUSALEM
(June 1986)

The Jerusalem Day procession was more exciting than I had imagined. Liz and I put on comfortable shoes, stuffed snacks into our backpacks and joined the multitudes that came to celebrate the nineteenth anniversary of the reunification of Jerusalem. Beginning at midnight from the Mercaz HaRav Yeshivah[22] in Kiryat Moshe, we joined the throngs of people making their way through the lively Jerusalem streets towards the Old City. I felt like we were all moving in a big wave, crossing like the ebb and tide of the sea—stopping at the red lights and rushing across with the green.

---

22 Torah academy.

When we reached the top of an upward sloping road, I stopped to take in the panoramic view of the scores of people parading en masse before and after us. There seemed to be no beginning or end to the crowds moving forward. Blue and white Israeli flags were everywhere, flapping and fluttering above the bobbing heads, or waving rhythmically from side to side. Group after group of celebrants singing Israeli and Zionist songs flocked past me as I watched, unable to pull myself away from the overwhelming scene.

The last march that had a strong effect on me was years ago when the neo-Nazis had wanted to demonstrate in Skokie. Now I was participating in something that would make Nazis everywhere go crazy. All around me was more than just the survival of the Jewish nation. It was its amazing revival. Israel and all of Jerusalem, including the Old City and the Western Wall, were once again in Jewish hands. The Jewish Land and its people were thriving and growing stronger every day. And there was no stopping us!

I was sure that, like many of the Arabs in the country, the protesting Palestinian students from my university days would also be furious if they could see what I was witnessing now. As for myself, I felt like belting out what everyone around me was singing with great passion: "*Am Yisrael Chai!*—The nation of Israel lives!"

"C'mon, Shelly." I felt Liz turn me around and push me forward. "We should keep moving," she shouted over the singing and clapping. "There's supposed to be dancing up ahead in the center of town where the roads are closed off. You wanna dance, don't you?"

We continued on with the rest of the marchers until we reached the first circles of dancers who were flooding the streets with overwhelming enthusiasm. I grabbed Liz by the arm and dragged her over to where the women and girls were kicking up their feet together.

"I have to take a break," Liz said after a while, breathing hard and pushing stray locks of her reddish-brown hair off her freckled face.

We rested for a few minutes and then moved on, stopping a couple of more times along the way for more dancing. Eventually, we reached the Old City and the plaza leading up to the Western Wall. Already overflowing with people, the plaza was filling up so rapidly that soldiers manning the security checkpoints were having a difficult time keeping up with the inspection of each person's bag or backpack.

Like an older sister, Liz took my hand and held onto it tightly. "We have to make sure we don't lose each other."

I was wondering how I would ever find Beth and Michelle, my two newest friends who'd come to Israel a couple of years before me. "I can't believe I told Beth and Michelle that I'd try to find them here," I told Liz.

"What?"

"I said," I raised my voice so Liz could hear me better, "it will be incredible if I actually find my friends in all of this. They were going to meet me near the women's section by the Wall." I stood on my tiptoes and stretched my neck up to see if I could spot them anywhere.

"If they're here somewhere," Liz shouted back, "we'll probably only find them later on in the morning, closer to dawn when it's less crowded. C'mon, let's try to get over to the Kotel."[23]

I was starting to feel tired, but the high-spirited atmosphere near the Western Wall reenergized me. A dancer at heart, I joined the whirling feet on the women's side of the Wall, stopping only when I noticed two familiar

---

23 Western Wall—remnant of the ancient wall that surrounded the Second Temple's courtyard.

faces standing close by. Beth with her fine brown hair and Michelle with her long, thick ponytail, both wearing sweatshirt jackets and mid-length jean skirts, were clapping and singing while they watched the dancing. I left the circle and ran over to them.

"Unbelievable!" Beth said, placing her hands on her narrow waist and shaking her head in disbelief. "I'm amazed that you spotted us."

"I'm so glad we found each other!" Michelle called out with a radiant smile. "We gave up the idea of looking for you when we saw how packed it was here. Hey!" Michelle suddenly noticed someone trying to get our attention. "Isn't that your friend Liz up there?" Liz was waving both of her hands excitedly in the air, gesturing for the three of us to come over. She was standing on the elevated grassy area off to the side.

"You're right!" I said, waving to Liz. "Looks like she's found a place for us to sit."

"Can't imagine how she managed that," Michelle said, "but let's go over there!"

We climbed up onto the triangular patch of grass and congratulated Liz for finding enough space for all of us to rest until sunrise. Michelle opened a small bag of roasted peanuts, while Beth pulled out a bottle of water from her backpack and Liz polished an apple on her skirt. I popped a thick pink Bazooka bubble gum into my mouth.

"A month ago, I was on my way here to the Old City to visit Malka," I said, chewing hard on my gum. "But the atmosphere was so different then. It was Holocaust Day and you could actually feel the sadness in the air." I stopped chewing and looked at my friends. "As I was walking, the memorial siren suddenly went off. I knew that all the people and the traffic on the street would come to a stop when they heard the siren. But I didn't expect everyone to get out of their cars and stand still in the middle of the road. People even stood up inside the buses."

"The whole country stops at the same moment," Michelle said, "to silently remember."

Beth sighed. "That's the least we can do to pay homage to our six million who perished."

"Are we supposed to be happy celebrating Jerusalem Day now or sad remembering what happened during the Holocaust?" Liz asked.

"Both." Michelle was lying on her back, her ponytail flipped up over the bunched up sweatshirt she was using as a pillow. "This is the bright refreshing day that comes after the long scary night." She folded her hands on her stomach and looked up at the stars in the sky. "It's the light at the end of the dark tunnel. It's the warm spring that comes after the harsh winter."

"Very poetic," Beth said.

"And true," Michelle smiled.

We watched as the crowds thinned and the sun began its slow ascent in the sky. It spread its faint early morning rays onto the remaining Jerusalem Day celebrants who were patiently awaiting its arrival.

"Everyone's going to the Kotel," I said, noticing the flocks of people slowly moving towards the Wall.

"C'mon," Michelle said, picking herself up off the grass. "Let's go too."

We inched our way up to the Wall. Small folded and crunched up pieces of paper were stuffed into the many cracks and crevices of the massive boulders. Some had fallen and were now scattered on the ground below. They were the handwritten pleas of the myriad of people from all over the world who had come to visit the ancient wall that once stood on the western side of the Temple courtyard.

All around us hundreds of women and girls were already deep in their morning prayers. I was standing next to a girl in a long flowered skirt who was in the midst of a silent prayer. On the other side of me, a young woman with baggy pants was standing with her face buried inside her prayer book. The elderly woman directly in front of me closed her eyes as she pressed her cheek against the Wall. Praying voices from the men's side floated over the partition and mixed with the cries of a weeping woman who was seeking comfort from Above.

Moving even closer, I squeezed into a tight spot next to the Wall and leaned my forehead on its hard, cool surface. In only a few short days I would be flying to Chicago for another visit. I was happy I'd be seeing my family again, but sad to be leaving Israel. Every day I lived in the country I felt my connection to the Land and to G-d becoming stronger and more alive in me. Nearly two years had passed since I'd first arrived and my attachment to the people and to the place was growing all the time.

Placing the palms of my hands against the stone in front of me, I closed my eyes and said my own prayer in my heart. *When I return, please let it be forever. I want to be part of the country's future celebrations, achievements and triumphs. I want to be a part of those who help overcome Israel's troubles and struggles, and who help strengthen the people and build up the Land.*

I opened my eyes when I felt a light tap on my shoulder. It was Michelle. "Are you ready to go home?" she spoke softly near my ear. "We're all finished here and pretty tired."

"I guess so," I whispered, lowering one hand from the Wall.

"Don't worry," Michelle caught the melancholy look in my eyes, "you'll be back soon."

I let the fingertips of my other hand slide slowly down the giant stones until they fell to my side. "I know," I said stepping away. "Let's go home and get some sleep."

Michelle and I held hands as we weaved our way through the women and girls who were still facing the Wall. We found Beth and Liz gazing out at the nearby ruins of the ancient City of David while they waited for us. We all walked slowly towards the lines of buses that were quickly filling up with people leaving the Old City.

"This was definitely an experience," Liz said, as we found seats facing each other on a bus.

"It was," Beth agreed, as she sat down next to Michelle.

"We'll have to do this again," Michelle said, stifling a yawn.

"Right." I was sitting by the window, watching the continuous flow of people coming towards us. "Next year in Jerusalem!"

"That's what we say on Passover," Liz told me, resting her hands on the backpack in her lap.

"And at any other time that it's appropriate," Beth added.

Michelle looked at Beth. "It's always appropriate to say 'Next year in Jerusalem. And in her case," she pointed to me, "it's appropriate to wish her back in Jerusalem *before* next year."

The overloaded bus drove through the Dung Gate, leaving the Old City and its surrounding walls behind. I turned away from the large double-paned window.

"Don't worry," I assured my friends, "I'll be back way before then."

•❧• CHAPTER 12 •❧•

"You're sitting down?" I asked Carol, who had just moved over to the chair at the side of my bed.

"I finished with you for today," Carol said, "and my next patient was cancelled. So I have extra time for our 'story hour.'" Carol leaned her elbow on the bed. "It seems like you're still telling us about your early years in Israel. When do we get to the later parts?"

"Don't rush her," Fran told Carol lightheartedly. Then, standing up to adjust the pillow behind my head she turned to me. "I can also stay longer today. So keep going. And please don't leave out anything."

"If we're going to do this every day, then I can take it slow," I said.

"Of course, take it slow." Carol agreed.

I waited for Fran to return to her chair and then I began again. "After I spent a couple of months in Chicago, I came back to live in Jerusalem. I was so happy to be in Israel again."

NO PROBLEM
(November 1986)

I'd made up my mind. I was making *aliyah*.[24]

My parents weren't happy about me living far away. But I felt wonderful in Israel. With each day that passed, the newly awakened Zionist within me intensified. And now I was ready to make Israel my new home.

But acquiring my Israeli citizenship and all the rights and benefits that went along with becoming an *olah chadashah*[25] was not as simple as I had hoped. I found myself hopping back and forth from one Jerusalem municipality office to another. Each was in a different location, was only open at certain times of the day and usually required waiting in long lines, sometimes for hours.

I knew that, as the country advanced, public services and administrative workplaces would begin to run smoother, including those that were involved with the process of making *aliyah*. But that had yet to happen.

Now, the bureaucratic red tape, the disorganization, and the lack of available staff in all the different departments left me incredibly frustrated. At one office I waited for more than two hours, only to discover that I didn't have the right forms filled out. I would have to return some other time. Another office closed for the day right before my turn, forcing me to return at a later date.

After three weeks of what sometimes seemed like fruitless running around to get the necessary requirements in order, I finally broke down and cried. I couldn't believe it when the clerk in one of the governmental offices

---

[24] Immigration to Israel; lit., "ascent."
[25] New Israeli immigrant.

informed me that my new landlord hadn't signed the form
I was submitting in all the appropriate spaces. I had
tracked my landlord down in the hospital, where he was
having medical tests done, in order to get his signature for
that form. Now the stony-faced, middle-aged woman
sitting in front of me was saying that I wouldn't receive my
monthly rent subsidies unless I came back with it signed
again, "in all the right places."

I jumped up from my chair. "Why didn't anybody tell
me he had to sign on the back too?" Although I was trying
to keep my emotions in check, I could feel tears pooling up
in the corners of my eyes. "Do you know how many times
I have had to go back and forth for everything?" I slumped
back down into my seat. "I can't go again to him now," I
said more quietly. "He's about to have an operation."

The carefully made-up woman in black slacks and a
cream-colored sweater watched the tears slowly roll down
my cheeks. She handed me a tissue and then frowned at
the form on her desk as I wiped my eyes. "Don't worry,"
she said in a more gentle voice, lifting her now softer gaze
to me. "I'll take care of it."

I stared questioningly at this clerk with the high-arched
eyebrows who, like a chameleon, seemed to be changing
her colors before my eyes. "But you said it won't be
accepted this way."

"Don't worry," she repeated. "I'll handle it for you. You
don't have to come back."

"You're sure?"

"Yes." She patted my hand resting on her smooth
formica desktop. It will be okay."

I sighed. "Thank you."

"No problem." The clerk watched as I stood and, filled
with relief and gratitude, slowly walked out of the office.

Wandering aimlessly around the center of town, I tried
to console myself. I wanted to sort out my feelings about

all that had transpired during the past few weeks while I was struggling to make *aliyah*. With my hands warming inside the pockets of my blue *dubon* jacket, I began walking slowly past a variety of cafés and stores. *The harder you work at something, the more you appreciate it*, I reassured myself. *No gain without pain. All beginnings are difficult.*

I stopped in front of one of the clothing store windows on King George Street in the center of town. Staring blankly past the clothing on display, I thought of how Malka always said that the Land of Israel is built on suffering. I knew she meant that sometimes it isn't easy to overcome the hardships that come with the country's rebirth. "But," Malka always added, "it's worth it."

Focusing on the dressed up mannequin in the window, I considered what Malka would say about how I was feeling now, and about all that I was going through to reap the benefits of living in Israel. *Malka would say, "The State is still new, and like anything new, there are still a lot of kinks that have to be ironed out."*

Recalling my own reasons for wanting to make *aliyah* in the first place, I felt my frustration and annoyance melt away. "Okay," I said out loud. And then with conviction, I told the mannequin in the navy lace-trimmed dress, "I'm not letting these little hassles and inconveniences get me down."

"Do you think she's going to answer you?" a cheerful voice from behind me broke my concentration. I whirled around to find my witty friend, Esther, grinning and batting her pale eyelashes at me. "You know, I was just thinking that if I walk down this way a little farther, I might find my friend Shelly talking to a window display," she teased. "And here you are! Can you believe my luck?"

"Ha! Ha!" I replied. "You scared me. I was thinking out loud."

"No, you were talking to that mannequin!" Esther

corrected. "If you come with me on some of my errands, I won't hold it against you. You can tell me what's on your mind, instead of telling *her*." Esther pointed towards the store window.

"Fine. Let's go." I was happy to have my friend's company.

Walking towards the intersection of King George Street and Jaffa Road, we noticed some soldiers stopping people on the sidewalk up ahead. A small crowd was gathered on both sides of the street.

"It looks like there's a suspicious object somewhere over there," Esther warned me as we got closer.

"They're not letting anyone pass," I pointed out. "I hope we don't have to wait long this time for the soldiers to find out if it's something that will explode, or not." All traffic on the two main streets was also at a standstill. A few soldiers had sectioned off a large area of about half a block in all directions. We could see a man in a special protective suit crossing in the middle of the vacated intersection. A small contraption whizzed ahead of him to the curb on the other side of Jaffa Road.

"I wonder what the suspicious object is that they're checking," I said. "The last time I was stopped with everyone like this, it turned out to be some kid's backpack that was left on the sidewalk by mistake."

"That's a classic suspicious object—a forgotten backpack or shopping bag accidently left behind." Esther was busy looking across the street at the small moving machine. Motioning towards it, she said, "That thing is the robot they use. If the suspicious object turns out to really be a bomb of some type, the robot sets it off inside some kind of special protected container," she explained.

I zipped my jacket, folded my arms across my chest and shifted my weight from one foot to the other. "It seems to be taking longer than usual," I said, wondering what exactly was going on up ahead. "I hope they don't discover that it's the real thing this time."

We waited with the others who were gathered behind the soldiers. Esther tightened the back knot of the trendy blue and green scarf covering her hair as she watched the man and the robot doing their job up ahead. I observed the people standing with us. Everyone was calm, including the two young children next to me who were nonchalantly licking their red strawberry-flavored lollypops. It was as if this was just another normal event in their day.

After a while, the soldiers opened up the streets and sidewalks. "Good, they're letting us go," I said.

"Looks like they determined that it wasn't a bomb," Esther stated matter-of-factly.

"Thank G-d."

Once again on our way, we turned down Jaffa Road and blended in with the rest of the people going about their business as usual. Buses, cars and trucks roared noisily past us. There was nothing in the air to suggest that less than a minute ago there had been a threat of an explosion.

"C'mon," I said, pulling Esther towards a nearby gift shop. "I want to buy something fun for myself. It's been one of those days."

A few minutes inside the shop was all I needed to find what I was looking for. "Oh, no," I groaned when I went to pay at the cash register. "I thought I had my checkbook with me, but I don't. And I don't have enough cash on me to buy this."

"Sorry I can't lend you the money," Esther said, apologetically. "I didn't bring my checkbook either and I need whatever I have with me for the errands I have to do after this."

"Don't worry about it," the balding store owner told me in broken English. "You pay me what you have, and next time you bring me the rest."

"Really?" I wasn't sure I'd heard right. "I can pay what I have now and bring the rest another day?"

"Yes. Just bring it next time you in the area," the owner repeated.

"But that probably won't be until next week. Is that all right?"

"Yes, yes. Dat's fine," he assured me.

"Thank you very much!" I happily placed my money on the counter.

"No problem." The man dropped my coins into the register and turned to his next customer.

I smiled at Esther, and then followed her out the door. "That was really nice," I said, making a mental note of the store's name and exact location for the next time I came.

"Yeah, some shopkeepers do that. It is pretty nice," Esther agreed.

"I bet some people forget to bring the money later, or just never bother to go back to the stores," I hypothesized.

"Usually, it's not a problem," Esther replied. "If they didn't pay at some point, then these guys wouldn't continue to trust people like they do."

"I guess that's true," I said. Then, pointing backwards with my thumb, I asked jokingly, "Want to meet me here again tomorrow?"

"I don't know. Will you be talking to a mannequin tomorrow too?" Esther teased, her smiling eyes glistening in the sunlight.

"I'll try not to." I gave Esther a squeeze on the arm as a goodbye and turned to leave. "I've got to get home. See you later."

We parted and I crossed over to wait for my bus on the other side of the street. "Oh no!" The words of alarm escaped my lips for the second time when I realized a few minutes later that I had left myself no money for bus fare. "This is just great," I muttered under my breath.

I didn't have my checkbook with me and unfortunately, my first Israeli credit card, which would also allow me to withdraw cash from an automated teller machine, was still on order. I considered running after Esther. *But who knows where she is by now?* Or, maybe I could find someone else I knew who might be shopping in the vicinity. Only, how long would that take, if there actually was anyone around? *And it's so far to walk home.* I was tired out from my emotional and eventful morning.

After checking all the different compartments of my wallet again, I had no choice but to ask a stranger for the bus fare. I knew that giving handouts to help the homeless was normal in Israel. But I wasn't homeless and wasn't sure I had the guts to walk up to just anyone and ask for money.

Feeling queasy, I began wandering around, hoping I would bump into somebody I knew. My predicament reminded me of an evening, years ago, when I was walking with my father in downtown Chicago. We had just parked the car and were on our way to meet my mother at a concert hall, when a scruffy-looking man approached us. He asked my father for a dollar to buy a cup of coffee. I knew that most people would have walked right past the man, ignoring his plea. But my father, hesitating for only a second, pulled a dollar bill out of his wallet and handed it to the beggar. The man thanked him, shoved the money into his own pocket and went on his way.

"I'm not sure he'll actually use the money to buy himself a cup of coffee," my father had admitted to me. I wasn't sure either, but I was proud of my father, that despite his doubts, he had been willing to help out a complete stranger.

Now, I'm the beggar! I returned to my unpleasant situation.

From half a block away, I saw my bus slowing down. When it stopped, the people waiting on the sidewalk flocked towards the opened doors and began haphazardly clambering up the metal steps. Running, I knew I would have to find the nerve to approach someone quick.

As I reached the bus, my eyes swept over the people crowding next to it. They rested on a short, thin woman wearing a light purple skirt and a matching purple beret. With a bulging shopping bag in one hand and a small brown purse hanging from her shoulder, she reminded me a little of myself.

Perspiring, I walked towards the woman in purple. I knew there wasn't any time to waste. *I can't believe I'm doing this!* Struggling to remain calm, I told myself that I shouldn't feel embarrassed about my predicament. I knew that people helped each other out like this all the time in Israel. Nobody would criticize me for what I was about to do.

"*Selichah.*"[26] My cheeks turned a deep shade of red, as I tried to catch the woman's attention. I could feel them burning, but I forced myself to continue on with my request in the best Hebrew I could manage. "I don't have money with me to pay for the bus. Could you help me out?" I held my breath, waiting for a response.

"Just a minute," the woman said. She put down her shopping bag and, placing her bus card between her teeth, began hastily fishing around inside her purse for her wallet. Without hesitating, she quickly pulled out some change and handed it over to me.

"*Todah rabbah,*"[27] I said meekly, allowing myself to breathe again.

---

[26] Excuse me.
[27] Thank you very much.

"*B'vakashah*, you're welcome," the woman replied before disappearing inside the bus.

I waited behind the last few people on the sidewalk, feeling extremely relieved and completely humiliated. I had seen people help pay for others on the bus who were a little short on the fare. But this was different. I didn't have any money at all! I replayed the scene over in my mind. *Why am I feeling so embarrassed? That woman didn't even bother to look me over. She barely glanced at me.*

Walking down the aisle, I spotted her purple beret towards the back of the bus. I went over to thank her again.

"No problem," she replied, giving me a smile and a slight nod of her head.

I plopped myself down in an empty seat a few rows behind her. "No problem," I whispered the two words I'd been hearing throughout the day. Then, with a sigh, I closed my eyes and leaned my head back on the seat. I wasn't only in the process of making *aliyah*... I was in the process of becoming Israeli.

❖ CHAPTER 13 ❖

EZRA'S STORY

(March 1987)

"*Le-hit-ga-ote,* to be proud." I covered the list in front of me with my hand as I tested myself on the words I was learning in my Hebrew ulpan class. Now that we'd both made *aliyah* and were officially Israelis, Liz and I were trying to improve our Hebrew.

"Very good," Liz said, pouring herself some herbal tea. She always brought along a thermos with a hot drink for the fifteen-minute break.

"Thanks," I said, removing my hand from the list of words. "I'm a real whiz at all of this, you know. I memorize the vocabulary and grammar one day, and then the next day I forget everything." I smiled. "Of course, that's so I can make room in my brain for the new stuff we'll be learning!"

"I know your type," Liz said. "You just can't be bothered to study at home. I'm in the midst of planning my wedding and I still open my notebook more than you do!"

Liz picked up the plastic cup of tea from her desk and raised it in the air towards me. "*Le'chaim.*"

"It's so much easier for the Europeans to learn Hebrew," I said. "They're used to hearing a bunch of different languages. And the Ethiopians here don't really have a choice. They have to pick it up quickly because nobody in Israel speaks Amharic."[28]

"Right," Liz agreed.

"And look at what's-his-name from Iran." I nodded towards the sturdy young man sitting up in the first row of seats.

"Ezra?"

"Yeah. We've been in the country longer than he has, but he understands and speaks Hebrew much better than we do. I heard him tell someone he already has a job working at Angel Bakery." I put my pen down and looked at Ezra's back. "I wonder if he knew any Hebrew before he got here."

"Did you?" Liz asked.

"Yeah, a little. But at the rate I'm going, it will probably take me years to get it down pat."

"Same here," Liz nodded. "So let's ask Ezra his secret."

"Okay. But what are we going to do—just tell him to come over here and start talking about himself?" I cupped my hands around my mouth and, in a low playful voice, pretended I was calling him. "Hey, Ezra! Let us in on why you're at the front of the class, so to speak, and we're at the back!"

"Are you talking about me?" Turning around in his seat, Ezra eyed us good-naturedly.

"Oops!" I nearly shrunk in my seat.

"I thought I heard someone say my name," he continued in Hebrew, leaving his desk and heading towards us in his faded blue jeans and flannel shirt.

"Oh good! Now we can get some answers!" Liz whispered, rubbing her hands together in mock delight as

---

28 The official language spoken in Ethiopia.

she watched Ezra approach.

Ezra straddled the vacant chair in front of our desks. Facing us, he asked, "So how can I help you?" His strongly accented Hebrew flowed smoothly.

"We want to know why your Hebrew is so good," I said, *my* words coming out more choppy.

"Yeah, what's your story?" Liz asked, raising her eyebrows as she slowly pronounced each word.

Ezra clasped his hands together and leaned forward on the back of the chair. "My story? *B'seder,*[29] I'll tell you my story. But it doesn't have anything to do with Hebrew."

"That's okay. We want to hear it anyway," Liz encouraged Ezra. It was much easier to listen and understand the language than it was to speak it.

Some of the other students also gathered around to hear what Ezra had to say.

"I'll tell you how I got to Israel," Ezra began. "It wasn't easy," his expression became more serious as he spoke. "I came with a group of Jews who were also trying to escape from Iran."

A French student wearing a silver Jewish star around his neck came closer. "How did you manage to do that?" he asked in his French-coated Hebrew.

"With careful planning," Ezra said. "We had to pay a lot of money for special secret escorts who guided us and helped us all along the way."

"Were you scared?" Liz asked.

Ezra's deep brown eyes narrowed. "Yes, very scared." He paused to think which Hebrew words to use as he continued. "Special drivers drove us part of the way. They had to sneak us through checkpoints. We didn't know who they were, but we had to trust them."

---

[29] Okay, fine.

Ezra shifted in his seat. "At one point I was sure the guards at the checkpoints knew we had fake IDs, because we were told to get out of the car. But then they just checked the car and let us get back inside."

Ezra stumbled over some of the Hebrew words, but was still able to relay his story fairly well. "We tried to act calm, but we were very nervous."

"Were you with your family?" another student asked.

"No. Only one of my brothers was with me." Ezra lowered his head and rubbed the middle of his forehead for a second with his thumb. "My parents and my younger brother and sister couldn't come because it was too dangerous."

Liz shot me a look of sympathy for Ezra. Iran was by no means Israel-friendly. Who knew when, or if, he would ever see the rest of his family again?

"We had to climb over the mountains, which was very difficult."

"Over the mountains!" Liz mouthed to me.

Ezra paused again to transfer his thoughts into Hebrew as he relayed to his captivated audience the details of his perilous journey. "We could only climb at night because we were afraid we'd be caught during the day. Nobody was even allowed to light a cigarette for fear that it would be seen. It was so dark we weren't always able to find our way."

"Did everyone make it over the mountains?" the French student asked.

"No." Ezra shook his head slowly. "Not everyone." His face was blank as he spoke. Nobody pressed him for details.

"We walked for a very long time until we arrived at a hiding place on the other side of the Pakistani border," Ezra went on. "Our escorts moved us from one secret spot to another so it would be hard to find us. We were all hungry and thirsty and very tired."

"Did you have anything to eat or drink in all that time?" I asked.

"Very little. We couldn't really bring anything with us. And after a while even the water we had ran out."

"So what happened when you got to these secret places in Pakistan?" Liz wanted to hear more.

Ezra cleared his throat while everyone waited anxiously to hear what would come next. "We were given passports and visas, and then a plane that I think must have been organized by Israel brought us from Pakistan to Germany."

"Germany? Why Germany?" the lanky Canadian boy sitting on the edge of the desk next to Ezra asked with surprise.

"Pakistan doesn't have diplomatic relations with Israel, so the plane took us to Germany. An El Al airplane flew from Israel to meet us."

I sat up straighter in my seat as Ezra continued. "We were so relieved to see that El Al airplane waiting for us. Getting on it was like entering heaven. When we finally arrived here in Israel," his eyes lit up, "we couldn't believe we had made it. We jumped up and down and we all hugged each other. And then we just cried and cried."

I also felt like crying. Everyone was silent for a moment, and then some of the other students began asking Ezra questions.

As he answered them, I turned to Liz. "I can't imagine having to go through all that," I said quietly.

"I know," Liz agreed. "All we had to do was the last part—get on a plane and fly over here."

"Was it worth it to come here," an Ethiopian girl with a head full of cornrow braids was now asking Ezra in her simple Hebrew, "even though it was so hard for you, and some of your family couldn't come with you?"

"Definitely," Ezra's answer came without hesitation. "It

was all worth it—to be able to live freely as a Jew in my own country." A small smile escaped his tight lips.

The Canadian student was about to ask Ezra another question when the ulpan teacher returned. The small crowd around our desks quickly broke up. Everyone went back to their seats and our teacher picked up where she had left off before the break.

I was having a hard time concentrating on the Hebrew lesson. I was thinking about Ezra's incredible efforts to reach Israel.

"And we thought we had it hard because we're here on our own," I whispered to Liz.

Liz leaned closer to me and whispered back. "Yeah," she replied. "But at least one thing is easier for him than for us."

"What?"

"Hebrew!" We both laughed. Then like young school kids, we pretended to be paying attention when the teacher glanced our way.

I listened to the lesson for a minute and then my thoughts strayed once more to Ezra. I had just learned lessons from him that were far more valuable than Hebrew grammar. Suddenly, I understood how privileged and free I had always been. I also realized, even more than before, how important it was to have a Jewish homeland.

Peering ahead, past the rows of new *olim*[30] in front of me, I could see the back of Ezra's head. In almost every way, Ezra and I were different. Yet both of us, like the rest of the students in the class, had a great deal in common. We had all made a major change in our lives, leaving our homes and our familiar lifestyles to come to Israel and start anew among our own people. Each of us was trying to

---

[30] Immigrants.

achieve something more for ourselves and hopefully also contribute something to the country.

I chewed on the back of my pen, staring ahead for another moment. I felt proud of Ezra for succeeding against extreme odds and challenges.

"Who knows how to conjugate this verb?" the teacher was asking. Hands shot up all around the room. My eyes rested on the Hebrew letters written on the chalkboard, then shifted to the raised arms of my fellow new Israeli classmates.

I wasn't only proud of Ezra. I was proud of all of us.

·❧· CHAPTER 14 ·❧·

"Wow!" Fran gasped. "I can't imagine having to deal with everything that guy Ezra did."

"No way," Carol shook her head. "I couldn't even think of my husband or my boys going on such a scary mission."

"And don't forget," I interrupted, "those guys went on that dangerous journey and made aliyah knowing they'd be on their own without seeing or possibly even hearing from their families for many years."

Fran crossed her legs. "It must have been a hard adjustment for them after they got to Israel."

"I'm sure it's an adjustment for anyone who moves to another country," Carol said. "It probably wasn't so easy for Shelly either. She didn't have her family with her when she made aliyah." Carol looked at me. "How did you manage, Shelly?"

"Actually, I think it was harder for my parents than it was for me," I admitted. "I *was* on my own, and there were cultural and language differences that made some things difficult in the beginning. But living in Israel was wonderful!" I flexed my foot slowly.

"My mother and father, on the other hand, weren't happy at all about my big move. They supported Israel, but they weren't big Zionists or anything like that. They didn't like the idea of me living across the ocean. In fact, when my mother was saying goodbye to me in the airport before my very first El Al flight, she told me, 'Just make sure you come back.' I guess she knew better than I did that I might love it so much I'd want to stay."

"And what about your older siblings?" Fran asked. "How'd they react to you moving so far away?"

"I remember my brother telling me that I should do whatever makes me happy. That was his motto—just be happy."

"And your sister?" Carol prompted me to go on.

"Well, I think my sister was actually able to relate to me a little. She married a guy from Texas, and like me, left Chicago and started a new life farther away than my father and mother would have liked. So she used to defend my decision to live in Israel whenever the subject came up."

Fran's thin lips turned up into a smile. "My sister and I used to defend each other too. Besides being Japanese, my parents are religious Buddhists. But my sister and I, as full-fledged Americans, didn't feel connected to Buddhism and became atheists. Whenever my mother and father would express their disappointment in our nonbelieving ways, we'd stand up for each other."

"I see we have something in common," I told Fran. "But I did the opposite of you and your sister. I became *more* religious than my family. That, by the way, wasn't easy for them either. The more I learned and experienced traditional Judaism, the more my faith in G-d and belief in the Torah grew, and the more my life became different from theirs."

"What was so different?" Fran asked.

"Oh, I can answer that one." Carol, who was holding my leg in an angular position, looked up at

Fran. "Maybe you've heard about eating kosher food and keeping Shabbat?"

"Hmmm," Fran pressed her lips together. "I've heard stewardesses on airplanes asking, "Who ordered the kosher meal?" And Shabbat, I got the general idea from Shelly's stories—it's your Sabbath day, right?"

"Right," Carol nodded, "though it's usually only the observant Jews who consider Saturday a day of rest. The majority of us like to spend it at the movies, shopping or doing errands and the like. Those of us who aren't religious don't worry about eating kosher food either."

"And that's what sometimes made it a little difficult for my family to relate to me and the changes I was making in my life," I explained. "It was especially hard for my mother. Whenever I flew to Chicago, my mother would be overjoyed to see me, but less thrilled about the "hassles" that came along with my visits. She wasn't into checking for a kosher symbol on food labels. And it took her a while to get used to me not cooking, using electrical appliances or doing other forms of work on Shabbat." I stopped flexing my foot. "Of course, there were more differences that came up over the years too."

"Like...?" Fran eyed me curiously.

"Like, gradually I started dressing more modestly. And after I got married, I wore some kind of head covering, such as berets or stylish hats over my hair like observant married women do. I knew my family probably thought I'd become a bit extreme and didn't think any of those things were necessary. But I felt good about who I was becoming and understood the importance and meaning behind my lifestyle changes."

"Sounds like it was a little challenging to be the new you when you were visiting in your old home," Carol acknowledged.

"Well, we managed okay with each other and with our different lives. But it *was* challenging at times," I agreed. "And there's no question that, as time went on, I felt more comfortable and more at home in Israel than anywhere else."

"I can understand that," Fran said. "But what I don't get is how you prepare all the special Shabbat meals if there's no cooking on Shabbat."

"Oh. We cook beforehand and keep the food warm on hot plates that we set up in advance," I said, with a little laugh.

"And that's funny?" Fran was wondering if she'd missed something.

"Not really. This conversation is just reminding me of a Shabbat experience I once had in Jerusalem with my Israeli friend Penina."

"'Shabbat with Penina,' Fran said, moving the palm of her hand across the air in front of her. "That would make a good story title."

"Penina and I had quite a few adventures together," I said.

"Okay. So, 'Adventures with Shelly and Penina,'" Fran's hand glided through the air again.

I looked sideways at Fran and smiled. "Actually, I was thinking more like, 'The Gabbai.'"[31]

---

[31] Custodian.

THE GABBAI
(October 1987)

I spent Friday preparing an assortment of dishes for the three Shabbat meals Penina and I would be eating together. My friend Penina was now studying at the Hebrew University in Jerusalem and would be spending Shabbat with me at my place. With my roommates away for a couple of days, we'd have the Kiryat Moshe apartment to ourselves.

Penina arrived about an hour before sunset. I'd already cleaned up the rooms and prepared the food. After setting up the electric hot plate, we took quick showers and put on our dressy Shabbat outfits. Then, before the sun went down, we each lit two thick, white candles, officially "bringing in" the Sabbath.

"*Shabbat shalom!*"[32] I gave Penina a hug, as the candles' little flames danced around, bouncing their soft light off the living room wall.

"*Shabbat shalom,*" Penina returned the greeting in a similar fashion.

The week had been a full one, and I was looking forward to resting and enjoying the more relaxing pace of Shabbat. Some friends would be joining us for the morning and afternoon meals. But tonight, Penina and I were eating on our own.

We walked to the nearby neighborhood of Beit HaKerem for Friday night services. Herzl Boulevard was much less noisy and bustling than on a weeknight. And as we neared the synagogue, tranquility blanketed the hushed Beit HaKerem side streets.

---

32 Have a peaceful Shabbat!

"*Shabbat shalom*," a woman wearing a black velvet dress nodded her head towards us as she passed by with her little boy in his crisp white shirt and fancy Shabbat pants.

"Shabbat shalom," we replied, turning to enter through the arched entranceway of the synagogue.

After services, Penina and I walked more quickly back to my apartment. The evening air had turned cooler. I buttoned my sweater and put my hands in the pockets.

"Oh my G-d!" I cried. "My key's not here." Stopping, I double- and triple-checked my pockets. "I don't have it! It was in my pocket."

Penina watched me turn my pockets inside out. "Did you take the key out after we left the apartment?" she asked, switching back and forth between Hebrew and English. "Maybe when we got to the *beit knesset?*"[33]

I bit my lip and looked down at the ground hard as I thought about Penina's question. "Yep, I did," I remembered. "You're right. It must be in the synagogue. I remember now that I took it out when I got a tissue from my pocket. I must have put it down by the prayer books on the shelf and forgotten about it."

"Let's go back," Penina suggested. "Maybe somebody will still be there."

I was doubtful. We were already more than halfway to my apartment. "The place will probably be locked up by the time we get there."

"Maybe," Penina admitted. "So let's just wait until tomorrow. We'll go back for the morning services and get it then. We can spend the night by one of your friends in Kiryat Moshe, can't we?"

"We *could* do that," I said, "but what about the food? It

---

[33] Synagogue.

will be on the *plata*[34] all night. It'll burn down to nothing and ruin my pots and serving dishes. The apartment will probably get all smoky." I was concerned. "Maybe we should try to get the key now."

Penina tugged at one of her long curls, as she considered our predicament. "Like you said, everyone might be gone, but we could take a chance and run back there."

I nodded, and without hesitation, we turned around and raced towards the Beit HaKerem synagogue. The streets were empty. It was Friday night in Jerusalem. Religious or not, Shabbat was a time when family and friends gathered together in their homes, often around the table, eating and talking, singing or playing games.

We arrived at the synagogue and found the doors locked. "Fantastic. We came here again for nothing!" Breathing hard, I leaned my weary body against the heavy glass doors and looked at Penina. "What are we going to do now?"

"We need to find the main *gabbai*,"[35] Penina said, holding her aching sides. "He'll have the key. He's in charge of everything here."

"How will we find him? I don't know who he is and I have no idea who would know where he lives." I paced back and forth.

Penina thought for a moment and then came up with an idea. "Let's walk around the neighborhood and knock on the doors of the houses or apartments that have Shabbat candles lit near a window."

I was skeptical. "This is a mixed neighborhood. There are probably as many non-religious Jews living here as

---

[34] Hotplate.
[35] Custodian.

there are religious. That already cuts our odds down by half. And besides, how many people do you know who light their Shabbat candles right next to the window?"

"None of that matters," Penina said confidently. "I think it's a good plan. Let's go." She gave me a little shove forward so we could begin our search.

I felt it was a shot in the dark, but since I didn't have a better idea, I went along with Penina's. We began walking up and down the quiet streets of Beit HaKerem, looking at every window. At first, no lit Shabbat candles appeared in any of them.

"This is pretty hopeless," I moaned.

Then Penina shouted, "Hey! Look over there!" She was pointing up to the second floor window of an apartment building across the street. Two bright Shabbat candles were vigorously flickering from side to side, as if they were beckoning to us.

"Finally!" I sighed with relief. "Now maybe we can actually find someone who knows the *gabbai*."

"C'mon." Penina grabbed my arm and started towards the building.

"What are we going to do if we find this *gabbai*—ask him to leave his family at the Shabbat table to open up the synagogue for us?" I was rushing alongside Penina. "I won't feel very good about doing that," I confessed.

"If we find him, we won't ask him to do anything," Penina reassured me. "We'll just ask him for the key."

"What? You think he's going to give us the key? He wouldn't do that." I was surprised Penina could even suggest such a thing.

"Well, first we have to find him," Penina reminded me. "Then we can decide what to ask him."

"Right," I agreed.

Climbing the stairs inside the building to the second floor, we arrived at the apartment. Through the door we heard the clattering of dishes and silverware, combined with laughter and lively conversation coming from inside. "They must be in the middle of eating. It sounds like they have company," I whispered to Penina.

"It's okay. They won't mind us interrupting," Penina whispered back.

I was glad Penina would be doing all the talking. She had more nerve, and being a Sabra,[36] she also spoke fluent Hebrew.

Penina knocked on the door. Almost immediately it swung open and a tall man with a short white beard stood in front of us. He was wearing grey slacks and a starched white shirt. A white crocheted yarmulke with various shades of grey running around its border rested on his head.

"*Shabbat shalom.*" I detected a European accent in his Hebrew. "What can I do for you?"

Penina explained our problem. When she finished, the elderly man told us to wait a minute while he got his jacket.

"Looks like he wants to bring us to the *gabbai*'s house himself," I whispered to Penina again.

Seconds later, the white-bearded man returned to the door without his jacket. "My wife doesn't think I should leave now, so you can go yourselves." I figured he was going to give us directions to the *gabbai*. Instead, he handed Penina a ring of keys.

"You came to the right place, girls," he smiled. "I'm the *gabbai.*"

My mouth dropped open. I couldn't believe it! What were the odds of Penina's plan working out so well?

"The big one is for the main entrance," the *gabbai*

---

36 Native Israeli.

explained. "Just make sure you lock everything up and bring the keys back to me afterwards."

Penina took the key ring without hesitation. "*Todah*," she said, and then turning to leave, added, "*Shabbat shalom.*"

"*Shabbat shalom.* See you soon," the man replied before closing the door and returning to his family and guests.

"C'mon. Let's hurry," Penina urged. "I'm getting hungry."

I followed my friend down the stairs in silence. When we reached the street, I couldn't hold it in any longer. "This is incredible!" I cried.

"Yeah. I had a good idea didn't I?" Penina was hurrying back towards the synagogue.

I walked quickly after her. "We are sooo lucky!"

"Uh huh," Penina replied over her shoulder.

"*He's* the *gabbai!*" My voice resonated through the streets.

"Yeah," Penina answered again nonchalantly.

Catching up to her, I grasped Penina by the elbow to get her to slow down. "How can he trust us with all his keys?"

Penina smiled and slowed her pace. "Why not?"

I stopped and stood still. Penina took a few more steps before noticing that I was no longer with her. She turned around and looked at me.

"What?" she asked innocently. "Why are you stopping?"

I went over to her. "He doesn't even know us," I said slowly, emphasizing every word.

"He does now," Penina replied.

"What's that supposed to mean?"

"It means... he saw us. He spoke to us. He trusts us. He gave us his keys. So c'mon, let's go." She gently coaxed me forward.

Putting my hand in the crook of her arm, we walked on together, moving more slowly now. "I guess it's not a big deal for you," I said. "You're used to this kind of thing."

"I guess so," Penina admitted. "And by now you should be too. You've been living in Israel long enough to know things are different here."

"You're right," I agreed. "I guess it's time to finally get rid of that old mentality I still have inside me about strangers. And the next time I accidentally leave my keys somewhere and we have to walk around looking for Shabbat candles in windows, and we end up knocking on some old man's door, who just happens to be the exact person we're looking for, and he willingly gives us all of his keys..." I paused to take a breath, "I won't be the least bit surprised or amazed, or anything. I'll just say, 'Thank you,' and walk away calmly. How's that?"

"That's great!" Penina said, with a smile. "Now, if you don't mind," she put her arm around my shoulder, "can we move a little faster? I'm starving."

·❧· *CHAPTER 15* ·❧·

INTIFADA "FRIENDS"

(February 1988)

"What's happening with my tuna platter, Mahmud?" I asked the Arab cook on the other side of the counter. "They're waiting." I nodded towards the couple sitting at the corner table.

Mahmud, the café's day manager and head cook, added a cucumber and tomato garnish onto the plate next to the big tuna ball. "*B'seder.*[37] It's coming," he said in his accented Hebrew.

I liked the idea of Jews and Arabs working together, and was glad to have the chance to get to know some of the restaurant's Arab employees firsthand. Mahmud and another cook, Fayyad, often joked with me, saying they would have married me instead of their own very young wives if they had met me first. And the two teenage dishwashers, Jamil and Sa'eed, who only knew a little Hebrew because they claimed it wasn't necessary to learn the language, liked to practice their English on me.

Although I got along well with the workers at the café,

---

[37] Okay, fine.

the violent intifada,[38] which began a couple of months earlier, was putting a strain on my liberal attitude about the Arab population in general. The intifada boasted a variety of terror tactics aimed at the Jews, including stabbings, bus bombings and pipe bombs. In the areas of Judea, Samaria and Gaza, where there were more Arab villages than there were Jewish towns, Arabs hurled Molotov cocktail explosives and deadly rocks at Jewish cars driving by. In Jerusalem's Old City, they stood on the Temple Mount with their Al-Aksa Mosque and threw rocks down on the Jews praying at the Western Wall.

The tension between Jews and Arabs increased with each attack. Many Jews even began to grow suspicious of their long-time Arab friends, neighbors and employees.

I knew that not all Arabs were responsible for the intifada. Wanting to give at least those whom I knew on a personal basis the benefit of the doubt, I tried not to let the events of the day affect my relationship with my coworkers.

Mahmud handed me the tuna platter and a tall glass of freshly squeezed orange juice. "*Todah*," I thanked him, whisking everything over to my hungry customers.

As I walked back towards the kitchen area, Penina, who was also waitressing at the café, grabbed me by my arm. "Let's take a break," she suggested.

"Now?"

"Yeah, we haven't had one yet. It's pretty quiet and all the customers have been served. We can get one of the other waitresses to check on our tables."

"*B'seder.*" I followed Penina over to the break table where she had already placed two glasses of juice and two cheese omelet platters.

---

[38] Arab uprising.

"It's a slow day," Mahmud said in English for my benefit, as he lit a cigarette and sat down to join us.

"You smoke too much," Penina told him in Hebrew, taking a bite of her omelet. Don't you know that smoking is bad for your health?"

Mahmud's lit cigarette dangled from his lips as he smiled in acknowledgment. "We're all going to die someday."

Mahmud's joke reminded me of the most recent intifada victim, who had died just hours before from multiple knife wounds. I wondered if he or the other Arabs we worked with were also disturbed by what happened.

Apparently Penina had similar thoughts. Unlike me, she didn't hesitate to address them. "Speaking of dying," she put her fork down and looked from me to Mahmud, "did you hear that the guy who was stabbed yesterday died this morning?"

"It's terrible, this intifada," I answered.

"It really is," Penina agreed. "What do you think of all these attacks, Mahmud?"

"What? You don't think that sometimes we're also afraid to walk down the street?" Mahmud was clearly offended by the question. "We could get it too, you know."

Penina nodded her head. "That's true."

Sipping my juice through a straw, I wondered if it really was true. *Would the Arab terrorists actually pick other Arabs for targets on the street or in their cars, or go around stabbing their fellow Arab workers? Their aim was to get the Jews... and the country. On the other hand, it was true Arabs also rode on buses that were being blown up.*

"But it's definitely more dangerous to be a Jew these days," I said out loud.

Penina turned to Mahmud. "That's true too," she told him.

"It's one thing to be persecuted somewhere else," I

looked at Penina, "but this is our country. Why should we have to be afraid of being hunted down or blown up here?"

Mahmud, who suddenly didn't feel like speaking to me in English, directed his comments to Penina in Hebrew. "How long has she been living here that she talks this way? I was born here. So why shouldn't I have more of a right to this country than she does?"

Penina turned to me. "Did you understand all of that?"

I got the gist of Mahmud's comments, as well as the bitterness in his tone. I wanted to respond to him and express exactly what I felt, but I knew it wouldn't go over well. He didn't understand, and probably wasn't interested in what Israel meant to the Jews in general, or to me specifically.

I knew he would laugh if I told him that G-d had given the Land of Israel to the Jews thousands of years ago. Most of the world believes that Israel only became a Jewish country in 1948 when the United Nations voted in favor of it becoming a state. I wasn't sure if Mahmud, his friends or his family even recognized Israel as a legitimate Jewish state. *For all I know, he might believe like many do that it should be Arab, just like the other twenty-two Arab countries around us.*

I doubted that I could make Mahmud understand that Israel belonged to me simply because I was Jewish. Would he care that, exiled and scattered throughout the world, often suffering persecution, Jews had always yearned for and tried to return to their homeland? Did it matter to him that, despite our wanderings over the centuries, there were always Jews in the Holy Land?

Now that Israel was back under Jewish rule, it was again flourishing and developing. Jews from everywhere were returning to settle it. I was one of them. And although I was a newcomer, my love and allegiance to the land and the people was just as great, if not greater, than some who were born in the country.

But I knew I couldn't tell Mahmud all of that.

"It doesn't matter how long I've been living here," I said.

Mahmud blew smoke in the air above our heads.

"Why does there have to be a problem with all of us living here together?" Penina asked nobody in particular.

"We have the same problems as you do," Mahmud said adamantly.

I didn't agree, but I didn't want bad feelings to develop between us, so I tried to lighten up the conversation. "Well, I didn't want to be the one to tell you, but you *do* seem to have a lot of problems," I poked fun at Mahmud.

"If that's true," he answered in English, "then *you* are definitely one of them!" he chuckled. "Now, as manager, I say it's time for you two to finish up here so you can go back to work and stop causing trouble!" Mahmud's tone of voice turned friendly again. I sensed that he also preferred to keep things on easygoing terms.

"Oof, we have to finish our break so soon?" Penina moaned.

Mahmud put out his cigarette and got up to clear away the ashtray. "You know," he smiled at me and Penina, who weren't moving from our seats. "I've noticed how much you two eat on your breaks. Do you come here to work or to fill your bellies all the time?"

"Both!" Penina smiled back at him.

"C'mon," Mahmud motioned with his hand. "People are coming in. We need to feed them more than we need to feed you, especially since *they're* paying customers."

When our shifts ended, Penina and I got our things and left the restaurant. Mahmud and his two cousins, Jamil and Sa'eed, did the same. We all said goodbye to each other and then began walking in the same direction.

"Where are you both going now?" Jamil asked, unconsciously fingering the thin scar on his chin as he spoke to Penina in English.

"Shelly's coming with me to my dorm at the university," Penina answered in her mixture of English and Hebrew.

"That's right near where we're going," Mahmud said. "My car's parked not too far from here. Do you want a ride? It's on our way home."

"Well," Penina hesitated, "we can get a bus."

"Okay. But if you change your mind, we could take you," Mahmud offered.

"*Todah*,"[39] Penina said, slowing down to walk with me.

Penina and I, both young and petite, stayed a little distance behind our three Arab coworkers as they continued on towards the car.

"What do you think?" Penina asked me.

"About what?"

"They want to give us a ride to the university. Should we go with them?"

I wasn't sure what to think. Penina was the Sabra. I trusted her judgment about these things better than I did my own. As we walked, I mulled over the idea. We did work together and we were all friendly with each other. Wasn't it almost like when we tremp and take rides from Jews we don't know?

I looked up ahead at the lean, dark, moustached Arabs walking in front of us. No, it really wasn't the same thing. The intifada had changed all that. *What do we really know about these guys? Can they be trusted?*

"I don't know if we should go with them or not," I finally said. "You would know better than I would. What do *you* think?"

Mahmud and his cousins had reached the car. Sa'eed, turned around and motioned for us to catch up to them. "I

---

39 Thanks.

think it's okay," Penina said. "C'mon. We could be at my dorm in ten minutes."

We hopped into Mahmud's car along with Jamil and Sa'eed, and the five of us drove off. Penina and I sat in the back with Sa'eed, leaving the front passenger's seat for Jamil. A small tree-shaped cardboard air freshener and a couple of metal necklace-type chains hung from the rearview mirror of Mahmud's dusty, white, slightly dented car.

Mahmud switched the radio on low. Penina leaned forward and began a conversation with him above the Arabic music. Every now and then Jamil turned around and exchanged a few words with Sa'eed in Arabic. I was content to be left alone to my thoughts as I looked out the back window. I was also glad that we agreed to accept the ride and were being open and friendly with Arabs, despite the situation in the country. On the other hand, I knew the intifada warranted us to be extra cautious.

Mahmud dropped us off at the university campus. He waved goodbye, and Penina and I thanked him for the ride. As we started walking away, Jamil stuck his head out the window and called out in his heavily accented English, "See you later!"

I knew the English was mostly meant for me. As the car began to pull away from the curb, I turned around and called back, "*Shukran!*" "Thank you" was one of the few Arabic words I had learned while working at the café.

We watched the car drive out of sight. "That was interesting," Penina said.

"Yep," I agreed. "It was."

"I was a little bit nervous, though," Penina admitted as we started towards her dormitory.

"Aha!" I exclaimed. "So I wasn't the only one."

"No. But it was nice of them to take us, and it turned

out well," Penina glanced at her watch. "Look how fast we got here!"

"I wonder," I said. "We're nervous about them because of the intifada. What would they be like if a major war broke out again? Would they be so nice? Would they offer us rides and take breaks with us and kid around with us like they do? Or would it all change?"

Penina kicked at a large stone in her way. "The intifada changed some things, and war usually changes things even more," she said. "We can't expect there to be love between us if our people are at war with each other."

"So what *can* we expect?"

"I don't know," Penina answered truthfully.

I looked down at my feet as we walked. I was feeling unsettled. "Well there doesn't seem to be much love out there for us Jews. Hate, however... there's plenty of that, isn't there?"

Penina sighed and shook her finger at me. "You know I don't have all the answers. And you just called out 'shukran' back there to those Arab guys, who were nice enough to give us a ride in their car. So what are we supposed to understand from all of this?"

"Good question," I admitted. "And I don't have the answers either."

"It doesn't look like anybody really does," Penina said. "Not even our leaders in the government seem to know what to do half the time."

"It's a tough situation."

"C'mon," Penina's tone suddenly changed, "let's not be so serious. Everything will be *b'seder*. It can't go on like this forever."

"True," I said. "All kinds of things can change in the future."

"Hopefully they'll change for the better, and not for the

worse." Penina held the door to the dormitory building open for me.

"*Shukran!*" I said in a singsong voice as I walked past her.

"*B'vakashah.*[40] And *shukran* to you too." Penina laughed and then followed me inside, as the door slowly closed behind us.

---

[40] You're welcome; lit., "please."

"Fran's not here today," I told Carol. "A different nurse checked on me earlier this morning."

"I know," Carol said. "I heard she called in sick."

I thought the empty chair where Fran usually sat looked lonely. "It's kind of strange that she's not here."

Carol opened the window to let in some fresh air. "I'll get her number and fill her in over the phone the best I can." She turned back to me. "So—you were waitressing with Arabs and Jews working together and then..."

"And then," I realized Carol didn't want to lose any time, "I got interested in special education. So I began working as a teacher's assistant in a school for autistic children where I got on-the-job training."

"That's a switch from serving soups and sandwiches." Carol gestured for me to start my exercises.

"Yep. It was hard at first." I pressed one hand on my rib cage and grimaced while straining to turn my leg sideways. "But after a while I actually started feeling close to some of the kids." I let my leg rest for a moment. "There was one boy, Yuval, who I watched sometimes on a private basis after school hours or on weekends. I'd bring him to my apartment and we'd play games, do puzzles and other things. I was always a little nervous on the days

I picked him up from his special school and we walked to my place. I had to make sure we both got there in one piece."

"Sounds like it was a little tricky."

"Oh, it was." I bent my knee slowly. "It definitely was."

YUVAL
(July 1988)

Eleven-year-old Yuval had lots of energy. I made sure to hold his hand tightly as we left the schoolyard, passed the other autistic children getting into their special school van and made our way down Herzl Boulevard. The afternoons I babysat for sweet-faced Yuval, he would often try pulling me in the wrong direction as we walked to my apartment. Sometimes he'd even break away from my grip and run into the street. I was always relieved when we arrived safely at my building.

Now Yuval clung to my arm as we slowly began walking up the stairs to the second floor. Wearing a Mickey Mouse T-shirt over his shorts and brown leather sandals, Yuval stomped his foot and then let out a loud grunt with each step we climbed. He stomped and grunted all the way up the twenty-five steps. When we reached my apartment at the top of the landing, Yuval looked blankly at the door, as if in a daze. Then, without blinking, he swiftly pulled off his left sandal and threw it over the side railing. I heard a thud as it hit the ground below.

"*Mah zeh,*[41] Yuval?" I was surprised and a little annoyed.

---

[41] What's this?

*I knew it was too easy getting here. Something **had** to happen.* Still holding his hand, I walked with Yuval back down the stairs. At the bottom, he eagerly grabbed his sandal before I could get to it. He insisted on holding it in his hand, rather than putting it on his foot.

Directing Yuval back to the stairs, we began climbing up for the second time. Once more latching onto my arm, he stomped on each stair and then grunted. This time only the foot that still had a sandal on it made a sound. Possibly to make up for the quiet bare foot, Yuval banged the metal handrail with the brown sandal he was holding and grunted afterwards. *Stomp, grunt, bang, grunt. Stomp, grunt, bang, grunt.* The rhythmic accompaniment continued until we arrived once again at my apartment.

"Okay," I said, reaching into my skirt pocket and retrieving my key, "we made it." I put the key into the lock. "Now we can..." The dull thud from below whisked my attention away from the door.

"Oh, come on! Not again." I couldn't believe I was going to have to drag Yuval back to the bottom of the staircase and then hike all the way up again, with all his rituals slowing us down. I looked at the skinny, dark-haired boy at my side who was hanging his head over the railing, searching frantically with his big eyes for the "mischievous" sandal he'd just dropped back down two flights of stairs. "This is crazy," I muttered to myself.

Finding the sandal once more, I was doubly quick this time to pick it up before Yuval could grab it. Carrying it in my right hand, I held onto his arm with my left, gently pulling him along with me up the steps. I was anxious for us to get inside the apartment.

I wanted to hurry, but Yuval was busy making sure he stomped, banged on the railing with his hand and grunted with each step. Relief filled me when I finally turned the key in the lock. The sandal was dangling by its strap from the last two fingers of my right hand as I unlocked the door. Suddenly, with one swift motion, Yuval reached over me and grabbed the sandal, hurling it back over the railing.

"Yuuuvaaalll!!" The familiar thump on the ground below was too much for me at that moment. Flinging the apartment door open, I pulled Yuval inside, quickly shutting and locking the door after us. "We are NOT going down and getting that sandal again," I announced, more for my own benefit than for his. I sat down hard on the living room couch. Folding my arms, I slumped deep into its soft cushions. Yuval stood next to me with a vacant, innocent look on his face.

"We'll get it later," I told him. "Now, we're going to have something to eat." I led Yuval into the kitchen. He sat down and looked at the games, puzzles and picture books piled up at the edge of the table. I was looking in the refrigerator when someone knocked on the door.

"*Ken,*"[42] I called out in typical Israeli fashion for the person to come in.

"It's locked," a muffled voice replied.

"Oh, right." I forgot I had locked the door to prevent Yuval from running out to retrieve his sandal again. Leaving him for only a second, I went to open it.

"Hi." It was my friend Rachel, who'd made *aliyah* from California and was also working at Yuval's school. Though Rachel was a couple of years younger than me, she had more experience than I did with autistic children and was blessed with a calm, confident disposition. I was thankful it was her standing in the doorway at the moment.

"Rachel! I'm *really* glad to see you!" Back in the kitchen, I relayed to Rachel the difficult time I had getting Yuval into my apartment. "His sandal is still somewhere down

---

42 Come in; lit., "yes."

below. Could you stay with him for a minute while I go look for it? And if you don't mind, while I'm down there I'll just check to see if I got any mail."

"Sure." Wearing a mustard yellow top that matched the color of her tawny hair, Rachel eyed the games and other activities set out to entertain Yuval. "We can do a puzzle," she said agreeably.

I took my keys and ran down the stairs. Finding the sandal easily, I quickly snatched it up and headed for the row of mailboxes on the wall. In my box I found a phone bill and a wedding invitation for one of my roommates. I was relieved there wasn't anything from an unidentified source. Home Front Command and Israel's National Security had previously warned the public to beware of any mail from unknown or unfamiliar people or places, since a group of letter bombs were discovered some months ago at the beginning of the intifada.

Trudging once more up the stairs, I thought about how the intifada was affecting even the smallest aspects of our lives. It was remarkable to me how Israelis kept on going, despite the many wars and attacks, and daily terrorist threats always hanging overhead. At the same time, I knew it wasn't always easy for everyone to stay positive. Sometimes it was hard to get back on the horse—to climb back up the steps. *But what's the alternative—to break down, be defeated?* Glancing at Yuval's sandal, now safe in my firm grasp, I knew that wasn't the answer. Not for Israel. *With every down there is an up.*

Back at the top of the landing, I pushed the apartment door open. "Okay, I got it!" I waved the sandal in the air for Yuval and Rachel to see. They were busy working on a fifteen-piece dog puzzle at the kitchen table. Rocking slightly back and forth in his chair, Yuval was trying hard to connect two pieces together. I noticed the great effort he was putting into the small task and felt a little guilty for getting frustrated with him before. *He has his own set of struggles.*

"Thanks for helping," I told Rachel, pulling over another chair. "I'll sit with him now."

Rachel made room for me next to the table. "I was in the area so I came over to ask you if you wanted to spend Shabbat with me and Yuval at the special needs kids' hostel."

Yuval didn't understand English. But hearing his name, he looked up from the puzzle and then ran abruptly over to the refrigerator, knocking over his chair in the process. I jumped up from the table and went after him. By the time I reached him, he had already opened the refrigerator door, grabbed an apple from the bin and was taking a huge bite out of it. I escorted Yuval and his apple back to the table.

"His family's spending Shabbat in Tel Aviv," Rachel continued as if there hadn't been any interruption, "and I've agreed to be with him here in Jerusalem."

I watched Yuval devouring the apple—seeds, core and all. When he finished, he wiped his mouth on his shirt. I wondered what kind of Shabbat it would be for the three of us if I helped Rachel babysit for overactive Yuval. I was sure it wouldn't be an easy or restful one. But I also knew that it was never easy for Yuval's parents. *They probably really need a break.*

Rachel took Yuval's hand in hers and looked through her glasses into his big brown eyes. "Do you want Shelly to be with you and Rachel on Shabbat?" she asked him in Hebrew. Yuval's eyes rested on Rachel's questioning face for only a split second before they wandered down to the half-finished puzzle. Staring at the pieces, he suddenly grabbed my arm and pulled it towards him with a quiet grunt. Rachel looked at me. "I'd say that's a definite yes."

I had a special place in my heart for Yuval. He reminded me of Israel. Despite everything he had going against him, he was so full of life. I remembered Yuval's father once telling me that he was glad his active autistic son wasn't the complacent or lethargic type, because that meant he still had some fight left inside him.

"*B'seder,*"[43] I told Yuval, who was still holding onto my arm. "I'll stay with you and Rachel on Shabbat."

"Great!" Rachel was happy.

"And," I looked from Yuval to Rachel with a smile, "I'll even help run up and down the stairs if anyone's sandal gets thrown overboard!"

---

[43] Okay, fine.

"Too bad Fran's not here," Carol said. "She would have enjoyed that story about Yuval."

I looked at Carol, who was lifting my leg slightly higher than where I had managed to raise it up from the bed. "More?" I asked her.

Carol nodded. "Yes, definitely more exercises." Then, looking from my leg to me, she added, "And, of course, more stories."

WHAT GOES AROUND...
(September 1988)

"I can't see a thing!" I felt like a real blind person as I walked around wearing special blackened sunglasses over my contact lenses. My newest Israeli friend, Navah, was guiding me through Jerusalem's dynamic outdoor food market, known as the Mahane Yehudah *shuk*, or simply the *shuk*. Navah and I were working on a homework assignment for a special education class. Our mission, as we made our way through the busy *shuk*, was to experience what it was like to be blind.

"Okay, I've had enough." I took the dark glasses off and placed them over Navah's eyes.

"Wow, you're right!" Navah exclaimed. "It's strange not being able to see." She was cautiously moving forward with one arm extended in front of her for protection.

"That's why I'm here." I took hold of Navah's hand. "You're supposed to walk *with* me, not ahead of me, especially since you don't have a walking stick or a seeing-eye dog."

It was a hot Thursday afternoon and the *shuk* was bustling with pre-Shabbat shoppers. I began slowly leading Navah in her summery dress and dark glasses through the crowded open section of the *shuk*. Eventually, we reached the covered shady area where we could get some relief from the blazing sun.

As I carefully guided Navah through the packed pathways, the strong scent of freshly ground spices replaced the fragrance of sweet summer fruits. Walking slowly past the fresh poultry, meat and fish stalls we turned into the even more congested main aisle of the covered section. People were choosing from the mounds of fruits and vegetables on both sides of the long aisle. In an effort to lure buyers over to their merchandise, vendors were calling out their competitive bargain prices for the food and housewares they were selling. Some shoppers were adding chocolates, pastries and assorted bakery goods to their plastic shopping baskets and two-wheeled grocery carts. Those who noticed us coming moved quickly out of the way so we could pass more easily.

"I want to try to buy something here without being able to see anything," Navah told me.

I brought Navah over to a stand of Golden Delicious apples and placed her hand on the pyramid of round yellow fruit. The young animated vendor shouting out his prices watched Navah out of the corner of his eye as she moved her fingers over the apples, feeling each one for bruises or soft spots. Although he was busy with another customer, he turned to assist her.

"*Shalom aleichem!*[44] Let me help you," he offered. "I can fill up a bag for you. Just tell me how many kilos you want." He instantly produced a small plastic bag from behind his stall. Then, leaning forward with his beer belly against the counter's low wooden edge, he began filling the bag with apples.

I didn't expect the vendor to rush to Navah's aid. I felt a twinge of guilt, as I watched his long fingers swiftly and eagerly picking out apples from the enormous pile, for the "blind woman in need."

"It's okay," I intervened. "She wants to do it herself."

"Oh," the young man said. "I understand." He smiled knowingly at me and threw a sympathetic look at Navah. Then, just as speedily as he had begun filling the bag, he turned it upside down and emptied it. I watched the golden apples roll back onto the mound.

Navah once again began choosing carefully, putting the apples one at a time in the bag I was holding open for her. I placed some shekels in Navah's hand and whispered to her, "The man is standing up on a platform behind the stall in front of us and a little to your right."

"*B'vakashah*,"[45] she called to the vendor, holding the coins out to him in the direction I had indicated.

Reaching over the apples, the vendor took the money from Navah. "You did very well!" he complimented her. "Come again whenever you want. I'm always here and I can help you if you ever need it."

"*Todah rabbah*,"[46] Navah replied, with a tilt of her head.

"No problem. Good luck."

I smiled and then gently pulled Navah away from the fruit stand.

---

[44] Hello to you; lit., "Peace be upon you."
[45] Here you go; lit., "please."
[46] Thank you very much.

"Whoa, do I feel bad!" I said after we were out of sight.

"Yeah," Navah agreed, whisking the dark glasses off her face. "He was really nice. It's good we didn't let him know we were just doing this for school. He would have probably felt foolish, after trying so hard to help me."

"Right. This could also be embarrassing for us if people discover we're just pretending, even if it is for educational purposes," I said.

"Okay, let's stop. I've got a pretty good idea what it's like not to be able to see. It's terrible and I'm glad this was just an experiment!"

Having completed our assignment, Navah suggested we take advantage of being in the *shuk* and do some real shopping. I liked the idea, "as long as we don't pass anyone who's already seen us walking around as 'blind people.'" We agreed to split up and meet afterwards on the other side of Jaffa Road, where we would catch a bus back to the apartment we were sharing in Kiryat Moshe.

I bought what I needed and then hauled my heavy grocery bags across the street to the bus stop. It was an unusually hot day and the sun had been scorching the city with its strong rays since the early morning. I hoped Navah would come quickly. I was looking forward to hopping onto an air-conditioned bus.

The shaded bus stop benches were all occupied with overheated shoppers. Some were fanning themselves with newspapers or a sun hat as they waited for their bus. Others were discussing the weather and the newsman's predictions about when the heat wave would break.

I set my bags down close to the curb and waited for Navah. Wiggling my toes in my sandals, I could feel the heat from the baking concrete sidewalk beneath my feet. I tilted my head back to drink from the giant plastic bottle of spring water I had been carrying around. There was only a small amount of water left, so I decided to save the rest for the short walk home after we got off the bus.

Just as I was about to replace the cap on the bottle, a frail-looking elderly man with dark leathery skin and lots of stubble on his face called out from his seat on the bench. "*B'vakashah*, please, let me have a drink from your bottle."

I was facing the street with my back to the man. I heard him speak, but didn't realize he was talking to me. After he repeated himself a second time, the large wispy-haired woman standing next to me decided to help him out.

"Why don't you give the man a drink?" she said, looking right at me.

I turned around to see the wrinkled man pointing his gnarled finger at my nearly empty water bottle.

"He needs your water," declared the young bleached blonde sitting on the bench next to the old man.

I didn't answer immediately. I felt everyone at the bus stop staring at me, waiting for my reply. Surprised by this stranger's request to drink from my own personal bottle, I needed a moment to mull over the situation. I'd bought the water to keep me hydrated throughout the blistering hot day. I was thinking that if I gave it to him, he might drink all of it. And if he left some for me, his germs would be all over the bottle and there was no way I would drink from it again. *What if he has some disease that I could catch?* The idea made me cringe.

"Go on," urged a teenage boy wearing a blue and white sweatband on his forehead, "let him have some of your water.

"He could dehydrate," reproached the large woman.

I realized that they all thought the only decent thing for me to do was to give up my water. *Okay*, I told myself, *they're probably right. He obviously needs it more than I do right now.* Without further hesitation, I walked over to the bench where the parched man was sitting. He watched me with anticipation as I approached.

"*B'vakashah*,"[47] I said, handing him my bottle.

Like a fish that had just been thrown back into the sea, the man quickly gulped down most of the remaining water. "*Todah rabbah*," he thanked me with a sigh and then handed me back the bottle.

The bleached blonde gave me a look of approval.

"Good going," the teenage boy praised me.

I went back to my overloaded *shuk* bags by the curb. The large woman with the wispy hair nodded in my direction with satisfaction. Everyone settled back into the mundane task of wiping their brows and lethargically fanning their faces while waiting in the sweltering heat.

I reflected for a moment on what had just transpired. Although I wouldn't be drinking the rest of my water, I knew I had done the right thing. I felt good that I'd helped the thirsty elderly man, thanks to the others who had pushed me to do so. At the same time, I wished that I had been more eager to aid him in the first place, like the vendor who'd been so willing to help a blind girl pick out apples.

After a few minutes, Navah came running awkwardly across the street, loaded down with two bulging plastic shopping baskets. "Hi!" she said out of breath as she reached the curb. "I thought maybe the bus had come already and we'd have to wait for the next one. But I see there are still lots of people here."

I glanced around at the now familiar group of travelers waiting at the bus stop. "Yep," I confirmed. "We're all here."

Our bus finally came. Despite the usual jostling of

---

[47] Here you go; lit., "please."

everyone trying to get on at the same time, we managed to pull our loads up onto the steps and find seats together in the back. The cool air-conditioning felt great, but my throat was dry and my cheeks felt sunburned.

"You wouldn't happen to have any extra water with you that you could spare, would you?" I asked Navah.

Reaching into one of her shopping baskets, Navah pulled out a small bottle of mineral water. "I just bought this." She looked at my flushed face. "I see you need it more than me."

"I'm glad you have good eyes," I said, alluding to our earlier experience—walking around like blind people. "You're sure you don't need it?"

"I've been drinking all day. I'm fine."

Tilting my head back once more, I gratefully drank some of Navah's water. I allowed the cool liquid to sit for a moment in my mouth before letting it slide down my throat. *Well,* I thought to myself, *what goes around, comes around.*

"*Todah.*" I wiped the mouth of the bottle before handing it back to Navah.

"Glad to be of help. And if you want more," Navah slipped the bottle back into her basket, "just ask. I wouldn't want you to dehydrate or anything like that."

"Good thing you weren't in the desert where you could really dehydrate fast," Carol said.

"Right. That wouldn't be fun," I agreed, resting my leg for a minute. "But actually, I love the desert. I still remember one of my first desert trips in Israel. It was when I rented a car with some friends and we went to the Negev together."

"Where's the Negev?" Carol asked.

"It's in the southern part of Israel, just before the Sinai Desert."

"So turn your foot towards me," Carol motioned for me to get back to work, "and we'll continue with your leg while you tell me all about your excursion to the Negev desert."

ATZMONA, DESERTS & WONDERS
(April 1989)

I was really looking forward to spending a few days of my Passover vacation in the southern part of the country. First, I'd be joining some of the new Machon Ora students on a visit to Atzmona, a settlement town in an area known as Gush Katif. Then, I'd be meeting up with Rachel, Beth and Michelle for a day of hiking on the sandy trails of the Ramon Crater in the Negev.

My first destination, Atzmona, was originally in the Sinai Desert and was one of the many settlement towns that Prime Minister Menachem Begin reluctantly handed over to Egypt in 1982. I was in college in the US when thousands of Jews living in the Sinai were forced to leave their homes and relinquish their towns to the Egyptians. I had learned about the emotional and dramatic evacuations from the news and from my friend Esther, who was already living in Israel at the time and had sent me a letter describing the traumatic and painful uprooting.

Some of the residents living in the Sinai had left their communities without a fight. Others, mainly from Yamit, the largest of the settlement towns, had refused to abandon their homes or leave any part of their country for what they believed would be an uncertain or, at best, a temporary peace. To get the job done, soldiers physically removed many families out of their houses, forcing some people down from the rooftops where they'd planted themselves in defiance. Living across the ocean, I was vaguely aware of how the devastating evictions tore the Israeli public apart.

Now, ten years later, I was in Israel visiting the reestablished Atzmona in Gush Katif, not far from the relinquished Sinai Desert. I was impressed by the families the Machon Ora students and I met there. Some of them were from the original Atzmona and I was inspired by their resolve to remain strong and to continue settling the less-populated areas of the country. I admired their faith that one day the land they'd cherished so much would be returned to its rightful owners.

After a couple of days in the new Atzmona, I traveled by bus to meet my friends who'd rented a car for our trip to the Ramon Crater. Stepping off the bus in the Negev city of Be'er Sheva, I heard a familiar voice calling out to me. "Shelly, we're over here!" It was Beth. She was wearing a

faded red sun cap over her thin brown hair. "I was a little
nervous that I wouldn't find you easily in this crowded bus
station," she said, relief showing on her face. "The others
are waiting in the car. We made good time. It's Michelle's
turn to drive. She wants us to hurry so we can get to the
Crater already."

Beth put my overnight bag in the trunk of the rental car
and I settled into the back seat next to Rachel. Tired from
the traveling and the heat, I napped in the car, awakening
just as Michelle turned into the entrance of the Ramon
Crater.

"We made it!" Michelle announced, her wide smile
revealing two rows of straight white teeth.

"Which trails should we go on?" Rachel pushed her
glasses up higher onto the bridge of her nose as she looked
at the map guide we'd picked up at the entrance.

"Let's figure that out when we get closer to them," Beth
suggested.

The Ramon Crater was so big, one could spend days
hiking through the enormous box canyon in the middle of
the Negev. We drove around until we came to one of the
easier trails. We hiked passed an assortment of rock
formations and scatterings of wild flowers, dusty-looking
shrubs and an occasional small tree. After a while, Michelle
stopped and sat down on a large flat rock. "It's so beautiful
here," she said, taking a swig from her water bottle. "I just
want to sit here and take it all in."

"Good idea." Rachel found a rock of her own on which
to perch.

I flopped myself down on the ground and leaned back
against Michelle's rock. "I wish I had some containers with
me to collect all the different colored sands that are out
here. I had no idea sand could be red or purple... or green."

Rachel bent down and touched the little pink flower

growing next to her foot. "Deserts are fascinating places. They're so dry, but animals and plants somehow manage to live in them."

"Fascinating and mysterious," I said.

Still standing, Beth pulled her cap off her head and began fanning herself with it. "What's so mysterious?"

"You know," I said, brushing sand off my arm. "For instance, where are all the animals that live in the desert? You never really see them, only sometimes their little footprints. And, like Rachel was saying, how do they and all the plants survive in the burning sun with hardly any water?"

"Yeah, well, what I'd like to know even more than that is, where are all the big, tall trees with lots of broad leaves that we could use right about now," Beth said.

Perching her sunglasses on top of her head, Michelle looked sideways at Beth. "Now you're talking like your practical self, aren't you?"

"Actually," Rachel dabbed some water from her bottle onto her perspiring forehead, "I wouldn't mind some shady trees myself right about now."

"C'mon guys," I said, standing up, "let's keep moving or we'll never finish this *tiyul*."

We hiked to the end of a second trail and then drove around searching for the beginning of a new one to begin. "It's getting late, and we seem to be going in circles," Rachel finally said. "We should probably start heading home."

For me, the drive back to Jerusalem was an added bonus. I loved the procession of barren sandy dunes on all sides, the tan desert mountain humps reaching up to the skies. I was also fascinated by the many bands of Bedouin nomad encampments spread out along the way.

"It must be hard for these Bedouins." I was now behind the steering wheel, glancing every now and then at the thick tarp-like tents off the side of the road. Some of the dwellings had dented rusty tin roofs. Others were covered with sheet-like cloths. "How do they live out here?"

"They live in tents." Beth answered matter-of-factly.

"Yea, but I meant, how do they manage in the desert without houses and plumbing and electricity?"

"And a regular supply of water!" Rachel added.

"And what do they do with themselves all day?" I wondered out loud.

"They herd their goats," Beth answered. "Their lives are much simpler than ours. They don't have the headaches of modern living with complicated technology and hectic schedules."

"Sounds boring," Michelle said.

Rachel rolled down her window and leaned a little way out to get a better view. "How do they walk around on the scorching hot sand, barefoot like that?"

"Well, they're Bedouins," Beth said. "They're used to it. The soles of their feet are probably like leather and don't feel what ours do."

"I would make a bad Bedouin," Michelle concluded. "I like my soft feet and I look forward too much to jumping into a nice, cool shower, warming up supper in the microwave and snuggling in my cushy bed with my Walkman!"

We stopped to change places. Beth slid into the driver's seat, Rachel came up front to the passenger's seat and I moved to the back, next to Michelle. Then we were off again. As Beth drove, I looked out the window at the scenery that was always changing.

"For such a small country, there are so many different environments and climates," I said. "And everything is just a short drive away. In only a few minutes time, we can go from boiling hot to freezing cold, from humid or rainy to dry and arid—and with no gradual change in between."

"Snowy mountain tops turn quickly into sandy deserts," Michelle embellished my point in her usual poetic fashion, "and tranquil beaches become bustling cities."

"It's amazing," I said, still watching the scenery pass.

"Okay everyone," Beth took one hand off the steering wheel and waved it in the air. "I've got some trivia for you. Did you know that Israel has a greater variety of birds year-round than just about every other country in the world? Plus, something like half a billion birds migrate through Israel every year."

"I didn't know that," Rachel said. "That's pretty interesting."

"What about people?" I asked.

"Yup," Michelle said with a nod, "we have people here too."

"Very funny," I elbowed Michelle. "I mean, we have so many different types of people here."

"Actually, most of us here are Jews," Beth pointed out.

"But look at how many types of Jews are here," I said. "Look at how many different places in the world we all came from. And how many different customs and backgrounds, professions and even languages we Jews have packed into this one teeny country."

Rachel turned halfway around to face both Michelle in the back and Beth driving at her side. "She's got a point there."

"It's not just the Negev," I went on. "The *whole* country is full of wonders."

"Very true," Michelle agreed. "And *that*, my dear," she reached over and playfully pinched my cheek, "is part of the reason we are all here!"

CHAPTER 19

"Wow. I think I'm going to have to plan a trip to Israel sometime," Carol said.

"I wish I could be planning *my* trip back there already," I said, feeling melancholy.

"You're progressing nicely. You'll see, in no time you'll be home again, walking around—up and down stairs, like nothing ever happened!"

"That would be great." I laid my head back on my pillow and repeated Carol's words. "Home again—up and down stairs..."

SWEARING IN
(June 1989)

Liz and I slowly made our way down the many stone steps to the Western Wall. "It's going to take a long time for me to climb back up," Liz said, holding on to the side rail.

"It's not so bad. You're just pregnant," I told her. "But don't worry, we can stop a lot so you can take deep breaths, maybe practice your breathing techniques. And if that doesn't help, I'll carry you on my back."

"That would be a sight... me on top of little you!" Liz held her big belly as she laughed.

Stopping on the landing midway down, we looked out

over the stone wall at the Mount of Olives in the distance. "I love coming to the Old City," Liz said, "especially, if we get to visit Malka before going to the Kotel."

"Me too." I turned my gaze down towards the Western Wall. "I just hope we won't have rocks thrown down on us while we're there."

"This crazy intifada," Liz scowled.

"Malka's been telling me how Arabs stand up there along with their Al Aksa mosque and Dome of the Rock and aim for whoever comes to pray at the Wall below them."

"Well, they can try to keep us away from here," Liz said, "but it won't work. Look how many people are down there right now!" She pointed to the open plaza leading up to the Wall where a large gathering had assembled. "It looks like there's some type of event going on."

"Let's go check it out." I led the way down the last set of stairs.

As we drew near, we discovered that the congregation of people standing together in a semi-circle was made up of Israeli families, not the usual groups of tourists who typically visit the Western Wall. "It's some kind of ceremony," Liz said, taking in the assembly of soldiers standing rigidly at attention in their olive green uniforms before the small crowd. Each soldier was holding an automatic M-16 rifle at his side.

My eyes danced with excitement as we positioned ourselves next to the other spectators. "We must have come in the middle of a 'swearing-in' ceremony!" I squeezed Liz's arm.

We watched as the new recruits gained their official acceptance into the army. By joining the Israel Defense Forces, the IDF, the sturdy boys lined up before us were entering a new stage in their lives. They were now taking on the important responsibility of defending their country.

"They look so young." Liz whispered to me.

"Most of them are just out of high school," I whispered back.

Many of the soldiers' fresh faces had a childlike innocence and wholesomeness about them. But I could see in their eyes as they were staring straight ahead, that they had strength and determination.

"It's too bad they have to go into the army at such a young age." Liz folded her arms in front of her indignantly.

"There's no choice," I sighed, "with so many enemies all around us."

"Yeah, I guess there isn't," Liz agreed.

"They must be proud to be serving in the army that's defending Israel," I said. "And I heard that many of them get some kind of education or training that could help them with a career in the future."

"True. But still, I'm sure sometimes it isn't easy for them or for their families and friends," Liz gestured towards all the people standing with us, "especially when there's a war."

I thought about how every Israeli soldier was dear and precious to all the people, as if he belonged to each one of us personally. Every soldier was somebody's son, or grandson, cousin, best friend or neighbor. The whole country was relieved and thankful when the army was successful. And the whole country felt a horrible loss when even one soldier fell in the line of duty.

Liz and I listened as one of the officers gave a speech about the honor of being a part of the IDF. Then the army rabbi recited a prayer for the new recruits. One at a time, the soldiers received a small, soft cover copy of the Bible. Each one responded with a clipped, well-practiced salute.

"Before I came to Israel, I used to be extremely anti-guns," I told Liz quietly as the ceremony proceeded. "I agreed with the conscientious objectors, who were exempt from being drafted into the American army because of their strong anti-arms belief."

"Really?" Liz turned to face me.

"Yep. But since I came to Israel, I learned how important it is that finally, after two thousand years, we Jews have our own army again to protect us."

"Right," Liz nodded. "It's actually those guns," she pointed with her chin, "that help keep us safe."

In unison, each soldier shouted out one of the two traditional oaths that pledged them to safeguard the people, the State and the Land of Israel: "*Ani nishba!*"[48] "*Ani matzhir!*"[49]

When the ceremony was over, the lines of newly sworn-in soldiers stood at ease. Their families and friends approached them with hugs and kisses, giving them care packages of food and other items from home, as well as good luck wishes and blessings to "be safe."

I noticed a couple of soldiers were standing by themselves. "Those two must not have anyone to fuss over them," I said, pointing.

"They must be new *olim*[50] without any family in the country," Liz said.

I was watching the two boys standing by themselves on opposite sides of the crowd. "They're called *chayalim bodedim*—'lone soldiers.'"

"If I would have known we'd be here for this, I would have baked those two cookies to take with them," Liz said.

"Really? You would have?" I was impressed.

"Yeah, I would have. I'm not a mother yet, but one day I may have a son defending us in this army. And anyway,"

---

[48] I swear!
[49] I declare!
[50] Immigrants.

she waved the back of her hand towards the soldiers in front of us, "aren't we all like family?"

I glanced once more at the two *chayalim bodedim,* and then at the other soldiers with their friends and relatives. "It's too bad we didn't know," I said. "I would have helped you make those cookies... for all of them."

PART THREE

September 1989—March 1991

"I understand you cut the time a little short yesterday," Fran said while she checked my ribs.

"Yeah, we didn't want you to miss too much," I joked. "But actually, my leg was getting tired."

"We'll make up for it today," Carol told me. "I scheduled you in for a longer time slot. You can rest for a few minutes halfway through, if you need to."

"Sounds good," I said. "I'm glad you're feeling better," I told Fran, "'cause guess what I've got in store for both of you today?" I laughed at how I, too, had begun to look forward to these story-telling therapy sessions.

"What?" Fran and Carol asked together.

"I'm getting engaged!"

"Yes?" Fran finished scribbling something on my chart and sat down next to my bed.

"Uh huh." I nodded. "And wait till you hear about my wedding."

"I'm happy I'm here for this," Fran pulled her chair closer.

Carol smiled at me. "So who's the lucky guy?"

YEHUDA
(December 1989)

"*That can't be him!*" I was staring at the hippie standing on the other side of the big clock next to the Mashbir department store in the center of Jerusalem.

For half an hour I'd been waiting to meet Yehuda for our first date. A young man with worn jeans, a scruffy-looking five o'clock shadow and an orange sweater that was unraveling at the bottom had also been standing around for a while. A small red yarmulke was clipped on top of his straggly hair. *He looks like he's also meeting someone.* I watched him smoke a couple of cigarettes and then eat a juicy orange while he waited. Every now and then he wiped his mouth on his sleeve and his sticky hands on his jeans.

Now I really wish I knew what Yehuda looked like.

Yehuda and I had become acquainted without ever meeting in person or seeing pictures of each other. Our story was very different from the way I'd ever dated or gotten to know a boy before. Yehuda and I were set up by Yehuda's younger sister and one of my Livnot friends who'd met in New York and had decided that we'd make a good match. While spending a few weeks in Chicago, I received a letter from my friend describing Yehuda a bit. It had seemed that he and I were on similar paths.

Slightly older than me, twenty-eight-year-old Yehuda had also come to Israel right after college. He'd toured the country, went to *ulpan* classes to learn Hebrew and studied Torah in a Zionist yeshiva,[51] gradually becoming more observant in Judaism. After living in Israel for five years, Yehuda had gone back to the US to get a master's degree in business.

That's when my friend's letter arrived. And *that's* when our relationship began.

Yehuda and I spoke a couple of times on the phone long distance while he was working on finishing up his studies

---

[51] Torah academy.

in New York and I was still visiting in Chicago. After I returned to Jerusalem we kept in touch through letters for a few months until Yehuda also came back to Israel.

Now, finally, we were meeting.

Could that be him? Pulling my coat tighter around me, I sat down on the concrete ledge near the tall clock and thought about how to determine if the person I was watching was actually Yehuda. *I pictured him differently.*

I considered leaving and later telling Yehuda that I'd waited for a while and didn't find him. But I decided that wouldn't be nice, after all our letters and phone calls. Yehuda had been quite friendly on the telephone, and our conversations had flowed easily. I'd begun to think that we'd get along well.

It wouldn't be fair to him if we didn't meet at least once. I decided to stay a little longer, hoping someone would come along and end up being the person this guy was waiting for. *Then I'd know he wasn't Yehuda. I wish I knew who Yehuda was already!*

I got up and glanced over to check again on my hippie buddy who was still there. Rubbing his hands together, he was also beginning to look anxious for *his* date to arrive.

Suddenly, an idea came to me. I could walk past him with my head down and call out Yehuda's name like a ventriloquist, being careful not to move my lips. *If he looks my way then I'll know he's Yehuda. But if he doesn't react, I'll know he's not.* What a plan! *Okay, I'm going to do this*, I psyched myself up. As far as I was concerned, this would be a very important test.

Gathering up my nerve, I began walking to the other side of the clock. As I drew closer, I lowered my head and called out "Yehuda" through my clenched teeth. The strong smell of cigarettes mixed with orange invaded my nostrils as I passed. *Please don't look my way*, I silently begged. *Don't move. Don't even blink!*

Out of the corner of my eye, I watched for some sign of recognition. Nothing. He didn't turn his head or even so much as twitch. He *wasn't* Yehuda!

I continued walking, as if I had somewhere to go. After a bit, I turned around and returned to my original waiting spot. Just as I was about to sit down again, I noticed a young man in the bustle of people coming up the street towards the Mashbir store. He was average height and build with a brown closely trimmed beard and brown almond-shaped eyes. Wearing corduroy pants, a blue pull-over sweater and a crocheted yarmulke on his head, he walked with quick and even strides. *It's him!* This time I was sure.

"Hi." He smiled in my direction as he reached the big clock. "Sorry I'm late. I missed the bus."

I'm right! One quick glance was all it had taken. There had been no doubt in my mind. I knew right away that *this* was who I'd been waiting for... Yehuda Kaplan.

CHAPTER 2

BIG NEWS AND BUS FARE

(March 1990)

I moved away from the Arab man standing next to me at the bus stop. Walking around the benches to the other side of the bus shelter, I waited with two teenage girls who were speaking French. I didn't like being suspicious of people. But these days, the circumstances called for taking extra precautions.

More than two years had passed since the intifada had begun. Although bus stop stabbings and other types of terrorist acts were still making the headlines, today I wasn't letting anything take away from my joy. I had exciting news to tell my coworkers at the small law firm where I'd started working part-time as a legal secretary. My friend Navah, who was now married and living near the office building where I worked, was also about to hear: I was engaged!

Since our first date, Yehuda and I had spoken on the phone every day and spent time together a couple of times a week, as well as on Shabbat. Our limited budgets had taken us to inexpensive cafes and on nature hikes. Often, we'd talk and walk the streets of Jerusalem until our feet ached. With each date, Yehuda and I had grown closer. Now, six months after our first phone conversation in the

US and four months after we'd met in Israel, we decided to get married.

I knew Navah would be thrilled for me. I had asked her to come to the office building so we could talk before I went in to work. Navah and I would often discuss how things were progressing with Yehuda and me, and now I could tell her that, as of last night, it was official!

I followed the two French girls onto the bus and found an aisle seat somewhere in the middle. The Arab man came on after us. He looked about thirty, was wearing a brown jacket and had a black and white checkered *kafiya* wrapped around his neck. After handing the driver money, he took a seat two rows behind me. Was I imagining it, or were the other passengers also carefully scrutinizing his every move?

A distinguished-looking elderly woman with short white hair, a long, thin nose and a cinnamon-colored overcoat came on the bus next. Holding onto a large umbrella with one hand and the metal side railing with the other, she pulled herself up the steps. I moved over to the window, allowing her to take the seat next to me. She sat down slowly, then turned to me and asked in a strong British accent, "Do you speak English?"

"Yes," I answered, with a nod of my head.

"How much do I have to pay again?"

I told her what it cost to ride the bus and then watched her rummage through her purse. The driver tilted his head backwards and called out in Hebrew, "*Geveret*,[52] what about your fare?"

Unaware that the driver was addressing her, the woman didn't respond. I could see her ghost white fingers with the brown spots pushing around the coins in her wallet.

---

[52] Ma'am.

"I've got it," she finally said, looking up and smiling at me. Leaning forward, she handed the money to the woman sitting in front of her, who passed it up to the bus driver.

The bus stopped at a red light. The driver counted the money the British woman had sent up to him. "Uh, *geveret*," he called to her again, "you gave me too much money." He peered at her through the giant rearview mirror.

Looking straight ahead, the woman, who didn't understand Hebrew, remained innocently silent.

"It looked to me like she paid the right amount," the Israeli woman who had passed the money forward answered for her.

"She gave me too much," the driver insisted.

The driver and the woman continued to discuss the British woman's bus fare across the bus for another moment. "This is like a beginner's math class," the driver laughed. "Give the lady this money back," he handed a shiny shekel and three ten-agurot[53] coins to a schoolboy sitting in one of the front seats.

"What's this money for?" the British woman asked when the boy handed her the coins.

"It's your change," I told her. "You paid too much."

"But I gave what I was supposed to."

"Don't worry," a man with a long beard and black hat sitting across the aisle told her in his thick Israeli English. "If de driver says it belong to you, den it's your money."

"Oh. All right. If you say so." The woman's white head bent back down towards her purse as she fished out her wallet for a second time. Dropping the coins inside, she turned to me. "It's always good to get money back, isn't it?"

"Yes," I replied, "it is."

---

53 Israeli coins, each worth one-tenth of a shekel.

The elderly woman zipped her purse shut and, shifting in her seat, made herself comfortable for the ride. "Do you live here?" she asked me.

"Yep," I answered. "I've been in Israel for almost six years now."

"That's lovely." She smiled at me.

"But I officially made *aliyah* about four years ago," I explained.

"How splendid! I just made *aliyah* myself." The woman's eyes danced excitedly. "So you're with your family then?"

"No. I'm just with me. But I have some relatives here. And," I couldn't hold it back, "I'm getting married!"

"Oh, that's delightful!" My elderly seatmate beamed. "*Mazel tov!*"[54] Her wide grin produced a map of fine white wrinkles that spread across her thin face. "He's a lucky chap to find a lovely girl such as you."

"Thank you," I said. "He's pretty nice too."

At my stop, I said goodbye and good luck to the friendly British woman. Then, passing the French girls and the Arab man with the kafiya, I got off the bus. As it pulled away, I spotted Navah coming up the street. She was wearing a fuzzy grey hat and a long belted coat that covered the small bulge of her pregnant stomach. I could see puffs of her breath in the cold air as she walked.

We met by the entrance of my office building. "Guess what?" I didn't waste a second.

"Don't tell me." Navah's big round eyes had a hint of excitement in them. "You're engaged?"

"That's right!"

"Ha!" Her smile stretched to both sides of her face. "I figured that was going to happen soon!" She threw her

---

[54] Congratulations!

arms around my neck. *"Mazel tov!"*

"I never imagined it would go so fast." I told Navah. "I guess when things click, you just know. And it doesn't have to take a long time. I feel like we've known each other for years."

"I can definitely see you two together." Navah gushed. "You're both smart and sociable and you're both so Mr. and Mrs. Eretz Yisrael![55] Have you told anyone else yet?"

"We're starting to tell everyone now. I spoke to Liz this morning and she's already offered to make us an engagement party."

"And I'm going to make you one of the *Sheva Berachot*[56] after the wedding. You'll tell me which night is good for you that week and then we'll make a list of friends to invite. If your parents are still in the country, they can come too."

My parents. I knew they were happy about us getting married. They just weren't happy about us getting married in Israel. They wanted us to live closer to them in the US and eventually have a family there. Yehuda's parents felt the same. But neither of us could imagine getting married or living anywhere but in Israel. We both considered ourselves privileged that one day our children would be Sabras—true native-born Israelis.

Now, though our families were far away, I was feeling very lucky to have good friends who would be helping us celebrate before and after we were married. "Okay," I told Navah. "When the time comes, I'll let you know which night would be good to make us a *Sheva Berachot*. But that's not for a while yet."

---

55 The Land of Israel.
56 Post-wedding celebration meals where seven special blessings are recited; lit., "Seven Blessings."

"Right. You're only at the engagement-announcing stage."

"And so far, I've only had a chance to tell my parents, Malka, a couple of friends and the nice English woman I just met on the bus."

"So what are you waiting for?" Navah took me by the arm. "Let's go tell everyone at your work." Laughing together, Navah and I disappeared inside the four-story Jerusalem stone building. It was time to begin spreading my big news.

·❖· CHAPTER 3 ·❖·

THE CUSTOMS AGENT

(July 1990)

I love presents—especially when I'm the one receiving them. While I was in Chicago for a family gathering, my mother's friends threw me a wedding shower. In only seven more weeks I was getting married! I was as anxious and excited about that day as I was about getting back to Israel. But now I was just focusing on packing all the new towels and linens I'd received as gifts and would be bringing with me on the airplane.

Jamie Goldberg, one of my high school girlfriends, was helping me fit everything inside my suitcases. Adventurous and capable, Jamie was short with light green eyes and a clear complexion. People often commented on how she and I looked alike. Before I began dressing in skirts and longer sleeves, some had even mistaken us for sisters.

Though Jamie and I were on distinctly separate paths with very different lifestyles and thousands of miles between us, we'd remained good friends. Whenever I flew to Chicago for a visit, we would spend many hours together shopping, going on walks and catching up on each other's lives. Sometimes we'd have positive self-searching talks about her future prospects or my growing connection to Judaism and Israel. Other times we'd disagree about everything from religion to politics to controversial social issues. But despite our different goals and ideals, we both had a strong Jewish identity and a mutual acceptance of one another.

Now, we were hunched over my suitcases, struggling to cram all my things inside them. "I'm a little nervous about getting stopped at Customs when I get to Ben Gurion Airport," I told Jamie.

Jamie waved the back of her hand at me. "Don't worry. You're not bringing anything expensive, like a food processor or one of those big video cameras."

"True, but we're packing presents that are new, and what about the electric can opener and that little hairdryer we wrapped inside my clothes?"

"And what about your wedding dress?" Jamie zipped my carry-on bag shut. "Do they charge for wedding dresses?"

"I don't know," I admitted. "It would be great if they just took one look and decided not to bother with me."

"Don't worry about it. Be optimistic. You'll be fine."

"Yeah, but look at all of this!" I swept my hand over all my new possessions.

"Well, you look young and innocent, and besides, there really isn't much of anything here for them to catch you with," Jamie said, trying to reassure me.

I stopped packing and sat on the carpet next to the open suitcases. "Truthfully, I'm not as worried about having to maybe pay taxes as I am about opening up all these bags, taking everything out and then packing them up again. It's hard enough stuffing everything in with two people working on it. It would be a nightmare having to do that all over again by myself in the airport after a long and exhausting trip."

I pictured my clothes, shoes and toiletries strewn all about on a low metal counter in front of the inspectors, the carefully folded new towels and sheets haphazardly opened and thrown into a heap. The small appliances I'd hunted for in a store that sold 220-voltage electronics would be discovered. And what about all the cheap cans of StarKist tuna we had fit into my shoes and sweatshirt pockets? I knew Jamie was right. There was nothing I could do but hope for the best.

The next night, when my plane arrived in Israel, I grabbed a free luggage cart and awkwardly piled my heavy baggage on it. I was careful to gently lay the hanging bag with my pearly white wedding dress on the top.

Here we go. Slowly pushing the weighted-down cart over to Customs, I gave myself instructions to try to calm my pounding heart. *Look straight ahead. Make sure to breathe. Blink normally.*

I figured it must have been the uneasy look on my flushed face, or maybe the sight of a small person pushing such a hefty load that caused the Customs agent to stop me.

"*Selichah, geveret,*"[57] he signaled for me to stop. "Let's see what you've got there."

I was panic-stricken at the idea of a possible suitcase rummaging. The stout, smooth-shaven man looked kindly enough. But I saw him as the enemy. I couldn't believe he was actually stopping me. *And now, of all times! This has never happened to me before —not with any of the flights I made back and forth.* I hoped he would let me go without a full-fledged investigation.

Facing my potential adversary, I tried to collect my wits and answer as nonchalantly as possible. "*Shalom,*" I said

---

57 Excuse me, ma'am.

quietly, attempting a smile.

"Where are you coming from?" he asked.

"From visiting with my family in the United States." My American accent was still fairly noticeable in Hebrew. I hoped my answer would make me seem young and innocent, as Jamie had suggested.

"And where are you going?"

"To Jerusalem."

"And these are all your things?"

"Yes."

"And what's that?" The man pointed straight at the bulky garment bag draped over my suitcases. "Your wedding dress?"

I stared at the man. Was he just guessing or was he accustomed to many other soon-to-be brides strolling past him, praying not to get stopped? In any case, I realized this was no ordinary Customs check.

"Yes," I answered warily, "it's my wedding dress."

"And you brought things back with you for *after* you get married?"

He was good.

"Yes." I sighed, wondering how all this was going to end.

Then suddenly, flashing me a big smile, the Customs agent slapped his hand down on the garment bag and said, "*Mazel tov*,[58] sweetie! Enjoy yourself."

What? I blinked hard. I couldn't believe it. *He's congratulating me and letting me go!* I looked at the intuitive, smiling man through new eyes. I felt like giving him a hug.

"*Todah rabbah!*"[59] With all the sincerity I could muster, I thanked my new friend, the Customs agent.

---

[58] Congratulations.
[59] Thank you very much, Thanks a lot.

Relieved, I slowly pushed my cart away and headed towards the crowd of people waiting outside for the new arrivals to appear. As I approached the area, I could hear the customary cheers and enthusiastic greetings in honor of those who had just come back home or had come to the country for a visit. From the open doorway, I watched reunited relatives and friends hugging and kissing, some with joyous tears.

Eyeing the garment bag with my satiny wedding dress snuggled inside, I took a deep breath and stepped outside into the warm sunshine. It was true. There really was no place like home.

·❖· CHAPTER 4 ·❖·

JUST THE BEGINNING

(September 1990)

    I brushed some rose-colored blush on my cheeks and then quickly smeared on a bit of clear lipgloss. Turning away from the full-length mirror, I handed my mother some hairpins to fasten on my veil crown of delicate white flowers.

    I was getting ready for my wedding in the apartment Rachel and I had been sharing. I wasn't interested in being hair sprayed or made up in a fancy hotel room like a doll. I wanted to be a natural bride. My dress did have princess-like puffy shoulders and flowery lace in the front, but unlike traditional wedding gowns, it fell to my mid-calf and not to the floor with a long, sweeping train.

    Rachel and my parents joined me in the decorated rental car for the ten-minute drive to the wedding hall. Unfortunately, my brother and sister, who were both married and each had a young child and a demanding job, couldn't be with us.

    Although I wasn't nervous about getting married, I was worried that all the wedding arrangements Yehuda and I had made might not go as planned. What concerned me most was whether my mother and father would feel comfortable with the traditional Jewish celebration. I knew that just about everything would be different from the weddings they usually attended. The ceremony under the *chuppah*[60] and the songs we'd be dancing to in separate areas of the dance floor would be in Hebrew and unfamiliar to them. Of course, the intifada passed through my mind as well. *G-d, please don't let anything bad happen. Please let everything go smoothly,* I had prayed countless times since my parents' arrival.

My parents were impressed with the décor of the hall. From the surprised expression on my mother's face, I could tell she wasn't expecting to see such a spacious and lovely set up. Beautiful red-and-white flowered centerpieces complimented the white tablecloths and red-cushioned chairs. Red cloth napkins were spread open like fans in the middle of each shiny white plate.

The photographer's lights and white flash umbrella were already set up. He asked me and my parents to step over to his "studio" for a quick photo session. Yehuda, whose parents and two siblings had already taken pictures with him, was now on the other side of the hall signing the wedding *ketubah*.[61] There would be plenty of time for pictures of me and Yehuda together, both during and after the wedding.

Guests began to trickle in, and then it seemed to me they were suddenly all there at once. Holding a small, but elegant lilac, peach and white bouquet, I took my seat on the majestic red velvet bride's chair. An enormous stand of red and white flowers, dotted with tiny white baby's breath towered over me from behind my chair.

My mother and father were sitting at my side as I greeted the guests who came with blessings and good

---

[60] Wedding canopy.
[61] Jewish marriage contract.

wishes. One by one, I acquainted my parents with the many friends, teachers, neighbors and fellow workers I had come to know during my six years in Israel. Some of Yehuda's co-workers and relatives also came over and introduced themselves.

Navah and Liz arrived at the same time, each pushing a baby carriage with their little one inside. Beth and Michelle came right after them. They all took turns hugging and congratulating me. "*Mazel tov! Mazel tov!*"

My mother's mouth opened wide when Esther approached. "Oh, I haven't seen Esther in years, since the two of you were in grade school together!" she exclaimed.

Jamie, who'd flown in for the wedding, was also excited to see Esther's familiar face from the past when she walked into the hall. A spontaneous reunion took place with my mother and my two friends from Chicago.

I left my chair and went over to greet Malka, who'd just come in wearing a fancy lemon yellow suit and a loving smile. Yehuda and I would be celebrating with Malka at *her* wedding next month, when she'd be marrying Yedidya, the retired doctor she was seeing.

While our Netanya cousins Gidon, Aviva, Yair and Tzvi exchanged warm welcomes with my parents, my friend Penina pulled me towards her. "Can you believe you're getting *married*?" she asked, squeezing my arm excitedly.

Before I could respond, the band started up. "He's coming!" I heard someone announce. The mingling stopped and I returned to my bride's chair. My mother and Yehuda's mother were now seated on both sides of me.

Yehuda, flanked by our fathers and escorted by an entourage of dancing and singing men, was slowly walking towards me from the other side of the hall. He looked handsome in his dark blue suit, white shirt and burgundy tie. On his head he wore a white hand-crocheted yarmulke with a blue and burgundy design around its edge. I saw the nervousness on his face as he came closer.

My friends and the other enthusiastic women who gathered along the sides of the long white floor runner in front of my chair began clapping and singing to the music. Yehuda, surrounded by all of his friends, continued moving forward through the parted sea of women until he reached me. Then, with the band growing louder and our exuberant guests all around us, he bent over and slowly raised my netted veil up from behind my head. His soft brown eyes looked into mine and, for a brief moment, it was as if the two of us were already one.

"This is exciting," I heard my mother say, as Yehuda carefully set the veil down over my face.

I couldn't have agreed more.

The energized procession of men now accompanied Yehuda outside to the *chuppah*. I joined him soon afterwards with our two mothers and Yehuda's sister at my side, and with the rest of the clapping, singing women following close behind us.

Standing next to Yehuda, under the *chuppah* and the stars, I was filled with a whirlpool of emotions. But mostly, I couldn't believe the night had finally arrived. *This is my wedding. I'm getting married... to Yehuda... in Jerusalem!*

When Yehuda's foot came down and broke the wrapped glass placed on the floor in front of him, all three hundred guests shouted "*Mazel tov!*" in unison. Yehuda and I smiled excitedly at each other and then joined the others singing the traditional heartfelt song, "If I Forget Thee O Jerusalem." It reminded all of us that even during our most joyous occasions, we are still yearning for the rebuilding of the destroyed Temple in Jerusalem. I glanced at my parents, who looked a little overwhelmed. I knew they weren't used to this kind of wedding. But it was what I had dreamed of for years.

"Where did all these people come from?" my mother

asked back in the hall after the first round of dancing had finished and the main course of the meal had been served.

"It's easy to get to know a lot of people in this country," I said, spooning glazed carrots onto my plate.

My mother swept her eyes around the hall. "And this is without our friends and relatives from back home."

We were just finishing the meal when Yonah and Steve from Livnot U'Lehibanot came over to say hello with their own new spouses. I was very happy that Arnon and Meira had also made it, all the way from Tzfat.

"Let's go! The band's starting up again," Michelle was now at the head table taking me by the arm. Beth was close behind.

"Up you go. Out of your seat, bride!" Beth and Michelle brought me over to the women's dance floor, where my friends were geared up for more action.

Yehuda and his friends also began dancing again in a gigantic circle on the men's side of the floor. With the band playing and singing one lively song after another, the hall once again came alive.

Adding to the joyful and festive mood, my friends threw confetti and balloons up in the air. Some put on funny hats and wore Hawaiian leis around their necks. Others were shaking tambourines or blowing plastic horns to the music. I danced in the middle of the woman's circle with both elegantly dressed mothers and then whirled around, Spanish-dancer style, with Yehuda's sister in her salmon-colored chiffon dress.

After a while, two of my friends began twirling a jump rope. All the women clapped while Malka jumped in the middle of the rope, beckoning me to join her. I wasn't surprised to see Malka, who was only slightly younger than my mother, jumping rope. I had seen her do it many times at her other students' weddings.

When the band played a slower-paced song, my father

came over to join me in his suit and tie and a rubber gorilla mask that someone had handed him as part of the entertaining spirit. We laughed as the videographer and the photographer both made sure they caught the young bride waltzing on the side with a gorilla!

Rachel then handed me a large, sky blue parasol with long blue and white crepe paper streamers hanging from its pointed edges. Standing on a chair, I held the open parasol above my head. As the music played on, my friends grabbed onto the ends of the long streamers and walked around me in a wide circle while I slowly turned around in place.

From up on the chair, I could see the men and boys dancing. Some of Yehuda's friends were moving around in the middle of the animated circle with Yehuda, our fathers and Yehuda's older brother sitting on their shoulders.

Suddenly, my friends whisked away the parasol I was holding and sat me down on the chair. "Oh, my G-d!" I cried, as they lifted me up off the ground and set me down on the dance floor next to Yehuda. Chairs were brought for our families and everyone crowded around as the entertainment continued.

"Now, watch this!" I shouted over the band to my mother sitting next to me.

Two of Yehuda's friends were dancing around in front of us and the circle of guests with full bottles of wine balanced on their heads. A third danced agilely to the music while balancing the tip of a fiery cardboard cone on his nose. Then another friend sat down on the floor and performed the fire-swallowing trick by dipping wads of cotton into a lit candle, one after another. My mother gasped when he held up the first wad of burning cotton for everyone to see and then dramatically popped it into his mouth. "He'd better drink some of that water he's got next to him!" she exclaimed.

Yehuda decided it was time to get into the action. Standing directly in front of me, he skipped like a deer with a jump rope. Everyone cheered as he hopped and jumped forwards and backwards, speeding up to double-time.

A few minutes later, my chair and I were back up in the air and I was returned to the woman's circle. Equipped with props and poster board signs, my friends put on a skit of their own for me. As the band played on, Rachel, Michelle and Beth began acting out an original comic pantomime of "This Is Your Life, Shelly!" It featured various significant events throughout my twenty-eight years, ending with my engagement to Yehuda.

"I don't believe this!" I exclaimed, as Liz and Malka also came on to play a part in one of the mini-scenes. I was amazed at how well my friends had put it all together.

After the entertainment finished, my parents and Yehuda's family each found their own set of Israeli relatives to converse with at the tables while Yehuda and I continued to let loose on the dance floor with our friends. Even when the band quit for the night, we kept singing and letting our feet carry us in all directions.

The last of the guests left after the seven blessings were recited over a glass of wine, marking the end of the wedding. Jamie stayed a bit longer to help me fix my hair in the bathroom for the last few pictures the photographer wanted to take before packing up his equipment.

Then, laden with presents, Yehuda and I followed our families out of the wedding hall into the quiet, empty parking lot towards our rental car. Our wedding was over. The exciting event we had planned and waited for had come to an end. But as we walked side by side in the cool midnight air, we knew, for us, it was just the beginning.

·❧· CHAPTER 5 ·❧·

"After we got married, Yehuda and I moved to Or Tzion, a settlement town just north of Jerusalem in the hills of Samaria."

"Why'd you leave Jerusalem?" Carol asked, tilting her head towards me.

"Yehuda was excited about joining the other thousands of pioneering couples and families who were settling the areas of Judea and Samaria in the middle of the country. I was less sure at first that a settlement town was where I wanted to live," I admitted. "Judea and Samaria are filled with amazing Jewish biblical and historical sites and many developing Zionist communities. But there are also a large number of Arab villages in the area and their residents aren't very happy about the Jews sharing the land with them."

"That could be a little unpleasant," Fran said. "How'd you feel after you moved there?"

"Well, I had to get used to the meuzzins' loud middle-of-the-night calls to prayer that come from the neighboring Arab villages. And it was a little nerve-wracking being on the lookout for rocks that might be thrown at our car while driving on the road to and from Jerusalem. But I soon began to understand and appreciate the important role that Or Tzion and the rest of the settlement towns play, especially for Israel's security. Our communities keep the areas from turning into a huge terrorist haven, which would eventually spread more terrorism to the rest of the country as well.

"So, you've created like a buffer zone," Carol said.

"Yeah, something like that." I stopped to concentrate on bending my knee. "We have to be more aware and take precautions, but we have quality lives and we feel good knowing that we're making positive contributions to the country just by living where we're living."

"Everyone must really appreciate what all of you are doing," Fran said.

"Well," I smiled to myself," not exactly." There are many who feel that the Jews in Judea and Samaria are making problems for peace."

"Why is that?" Fran asked.

"Well, when Israel won the 1967 war and liberated Judea and Samaria from the Jordanians, the government didn't rush to annex them because they were populated with hundreds of thousands of anti-Israel Arabs. But, not long afterwards, we began settling those areas and Jews have been building up that part of the country ever since."

"That probably doesn't sit well with the Arabs, does it?" Carol acknowledged.

"No, it doesn't. The Arabs claim that Israel has no rights to the land in Judea and Samaria." I bent my knee again. "Actually, the Arab terrorist organizations, the majority of the Arab countries and a good percentage of the Muslims around the world don't even recognize Israel as a Jewish state or a Jewish country. As far as they're concerned, we don't have the right to any of the land at all."

"But didn't Egypt and another country sign peace treaties with Israel at some point?" Carol asked.

"Yeah, Egypt did in '79 and Jordan did afterwards, in the '90s. But just about everyone else still uses Judea and Samaria as a reason for not agreeing to make peace with Israel. They insist we're occupying their land."

"Is that why Israel hasn't officially annexed those areas yet?" Fran was wondering.

"Well, unfortunately, when it comes to the question of whether we should annex Judea and Samaria or send nearly half a million Jews packing, there are differences of opinions and disputes among the Jews in Israel as well. The Zionist right wingers have no doubts about being the rightful owners of those areas and aren't willing to risk the security of the people by handing them over to the Arabs. The more liberal left wingers, on the other hand, believe that the most just and peaceful move would be for the government to do just that— return control of that part of the Land back to the Arabs.

"So what pulls so many Israelis to live there is basically the matter of the country's security?" Fran asked.

"That, and also because we don't want to lose any part of our homeland," I added. "Judea and Samaria were part of biblical Israel. When the Land was first given to the Jewish people, thousands of years ago, Jews acquired the right to settle those areas along with the rest of the country."

"That was a long time ago," Fran pointed out.

"Yep, Jews have been living there and all over Israel since ancient times. The only time in more recent history that Jews weren't allowed to live in Judea and Samaria was between 1948 and 1967 when Jordan took control over the region."

Carol tucked strands of her short blond hair

behind her ear. "So does that mean that during that period of time those parts belonged to the Arabs?"

"Well, in order for an area of land to officially belong to any particular nation, the people have to hold some sort of broadly recognized sovereignty over the place. For centuries, going as far back as the times of King Saul and King David, Israel was sovereign over the Land. And today, the State of Israel has sovereignty over it. But during Jordan's nineteen years of rule, nobody, except Britain and Pakistan, recognized its claim to Judea and Samaria."

"So you and Yehuda moved to a town in Samaria, along with lots of other people, to help keep Israel whole and safe," Fran summarized.

"Right. We set up a modest home in the town of Or Tzion," I replied. "At first, we lived in a caravan."

"Which is..." Fran fixed her eyes on me and waited for an explanation.

"A caravan is like a large trailer home without the wheels. Young couples or small families sometimes live in a caravan until they can afford to rent or buy a bigger or more permanent place. We lived in one for three years." I carefully straightened out my leg again. "Oh, except for that month during the war."

"The war?" Carol took her hand off my foot and looked at me.

"The Persian Gulf War."

"You were in a war?" Fran leaned closer to me. "How can you act so calm and nonchalant about being in a war?"

"Oh, believe me, at the time, I was anything but calm." I looked over my glasses at Fran. "And, I wasn't nonchalant either."

PREPARING FOR THE WORST
(January 1991)

"Can you pass me the tape?" I held my hand out to Yehuda.

"Here." Yehuda tossed me the wide roll. "I'll need it back though."

Using my teeth, I tore off a long piece of tape and stuck it onto the edge of the thick sheet of plastic I was using to cover a window. Yehuda and I were busy sealing a room to prevent the infiltration of deadly chemicals in case war broke out the next day.

The threat of war began after Iraq invaded Kuwait six months earlier. Iraq's main goal was to get out of paying back the huge debt it owed the smaller, oil-rich country. The United Nations immediately jumped in to defend Kuwait. It imposed sanctions on Iraq and set January 15 as the date by which Iraqi President Saddam Hussein had to withdraw his troops. If Hussein failed to meet the deadline, US President George H.W. Bush, together with an international coalition, would use all means necessary to force Iraq out of Kuwait. For his part, Saddam Hussein made it clear that if his country was attacked, he would not only strike Saudi Arabia, where US soldiers were positioned, but he would also use far-ranging chemical weapons on Israel.

"It just goes to show you," I said, smoothing the tape at the edge of the plastic onto the window frame, "it doesn't matter whether or not we're involved in any particular political situation, economic problem, social dilemma, or anything else. We always get sucked in by our enemies for no reason other than pure hatred. We don't have anything to do with this war! They're just finding another way to get at us, to let out their hostilities towards us... as if this intifada that's still going on isn't enough."

"I think the word you're looking for," Yehuda said, "is scapegoat."

"I can't believe tomorrow is January 15 already." I ripped off another strip of tape before returning the roll to Yehuda.

We were preparing one of the bedrooms in Malka's new apartment in Jerusalem. When Malka asked us to housesit for a month while she was in the States, Yehuda and I readily agreed.

I loved the fresh air and open space in Or Tzion where Yehuda and I had already begun to feel very much a part of the community. Settling the Land and building up Jewish towns and cities where Arab towns and villages threatened to take over was becoming important to me, as it already was to Yehuda. But being five months pregnant, I'd really liked the idea of moving for a while into Malka's comfortable, more conveniently located Jerusalem apartment.

With quieter, muezzin-free nights and easier access to both work and shopping, we were enjoying the temporary arrangement. Unfortunately, Iraqi troops had remained in Kuwait and January 15 had quickly crept up on us.

"Doomsday's coming," Yehuda quipped lightly.

I wasn't amused. I had hoped we would just be able to relax and have a nice time while in Jerusalem. With the threat of another war hanging over the country, we were left with no choice but to get ready.

Israel took Saddam Hussein's warning seriously and prepared for chemical warfare. Overnight, gas masks, Scud missiles and sealed rooms became Israeli household words. The government distributed emergency kits, housed in brown cardboard boxes with long black plastic straps. The population was instructed on how to wear the enclosed gas masks, as well as when and how to use the supplied syringe of atropine—an antidote to nerve gas.

If a loud siren screamed out its warning that a tactical ballistic Scud missile was on its way over, there would be two minutes to hurry into a sealed room and don the masks. Parents would have to work fast to help their children and to put their babies into their plastic, protective tent-like cubicles.

"Okay. The window's done," I announced. "How's the door?"

"It's ready," Yehuda said. "If the time comes, all we have to do is smooth down the tape onto the doorpost."

"Here's some towels to stuff into the space between the door and the floor," I dropped two grey towels in the corner behind the door.

"Good. Are we done here now?" Yehuda wasn't as concerned as I was about getting things ready before there was an actual need to do so.

I looked around. "We need to bring in a radio and a flashlight. And maybe we should go to the supermarket now to stock up on food, bottled water and batteries."

"No, let's wait till tomorrow and see what happens. There's still a chance Saddam Hussein will come to his senses. Why buy a bunch of stuff we may not need?"

"Come to his senses? It doesn't look like that will happen." I thought Yehuda was in denial. I didn't like the idea of last minute shopping, but agreed to wait until the next day. There *was* a slim chance things would turn around. "Fine, we can wait with the food," I said, "but I'm bringing a bucket into the room now. Please don't take it out. I might need it if we end up being stuck in here for any length of time," I instructed.

"What do you need a bucket for?" Yehuda asked innocently.

"Well, some of us need to go the bathroom on a regular

basis these days. I don't want to take any chances that it might be one of those times right after a siren goes off."

"You're kidding. You'd use a bucket?"

"Well, maybe you're right. It *would* be better if you pulled out the toilet and cemented it onto the floor right here," I pointed with my foot to a spot near the window.

"Okay. Bring in the bucket. But don't expect me to use it. No his and her buckets in *our* sealed room!" Yehuda teased.

I wished I could feel more relaxed, but the uncertainty of everything was frustrating and scary. I knew that, although Yehuda was less stressed about the possibility of war, he was also starting to feel anxious. There probably wasn't a soul in all of Israel that wasn't concerned about what would be.

That night, the country went to sleep unsure whether or not the dark threatening blanket of war would come the next day to smother us. We hoped and prayed that it wouldn't.

·❧· CHAPTER *6* ·❧·

SCUDS, GAS MASKS, SEALED ROOMS
(January 15, 1991)

"Iraq's not budging," Yehuda said, switching off the radio. "Looks like this is it." The news reports confirmed what everyone in Israel, the United States and many other parts of the world had feared. "There's going to be another war."

Time was up. President Bush and his coalition were ready to punish Saddam Hussein. They would fight him to free Kuwait.

"C'mon," I said, wasting no time. "We have to get over to the supermarket."

Now that war was imminent, Israeli shops and streets suddenly filled with people hurrying to stock up on plastic, tape, food, batteries, small radios and flashlights. Supermarkets and smaller local grocery stores were bursting with panicky shoppers rushing to grab double-wrapped and canned food items from the shelves and freezers.

"Oh my G-d, look at this place!" My mouth hung open as I stepped into the supermarket across the street from Malka's building. "It's like a madhouse in here."

The lines of people waiting to pay went from the cashier

in the front of the store all the way to the butcher counter in the back. One line wound around and into the next aisle.

"This is crazy!" I stood in the doorway, staring.

"C'mon,' Yehuda said, nudging me forward, "let's hurry and get what we want or we'll be here forever."

With no shopping carts available, we began loading up small plastic grocery bags that were strewn about the fruits and vegetables section. Ready-made food that didn't need to be cooked, wouldn't spoil quickly, and was sealed well against chemical contamination was scarce to find on the rapidly emptying shelves. The food was clearing out so fast that Yehuda and I found ourselves rushing up and down the aisles, grabbing whatever we could before there was nothing left. When we had enough to last a couple of weeks, we went to wait in line.

"This will take all day," Yehuda complained.

"I hope not. I want to get back to the apartment before something starts to happen. I didn't expect to be out for so long."

"Maybe we should have brought a bucket with us," Yehuda joked. Noticing I wasn't laughing, he offered me a smile. "Well at least we managed to find something to eat."

"Yeah, we can feast on rice cakes, dry tuna and canned apples every day! Wonderful." I was less than thrilled with what we were purchasing, and even more anxious about being away from our sealed room and gas masks.

As it turned out, the US-led coalition attacked Iraq two days later, on January 17. Iraq's response slammed into Israel the next night at 2 AM. Those who were awake listening to the radio heard the Hebrew code words "*nachash tzefa*"[62] just seconds before air raid sirens went off across the country. From the city of Kiryat Shmona in the

---

[62] Viper snake.

far north to the beach resort town of Eilat in the south, a low-pitched whine rose to a high-strung wail, warning everyone of incoming danger. Sleepy Israelis sprang from their beds and scrambled nervously into their sealed rooms.

Yehuda and I remained sound asleep through it all.

For some reason, the siren in Malka's neighborhood didn't go off! We awoke in the morning to discover that everyone else had been up in the middle of the night, wearing their gas masks. Phones were ringing off the hook as friends, neighbors and relatives both in Israel and outside the country called to check on each other and talk about their experience. Reactions ranged from fear and panic to relief that nobody had been hurt.

Though the first set of missiles Hussein sent over had landed far from Jerusalem, I was distressed by the fact that Yehuda and I and the rest of Malka's neighborhood had been completely unaware of the attack.

"I don't believe it! Everyone was up and in their sealed rooms. And *we* slept through the whole thing!"

"There must have been a problem with the siren in our area," Yehuda figured.

I was horrified. "What if a missile had landed around here? Can you imagine? I don't believe this!"

Apparently my cries echoed those of many others in the vicinity, for the neighborhood's loudspeaker was working extraordinarily well by the next attack. The siren rang out so loudly, Yehuda and I both jumped at its unexpected blare. It took an instant for us to absorb what was happening. Then something close to hysteria set in.

"Hurry," I instructed Yehuda. "To the sealed room! Get your mask! Wait, I have to take out my contact lenses!"

"I have to shave my beard!" Yehuda exclaimed as he ran to get scissors from the drawer before ducking into the room. "Or the mask might not fit properly."

"You were supposed to do that in advance!" I reminded

him, slamming the door behind us.

"I know—wishful thinking. I guess I was hoping there wouldn't really be a need for any of this."

"Well, let's get this door sealed up first!"

I ran the palms of my hands over the tape on the edges of the plastic. Yehuda quickly reached up to the top of the door and smoothed the tape down with one hand while haphazardly cutting at his beard with the other. I searched around for my contact lens case, which had fallen from the shelf with all the rushing around.

After what seemed like an eternity, the door was sealed, the space near the floor was stuffed with towels, lenses were off, beard was mostly cut, gas masks and radio were on. Yehuda told me to put my hand over the filter part of the mask the way everyone had been instructed, to check if it was working. My heart was beating fast as we sat down together in the still room. Tense and worried, we held hands and listened anxiously for the all-clear siren and a radio announcement. It would tell us which areas of the country were no longer in danger, and when we could remove our masks and leave the room.

This wasn't how I had imagined it would be. I wasn't only nervous about the missiles flying overhead, I was also upset about how sloppy and unprepared we'd been. *We were a chaotic mess.* I was sure we had gone way over the two minutes allotted to run for cover and prepare oneself before a missile actually struck. Plus, the gas mask was anything but comfortable.

"I'm pretty hot in here," Yehuda said, tapping the thick, black rubber over his head.

"It's not so easy to breathe with this thing on," I complained. "And I can't see anything when I'm not wearing my contact lenses."

"You're supposed to try to remain calm and not breathe too hard," Yehuda reminded me.

Remain calm— with Scuds whizzing around! Listening to the soothing melodious music that was now playing on the radio, I tried to slow my breathing down. "What're we supposed to do if we need to throw up or blow our noses or something like that?" I wondered out loud.

"Wait, I guess."

Wait. It seemed like that was all we were doing lately, waiting. Waiting to find out if there would actually be a war. Waiting through the anxiety-ridden days and nights to hear whether there would be a siren. Waiting each time to see if America's Patriot anti-aircraft missiles would succeed in shooting down Iraq's Scud missiles that were headed our way. Waiting for the all-clear siren and the radio to announce it was all right to leave our sealed room. And on top of all of that, the whole country was shut down and on hold, waiting to come alive again.

A few more tense minutes passed before we were free to move about outside the room. Yehuda and I removed our masks and pulled back the tape and plastic from the door. Then we sat back down next to the radio to listen for the broadcast that would soon tell where the Scud or Scuds had landed, and whether there were any injuries this time.

"That was not an experience I want to repeat again soon," I said, as we waited to hear more information.

"You did look kind of funny," Yehuda said, trying to lighten the atmosphere. "Like an alien from Mars or maybe Saturn."

"Ha! I wouldn't talk, if I were you." I was beginning to loosen up a bit. "You should see what you look like now, and that's *without* your mask!"

Yehuda rubbed his hand over his red, perspired face, and then over the smooth and rough patches of his scrappily cut beard. "Okay, you're right," he said more seriously now. "I'll also be happy if we never have to go through *this* again."

·❖· CHAPTER 7 ·❖·

WARTIME

(February 1991)

Iraq mainly attacked Israel after dark. During the day, the country slowly came back to life. Buses and trains began running again, and private vehicles were back on the roads. Businesses reopened and people started back to work. Hospitals running under emergency conditions began to operate normally. And schools held missile drills with volunteers on hand who would calm the children or help them with their masks in case of a real attack. Most schedules were rearranged so that meetings, functions, special events and weddings were held during the daylight hours. Wherever anyone went, their brown cardboard gas mask boxes went with them.

At nightfall, people retreated to the security of their homes to wait. Would it be a peaceful night or would we hear "*nachash tzefa*," a wailing siren and, in some areas, a deafening boom?

While the United States agreed to help protect Israel with Patriot missiles, President Bush repeatedly urged the Israeli government not to actively participate in the war. He was concerned that if Israel retaliated for the attacks, the Arab partners in the coalition against Iraq would leave the alliance and lessen the chances of defeating Saddam

Hussein. Israel, ready, able and itching to properly defend herself, reluctantly agreed to cooperate with America's request to refrain from launching counterattacks.

Israelis' reactions to the missile attacks varied. Some believed that only G-d could keep them safe from harm. When sirens went off, they threw themselves into their prayers instead of their gas masks and sealed rooms. Others stood and watched as the missiles soared through the air. They felt that when it was their time to leave this world, it was their time, and "anyway, the missiles are landing far from where we live, so why carry around masks and tape up windows and doors?" But most people did whatever was physically possible in order to safeguard themselves and their families. For them, gas masks and sealed rooms were an almost nightly reality.

Those living in the heavily populated metropolitan centers of Tel Aviv and Haifa felt the fears and stresses of war the most, as Iraq's Scuds were landing mainly in those areas. Many left their homes, temporarily moving to less dangerous parts of the country. For those who remained, coping with the terror and trauma of the war was especially difficult. More than once, Yehuda and I called to check on our friends and relatives living in or near Tel Aviv or Haifa. Each time, we were relieved to hear that everyone was okay.

"Why don't you come back home to live, at least until things calm down?" some of our concerned family suggested when they called from overseas. Yehuda and I both knew that it was difficult for them to understand that, war or no war, we were committed to staying in Israel.

But now, nearly three weeks after the first Scud missiles hit Israeli soil, we were about to leave the country. Months before, we had made travel plans to visit our families in the US, most of whom weren't able to be at our wedding. Though our families were important to us and we knew we couldn't disappoint all the friends and relatives who were expecting us, we wished we were going for a pleasure trip at a more peaceful time.

"I feel like a deserter," I admitted to Yehuda that evening after supper. "Everyone here will be living with anxiety, fear and worry—never knowing when or where another Scud will hit. And we'll be over there, far away from it all—eating, drinking and being merry." I left Malka's dining room table where we'd just finished supper and went to sit on the couch in her living room. "I don't feel good about that."

"I'll be eating and drinking over there," Yehuda said, wiping his hands on a napkin and joining me on the couch, "but I'll be thinking too much about everything that's going on here to be merry."

"I wish the war would end before we leave," I said, leaning over and resting my head on Yehuda's shoulder. "Then we could enjoy ourselves without worrying and without feeling guilty."

"There's not much chance of that happening." Yehuda said. "We have less than thirty hours before our plane takes off. It doesn't look like Saddam Hussein will surrender or be defeated before then."

I sat up straight and turned to face Yehuda. "We're leaving in less than thirty hours and we haven't even started packing or cleaning up this place! We put it off for too long." I tugged at Yehuda's arm. "C'mon, we've gotta get moving or we won't be ready on time!"

"Do we have to?" Yehuda didn't budge.

I sighed. "Yeah, we do." Then, following Yehuda's example, I slouched back onto the couch. "But I really wish we didn't."

CHAPTER 8

LAST-MINUTE FRENZY

(February 1991)

I wasn't moving as quickly as I would have liked. Being pregnant and still feeling nauseous at times slowed me down. We'd started packing our things and cleaning up Malka's apartment the night before. But the pace was slow and there was still plenty left to be done. To make matters worse, it was already close to noon and I couldn't find some of the clothes I wanted to bring with me on the trip.

Dialing Yehuda's work number, I spoke quickly into the phone. "I think we forgot to bring those outfits I had hanging on the closet door back home in Or Tzion."

"Well, guess what?" Yehuda sounded agitated. "I think we also must have forgotten to bring our passports."

"No. I've got them in the side pocket of my overnight bag," I said.

"Those are only our Israeli passports. I looked around for our American passports this morning while you were asleep, but couldn't find them anywhere. I was about to call to see if you knew where they were."

I leaned my elbow on the wall and rested my forehead in the palm of my hand. "Great. What are we going to do now?"

"I'll have to go to Or Tzion after work tonight and get everything."

"What? That's insane." Gripping the cord of the phone, I pulled it with me as I walked in circles. "You can't go then. It'll be dark! What if there's a missile? Plus, there's no time. I need your help getting this apartment in order for when Malka returns. And we didn't finish packing." Standing still, I spoke more quietly. "I have to go to work now. How am I going to finish everything by myself?"

"I'll come back for half an hour or so after work to help you before I leave," Yehuda promised.

Resigned to the fact that it would be a crazy day, I grabbed my gas mask box and left the apartment. On the bus, I wondered how we would be ready on time. The Nesher taxi would be picking us up at 9:30 PM to take us to the airport. I had planned everything so that we would be finished cleaning and packing with some spare time to relax before then. But it didn't look like it would happen that way.

And it didn't.

At six thirty that evening we were back at Malka's, making the beds and washing dishes. Yehuda left soon afterwards to catch the bus to Or Tzion. While I swept the kitchen floor, I worried about Yehuda being outside at night with the car as his only shelter. *He has his mask with him*, I told myself. *And chances are slim that a Scud will strike at exactly the time he'll be traveling on the road. Even if it does, he won't be anywhere near Tel Aviv or Haifa.* I put Yehuda's situation out of my mind and neatly packed a few more items.

Time was flying. I found myself starting to worry about other things as I worked, like what if Yehuda didn't find the passports? And what if the taxi came to get us before Yehuda got back?

The phone rang loudly. I dropped the clothes I was holding and ran to answer it. "Okay, I've got everything," Yehuda was breathing hard. "The bus leaves too late for me to make it back to Jerusalem on time, but I found someone in Or Tzion who will drive me. I should be there in about forty minutes."

"That's great that somebody's willing to take you in the dark." My anxiety about the time lessened after talking to Yehuda. But just as I returned to my packing, the phone rang again. It was the Nesher taxi driver informing me that he was on his way.

"You're first on the list of passengers I'll be picking up," he told me. "I'll be there in about fifteen minutes, so please be waiting outside with your luggage."

"Fifteen minutes? That's impossible." *He's early!* I clutched the phone receiver tightly and talked into it with urgency. "My husband is on his way and we're not ready," I explained, trying to formulate my Hebrew words clearly, under the pressured circumstances. "Could you please get the other people before you come to us?" I pleaded.

The driver wasn't happy. It was out of his way to pick up the other passengers first. But, reluctantly, he agreed to come for us last.

Working like a madwoman, I ran from room to room, collecting the rest of our belongings and throwing them into the suitcases. Suddenly, the loud, rising shrill of the siren screamed out its two-minute warning, blasting through the partially opened window and filling the apartment. I froze.

It can't be! I closed my eyes in disbelief. I had never been on my own before when the siren went off. *Not now! Yehuda's in the car! I'm alone! I need to finish packing!* Hurling Yehuda's running shoes and sweat pants into the nearest suitcase, I ran to the sealed room and slammed the door shut. A second later I ran back out for my gas mask, which was sitting by the front door, waiting with other bags to be brought out to the taxi.

Back in the room, I quickly taped up the door and

fumbled to open the brown cardboard box. A minute later I was sitting in my maternity jumper on the bed, breathing impatiently into my mask and listening for the all-clear signal. *What was going on with Yehuda?* I wondered. *Did he and his friend keep driving or did they stop and wait somewhere on the road with their masks on? Maybe they got out of the car and found some shelter somewhere. And what about the Nesher taxi guy? Was he still on his way or was he in one of the other passenger's sealed rooms?* I hoped he had stopped somewhere to take cover. That would be safer, and it would buy us more time.

What a nightmare! Stressed out and feeling helpless, I sat with my unanswered questions—and waited.

When the announcement came on the radio that the Jerusalem area was no longer in danger, I bolted out of the room. Throwing my mask into its box, I tossed it back over to the front door. Then, I began shoving the remaining clothes into the last suitcase.

A loud buzz came from the building's intercom. I shrieked. "No, wait!" I knew it was the taxi driver buzzing for me to come down. "Give me a few more minutes!"

When I pushed the button on the wall and spoke into the intercom, I tried to sound more relaxed. "You're here? And waiting for us downstairs? Okay, we'll be there in a couple of minutes," I told him, praying Yehuda would arrive at that exact moment. *Where is he?*

The driver told me that he was already late. "Sorry, geveret,[63] I can't wait any longer. I'm responsible for getting everyone to the airport on time."

I was about to cry when Yehuda burst through the door. "I'm here," he called out, panting. "What's happening?"

---

63 Ma'am.

"Oh, Thank G-d!" I ran over to give Yehuda a hug. Then returning to the luggage, I told him, "We have to hurry! Start bringing everything outside!"

"Here, take these!" Yehuda tossed me the outfits he'd just brought back from Or Tzion. "Hey, were you crying?" he asked, noticing a tear on my distraught face.

"I was thinking about it, but then you came. So, now I don't have to." I knew that sounded completely ridiculous. "I was so worried about everything."

Yehuda came over and wiped the escaped tear from my cheek with his finger. Loud honking from the taxi outside snapped us both back into action. "Are you finished with everything?" Yehuda asked, grabbing a suitcase and our carry-on bags and heading back out the door.

"Not exactly," I called after him. "But tell the driver we're ready."

I wanted to sit down and calm my nerves, now that Yehuda was here. But the seconds were flying. I ran around the apartment checking under the beds and dressers and in the bathrooms, making sure we weren't leaving anything behind.

"I can't get this suitcase closed," I said, as Yehuda rushed back into the apartment for a second load. The suitcase was bulging on all sides from my unconventional packing job.

"Sit on it," Yehuda ordered. With me weighing it down a bit, Yehuda managed to get the suitcase halfway closed before we heard another honk from outside.

"We have to go!" Yehuda stopped tugging at the zipper and helped me stand up.

"But," I protested as we locked the door and ran outside, "things are falling out!"

Two pairs of socks, one of Yehuda's undershirts, a light blue cable knit sweater and a black shoe were strewn along the sidewalk, making a trail from the building to the taxi.

Yehuda handed the suitcase to the driver and then ran back to help me gather up the items that had fallen.

The driver glanced at the half-opened suitcase and then at our frantic faces. "Rough day, huh?" he said.

"We're sorry," I apologized breathlessly, shoving one of the socks that had fallen out into my purse.

"It's okay. I understand." With swift motions, the hefty driver removed a few bags from the taxi's large trunk and heaved them up onto the luggage rack. "It isn't an easy time for any of us."

Feeling a bit calmer now that the driver was taking over, I smiled feebly and nodded in agreement. We were all in this together.

The driver took another moment to maneuver some of the luggage around so that our partially opened suitcase would fit inside the trunk. "If we put this one up on the rack, there'll be nothing left inside it by the time we get to the airport!" He flashed us a smile, exposing his tobacco-stained teeth. Then, gesturing for us to quickly find a seat inside the large vehicle, he added, "We're on our way!"

I sat in the far back, between Yehuda and a woman who was holding her purse on her lap with one hand and her gas mask box with the other. The woman smiled at me knowingly. The driver pressed on the gas. "Now everyone just relax and leave it to me to get you there," he said with confidence.

We drove off in silence. I felt a little nervous heading towards the airport, near Tel Aviv, at night. Even more so, I was unhappy about leaving the country at such a crucial time.

As we sped down the Jerusalem-Tel Aviv highway, Yehuda squeezed my hand. I understood his unspoken message: *Don't worry, we'll be fine. And we'll be back... soon enough.*

·❖· *CHAPTER 9* ·❖·

NANNA

(February 1991)

"OPERATION DESERT STORM—THE GULF WAR" came onto the television screen for about the hundredth time that day. The news flash with its dramatic musical accompaniment once again filled the family room in Yehuda's parents' condominium in New York. Yehuda and I were glued to the latest news reports.

Although the almost minute by minute CNN updates were keeping us informed about the war, it was still difficult to be so far away from Israel. Iraq was firing Scuds on a regular basis into both US-manned Saudi Arabia and Israel. Yehuda and I felt anxious each time we heard a siren wailing on the television. The news bulletins described what was happening at the scenes of the missile attacks, but we didn't know exactly who was getting hurt or how everyone back home was managing.

Now, the latest danger alarm, blaring from thousands of miles away, was warning that yet another Iraqi launched missile was heading towards Israel. Sitting tensely on the edge of my seat, I watched the people on the screen running for shelter.

"It's so frustrating seeing everything happen from far away," I said.

Unconsciously rubbing his hands back and forth on his pant legs, Yehuda leaned forward to get a closer look. "I feel disloyal for not being there with everyone."

Many of our family members felt differently about where we should be. They believed the best thing for us was to remain in the US, at least until the war was over. We appreciated their concerns and appeals not to return to Israel, but we couldn't be persuaded to stay longer than the two weeks we had originally planned.

After spending a week on the East Coast with Yehuda's family, we flew to Chicago to be with mine. That's when my eighty-six-year-old grandmother, Nanna, also tried to convince us not to leave. Still sharp-witted, Nanna was a short, gentle woman with ivory skin and thick round glasses. Though she'd strayed from traditional Judaism after moving from Lithuania to America in the early 1900s, Nanna was proud that I, her youngest grandchild, had returned to it.

Nanna was also delighted that I'd made a connection with her nephew, Gidon, and his family in Netanya and that I was living in Israel. Whenever she'd introduced me to her elderly friends and acquaintances, she would always say the same thing: "Meet my religious granddaughter Shelly who lives in Israel, near Jerusalem!"

But now, the Gulf War had Nanna worried. Two days before Yehuda and I would be leaving the US, she came to my parents' house to see us one last time. After we finished eating lunch together, Nanna handed me an envelope. Without a word, she waved me and Yehuda off to open it in private. Yehuda and I exchanged looks before going to the dining room.

Curious, I quickly broke the seal of the envelope. "There's a note," I announced, pulling out a neatly folded piece of flowered stationery, "and a check." I held up the check for Yehuda to see. It was written out in our names for the sum of $20,000.

A quiet whistle escaped Yehuda's lips when he caught sight of the amount. "What's the note say?" he asked.

Sitting down on one of the dining room chairs, I opened the piece of stationery and read out loud what my grandmother had written:

> To my precious grandchildren,
>
> I am worried about you. It would make me very happy if you would stay here. I have enclosed a check for you to use in order to rent an apartment in the area. I hope you will accept my offer and will remain in the United States.
>
> With much love,
Nanna

I looked at Yehuda. "In other words, the money is ours as long as we don't go back to Israel."

"Ever?"

"Who knows." I set the note and the check down on the dining room table. "I didn't expect this."

"Neither did I." Yehuda sat down next to me. "Nanna doesn't have this kind of money to give away, does she?"

"Not that I know of."

Picking the note up from the table, Yehuda read it for himself. "She's made the conditions pretty clear."

We stared at the check for a moment. I was the first to turn away. "Well?" I looked at Yehuda.

"Well," Yehuda said, shaking his head, "this isn't going to be easy."

"How are we going to tell her no?"

"We'll have to say it nicely."

"I feel so bad." I glanced at the check. "She'll be upset."

"And she probably won't be the only one," Yehuda

added. "I'm sure your parents are also hoping we'll take the money."

"Do they really think we won't go back?" I replaced the note and the check inside the envelope and let it drop back onto the table. "They don't understand us."

"We probably seem a little crazy to some of my family too," Yehuda replied with a half-hearted laugh. "C'mon, let's just get it over with." He picked up the envelope and held it out to me. "We'll just say thanks, but no thanks as politely as possible. Then our position will be clear, and that will be it."

"Okay, let's go." I took the envelope from Yehuda and started out of the dining room. Walking through the tidy, color-coordinated rooms of the house where I grew up, I wondered if the guilt would ever leave me. *As long as we live there, someone will always be upset that we don't live here.*

We paused just before the doorway to the family room. Nanna was in there. We could hear the *click, click, click* of her knitting needles. I peeked into the carpeted room with its Western desert-like décor. Nanna was sitting on the couch in her black wool slacks and a cherry red turtleneck sweater, staring out the window. Her hands moved automatically in the rhythm of her clacking needles as they wove in and out green-and-white-speckled strands of yarn.

"Ready?" I whispered to Yehuda.

Nodding, Yehuda gestured for me to proceed.

I hesitated, nervously tapping the envelope against the palm of my hand. Then, I stepped into the family room and sat down with Yehuda to face my grandmother. Nanna put her knitting down, folded her hands in her lap and looked at us.

"Thank you, Nanna, but I'm sorry," I said gently, "we can't stay."

Nanna's shoulders dropped. "I had hoped for a

different answer," she said quietly. "But," she sighed, "I understand."

I was relieved. "We understand you too, Nanna." I handed the envelope back to her. "We're leaving in a couple of days, but don't worry, you'll be seeing us again before you know it."

"Right," Yehuda agreed. "And we won't complain if the next time we come, you hand us another envelope with a big check inside," he joked.

I punched Yehuda playfully on the arm and then gave my grandmother a hug. "You know, Nanna, despite what it seems, we actually live in the safest place in the world."

Nanna pulled out a tissue from her sweater sleeve and wiped her damp eyes from under her bifocals. "I know," she said, now softly blowing her nose. "You have G-d with you." Smiling wanly, she went on. "And don't *you* worry," she told Yehuda. "This," she waved the envelope at him, "probably won't happen again so soon," she teased. "But I always do my best to help out my grandchildren."

"We know that, and we thank you," Yehuda returned the smile.

"You really love it there don't you?" Nanna asked.

"Yes, we do." I answered for both myself and Yehuda.

I knew my grandmother had visited the country a few times, many years before, when the State was still young. "You know, Nanna, things have changed a lot since you were in Israel."

"I'm sure they have. I've always wanted to go back there again for a visit."

"Why didn't you?" Yehuda asked.

"Oh, I don't know," Nanna tilted her head to one side. "I just didn't, for one reason or another. But now," she took my hand in hers, "you'll be going back for the both of us."

"Right." I nodded.

"And I'll be here," Nanna said, "praying every day that

you'll both be safe, please G-d." She picked up her knitting needles. "Now, you two go and enjoy yourselves." She waved us away with her hand, just as she had done earlier when she'd handed us the envelope. "I've also got things to get back to."

We went outside for a walk around the block, leaving Nanna to her knitting and her thoughts. As I buttoned my coat over my round belly, I noticed a Robin Redbreast take flight from the branch of a nearby tree. *Very soon we'll also be taking off*, I thought as I watched the bird wing its way towards a smaller, fuller tree down the block.

We'll be flying back to another world. Back to a war, and back to the life and place we love. I lifted my head up to the clear blue sky. *Back to Eretz Yisrael.*[64]

---

[64] The Land of Israel.

CHAPTER 10

"They actually went back to the war," Carol said, looking over at Fran.

"They went back home," Fran reminded her.

Carol turned back to me. "So what was it like when you got there? What was going on?"

I smiled as I remembered our return to Israel. "It was like getting back into an action-packed drama after a long commercial break."

ALARMING ARRIVAL
(February 1991)

"Excuse me, do you speak English?" a modestly dressed American woman in her twenties asked us at the baggage claim area in Ben Gurion Airport.

"Yes, I do," I answered, turning away from our luggage cart to face her.

"I came here from New York for a few months' visit," the young woman said proudly. "I was told I would receive an emergency kit with a gas mask as soon as I reached the airport. Do you know where I can get one?"

"We just picked ours up over there," I pointed to a nearby counter with an assortment of small cardboard boxes piled up. An airport attendant behind the counter was busy handing out some of the boxes to a family who'd also just arrived. "But," I continued, "I'm pretty sure those are just for returning Israelis who turned in their masks before leaving the country. I'm not sure where they're distributing visitors' masks." I wished I could be more helpful.

"Thanks. I'll go ask them over there," the woman replied, heading straight for the counter.

"Good luck," Yehuda said.

Yehuda and I watched as the attendant directed the American visitor to a different distribution desk a little further away.

"Wow!" I said. "I can't believe she came here now." I looked at Yehuda. "That's pretty incredible, don't you think?"

"We also came here now, didn't we?"

"That's different. We live here."

"She must have strong feelings about Israel," Yehuda said, "or she wouldn't be here."

The conversation ended when a sudden low-pitched moan grew into a louder wail that echoed throughout the airport. "Oh, here we go," I groaned. "And we just got here!"

Yehuda whisked his box off the cart and pulled out the gas mask. I was already shoving mine on my head like a pro. *It's like riding a bicycle.* "Some things come naturally after a while," I said, my voice muffled, "even if it has been two weeks since we've had the pleasure of strapping these monstrous things over our faces!"

Through my mask, I saw the woman from New York we had just spoken to a few minutes earlier rushing towards us with a brown box hanging from her shoulder. "Whoa! She's lucky," I said. "She got hers just in time."

"You need help with that?" Yehuda asked the woman as she approached.

"Yes!" she gasped, pulling the black strap off her

shoulder. "What do I do?" Her hands were shaking as she opened the box.

"You have to take out the filter plug before you put it on," I quickly instructed. After the mask was in place, I helped her adjust the straps so it was tight against her face. "It's supposed to be a close fit on all sides."

"Now put your hand over the filter and take deep breathes to check if it's working properly," Yehuda directed. "Like this." He demonstrated with his own mask. "You should feel your breath."

"Thanks," the anxious woman said, trying to slow down her breathing. "What a welcome I'm having!"

"This must not be easy for you," I sympathized.

"Well, I knew what I was getting into, but I didn't expect it to be the minute I stepped foot into the country!" She was acting brave, but I could tell her nerves were frazzled.

I was appreciating my own calmer, more experienced state when reality suddenly hit me. *We're not in Jerusalem.* "We're right near Tel Aviv!" I said to Yehuda when our visiting companion turned away for a moment. "We've never been in this area when a siren went off. If a Scud hits around here, we could be right in the middle of it all!"

"That's true."

I couldn't read the look on Yehuda's face through his mask, but he didn't sound too worried. "Look over there," he nodded towards a man getting his baggage off the conveyor belt. "That guy didn't even put on his mask. The security guard over there didn't either," he said, pointing ahead of us. "And check out the one over at Customs. He's working without one too."

I noticed that everyone around us was carrying on—business as usual. Most were wearing their gas masks, but some weren't. *We've been out of it. These people have been dealing with the war longer than we have. They've been under attack nearly every night and are probably more used to this by now*, I reasoned, *at least as much as one can be in such a situation.*

We said goodbye to the American woman, who thanked us through her mask before going off to grab her luggage from the revolving belt. As we went on our way, we passed the plain-clothed security guard. Yehuda asked him why he wasn't wearing a gas mask.

"It's not easy working with that uncomfortable thing on," he told us, his Hebrew clear without a mask. "Do you know how many times I've had to take that thing out and stick it over my face? So many Scuds have landed around here. I'm fed up with it." He waved his arms around as he spoke.

"But," he added more calmly, "thank G-d there have been lots of miracles. Many of the missiles missed their target and landed in unpopulated areas. And those that hit buildings unbelievably missed the people inside. So why get so worked up about these masks?" He winked at us. "We're all going to be fine."

"From your mouth to G-d's ears," I said.

"All the best," the security man replied.

We passed Customs and moved on towards the exit door. A small crowd of masked arrivals were there, waiting inside with their suitcases for the all-clear siren.

"I'm glad we're back," I said, as we stood alongside the others. "But this really *is* a hassle. My nose is itching and I still have my contact lenses on. They'll dry out if we have to wear these things for a long time."

"What? Can you speak a little more clearly? I can't understand what you're saying!" Yehuda kidded me.

"Just so you know, since you can't see my face—I'm *not* laughing," I answered, smiling secretly. "And," I pointed to my stomach, "neither is this baby, who's probably also not happy about getting rubbery oxygen at the moment."

"Okay, no more jokes until later," Yehuda promised. "Anyway, we'll probably be able to take these contraptions off soon. It's already been about fifteen minutes." Just as he finished speaking, the all-clear signal sounded.

"Ha!" I laughed, pulling off my mask and readjusting the beret on my head. "What are you, a prophet?"

"From your mouth to G-d's ears," Yehuda chuckled. "C'mon," he said, throwing our mask boxes back on top of our bags and maneuvering the cart out the door. "Let's get a Nesher taxi and go home."

·❖· *CHAPTER 11* ·❖·

DOUBLE CELEBRATION

(March 1991)

I was wearing a mask made of feathers over my eyes.
But I could see perfectly as I helped Yehuda pull the sheets
of plastic off the door and window of our caravan's sealed
room in Or Tzion. The Gulf War was over. Six weeks after
the January 15 deadline, the Coalition forces defeated
Saddam Hussein.

Israelis were in the middle of celebrating the festive
holiday of Purim when President Bush called for a ceasefire
and the liberation of Kuwait. Coincidentally, Saddam
Hussein and his malicious plan to wipe out the Jews in
Israel were thwarted the same day the evil Haman's plot
to destroy the Jews in Persia was miraculously foiled two
thousand years earlier. This year, Purim celebrations were
marked with an added enthusiasm and appreciation, as
children and adults traded their sealed rooms and gas
masks for festive costumes and Purim masks.

"There's no 'here today, gone tomorrow' for us," I said,
stuffing the plastic into the garbage pail. "We're here
today," I opened the window wide, letting in a gust of fresh
air, "and we'll also be here tomorrow."

"And the next day and the next," Yehuda said, pushing

back the floppy clown hat that had fallen over his forehead. "And not only that," he continued, rolling the last bit of tape between his fingers and flicking it into the garbage along with the plastic, "but tonight we'll actually get a good uninterrupted sleep."

"Thank G-d."

Thirty-nine Scud missiles had been shot into Israel during the war. Though, thankfully, none of them had actually carried a chemical warhead, all of them had caused physical, financial and psychological damage.

Two Israelis had been killed by missiles. Others had died of heart attacks or from asphyxiation due to the improper use of gas masks or heaters in their sealed rooms. More than two hundred people were injured, and about the same number suffered from unnecessary atropine injections because they'd panicked or misunderstood when to use the antidote. About one thousand five hundred families were forced to evacuate their homes. At least four thousand buildings, including residential dwellings, public and educational institutions, shops and businesses, were damaged or completely destroyed.

The amount of psychological harm could not be measured.

"We suffered a lot because of this war," Yehuda told me after we'd heard the good news that day. "But it could have been much worse, considering the advanced weapons Iraq was using."

"And the threat of toxic chemicals," I added, looking at Yehuda through my colorful feathers.

Most agreed that despite the trauma and destruction, Israel had endured the war remarkably well. Major casualties had been expected and the country had been stockpiled with medical supplies. Hospitals, special emergency facilities and medical crews had been prepared for the worst. Although Hussein's madness did inflict pain and cause tragedy, most Israelis walked away from devastated missile sites with light wounds or no wounds at all. Whole neighborhoods were all but destroyed, but to everyone's relief, the death toll remained low and the injuries reported were mostly minor.

"It's amazing that so many people made it out alive, while their homes crumbled or collapsed all around them." I slipped white feathered wings over my shoulders.

"Or caved in from under them," Yehuda added, referring to the multi-leveled apartment and office buildings that had been hit.

Countless times over the centuries, the Jews, and more recently the State of Israel, had been faced with threats of obliteration. Incredibly, the nation and the country were still going strong. Many realized that this war, in which Israel wasn't even allowed to fight back, was yet another opportunity for the people to see and understand that they were being protected. For Yehuda and me and many others like us, it was clear Who was running the show.

I glanced around the room. "I'm looking forward to getting all of these emergency supplies out of here."

Ignoring the boxes filled with stocks of bottled water and canned food, Yehuda went straight for the red plastic bucket in the corner. "This," he said, lifting it up high by its metal handle, "will be the first thing to go!"

"May we never need to use *that*, a sealed room or gas mask ever again," I said, sitting down to rest on a chair next to the opened window. The cool air from outside felt good. "Thank G-d the war is over," I went on. "Everything was beginning to get on my nerves. Any loud noise that rose in pitch made me jump, like when a motorcycle passed by. And all those nightmares I was having about being caught outside with no gas mask and no place to run to when a siren sounded."

"I didn't have any bad dreams," Yehuda said. "But I *was*

getting sick of those bulky boxes we had to carry around with us everywhere."

I looked pensively at the floor for a moment. "Think how hard all this must have been for the new *olim*[65] who came just before the war. Those poor Ethiopians, and all those Russians who came right in the middle of everything."

It was both exciting and overwhelming when the Soviet Union finally threw open its iron curtain and hundreds of thousands of Russians poured into the country. Even as the Scud missiles were traumatizing the nation, Israel transported home myriads of Soviet Jews.

"They waited so long to come here," I went on. "And what was the first thing they received when they arrived?"

"A gas mask."

I sighed. "At least now we can all breathe easier." I laughed at my pun.

"Yehuda and Shelly— are you guys coming over?" We could see our neighbor's frizzy purple-and orange-sprayed hair through the window. "Everyone's waiting for you, and my wife says the food's getting cold."

"We'll be there in a minute," Yehuda called out the window. Then, dropping the red bucket back into the corner, he turned to me. "Ready to go to the Purim *seudah*,[66] so we can eat, drink and be merry?"

"Yep." Standing up, I straightened my wings. "And this time, we're really going to do that." I followed Yehuda out of our now unsealed room. "For tomorrow, we *won't* die."

---

[65] Immigrants.
[66] Festive meal.

PART FOUR

June 1991—October 2003

·❧· CHAPTER 1 ·❧·

When Carol arrived the next morning, I was sitting in a low arm chair.

"Oh good," she said, smiling at me from the doorway. "I'm glad to see you out of that bed. We're going to try to actually use that leg today." She came over and helped me stand up.

"I'm not sure I'm ready for this," I admitted. "And what about my ribs?"

"Don't worry. We won't do anything drastic," Carol assured me. "And it will only be for a few minutes. You can sit for the rest of the time."

I leaned on Carol and tried to take a small step. "Fran was here already," I said. "She had to leave, but she said she'd be back in about ten minutes."

"That'll be just enough time for us to work on you in an upright position."

Fran came in just as Carol was easing me back into my chair. My first attempt at walking had been very brief, but I was relieved to be sitting down again.

"I was thinking," Fran said, bringing her own chair closer to mine. "We've got to speed things up if we're going to get to the end of your saga before you leave this place."

"Didn't you say the opposite last week, when you told me not to have Shelly rush through it?" Carol looked sideways at Fran.

"Right. But now I'm thinking we might not get to

hear everything at the slow pace we're going."

"I was planning to move things along anyway," I told my two companions. "Last night I thought about a bunch of different happenings to tell you about this morning. And I think that, from now on, I'll just do one or two stories from each year—just to give you a glimpse. You can use your imaginations to fill in the gaps."

"I think we can handle that." Carol placed a small therapy bench under my leg.

"So," Fran leaned back in her chair and crossed her arms, "you're a pregnant war survivor."

"Not anymore," I smiled.

"What, no longer a survivor?" Carol winked at me.

"No," I patted my stomach. "No longer pregnant..."

HADAS

(June 1991)

"She looks just like a little peach." Malka was staring affectionately at the angelic newborn sleeping in the hospital bassinet. "Her complexion is so clear and her cheeks are so pink." She gently pulled the little blanket up higher over the infant's delicate shoulders. "No wrinkly or peeling skin anywhere."

At four-thirty in the morning, after twenty-one hours of back labor, I gave birth to a beautiful baby girl who we'd decided would be named Hadas. "It was such a long labor," I told Malka in the hospital that afternoon. "Thank G-d Yehuda's sister is visiting for the summer and was around to massage my back during the hardest contractions."

"You did well," Malka said, her blue eyes shining at me. "And look what you got for all your hard work," she continued, gesturing towards the tiny figure curled up in the transparent bassinet next to my bed. "She's beautiful! And thank G-d, she's healthy."

"Thank G-d," I nodded.

"Malka, you're here!" Yehuda called out, breezing into the room, his shirt half out and the lace of his untied shoe dragging on the floor. After the birth, Yehuda had left the hospital for a few hours while I was napping. Returning by bus, he'd raced through the hot parking lot and down the long corridors to the room I was sharing with two other women.

"How do you like our baby?" he asked Malka, wiping droplets of perspiration from his forehead with a tissue. "She's our full-blooded Israeli Sabra."

"I love her," Malka replied. "*Mazel tov!*"[67]

Yehuda looked at me and a wide grin spread across his face. By his disheveled appearance, I figured he was feeling a little harried.

"I started calling people and telling them about the birth," Yehuda told me. "Everyone's excited for us. Your parents are waiting to speak to you when you get home. My coworkers want to buy us a big present. So we have to let them know what we need." Yehuda pulled over a chair from the other end of the room and sat down. "Oh, and Benny and Yaffa are really happy for us. They send you a big *mazel tov.*"

It was Yehuda's best friend, Benny, who drove me to the hospital from Or Tzion. Yehuda was in Jerusalem at work when my contractions grew stronger. He rushed over to the hospital and met Benny and me shortly after we arrived.

---

[67] Congratulations!

At the hospital's entrance, Benny let me out of the car and told me to go up to the delivery ward while he found a place to park. I went inside and obediently began walking up the stairs. Halfway up, I stopped and leaned against the wall to breathe through a contraction.

"What are you doing climbing the steps?" an Australian accented voice asked me from above, just as another wave of pain subsided. It was Benny. He was standing at the top of the staircase looking down at me in his starched blue shirt.

I looked up and saw his questioning face. "How'd you get up there?" My brain felt a little fuzzy.

"I took the elevator," Benny said matter-of-factly. "And *you're* taking the stairs!"

"I didn't think about an elevator." I felt a little foolish as I walked up the last few steps. "I saw the stairs, so I started going up."

Outside the delivery ward, Benny instructed me to sit down while he went to get a nurse. That's when Yehuda showed up.

Now, a day later, Yehuda was describing the different conversations he'd had while announcing our exciting news. "And the neighbors are making food for us for a couple of weeks so we won't have to cook for a while," he told me.

"Thank G-d for that," I said. "I'm so tired. I can't even begin to think of cooking when I get back home."

A faint whimper stopped our conversation. Yehuda, Malka and I turned to see Hadas' lips pucker and her smooth little face scrunch up like a raisin before relaxing and becoming peaceful again.

"It's so funny when she does that," I said.

Yehuda leaned over the bassinet. "I can't believe she's our baby!"

"Babies are such miracles," Malka said.

A nurse walked into the room and announced that visiting hours would be over in a few minutes. Malka hadn't been my only visitor that afternoon. Navah had also stopped by. Beth and Rachel said they'd be coming tomorrow, and some of my new Or Tzion friends left messages at the nurses' station congratulating me.

"I have to pick up the things we ordered from the baby store," Yehuda said, jumping up off his chair. He was feeling nervous about everything he needed to do before the baby and I came home. "It'll be a challenge taking the carriage, the baby bathtub and everything else by bus."

Malka noticed how overwhelmed Yehuda seemed. She knew the custom among many couples was to wait until the baby was actually born before bringing home all the baby equipment and paraphernalia. "I've got my car here," she told Yehuda. "I can take you to pick everything up, if you want." As generous as she was wise, Malka thrived on helping others and was hoping Yehuda would agree to let her help him now.

"That would be great!" Yehuda, clearly relieved, gladly accepted her offer.

Little Hadas woke up soon after Yehuda and Malka left for the store. "She has such a cute cry," the young Israeli woman in the bed next to me said from behind the turquoise divider curtain. I was pleasantly surprised when I'd discovered earlier that morning that I knew the new mother on the other side of the curtain. She and her husband lived a few blocks away from us in Or Tzion.

"*Todah*.[68] Your baby's a cutie too," I said, opening the curtain so we could talk face to face. I brought Hadas into bed with me, tucking her miniature body in the crook of my arm, as I shared pregnancy and first birth stories with

---

[68] Thank you.

my Or Tzion roommate.

When Hadas fell back to sleep a few minutes later, it was a good time for me to do the same. I kissed her soft cheek and gently placed her back in the bassinet next to my bed. Happy and exhausted, I laid my head back on the pillow and closed my eyes. I pictured Yehuda rushing from the hospital that morning to Or Tzion to shower and spread the news before hurrying back to Jerusalem for a couple of hours of work and another hospital visit. Now he was on a trip with Malka to the baby shop and then back home to set things up. *He must also be tired.*

As I sunk deeper into my pillow, the world seemed to slowly fade away. My own world lay between the enveloping turquoise curtain on my left and the wall on the other side of my bed. My arms and legs felt like heavy weights. All I wanted now was sleep.

Sleep, and my little Sabra.

CHAPTER 2

SNOWBOUND

(January 1992)

The snow fell in a fury. Within hours, Or Tzion and many other parts of the country were covered in white. One of the biggest snowstorms Israelis had ever encountered, it was both worrisome and exciting. Even *my* adrenalin was rushing as the big wet flakes quickly and continuously piled up.

"You're from Chicago," my friends reminded me. "This isn't a big deal for you, is it?"

"It's been a long time since I've seen this kind of storm," I explained. "And, I never expected something like this in Israel!"

As soon as the first layers began to stick, everyone in Or Tzion ran outside to enjoy the uncommon phenomenon that had caused schools and workplaces to close. Laughter and joyous shouting filled the snow-covered streets and sidewalks, as families shared in the fun of making snowmen, packing snowballs and sliding around on makeshift sleds.

While baby Hadas was inside napping, Yehuda and I bundled ourselves up and went outside to join the action. "I'm going to make a snow angel." I lay down on the thick white snowy "carpet" next to our caravan and started moving my arms up and down to create wing imprints.

"Do you think Israelis know about making snow angels?" Yehuda was now lying on his back next to me.

"If they don't," I looked sideways at him, "we'll teach them!"

Snowflakes steadily landed on our cheeks and eye-lashes, as Yehuda and I swished our arms and legs about on the cold white ground.

"You're looking pretty funny down there," a voice from above us laughed. "I think you've both regressed a little!"

"Benny!" Yehuda jumped up to greet his friend with a gloved slap on the back. "Isn't this great? Roads are closed, offices are closed, no traveling to Jerusalem for work. Just fun!"

I stood up to see how my angel had turned out. "Hey! Not bad for a rusty Chicagoan gone Israeli!"

"Now," Yehuda bent down to gather some snow, "it's time for a snowball fight."

Benny grinned slyly and then threw a wet, packed ball at his friend. "I thought you'd never say that!"

As Yehuda straightened up, the snowball smacked him on the arm. "You were hiding that, weren't you?" Yehuda wasted no time whipping his fist full of snow back at Benny.

"You guys are going to get it!" It was Benny's bubbly Australian wife, Yaffa, coming towards us with a huge snowball poised above her head. Benny and Yaffa, who'd made aliya from different parts of Australia, were married a couple of months ago. We were thrilled when they moved into the vacant caravan next door to us. Yaffa was a few years younger than me and about a head taller. Confident and good-humored, she was perfect for serious but easygoing Benny. I was glad to have her as a new friend and neighbor.

Now, eager to get in on the action, I scooped up chunks of snow as fast as I could. Yaffa and I shrieked as the four of us ran around hurling snowballs at each other.

The storm persisted throughout the day. Or Tzion began to look like a town in Alaska. Snow was covering the cars and hiding the houses' red rooftops. High drifts formed and tree branches and bushes were bending under the weight of the snowy layers.

I went inside early to check on Hadas and to warm up. Half an hour later, Yehuda finally said goodbye to Benny and Yaffa and came inside to change into dry clothes.

"Good thing I didn't even try to go to work," he told me. A small puddle was forming on the kitchen floor where he'd hung his coat over the back of a chair.

"Yep, good thing," I agreed. "I was just talking to Navah on the phone. She said nothing's moving in Jerusalem. Except for everyone playing in the snow, the whole city has stopped."

Just as I finished speaking, the lights went off in the caravan. "Ohhh," I groaned. "I hope this isn't a serious blackout."

Yehuda checked the fuse box. "Everything seems to be fine here," he announced. Then determining that none of the electrical appliances were working either, he began dialing friends in other neighborhoods to see whether they had power. "It looks like the whole *yishuv*[69] is without electricity," he reported his findings to me. "The lines must have fallen from all the snow."

"If it isn't the Arab electric company turning off our electricity whenever they feel like it," I said, pulling a gas heater out of its storage box, "then it's the weather bringing on these power failures."

---

[69] Settlement town.

"At least when the Arabs shut us down, they eventually turn everything back on," Yehuda said. He looked out the window at the white blizzard coming down hard. "Who knows how long it will take to get someone out here now to repair those broken lines."

"It's going to be candles and flashlights tonight," I said matter-of-factly.

Benny came back over. "Our place is freezing. Oh great, you have a gas heater."

"Stay with us," I said. "I'll make some hot tea."

"We bought that gas heater last year because of the electricity problems we're always having," Yehuda told Benny.

"We should probably buy one too." Benny placed his wet coat over the chair next to Yehuda's coat and then called Yaffa to tell her to come over. "It's time they switched all us *yishuvim*[70] over to the Israel Electric company." Hanging up the phone, he returned to the warm heater. "We shouldn't be treated like second-class citizens because we live in a settlement town."

"Oh no! Guess what, guys." I was standing at the kitchen sink, turning the water tap on and off. No water was coming out of it.

"The pipes must have frozen," Yehuda said.

A knock at the door diverted our attention away from the faucet. "*Ken*,"[71] Yehuda called out for whoever was there to come in.

"Anybody home?" Yaffa joked as she walked inside all bundled up. "Wow, it's great you have heat here!" She quickly pulled off her wet hat and gloves.

"We have heat, but no running water." I told her.

---

[70] Settlement towns.
[71] Come in; lit., "yes."

"Wonderful. That's gone too?" Yaffa grimaced and then went to warm up by the gas heater I had strategically placed between the open kitchen and living room areas.

"Looks like we're in for an adventure!" Benny said, grinning.

"Well, we might as well make the best of it," I said. How 'bout a game of Monopoly?"

I took Hadas out of her crib, changed her diaper and got out the Monopoly game. Benny and Yehuda went back outside to collect clean snow to melt for hot drinks. Yaffa began setting up the game on a low table near the heater.

"What's this?" I asked Yehuda a few minutes later, as I peered into the pot on the gas stovetop. "How could it be that those huge bowls of snow you and Benny brought in melted down to so little water? It looks like only enough for three cups of tea!"

"We're getting a lesson in science," Benny said lining up his Monopoly money in a neat row alongside the edge of the game board.

"Actually, it's more like new math." Yaffa was organizing the property cards. "Two big bowls of snow equals three small cups of water—or in our case, three cups of tea."

"I wonder how much snow we'd need to wash dishes," I said, placing bowls of pretzels and potato chips on the corners of the table.

"Forget about the dishes. Think how much we'd need to take a shower!" Yehuda grabbed the two now-empty bowls and headed back outside for more snow.

The game went on into the evening hours. Yehuda lit some candles while I made sandwiches for a light supper. "Tomorrow we'll have to go shopping and pick up some bottled water and something to eat that doesn't need to be washed or cooked," I said, "unless we have water and electricity by then."

"Don't count on it," Benny said. "We could be in this situation for a while."

Eventually, the snow stopped falling. But by mid-morning the next day there was still no relief from the cold, the electric outage or the frozen water pipes. Benny and Yaffa offered to babysit for little Hadas while Yehuda and I trekked the few blocks over to the grocery store.

The streets, sidewalks and backyards were buried in white. Even the many steps leading up to the Shaarei Avot Synagogue had disappeared under a thick blanket of snow.

"Wow!" I said. "We should have brought the camera to take pictures."

Snowmen with hats, scarves and vegetable faces appeared to be guarding every second or third house. Shouts coming from rowdy boys in the midst of a snowball fight up ahead resonated through the now relatively quiet streets.

I sunk thigh-deep into the snow with each step I took. "This is unbelievable!" I exclaimed as I trudged onward. It was an effort for me to lift my legs up high and try to match the indentations of Yehuda's wider steps ahead of me. "There's got to be about two feet of snow!"

"If you weren't so short, you'd be able to manage better," Yehuda said, waiting for me to catch up. "Maybe if you had eaten your Wheaties when you were younger, you wouldn't be in this situation now!"

"Ha!" I held my hand out for Yehuda to take. "How 'bout if you just help me get there!"

The grocery store was buzzing with friends and neighbors conversing in Hebrew, English, French and Russian. "How long do you think we'll be without water and electricity?" A short bearded man in rubber boots asked a taller, clean-shaven shopper in the canned goods aisle.

"I don't know," the taller man answered, "but I love all

this snow. With the roads buried, I get a vacation from work!" he laughed.

Near the dairy refrigerator I overheard two mothers talking. "Everyone was really excited about playing in the snow yesterday," one mother told the other. "But today it's so deep my little ones are staying inside."

"Having everyone home for a day or two is fun," the second mother replied. "I wouldn't complain, though, if everything would melt fast so the kids can all go back to school and I can have a little more quiet time!" she admitted.

"Our house is so cold, we're all wearing coats and hats indoors," a young woman picking out cucumbers with her purple gloves on commented to the older woman next to her who was filling a bag with tomatoes.

"My *abba*[72] couldn't get home from Jerusalem last night because of the icy roads," the teenage girl behind us in the checkout line was telling her friend. "He had to walk to my aunt's house and now he's stuck in the city."

At the cashier, Yehuda and I met up with Rafi, the "dark and handsome" Israeli bachelor who lived on our block. Rafi was friendly with all the young couples and families in our small neighborhood of caravans, never missing an invitation for a Shabbat meal or a chance to drop in and visit during the week. Now he was standing before us in line, placing his purchases on the counter. "I saw they were starting to plow the streets," He told us in his deep baritone voice.

"Great!" Yehuda said. "That will make it less problematic for Shelly to walk around outside. I had to keep her from getting lost in the snow banks out there!" he teased.

---

[72] Father or dad.

Rafi laughed. Then, taking his bag of groceries, he waved goodbye to us and left the store to brave the weather.

We paid the cashier and started back to our caravan where Yaffa, Hadas and her toys were keeping warm, thanks to the gas heater. "We made it!" I exclaimed, stomping my feet at the door to shake the snow off my boots. "It took us a little while to get there and back. But we did it!"

"Benny just went out for a few minutes to see what the group of people gathered at the corner were talking about," Yaffa told us after Yehuda and I were both inside. "Apparently, there's a rumor going around that someone was found unconscious in the snow. But nobody knows what happened."

Or Tzion was a close-knit community, and I felt unsettled not knowing who the person was or in what condition he might be. "I wonder who it is." I put the water bottles on the kitchen counter. "I hope it wasn't some little kid who wandered outside."

"No, supposedly it's a man," Yaffa said.

We heard a knock and then Benny appeared at the door. "I couldn't find out much," he told us. "Apparently he was just found a few minutes ago and nobody has any real information yet."

Yehuda put the grocery bags down and pulled off his wet boots. "When Benny and I go out later to *daven Minchah,*[73] we'll try to find out more. Maybe someone at the synagogue will have some details about what happened.

---

[73] Recite the afternoon prayers.

"So what's the story?" I asked Yehuda and Benny when they came back from the afternoon prayer services.

"It's pretty bad." Yehuda's shoulders were slumped and his eyes lacked their usual spirit.

"What happened?" I pulled over a chair and sat down in front of Yehuda and Benny, who were sitting on the couch, still wearing their coats and hats.

"He had a heart attack." Yehuda said quietly.

"Who did?"

Benny answered this time. "Rafi."

"Rafi?"

Yehuda nodded. "Nobody's sure exactly what happened, but it looks like he was running or jumping through the high snow drifts with his heavy grocery bags and the stress was too much for his heart."

"But we just saw Rafi in the grocery store a few minutes before then," I looked from Yehuda to Benny. "We were talking to him about the snow while we were waiting in line to pay."

"It happened while he was on his way home," Yehuda said, "right after we saw him."

"Is he going to be all right?" I asked.

Yehuda shook his head slowly from side to side.

Benny looked at the floor. "The funeral's tomorrow."

"What? I don't believe it," I whispered. "He was too young to have a heart attack." I could still see his smile as he said goodbye to us before he left the store. "He didn't seem to be in such a hurry when we were talking to him."

"We'll never know," Yehuda shook his head again.

Benny got up to go tell Yaffa, who had gone back to their caravan to make supper. I sat down next to Yehuda on the couch. We were both quiet. "I'm sorry," I said in a low voice, taking Yehuda's hand in mine.

Yehuda sighed, "I am too."

The next day I stayed home with Hadas while Yehuda and the other mourners slowly made their way along the snowy streets and sidewalks to Or Tzion's cemetery. In our caravan, I stood staring out of the frosty living room window. *Just a few days ago the snow had seemed so beautiful and pure. So thrilling. So perfect.*

I turned to Hadas, who was bouncing next to me in her springy chair, her cheeks as rosy as her pink outfit. "Nothing's perfect in this world," I informed her.

After nearly three days without power and running water, the sun finally began to thaw the packed snow and ice. Water flowed from the taps again and repairmen came to fix the electricity. Unfortunately, nobody could fix what had happened to Rafi.

By the end of the week the last remnants of the storm had melted. But, for many of us, the fun, the adventure and the unfortunate tragedy would take much longer to fade away.

·✦· CHAPTER 3 ·✦·

"We can't know what's going to happen from one day or one minute to the next, can we?" Carol said.

"That's for sure," I agreed. "Especially in Israel, where things are dynamic and always changing."

"It seems the one thing that never changes there," Fran noted, "is the need for peace."

"Yeah, that's true." I nodded. "But for that, you have to have real peace partners."

PEACE FOR SURE
(September 1993)

Oh, we're definitely going to have peace now. I turned away from the newspaper stand on Jaffa Street. The headlines said that Israel had officially signed the Oslo Peace Accords with the PLO.[74] *But really*, I muttered under my breath as I began pushing Hadas in her stroller up the street, *it looks like we're going to have worse troubles.*

The Oslo Accords called for Israel to give up its sovereignty over certain Arab populated areas in Judea and Samaria, as well as a portion of the Gaza strip in the southern part of the country. The Jewish state would also

---

[74] The Palestine Liberation Organization terrorist group.

eventually be responsible for providing weapons to the new Arab police forces in those areas. In return, terrorist leader and PLO chairman Yasser Arafat was to officially recognize Israel's right to exist as a Jewish state. He was to stop incitement of terror and remove the clause in the PLO charter that called for the annihilation of Israel. Also, promising to end the violent intifada, Arafat was, in short, to abandon his hostile ways.

Do they actually think he'll do all of that?

I couldn't understand how so many people had allowed themselves to be so easily fooled by Arafat's alleged sudden change of heart. I was amazed how quickly and successfully he'd manipulated the world into believing that he was now a reformed "good guy," ready and waiting to make peace.

Many of us right-wing Zionists were furious with the government for promoting Arafat's charade with the Oslo Accords. We had a strong nationalistic ideology and considered Israel to be much more than just a safe haven for Jews. We believed that it was the natural, historical and inevitable destiny for the nation of Israel to live in the Land of Israel. And that meant not just settling the land, but also protecting it from anyone who wanted to take away or destroy any part of it, including Yasser Arafat.

Many left-wing Israelis were, however, thrilled with the signing of the Oslo Accords. They felt that, despite the Arab leaders' resolve to destroy Israel and push all the Jews into the sea, harmonious Jewish-Arab coexistence was attainable. They believed it was necessary at times to make "painful sacrifices," like setting terrorist prisoners free or giving up some of the land, in order to move towards that goal. They had high hopes that the Oslo Accords would succeed and would mark the beginning of a new era of peace in the Middle East.

I turned right onto King George Street. Pushing

two-year-old Hadas' stroller and pregnant with my second child, I felt heavy. But really, at the moment, it was my heart that was the most heavy. *We're being pressured to make major concessions, but without any guarantee of peace in return.* I remembered how difficult it had been for many of us when it was revealed that some of Israel's leaders had been holding secret meetings with Yasser Arafat in Oslo, Norway. Israel had never negotiated with terrorists before. "Why start now?" we'd asked.

"It's always good to talk," my mother had told me on the phone at the time.

"Mom, Yasser Arafat's been our enemy for decades! He's responsible for the murder of thousands of Jews all over the world. He's organized tons of terrorist attacks in Israel. And now we're supposed to believe that he suddenly accepts us and wants to live with us in peace and harmony?"

"Well, it hasn't worked any other way. And I don't think Israel should give up the chance to try to work out its problems through negotiations."

I felt like yelling into the phone. "We're talking about the PLO here!" I forced myself to remain calm. "Arafat was also the mastermind behind the intifada uprising. And he didn't only murder and injure Jews all these years. He had hundreds of Arabs tortured and executed too."

"Maybe things will be different now," my mother had offered.

"I don't think we can expect that," I stood my ground. "He's evil to the core."

But enough people believed, or wanted to believe, that Yasser Arafat had really turned over a new leaf. So the Oslo Accords were signed. Israel's Prime Minister Yitzhak Rabin and Foreign Minister Shimon Peres shook hands with Arafat and suddenly he was no longer a poverty-stricken refugee terrorist in Tunisia. Now, in the eyes of the world, he was a transformed, legitimate negotiating partner. And soon, he'd be using his money and power to control certain areas of Israel.

I stopped to rest on the low stone ledge near the Mashbir department store. "Yep," I told Hadas, who had fallen asleep in her stroller, "now, for sure, we'll have peace."

·❖· *CHAPTER 4* ·❖·

NO TURNING BACK
(July 1994)

The crowd was squeezing through the Flower Gate, one of the seven arched entrances into Jerusalem's Old City. Yehuda, Hadas and I were inching forward with the large procession that was heading inside the gate and on to the Western Wall. Baby Yael, born nine months earlier, sat wide awake as I pushed her along in her stroller.

The protest march we'd joined had started out as a massive rally in the city's center against both Yasser Arafat and the recently signed Oslo Accords. The Oslo Accords had allowed Arafat to reenter Israel after 27 years of exile. As the head of the newly created Palestinian Authority legislative body, Arafat gave a speech before hordes of his followers in the southern Arab town of Gaza City. In that speech, he declared that it wasn't enough to have control over the areas the Israelis had surrendered to Arab autonomy. He had a greater goal. He would also take over Jerusalem and make it the future capital of a Palestinian state.

In response to Arafat's return visit to Israel and to his speech in Gaza, Jews gathered in a giant demonstration at Jerusalem's Zion Square. The predominantly right-wing

Zionist crowd publicly blasted the terrorist, the Oslo Agreement and Prime Minister Yitzhak Rabin, who they believed had made a pact with the enemy.

"What Arafat really wants," opposing Likud party leader Binyamin Netanyahu's voice echoed from the loudspeakers, "is not an Arab state beside Israel, but an Arab state *in place* of Israel." In his speech, Netanyahu went on to say that the prime minister "should proclaim absolutely that Arafat will never enter Jerusalem!"

Israeli flags, signs denouncing the Oslo Accords and anti-Arafat banners accompanied the protesters, as they now marched down the streets of Jerusalem and through the Old City's Flower Gate entrance. I gripped the handles of Yael's stroller tightly and Yehuda hoisted Hadas up onto his broad shoulders as we passed through the gate and continued down the crammed walkway.

The Flower Gate, which leads directly into the Muslim Quarter of the Old City, was one area neither we, nor most of the people with us had ever been to before. Usually, only Arabs entered through it. But this time was different. Those leading the way that evening decided there was no reason why Jews couldn't, or shouldn't, go to the Wall via the Flower Gate, or any other Old City entrance. Everyone following along agreed. "The Arabs go wherever they want, and without fear. Why shouldn't we be able to do the same?"—we had all asked that question many times.

As we inched our way down the passageway that would eventually bring us to the Western Wall in the Jewish Quarter, I noticed the Arab onlookers staring at us.

"They're not used to seeing Jews here," I said to Yehuda. "Especially not so many of us."

The Arab women and children who were intently watching us from the sides didn't worry me. But I wondered how the Arab men would react to our strong presence.

My concerns were replaced with wonder when, for no apparent reason, our march came to an abrupt halt up ahead. People were still coming from behind and I started to feel crushed by the crunch of bodies all around us.

"What's happening?" I asked Yehuda.

"I'm not sure." Holding onto Hadas' dangling legs, Yehuda stood on his toes and strained to see what was going on up ahead. "Looks like they're telling everyone to turn around."

"Turn around?" I cried out in disbelief. "How do they expect us to do *that*?"

"Horsies!" Hadas, who'd recently celebrated her third birthday, called out what she was seeing from her high perch. "Pleesman!"

"They're not letting us go any further," Yehuda explained. "Maybe they're afraid of the security situation."

I wondered whose security they were worried about, the Jews' or the Arabs'. After years of terror, the intifada had at last come to an end. But tensions remained. *Did they send out mounted policemen because they thought the Arabs were going to suddenly start attacking us Jews, or did they think it might be the other way around?*

I felt it was absurd that we were being forced to leave just because we were Jewish. We were in our own country. The police should be there to protect us, not to throw us out. What kind of a message was this for all of our children—that we have to learn to stay on our own turf, like "good little Jews"? And what kind of message was this for all the Arabs who were observing the Jews being thrown out of *their* Quarter, *their* road, *their* gate?

It took a while, but eventually we all managed to turn ourselves, our strollers, our children, our flags and our signs around. Slowly and somberly, we walked back towards the Flower Gate. Once outside and again on the street, Yehuda set Hadas down and stretched his arms and back muscles.

"Why didn't we go to the Kotel?" Hadas, standing on the sidewalk in her little flowered sundress, was looking at us with her head and curly pigtails tilted to one side.

I glanced at Yehuda and then turned to my bright-eyed daughter. "We're going. We're going there now," I answered with determination.

Most of the crowd had the same resolve and began to make their way up the street towards the Jaffa Gate, where people of all backgrounds and religions always came and went freely. Passing along the Old City's outer walls on our way to the Jaffa Gate, we came first to the Damascus Gate. Although some Jews would go through the Damascus Gate, it too led directly into a section of the Muslim Quarter and was used mostly by Arabs.

"Look!" Hadas pointed towards clusters of people who were deviating from the route to the Jaffa Gate and heading instead down the path to the Damascus Gate. A group of soldiers were standing guard inside the arched stone entranceway, which was just below street level. We stopped to watch as the area below us began filling up with many more demonstrators now rushing towards the open gate.

"Whoa, look at them go!" Yehuda said, sitting Hadas down on the low wall in front of us. "They're angry about what happened at the Flower Gate."

"I'm upset too." I took Yael out of the stroller and held her in my arms while we observed the scene before us. "Why shouldn't we be allowed to go through Flower Gate, Damascus Gate, or any other gate?"

Just as the crowd reached the Damascus Gate entrance, its two massive iron doors began closing from the inside. "They probably called for reinforcements to help keep people out and to turn everyone away again," Yehuda said.

"But so many people are going there now, it doesn't look like it's going to be so easy to do that."

Within minutes, the Damascus Gate was swarming with people impatient to pass through its now narrower opening. As the enormous doors were slowly closing, the mob tried to keep them open so everyone could pass through. With strong forces on both sides, the situation became a stalemate. The doors stood halfway opened for a few minutes and then once again began shutting the people out.

"This is really something else!" I exclaimed.

I wanted the protesters to shove open the gigantic doors. I hoped they would break through the barrier of soldiers, or whoever was on the other side, so they could continue on to the Wall. But I also felt sorry for the soldiers who were compelled to obey orders. I knew they had no choice but to make sure that the Jewish marchers didn't pass through that gate.

For about twenty minutes, we watched as the area in front of the Damascus Gate became more packed, and the struggle at the entranceway continued. The thick iron doors remained more closed than open. There was no sign of them opening further or shutting altogether. With no progress in either direction, the people grew restless and agitated. Yehuda and I were also feeling anxious as we listened to the commotion below and wondered what would be.

"Are they going inside?" Our precocious Hadas was as curious as we were.

"Well," I began, but before I could say more, the doors suddenly started moving again.

Cheers and shouts burst forth as gradually, little by little, the passageway opened wider. Then, like a dam that suddenly broke, the sea of people began pouring through the Damascus Gate.

"Yes!" Yehuda and I slapped each other high-fives in the air.

We didn't know whether the soldiers on the other side had been given the okay after all to let everyone through, or whether the physical strength and passionate will of the people had actually triumphed. Either way, I felt it was a successful ending. I hugged Yael and then bent down to Hadas to finish answering her question.

"Yes, cutie," I said with a big smile, "they are all going to go inside."

·❧· CHAPTER 5 ·❧·

Fran's cell phone was ringing. "Hold on one second," she said, flipping up the little black cover to check which number was appearing on the miniature screen. "It's okay. I can call her back later," she said, snapping the phone shut.

"Are you sure?" I asked. "We can wait."

"Positive. It was my sister. She knows I'm usually in the middle of our story sessions at this time of day. If it's anything important, she'll send me a message."

"Oh yeah, I forgot that you tell your sister these stories," I said.

"Only the ones that pop into my head when we meet for lunch, or if I happen to talk with her on the phone right after I leave here," Fran explained.

"Is she also starting to get a better picture of Israel?" Carol asked Fran.

"Well, she agrees with me that our parents made a mistake by skipping over Israel years ago during their business trips to the Middle East. And I think she was a little bit jealous when I told her the other day that I'm considering going to visit there myself sometime."

Carol's voice had a little ring of excitement to it as she leaned over me and pointed her finger at Fran. "You're not the only one who's considering doing that these days! Remember I told you and Shelly that my mother chose to live in the States and wanted to hide her Jewishness for a while after the Holocaust? Well, now she's glad that my husband's Jewish and that our children have some kind of connection to Judaism. And I think she'd actually be happy if I spent some time in Israel and maybe even checked out my Jewish roots a bit."

Fran's narrow brown eyes met Carol's light, round eyes. "Is that what you want to do?"

"Maybe." Carol stole a sideways glance at me and then returned to her working position. "I'd probably have to wait until my twin sons grow out of their "terrible teens" first, so my husband and I could get away for a while without worrying about them. But, in the meantime, I'd love to take a trip to Israel for a vacation."

"Well," Fran let out a loud, melodramatic sigh, "for now we'll just have to settle for virtual visits to Israel through Shelly." She turned to me. "Where will you be taking us to next?"

I leaned my head back on the armchair to think for a moment. A silly smile came over my face as I remembered another experience worth telling. "How 'bout Kibbutz Yavneh?"

"Kibbutz Yavneh okay with you?" Fran asked Carol jokingly, as if they both knew something about the place.

Carol shrugged. "Sure. A kibbutz[75] is probably as good a place as any for a unique or interesting Israel story." She nodded her head towards me. "Right?"

"Yep," I let out a little laugh. "And I think you'll find this next story somewhat interesting and *very* unique."

---

[75] A cooperative agricultural or industrial community.

DEFINITELY MORE ISRAELI
(September 1994)

"Are we really going to do this?" Yehuda asked me, as we walked up the pathway leading to the little stucco house. "This could be embarrassing."

"Well, are we becoming more Israeli or not?" I replied. "Besides, this is a kibbutz. It's like Or Tzion. Everyone's open and friendly to everyone else here, even more than in the city."

"Okay. But this isn't an everyday request," Yehuda said.

I knew Yehuda was right. Even though we were in Israel and the wedding we were invited to was on a laid-back kibbutz, knocking on a stranger's door and asking to borrow a slip might just be a bit too much.

"Well, what am I supposed to do?" I asked. "We were rushing to leave the house and I didn't notice until we got here that I forgot to put on a slip. I can't walk around in this pale pink dress without one."

"I'm still not sure this is a good idea," Yehuda said. "Maybe if we knew somebody who lived here besides the bride, it would be easier."

"But we don't."

"Right."

"So, what choice do we have?"

Yehuda threw out a suggestion. "When we get to the wedding hall, you could ask your friends if one of them happened to bring an extra slip, maybe stuffed in her purse or something. Women do things like that, don't they?"

I stopped walking, crossed my arms in front of me and looked hard at Yehuda.

"Fine," Yehuda said. "Let's knock. But *you're* doing the talking."

"Fine," I said. "Even though your Hebrew is better than mine, I'll be the one to speak. But *you* knock." I needed the extra couple of seconds to figure out the best way to approach the subject with whoever answered.

The smell of cows was in the air as Yehuda, in his dark dress pants and crisp white shirt, stepped up to the door and rapped lightly. "I can't believe we're doing this," he whispered from the side of his mouth.

My heart was pounding. *It's not such a big deal,* I told myself.

After the second knock, a pleasant-looking woman, presumably in her forties, opened the door. She was wearing a peach dress, flat white sandals and a fancy peach and white hat. "*Shalom,*" she greeted us.

"*Shalom,*" Yehuda said, quickly moving to the side and indicating to me that his part of the plan was over.

"*Shalom.*" I stepped closer to explain my predicament to the woman at the door. "I'm Shelly and this is my husband Yehuda." I smiled awkwardly, fidgeting with the delicate gold chain around my neck. "We're here for a friend's wedding and we were in such a rush to be on time that I forgot to put on a slip," I said in one breath. "So... I was wondering if, by any chance, you might have one I could borrow? Or, maybe you might know of somebody who wouldn't mind lending me one—only until after the wedding, of course."

"Come in," the woman said, motioning with her hands. "I'm in a hurry because the bride, your friend who's getting married, happens to be my niece. I just came back home for a minute to get something I forgot."

"Oh, I'm sorry to take up your time," I said. "We could try somewhere else."

"No, that's all right," the bride's aunt replied. "Let me just see quickly what I might have for you to wear." She eyed me. "You're definitely a size small," she said before disappearing into one of the back rooms of the house.

Yehuda and I sat down in the quaint living room and waited. "I feel a little foolish," I admitted to him.

"Not me," Yehuda said. "I don't feel a little foolish. I feel a lot foolish!"

"Well, I'm *really* relieved this is working out so well."

The aunt returned with an eggshell-white, full nylon slip that looked almost exactly like the one that was sitting in my dresser drawer at home.

"I have one just like that!" I exclaimed as I jumped up off the couch. "I'm sure it will be fine." *I am so glad we knocked on this woman's door!*

"It's at least one size bigger than what you need, but if we pin it up, it will probably do the job," the aunt replied. "You go into the bedroom and put it on while I look for some safety pins."

I smiled excitedly at Yehuda and hurried out of the living room.

"Let's see what we can do here." The nice woman began pulling up, folding over and pinning the shoulder of the slip.

"Shouldn't you be going now?" I asked. "I don't want you to be late for the *chuppah*[76] on account of me."

"Don't worry, sweetie. I'm just going to do this side and you can do the other one on your own." In a few seconds the woman in peach had finished her part and was on her way.

"Enjoy the wedding," she told us as she walked out of the house. Then she popped her head back inside, "*B'vakashah*, please just make sure you close the door when you leave."

I finished the job and then checked my dress in the mirror.

---

[76] Ceremony under the wedding canopy.

"Perfect!" I was all smiles. I couldn't believe how lucky I was that my crisis had been so easily resolved.

"We'll probably even be in time for the *chuppah!*" I told Yehuda, shutting the front door behind us.

Halfway through the wedding, I spotted the bride's aunt standing near one of the tables. "I just wanted to tell you how much I appreciate your help," I said. "And I'm sorry I won't be able to wash your slip before returning it to you tonight."

"Not to worry," the aunt assured me. "I'm glad I could help. The door's not locked, so you can just leave it on the couch before you go back home."

"*Todah rabbah,*" I thanked her.

"No problem. And you know that if you ever need to borrow a slip again, you can always just knock on my door!"

We both laughed.

"I don't care what anyone says," I told Yehuda after I returned to our table. "I'm definitely more Israeli these days."

"What about me?" Yehuda straightened his shoulders and grinned proudly. "I did the knocking."

"Okay," I agreed. "We both are."

·ᑀᕽᑀ· *CHAPTER* 6 ·ᑀᕽᑀ·

LEAVING ON A JET PLANE?

(June 1995)

My friend Michelle had spent the past two months preparing for her big move from Jerusalem back to her hometown in Canada. She'd soon be starting a new life in Ontario with her fiancé, who she'd met while visiting her family there last winter.

I was happy about Michelle's engagement, but sad about her leaving Israel. It was bad enough that a couple of years ago my good friend Liz unexpectedly had to return to her hometown in the US with her husband and baby for an indefinite period of time. Now Michelle would also be gone, and who knew when she'd be back?

For Michelle, tying up loose ends at her job was the easy part. Sorting out what to store in Israel, give away to friends or bring with her to Canada was harder. And visiting all her favorite people and places one last time was the most difficult.

"It was pretty painful for Michelle to say goodbye to everyone she'd become close to these past thirteen years," I told Yehuda on the way to picking Michelle up from her apartment. We had offered to drive her to the airport for her six o'clock flight that evening.

"I'm not happy about her leaving either," Yehuda admitted. "She's been kind of like a sister."

It was almost three o'clock in the afternoon when we arrived at Michelle's building with four-year-old Hadas and Yael, nearly two, strapped into their car seats. I waited with the girls in the car while Yehuda ran up the three flights of stairs to collect Michelle and her luggage. He returned a few minutes later, alone and empty-handed.

"Where's Michelle?" I was surprised not to see her or any of her suitcases.

Yehuda just shrugged his shoulders and looked confused.

"What's going on? We have to get moving or she'll be late."

"She's not exactly ready," Yehuda finally said. "I think maybe you should go up and check things out."

In my eighth month of pregnancy, wearing an oversized maternity top and a stretchy-waistband skirt, I slowly began the climb to Michelle's apartment. When I got there, the door was slightly ajar. I knocked lightly and stuck my head inside.

"Michelle?"

"In here," came a faint reply from one of the back rooms.

Passing through the living room towards the bedrooms, I immediately understood why Yehuda seemed so bewildered. Boxes, bags and suitcases of different shapes and sizes were everywhere. Some were taped shut. Others were half-filled or still empty. Clothes, books, knickknacks and many of Michelle's other possessions were lying about waiting to be packed, discarded or put into the "give away" pile.

I found Michelle sitting on her bedroom floor surrounded by her belongings, attempting to sort through them. A swift assessment of the rest of the place threw me into a sudden state of alarm.

I wanted to shout, "What's going on? We have to leave now! You'll miss your plane!" But I managed to just say "hi" as calmly as possible.

"Hi." Michelle briefly looked at me before continuing with her work on the floor. Her voice was tense and she moved stiffly as she tried to quickly go through her things in some kind of organized fashion.

I sensed my friend was struggling to suppress her own feelings of hysteria. Her usual fun-loving big smile was nowhere to be found. And her long lashes couldn't cover up the anxiety I'd just seen in her eyes when she looked up at me. "Can I help?" I asked in the friendliest voice I could muster.

"No, yes, I don't know," Michelle replied without pausing or looking up. "I don't know what you could really do. I'm the only one who can figure out what needs to go where."

I watched for a few seconds as Michelle hastily sorted through the many items crowding her space. She stopped only to take swift glances around the room or to grab something and plunk it down into a box, suitcase or plastic bag.

"This whole moving away thing has been really hard for me," she admitted.

Although Michelle was looking forward to seeing her fiancé and to getting married, she wasn't happy about leaving Israel. Emotionally, I understood how she was having a hard time doing that. And now I was seeing how it was also difficult for her to physically get ready as well.

"Well..." I shifted my eyes from the objects scattered around the room back to Michelle. "Just tell me what to do and I'll do it." I was hoping that, somehow, together we could make some headway.

"Okay," Michelle finally agreed. "If you bring that stuff

from the bathroom over to here, then I'll take care of it."

For the next half-hour Michelle and I vigorously worked on packing up and clearing the rooms of the apartment. Time was speeding by like a racehorse. I could tell Michelle was trying hard to relax.

"I don't know what happened," she told me, as we scrambled to get things in order. "I started packing days ago. I even stayed up all night trying to get everything ready, so I would be on time." She speedily shuffled through some papers that were lying on the kitchen table. "Everything just took so much longer than I expected."

With every passing minute, our concern about making it to the airport on time became greater. I stopped working for a few minutes to give my back a rest. "I want to try to get in touch with the airline," I told Michelle, who was now wrapping some of her dishes in newspaper. "If Air Canada is running late, then there's still a chance we could make your plane."

I went into the living room and picked up the phone. "The recording at the Air Canada office in Tel Aviv says it's 'closed at this time,'" I called out to Michelle after a few minutes. "And the number at the airport is constantly busy."

Michelle didn't answer. I guessed she was contemplating whether it was still worth rushing, if the plane might leave without her anyway.

At that moment, Yehuda came through the door with Hadas and Yael, who were wearing matching pink and purple outfits. "How's it going?" His eyes were searching around the apartment for clues. "Doesn't this remind you a little of us?" he whispered to me so Michelle couldn't hear.

I knew exactly what Yehuda was referring to. "You mean during the war when *we* were trying to get to the airport. Yeah, it does."

Michelle came into the living room with a box of

wrapped kitchenware.

"I know what I'm going to do," I announced, still holding the receiver in my hand. "The minute I get through to the airport I'm going to pretend that I'm the one getting married and that I absolutely *have* to get on that plane. I'll beg them to keep the check-in counter open just a little longer."

"They probably won't do it," Yehuda said realistically.

"I don't know anymore," Michelle groaned. She put the box down and began walking from room to room, collecting, packing and discarding her things a few at a time. The place was starting to shape up, but there was still more to be done.

"Well, that's what I'm going to do," I announced, as I began dialing again.

Yehuda took the girls back down to occupy them, and to wait. Michelle picked up her pace. I dialed and redialed the phone until finally the line cleared.

"*Shalom!*" I straightened my back and cleared my throat. "I'm supposed to be on flight 213 and I got stuck in Jerusalem," I began.

There was a brief pause while the woman on the phone checked the flight schedule. "That flight," she said, returning to me, "is due to leave in just a little over an hour. But the check-in counters close up way before then."

We'll **never** *make it on time.* "But," I persisted, "I'm getting married. I *have* to be on that flight!" I insisted.

"Are you on your way now?"

"Well, not yet. But I will be very soon."

"So get into your car *right now* and hurry!"

I slammed down the phone receiver and shouted, "We have to hurry! The woman at the airport said we should get in the car and come *right now!*"

"Are they going to wait for us?" Michelle asked in disbelief.

"I don't know. But *c'mon!*"

In a frenzy, we began throwing things into bags and suitcases and smashing boxes shut. I called out the window for Yehuda to "come up fast!"

Michelle rapidly explained things to me. "Okay, this bag stays here for my roommate when she gets back from visiting her family in England. And this one goes to the Steiners. This box is for charity, and those boxes and that suitcase over there are for storage at the Hirsch's."

I made mental notes of everything, hoping I would remember it all later. Michelle pushed her suitcases out the door and Yehuda hauled them down to the car, while I waited down below with Hadas and Yael.

"We'll have to come back later for the stuff that will be going into storage," I told Yehuda as he put the last bag in the trunk. "There's no time or room to bring anything extra now."

After the car was speedily loaded up, Michelle climbed into the backseat with Hadas, Yael and two plastic bags that she would be sorting through on the way.

"We'll have to fly to make good time," Yehuda informed everyone, chuckling to himself at his play on words.

From my seat, I watched the speedometer needle rising rapidly as we sped down the Jerusalem-Tel Aviv highway. In the back, Michelle's high ponytail was swishing from side to side like a horse's tail as she went back and forth from one bag to the other, busily pulling things out and rearranging them as best she could so that everything would fit into one bag. The girls were giggling and having a grand time enjoying the exciting trip.

"Maybe you should slow down," I cautioned Yehuda.

"Don't worry," Yehuda reassured me. "I have everything under control."

As we entered Ben Gurion Airport, about forty minutes later, Yehuda gave out orders. "Okay, I'll pull up as close as possible to the Air Canada section. You two get ready to jump out and rush inside. Find out if, by some slight chance, they kept the check-in counter open for Michelle. Then come back and tell me whether I should bring in the luggage or not."

I was skeptical. *Why would they consider staying open just for us?* I doubted there would be any airline personnel hanging around so close to the take-off time of an international flight.

"It would be a miracle if they actually waited for us," I said.

"I really hope they did." Michelle was trying to be positive, as she moved the bulging plastic bag she had just organized off her lap.

Yehuda stopped the car at Departures and Michelle and I scrambled out. With my big stomach leading the way, we dashed as fast as we could over to the entrance of the building.

"Please let them be there," Michelle prayed as we went through the big glass doors and continued on towards the large Air Canada sign in front of us.

The area was quiet and empty. There were a couple of plain-clothed security guards, a stewardess pulling her small suitcase on wheels and—I was ecstatic—a lone woman was sitting behind one of the check-in counters!

"They waited for us!" I shouted.

The woman saw Michelle and me scurrying over to her and called out in Hebrew for us to hurry. "Are you the bride? Fast! Fast! The plane is about to leave! Let me see your ticket and your passport," she ordered.

Michelle struggled to pull out the required documents from her purse as fast as she could, while I waddled back to Yehuda and told him to *"run* with the luggage!"

After Yehuda rushed over the cart of suitcases and returned to the car, I hurried back to Michelle. There was no time to discuss the extraordinary thing that had just happened or to say goodbye properly. So, teary-eyed, Michelle and I just hugged each other tightly.

"You have to hurry!" the woman behind the counter exclaimed. She had already called someone over to whisk Michelle up the back stairs and through all the different checkpoints that would bring her to the boarding area on the second floor.

Michelle bent down and picked up her carry-on bag and the plastic bag that she hoped they would somehow allow her to also bring onto the plane. I draped the hanging bag with her wedding dress over one of her arms and gave her another hug. "*Mazel tov,*"[77] I said with emotion.

"Thank you," Michelle said, managing to give me a quick kiss on the cheek before her escort took her away.

"Good luck with everything!" I called after her as she went up the stairs with her bulky load.

Michelle raised one of her bags in the air as a silent reply while she and the airport attendant continued walking up. I stood and watched until they reached the top and disappeared.

Outside, I found Yehuda leaning against the car with his arms folded over his chest, waiting for me to return. Hadas and Yael were sitting on the curb eating whole wheat pretzels from little plastic sandwich bags.

I leaned on the car next to Yehuda. Exhaustion, sadness and amazement simultaneously fought for my attention. For a moment I stared blankly at the glass doors from which I had just exited. Only minutes before, Michelle and I had run through them in a mad rush to get inside. Still dazed, I finally spoke.

"I can't believe it," I told Yehuda.

"I know." Yehuda replied. He was also staring at the doors. "It's unbelievable."

---

[77] Congratulations.

·❧· CHAPTER 7 ·❧·

"That last story reminds me of the famous song John Denver used to sing back in the seventies," Carol said. "Remember?"

"Yeah, I remember." I cleared my throat and began singing, "I'm leaving on a jet plane, don't know when I'll be back again..."

"Oh babe, I hate to go..." Carol joined in.

"That song was before my time," Fran said.

"Well actually," I stopped singing, "I think it was originally performed by Peter, Paul and Mary in the sixties, which was before our time too."

"If you say so," Fran shrugged. Then, turning to Carol she asked, "As long as we're speaking of time, what's our situation? Do we have enough time for more stories?"

Carol glanced at her watch. "We could probably fit in one or two more."

Fran turned away from Carol and looked at me. "We're good for one or two more stories. What about you?"

"Yep," I answered happily, "I'm good."

DEFROSTING THE FREEZE
(August 1995)

Why doesn't he just take a leave of absence so everyone can move in? I asked myself the same question each time I passed the casually dressed watchman. He was dutifully guarding the row of vacant buildings in Or Tzion's newly completed neighborhood. Handgun at his side, the watchman was to make sure all twenty-two apartments remained empty. Arriving early every weekday morning and leaving after sundown every night, he never missed a day. It was a boring job. But his presence guaranteed that the neighborhood would never come to life.

There were now nearly 150,000 Jews living in the settlement towns of Judea and Samaria. Though the Jews were grossly outnumbered by the Arabs in the villages surrounding them, Prime Minister Rabin still ordered a freeze on all building and development in the Jewish settlements. It was a gesture he offered to the Arabs and world leaders who claimed there could be no peace as long as Jews continued to build and help secure those parts of the country.

For Or Tzion, Rabin's freeze meant that, along with other building prohibitions, the new neighborhood was to stay unoccupied. The families who'd already signed contracts to rent or purchase the apartments would be forced to find somewhere else to live. As long as the young watchman hung around reading his book or pacing the bloc of empty apartments every day, there would be no settling into them. He was there as proof that Rabin wasn't going to stand for right-wing settlers planting any more of their roots in the Land.

Then one Thursday night, without much warning, it

actually happened! The bored, but faithful watchman finished his last shift for the week and left, just as he had done at the end of all the previously uneventful weeks. Only this time, he had no idea that when he returned on Sunday morning, he'd be out of a job. He didn't know that as unwavering as Rabin was about the building freeze, the town of Or Tzion was just as adamant about the families moving into their new neighborhood.

The plan was quickly devised and even more swiftly put into action. The town was secretly buzzing all day in anticipation of the night's event that lay ahead.

"Do you think it will work?" we all asked each other.

"I hope so, for the sake of those who've been waiting to move into their new homes."

"My kids want to stay up to help."

"There's so much organization involved; I hope nothing goes wrong."

Michal, our third baby girl, was only three weeks old. So I wouldn't be able to help much with the "Great Move." But I planned on giving my support and encouragement to the volunteer movers and to the families who would soon be living less than a block away from our own newly built house.

Resting on the living room couch, I wondered how our beloved watchman would react when he came to work on Sunday morning and found the quiet, barren neighborhood he'd been ordered to safeguard filled to capacity with twenty-two lively families and all their belongings. Would he be more shocked or confused? I decided it didn't really matter. *He shouldn't be there keeping people from moving into their new homes in the first place. And we shouldn't be prevented from building in our yishuv*[78] *in order to please other people, or*

---

[78] Settlement town.

other countries. I rocked the baby carriage at my side with one hand to keep little Michal calm. *Law-abiding citizens shouldn't be forced into a position of civil disobedience.*

As soon as the guard left for the weekend, the town sprang into action. Residents from all over Or Tzion volunteered their time and services in a gigantic effort to collectively move the families into their new apartments. Very little notice had been given to the community beforehand, as the small core of planners was careful not to leak the information until the timing was right.

After putting our two preschoolers to bed, Yehuda went to help the others. I went outside with sleeping Michal to watch the great efforts in progress. Convoys of privately owned cars, minivans and trucks loaded up with furniture, boxes and suitcases of all sizes arrived at the site. Men, women, teenagers and even younger children were unloading the vehicles and carrying the contents into the apartments. A few children also passed around homemade brownies, while popular songs played from loudspeakers that had been attached to the roof of someone's car.

I knew it wasn't just my hormones causing me to feel emotional. This was *Am Yisrael*[79] at its best—*coming together to help, to give, to encourage and to stand up for what was right.* Suddenly, I didn't feel good hanging around and doing nothing. Taking Michal with me in the carriage, I went to help my friend Ilana and her family. They'd been renting a small house a few doors away and were now moving into one of the "frozen" apartments they'd recently bought.

"Is there an easy packing job I can do?" I asked Ilana. Yehuda and Ilana's husband had already gone to the new neighborhood with some boxes and a few small furniture items.

---

[79] The Jewish people.

"If you're feeling up to it, you could put the food I just emptied from the fridge into these boxes." Ilana pointed to some cartons lying on the floor. "Someone will be coming soon to take them, along with the refrigerator and the oven."

Those who owned vans or trucks volunteered to go from family to family collecting and delivering heavy furniture and larger appliances. As they arrived at each home, the "moving men" called out, "Okay, let's have your washing machine!" or "Time to give us your beds!"

Yehuda and I periodically checked on Hadas and Yael, who slept through all the commotion. Music, singing and hastening feet could be heard on the streets, stairways and pathways into the early hours of the morning. I had a hard time tearing myself away from watching the action, but I eventually went off to bed.

By sunrise Friday morning, the news was already spreading throughout Or Tzion. The overnight moving mission was a success! All twenty-two apartments were inhabited. They didn't have electricity yet and there was plenty to be unpacked and organized, but the exhausted, excited families were all finally residing in their new homes.

"Neighbors in the area brought over food for our breakfast and lunch," Ilana told me when I went to welcome her family into the new neighborhood that afternoon. "And we've already gotten invitations for Shabbat meals."

"I hope there won't be problems with the government," I said, watching Ilana unpack a box of sheets and towels.

Though she was usually optimistic, Ilana was now also wondering what the future would bring her, her husband and their two young children. "The main event is behind us," she said. "But who knows what will happen next week after we're discovered. I hope they won't kick us out."

Sunday came and went, and Mr. Watchman with it. I don't know if anyone actually saw him that morning. But when the police showed up the next day, everyone knew that he'd seen the empty apartments fully inhabited.

"I was nervous when a policeman knocked on my door and asked how long we'd been living there," Ilana told me when she came over with her three-year-old daughter that afternoon for a break from unpacking.

"What'd you tell him?" I asked.

"I told him that it seemed like we had been living in the apartment for a while. I hoped that because I still have a pretty strong American accent, he'd think I didn't know much Hebrew and wouldn't bother trying to get me to answer any more questions."

Ilana poured milk into her coffee and then into a plastic cup for her daughter. "But then, he asked me why there were still so many boxes all over the place. I explained the best I could that it was just taking time to unpack all of our things." Ilana took a few sips of her coffee and then went on. "Actually, I'm less concerned now than I was because I found out that there's some kind of squatter's rights that supposedly make it a little harder to get rid of us after we've been living on the premises for a certain amount of time. And by the time any kind of legal action gets under way, we'll have already been there for a while," she explained.

"Well, so far the government isn't threatening to do anything drastic," I said.

"Thank G-d." Ilana wiped her daughter's cookie and milk face with a napkin. "We all have contracts that are legal, so they'll probably just leave us alone," Her optimism was returning. "How could they throw us all out anyway, especially after we moved in with our kids and all our stuff? I don't think they would do that."

"I don't either," I agreed.

"I guess that means we should go do some more unpacking." Ilana made a face at the idea and then, finishing her coffee, got up to leave.

"Never a dull moment," I said, opening the front door.

"That's right!" Ilana's eyes glimmered in the sunlight as we walked outside into the warm air. "Thanks for the break," she called to me over her shoulder.

"Anytime," I replied, watching Ilana and her little girl, as they walked down the block towards their family, their boxes, their new neighborhood and... their new home.

·❧· *CHAPTER 8* ·❧·

NATIONAL SHAKE UP

(May 1996)

It was six months after the assassination and the country was still in shock.

Nobody had expected Prime Minister Rabin to be murdered. It shook up the country like an earthquake. It stunned the world. And it widened the chasm in Israeli society to exaggerated proportions.

The left-wingers couldn't believe he was gone. The right-wingers couldn't believe they were being blamed for his death.

Yigal Amir, a young religious Zionist from Herzliya, was accused of the murder and sentenced to life in prison. While some questioned whether he was really guilty, others claimed that he wanted to kill the prime minister because he believed that Rabin's Oslo Accords were destroying Israel.

"Those Oslo Accords haven't brought us anything good," I said, as Malka and I had lunch together at an outdoor café in the center of town. "Arafat and the PLO charter haven't changed at all."

"That's true," Malka agreed, looking both regal and down-to-earth as she sat across from me in her long print skirt, plain white hat and shiny gold earrings. "I never understood how they thought Arafat could be trusted in the first place." Malka poured Thousand Island dressing over her salad. "We upheld our end of those agreements right away. We granted the Arabs autonomy over certain areas, and then, after the second set of Oslo Accords last year, we even supplied their police forces with all kinds of guns."

I pulled my chair closer to the table. "I wonder what they'll do with all those guns."

"Right." Malka said, understanding my concern. "Could anyone really expect the PLO to stop its violence, respect our holy sites and amend its charter calling for Israel's annihilation?"

Our doubts and worries reflected what the right-wing camp had been expressing for years. Unfortunately, the desperate pleas and cries for Israel not to give in to the enemy had fallen on deaf ears. And now, the Oslo Accords were failing to bring peace and Prime Minister Yitzhak Rabin was dead.

Tensions rose and hostile feelings intensified as outraged and mourning left-wing Rabin loyalists held not only Yigal Amir, but the entire right-wing population responsible for the prime minister's death.

"You can *feel* their fury towards all of us." I stirred my cream of broccoli soup to cool it off. "Like each one of us personally shot him."

"The whole thing is so awful," Malka said.

"Even if it could be proven one hundred percent that it was Yigal Amir who'd committed the crime, does that mean we should *all* be blamed? Did any of us plan the murder, buy the gun or pull the trigger?"

Malka looked at me. "Unfortunately, those who loved and believed in Rabin are so upset about his death they're convinced that our ideologies and principles caused this to happen."

"How can people think we believe it would be right or good to go out and kill the prime minister?"

"We all want the same thing," Malka said. "We all want peace. We just see the solution differently. Some see it as giving up parts of the Land, and we see it as holding onto every bit of it. But it's no secret we didn't want Rabin to continue leading the country," she reminded me.

I looked up from my bowl. "That doesn't mean we thought someone should murder him."

"That's true. And now we're all suffering, in one way or another. If we could deal with our differences better, we wouldn't have these problems." Malka waved for the waitress to come to our table. "What the Torah says about us being a stiff-necked people is right. We're stubborn, especially here in Israel, where we all need to be..."

"Tough," I finished the sentence for her, stabbing the air with my spoon.

"Tough," Malka repeated, with a nod of her head, "and also soft. Like the fruit of the sabra cactus—tough on the outside, but sweet and soft on the inside. That's a Sabra."

"Do you need anything else?" The young waitress asked us.

"Just more water please," Malka replied.

After the waitress left, Malka and I sat back and listened to the cheerful voices and laughter coming from the tables around us. I looked at Malka. "You'd never know there were problems underneath it all, would you?"

The waitress placed a glass pitcher of water with floating lemon slices on the table. "It's how we keep going," Malka said, pouring us both some water.

I glanced at my watch. It was getting late. "I should get back home. I don't want to keep the babysitter waiting for too long."

"You go ahead and catch your bus. I'm sitting here for a few more minutes," Malka said. "I'll pay the bill," she told me, reaching for her purse.

"Thank you." I grabbed my own purse and leaned forward to give Malka a hug. "I'll speak to you soon."

Malka took my hands in hers. "Remember how so many Jews who survived the Holocaust longed to come here? They so badly wanted to live in *Eretz Yisrael*,[80] despite the awful conditions on the ships that brought them over and the difficulties they faced after they finally arrived. That's because they knew that, as Jews, this was where they belonged."

Looking into my eyes, Malka went on, "G-d gave this Land to us thousands of years ago, and we've been here ever since. It's like a marriage. *Am Yisrael* and *Eretz Yisrael*, the nation and the Land—eternally connected; together, through the highs and the lows, through good times and bad... for better and for worse."

"A match made in heaven." I smiled. The cliché fit so perfectly. Then, letting my hands slip away from Malka's, I thanked her again and got up to leave.

Sometimes it was a challenge to remember, but I knew Malka was right. *Through good times and bad, for better and for worse.*

---

[80] The Land of Israel.

·❧· CHAPTER 9 ·❧·

"It's story time!" Fran came breezing into the room. She looked like a Japanese china doll today, with red rouge highlighting her high cheek bones and her shiny black hair gathered in a bun on the top of her head.

"We've been waiting for you," Carol told Fran as she gently massaged my leg to get the circulation going.

"Today I thought I'd start out by reading a letter," I told my two faithful listeners.

"A letter? What kind of letter?" Carol asked.

"I e-mailed my husband, Yehuda, last week and asked him to scan me some old writings and articles that I'd saved over the years for a book I've been writing. Thank G-d I brought my laptop with me from Israel. I can be in touch with everyone there, and writing helps pass the time while I'm lying here all day."

"So he sent everything to your laptop," Carol said matter-of-factly.

"Yeah. And while Yehuda was going through my papers, he came across some old letters I'd saved, and even some photocopies of a few letters I'd sent to other people over the years. I don't remember why I kept those. I probably thought they'd come in handy one day for my book."

"So what's this letter that you want to read to us?"

Fran started her routine checks on me as she spoke.

"I wrote it years ago, to my friend Jamie in Chicago. It fits perfectly into the part of the story we're up to."

"I remember Jamie," Carol said. "She's the one who helped you pack your shower gifts and flew to Israel from Chicago to be at your wedding."

"Yeah, that's her."

"I've got to leave earlier today," Fran suddenly informed us. "So we should probably get to it."

"You have to leave earlier today? Why? Gotta date?" Carol winked at Fran.

"The only date I have today is with the dentist at two-thirty."

"Your teeth are so perfect and white," Carol said. "Your appointment probably lasts two minutes."

"Yours look like they're in pretty good shape too," Fran replied.

"Not really." Letting my leg go, Carol walked over to Fran. "You see these two on the top," she opened her mouth and pointed for Fran to look at her teeth. "See how crooked they are? I should have had braces when I was younger."

"They're not that bad," Fran was looking inside Carol's mouth.

"Okay," I said in a loud voice, pulling my laptop closer and clicking onto the old letter I was about to read. "Are we ready?"

Turning away from Carol's teeth, Fran and Carol both looked at me as if they'd suddenly remembered I was there. Then, quickly returning to their places, they answered together, "Ready!"

DEAR JAMIE
(October 1997)

Dear Jamie,

How are you doing? We're all fine, except that my house is full of dust. We're building a second floor and it's a little crazy because we're still living on the first floor while the building is going on! But I'm actually very happy. When we moved into the house about three years ago, I didn't think we'd be able to add on to it so soon. We had to take out a loan, of course, and like just about everyone else in the country, our account is in overdraft. But the banks allow it and, thank G-d, soon we'll have a bigger place for our growing family!

These days there's a lot of building going on in Or Tzion. People keep moving here all the time. When we came seven years ago, there were three hundred families. Now there are about five hundred. And there's a long list of people waiting to join us. At this rate, in another ten years, we'll have close to a thousand families!

I've been thinking—maybe it's time for you to come for a visit. You haven't been to Israel since my wedding. It would be fun to have you spend some time here with me and Yehuda, and of course the kids. They've really grown from when you saw them on our last trip to the States. Hadas is already six, Yael is turning four and little Michal is two. You've never met Michal, since I haven't been back to Chicago in a while.

Sometimes I think about how my dad also never met her. He didn't have a chance to really get to know any of the girls before he passed away. I can't believe that was four years ago already. I remember my dad's last trip here with my mother. I arranged for him to see his cousin from

California who'd made *aliyah* with her husband and kids back in the sixties. My dad really enjoyed that reunion. I didn't even know I had more relatives here until one day they found out about me and called to see if I wanted to meet them.

That's Israel—everyone connects with everyone at some point. I've met people here who lived on my block in Chicago, but our paths only crossed when we ran into each other in Jerusalem!

So what are you doing with yourself these days? I'm pretty busy. I decided not to continue on with the small catering business I'd started a couple of years ago. The hours were too crazy for me. So I'm going to try something completely different with my friend, Ilana. We'll be opening a private nursery school soon. We already have fifteen toddlers signed up and we're hoping we'll have twenty by the beginning of the school year. Wish us luck!

Okay, gotta go wipe down the dusty kitchen counters and make lunch before Michal wakes up from her nap, and Hadas and Yael come home from school and pre-school.

Hope everything's good with you. Write me back soon, okay?

Love,
Shelly

·❧· *CHAPTER 10* ·❧·

"Great letter for getting us caught up on things." Carol took the laptop and set it down at the foot of my bed. "Now let's get you into a chair so we can begin your therapy."

"I think it must be time for another holiday," Fran said with a chuckle, as Carol helped me off the bed. "There seem to be so many of them." She smiled at me. "But I must admit, I'm actually enjoying learning a bit about all your Jewish and Israeli holidays. They're so different from the Buddhist ones I learned about or the American ones I grew up with."

"You want to hear about Lag B'Omer?" I asked.

"Lag B'what?" Carol was now easing me into the chair.

"Lag B'Omer. It comes in between Passover and Shavuot," I said matter-of-factly.

"Never heard of it," Carol said, turning to Fran with a shrug.

"Don't look at me," Fran laughed. "I've certainly never heard of it."

"Okay," I said. "I'm going to tell you about Lag B'Omer."

FIRE AND LIGHT
(*May 1998*)

I stood at the edge of the bonfire and dropped five potatoes wrapped in aluminum foil into the flames.

"Where should I put all this food?" Yehuda asked me. He had a white shopping bag in one hand and a plastic bottle of water in the other.

"Over there," I pointed towards the two portable tables some of the neighbors had already set up.

It was the eve of the holiday of Lag B'Omer, traditionally celebrated with large bonfires in commemoration of the great sage and mystic Rabbi Shimon Bar Yochai. A prominent Jew who lived two thousand years ago, Rabbi Shimon Bar Yochai was pursued relentlessly by the Romans for criticizing the anti-Jewish Roman government in power at the time. Taking refuge in a cave with his son, the Rabbi spent thirteen years in hiding. All that time he learned Torah and the deeper, hidden secrets and mystical dimensions of the Torah called Kabbalah. On the day Rabbi Shimon Bar Yochai died, he revealed all the Kabbalistic secrets he'd learned, passing enormous spiritual light on to the world.

"My teacher told us that when Rabbi Shimon Bar Yochai died, he left everyone lots of light," Hadas said, watching me throw the last potato into the fire to be baked.

I turned to my bright first grader. "Did your teacher tell you that Rabbi Shimon Bar Yochai died on the Hebrew date Lag B'Omer and that's why every year on that night we remember him with the light from bonfires?"

Hadas nodded. "And she also said that he told his students that everybody should be happy and have fun on the day he died."

"C'mon, let's have fun!" Yael cried. "Are we going to go see lots of other bonfires too?" she asked.

"Maybe a little later on," I said, "if Michal doesn't get too tired and need to go home to sleep."

Every year, children in Or Tzion and throughout the country spend the weeks leading up to the holiday collecting scrap wood and broken tree branches for the large bonfires that light up the night all over Israel on Lag B'Omer. Friends and family gather around the fires to celebrate with music, singing, story telling and plenty of food.

"Let's go help Abba[81] unpack the food we brought," I told the girls. On our way to the tables, I saw Benny and Yaffa with their young twins. They were eating whole onions wrapped in aluminum foil that had just been fished out of the hot fire.

"Hey, Yaffa!" I called out.

"Hi!" Yaffa called back, her smiling face shining in the moonlight. "Have you ever eaten baked onions like this? They're delicious!"

"Nope. Must be a funny Australian thing," I teased. Then turning around, I saw my friend Efrat, who was a music teacher, coming our way.

"I brought my guitar this time," Efrat said, handing her daughter marshmallows to roast in the fire with the other children.

"I'm hungry," Yael said, eyeing the hotdogs lined up on a little makeshift grill some of the older boys had put together with stones and bricks. "When will our potatoes be ready?" She moved closer to watch the boys who were kneeling on the ground, fanning the small flames.

"They won't be ready for a while," I told her. "But you

---

[81] Father, daddy.

can eat these in the meantime." I handed Yael and three-year-old Michal each a large cluster of grapes. After popping a few into their mouths, the two sisters ran over to Yehuda, who was watching Hadas roast marshmallows with a couple of her friends.

I noticed that both Efrat's and Yaffa's kids were also off with their fathers. So I suggested that the three of us steal away together for the few minutes we miraculously had free.

"You know," I told them after we moved our chairs off to the side, "the best Lag B'Omer I ever had was when I went up to Mount Meron."

"You went to Meron?" Yaffa sounded interested. "I've never been there."

"What was it like?" Efrat asked, looking funky in her brightly-colored patchwork top and long, twisty copper earrings.

"Well, I'd been in Israel for about a year or so and happened to be in Tzfat visiting the Livnot U'Lehibanot program on Lag B'Omer," I began. "At about eleven o'clock at night, a group of the Livnoters mentioned they were planning to take a bus over to the celebrations on Mount Meron. So, I joined them."

I paused to open a bag of potato chips. "It's only a few minutes' ride to Meron, but we had to wait for a while to get on a bus because the central bus station in Tzfat was packed with everyone trying to go over there. When we finally made it to the mountain, it was hopping! People were all over the place."

I took a few chips and held the bag out for Efrat and Yaffa to do the same.

"The first thing we saw was a long line of parked buses and taxis. The taxis kept coming, and busload after busload of people were arriving. We overheard a man next to us explaining to his children that many of the people had come straight from the airport, and that some were still flying into Israel from around the world just to be on Mount Meron for Lag B'Omer! One of the girls with us couldn't believe it. So we went over to a bus driver, who was smoking a cigarette next to his bus, and asked him if people really flew in just for the celebration.

"The bus driver could tell that we weren't Hebrew speakers, so he answered us in English. 'Dey come from de airport,'" I was trying to speak like the driver had, with a thick Israeli accent. "'Some of dem are from New York in America and some from udder countries. Dey come here tonight from all over deh world. Many of dese udder buses you see also just came from de airport.'"

Switching back to my own voice, I went on. "One of us must have made some kind of disbelieving face that the bus driver noticed, because I remember him blowing smoke simultaneously out of his mouth and nose, and then saying, 'You are surprised? It's Lag B'Omer! We bring sousands and sousands of people here every year.'"

"It must have really been crowded," Yaffa said.

"That's an understatement!" I exclaimed. "*Everybody* was there—religious and non-religious, Sephardi, Ashkenazi, Yemenite, Sabras, new *olim*,[82] tourists, young, old... you name it. They all came to Mount Meron for Lag B'Omer!"

"What was everyone doing?" Efrat asked.

"All along the way to Rabbi Shimon Bar Yochai's burial site, we were surrounded by people mingling about and lots of souvenir booths. Vendors were selling trinkets, religious objects and all kinds of gifts. Some old women were handing out little red strings to tie on our wrists for "good luck," while others called out blessings to whoever

---

[82] Immigrants.

passed by. And, of course, there were *lots* of food stands. We didn't know what to do or where to go first!

"And get this!" I sat up straighter in my chair. "In the middle of the mobs of people, we saw a row of about ten long tables joined together, one after the other, like a train. They were covered with tablecloths, and all the makings of a great feast were spread out across the length of them. It looked like a huge family and probably lots of their friends had gathered for the occasion. It was one o'clock in the morning and they were all seated around the tables, eating, laughing and passing the food and drinks back and forth! Lots of other, smaller tables with people sharing banquets together were also mixed in with all the vendors selling things and everyone walking around. It was such an unusual scene. I remember saying, 'Is this for real?'"

"Sounds wild!" Efrat said.

"But that wasn't the main part of it all," I went on. "When we finally got close to Rabbi Shimon BarYochai's burial spot, we realized that was where the real celebrating was taking place."

Yaffa and Efrat were drawn in as I told them about the gigantic raging bonfires with their enormous flames reaching up to the heavens. Men and boys, many dressed in traditional black Hassidic garb, were singing and dancing excitedly around the fires.

"It was really a sight! They were jumping and twirling around like mad as they danced," I explained. "We watched them for a while and then we looked around for Rabbi Shimon Bar Yochai's tomb. There were so many people everywhere—it took us a few minutes to find it. Then, we came to a slightly calmer area that was set back from the rest of the action."

"And that's where it was," Yaffa jumped in.

"Right." I nodded.

"Hey, what are all of you doing over here, Ema?"[83] Hadas called out, running over to us in her cute jumper with the butterflies. She had left the bonfire to come look for me.

"Hi sweetie." Pulling her closer, I could smell the scent of smoke in her soft, wavy hair. "We're talking about Mount Meron, where Rabbi Shimon bar Yochai is buried." I helped Hadas onto my lap.

"Anyway," I turned back to Efrat and Yaffa, "at the tomb, there was a men's section and a women's section. So our group split up. The two Livnot girls and I started towards the line where other women and girls were waiting to get up close. I stopped to watch the short, wrinkled old woman at the front of the line. She was bending over a low ledge near the tomb, lighting a little candle. The ledge was coated with wax from hundreds of other candles that had already melted." I still had a clear picture of the scene in my mind. "The old woman was wearing a brown and orange patterned head scarf that didn't go at all with her green and purple outfit. Her hand shook as she touched the match to the wick of her candle. After the candle was finally lit, she stood up and placed both of her hands on her heart. Then she bowed her head to her chest, closed her eyes and whispered a prayer."

"Why did she light a candle?" Hadas asked.

"A candle is like the light of a person's soul," Efrat explained, hoping Hadas would understand.

"We light a candle every year to remember someone close to us who died," I added.

"Plus, during Lag B'Omer, candles and fire remind us of the great light Rabbi Shimon BarYochai left behind," Yaffa said.

---

83 Mommy, mother.

"Did you also light a candle, Ema?"

"Well, I waited in line with the others," I went on. "But when it was my turn at the tomb, I wasn't sure what to do. Everything was still new to me back then. So I crouched down to look at all the burning candles flickering quietly on the ledge below. There was a lot of laughing, music and milling around in the background, but I was focused on watching the candles slowly melting. I remember wishing I had brought a candle of my own to light." I smiled pensively, as the fond memory lingered.

Leaning forward in her chair, her long earrings dangling in the air, Efrat drew closer to me. "What did you do afterwards?"

"Well," I said, pulling a few potato chips out of the bag and putting them in Hadas' outstretched hand. "We left the tomb. And after meeting up with the others, we decided it was time to return to Tzfat. I remember it was already really late. So we walked back past the bonfires and the dancing, all the vending booths and stalls, and everyone praying and eating their three o'clock in the morning feasts. When we finally reached the buses, we couldn't believe what we saw."

"Let me guess," Efrat said, "more taxis and more buses were coming."

"Yep. Tons of people were just arriving! And they were all rushing to get in on the excitement and to pray at Rabbi Shimon Bar Yochai's tomb."

Yaffa slapped her hand down onto her chair. "I've got to talk to Benny about going there one year!"

"It sounds like an experience," Efrat agreed.

"Oh, here you are, Shelly!" Yehuda came over, holding Michal's hand. "We were looking for you."

Hadas hopped off my lap and went over to Yehuda. "Can we go to Rabbi Shimon Bar Yochai?"

"She means she wants to go one year to Mount Meron

for Lag B'Omer," I explained.

"Mount Meron on Lag B'Omer," Yehuda said, raising his eyebrows. "I'd be a little afraid of losing you in all the crowds. Hey! How 'bout if we go get those potatoes out of the fire before they burn to a crisp."

Yehuda turned to us. "I left Yael with Benny and the twins guarding the potatoes with their lives so all our hungry friends and neighbors won't get to them before us!"

"Oh man," Efrat said, dramatically rolling her eyes upward.

Yaffa squinted sideways at Yehuda. "You just want to eat them all yourself," she joked. "We know about you!"

"I want a big potato." Michal was tugging at Yehuda, trying to pull him back to the bonfire.

"We really should be getting back," Efrat said.

"Okay, let's go." I picked up my chair and followed the others.

"Can we go to Mount Meron sometime, Ema?" Hadas asked, skipping alongside me.

"Maybe we'll see about going one Lag B'Omer when you and your sisters are a little older."

Slowing to a walking pace, Hadas looked up at me. "Can I bring a candle?"

"Of course," I nodded. "We wouldn't go without one."

"So we can make more light," Hadas added, "like Rabbi Shimon Bar Yochai did."

"Exactly." I set my chair down by the food table. "But for now," I pointed to the large bonfire burning next to us, "we have our own giant candle, and *lots* of our own light."

CHAPTER 11

"What a cute girl that Hadas is," Carol said.
"Her sisters are too," Fran smiled at me.
"Time for a boy," I said.
"What?" Fran and Carol looked at me.
"I said, time for a boy."

THE BABY SECRET
(September 1999)

"When's it going to pop out?" Michal poked my belly with her small skinny finger.

"Not quite yet," I answered my anxious four-year-old, smoothing my maternity jumper over the round bump that was once my flat stomach.

"I want it to be a boy this time." Hadas, now eight, was sitting next to me on the bed.

"Yeah, we want a boy." Michal began bouncing up and down on the thick mattress, her dark, silky hair flying about.

"A cute boy," added Yael.

I looked at my three daughters and decided I could no longer hold back what I had known for a while. "Okay, girls, listen." I put the open Berenstein Bears book that I was about to read them face down on my lap. "I'm going to tell you a secret." Michal stopped bouncing. Hadas and

Yael inched closer to me. "Can you keep a secret?"

All three girls nodded in unison. "Yes!" Yael answered for all of them. "We can keep a secret. What is it?"

"Your Abba and I thought it best not to tell people now whether the baby's a boy or a girl, just to be sure. But since there are only a couple of weeks to go and you're all so excited about it, I'll tell you what the ultrasound pictures show."

"Is it a boy?" Hadas prodded me.

"Well," I purposely paused for a dramatic affect. "Now, remember," I reminded them, "it's your secret with me and Abba."

Michal and Hadas nodded again. Yael couldn't take the suspense. "So, what is it?"

Smiling, I shifted my eyes from daughter to daughter and then said, "It's a boy!"

"Yay! Yay!" Hadas and Yael hugged each other.

"Yay!" Michal lay back on the bed and kicked her feet in the air.

"Really Ema?" Hadas was the first to turn back to me.

"Yep, it looks like you're all going to have a baby brother."

Yael looked at me. "What are we going to call him?"

"Yeah," Michal stopped kicking her feet. "What's his name going to be?"

"*That*, you'll find out *after* he's born."

"I'm going to have a little brother!" Michal enthused.

"We're going to have fun with him," Yael said. "And if we want him to be different, like when we play Ema and Abba, then we can just dress him up like a girl!"

"Hmmm." I smiled. "I think it might be all right to do that on Purim, *if* he likes the idea."

"Okay," Yael agreed.

"So Ema," Michal said, patting me gently this time, "when's he going to pop out?"

·❧· CHAPTER 12 ·❧·

"Hello. Sorry to disturb you." It was a new day and we were just about to begin again when the elderly woman from across the room called out to us. Sitting up in her bed, my white-haired roommate waved her hand in our direction from behind the half-opened curtain. "I'm ashamed to say that I've been listening to the three of you for a while," she admitted. "I sleep a lot and sometimes I'm not in the room when you're all huddled together over there. But yesterday I overheard more of the stories and today I decided to ask if I could be a part of your little gatherings."

Fran laughed. "Mrs. Weissberg! We didn't know you were an eavesdropper!"

"I should be embarrassed," Mrs. Weissberg told us, "but I found myself becoming more interested with each story."

"Don't be embarrassed." Carol went over to her bed. "What do you think *we're* doing here every day?"

"Should we include her?" Fran whispered to me.

"Why not?" I whispered back. "Come join us Mrs. Weissberg." I motioned for her to sit with us.

"Oh, thank you, dear." Mrs. Weissberg held onto Carol's steady outstretched arm and slowly moved from her bed to her wheelchair. A simple woman who was courageously tackling the aftermath of a stroke, Mrs. Weissberg had a slight double chin, a sunny smile and bright scarlet-colored cheeks.

I positioned my leg on the small therapy bench in front of me while Carol wheeled the friendly woman over to us. "I never made it to Israel myself," Mrs. Weissberg said. She was happily sitting next to Fran in her powder blue robe and matching slippers. "My son went there years ago, after college. And my daughter and her family have been there a few times," she went on. "They all told me a bit about the country. But not like what you've been saying." She looked at me.

"Well, I just want to let you know," I told Mrs. Weissberg, "some of these next stories might be a little disturbing because of the second intifada."

"Another intifada?" Fran interrupted. "As if living through the first intifada and the Gulf War wasn't bad enough."

"Whatever it is you have to tell," Mrs. Weissberg said, folding her hands in her lap, "is just fine with me."

THUNDERING SECOND INTIFADA
(September 2000)

I bolted out of bed like a scared rabbit. I'd never heard anything like it. The boom was so loud, it sounded like it was coming from our backyard.

Ten days earlier, on Rosh Hashanah, a second intifada stormed into our lives like thunder and lightning. Every peace treaty, including the most recent Oslo Accords, had failed to bring peace. And now the country was again thrown into a state of high alert. Nobody knew where or when the next attack would occur.

The loud boom in our neighborhood came an hour before the end of Yom Kippur, throwing everyone who heard it into a panic. With Arab villages all around us, I worried about the possibility of a terrorist infiltration into Or Tzion. Running down our second floor hallway to make a quick investigation out the front window, all I could think was, "Oh my G-d, they must have gotten into the *yishuv!*"[84]

From the window, I had a good view of the chaos on the street below. Mothers were grabbing their little ones and shouting for their older children to hurry into the house. Babies were crying, and kids of all ages were running in different directions, trying to quickly reach their homes.

Still not sure what caused the frightening sound or what it meant for all of us, I wished it would have happened an hour later. Yehuda and the rest of the men in the neighborhood would have been home from synagogue by then. But this was no time for wishful thinking.

I left the window and ran back down the hallway. Nearly jumping down a full flight of stairs, I made for the front door in mad pursuit of my children who were playing outside. *Thank G-d baby Eitan is safe in his bed.*

I whipped open the front door and dashed outside barefoot. I had to find my three girls. *Where are they?*

"EEmmaaa!" I didn't get far before Hadas, followed by her sisters and two of their friends, came running breathlessly towards me. "What's happening? What was that noise?" the girls blurted out at the same time when they reached my side.

"I don't know!" I exclaimed. I was resting when I heard it." Taking in their frightened faces, I motioned for the girls

---

84 Settlement town.

to continue moving towards the house. "Just c'mon. Fast!" I commanded, practically pushing them inside.

Slamming the front door shut, relief washed over me—just knowing that we were all in the house. I made a mental note to inform the two friends' families of their whereabouts as soon as possible. I didn't feel it was safe to send them home and, at the moment, there was no time for anyone to even catch their breath. Double locking the door with the latch, I called out orders to the girls.

"Quick, close and lock all the windows! And close the blinds and curtains! Somebody run and take Eitan out of his crib; he's crying!" The girls ran around the house with me, dutifully carrying out all of my orders. "Now hurry, everyone into my bedroom." I was trying to keep my tone of voice steady, hoping I didn't sound as hysterical as I felt.

Rushing all the kids up the stairs to my bedroom, doubts began to fill me. *Who really knew where it would be safest? Maybe it would be better down in the playroom where we could all climb out the window if we needed to. And what about Yehuda? What if he comes home now and needs to get inside fast. Would we even hear him knocking on the locked door from upstairs?* I had no idea which was the best place to be, or even from what we were trying to be safe. But since my bedroom was upstairs at the back of the house and farthest away from the street, I decided that would have to be where we stayed for now.

"Okay," I began, once we were all inside my room. "Now," I was trying to think of what to do next, "Everyone stay here and watch the baby for a minute while I try to find out what's going on."

Get a grip, I told myself. *You're responsible for everyone here. You have to stay calm.*

Since it was Yom Kippur, I struggled with the idea of "breaking" the holiest day of the year by calling someone for information. Who was there to call anyway? Nobody was working in any of the town's offices on Yom Kippur!

The synagogue was about three blocks away. I wondered if Yehuda had even heard the boom. *Could he be dashing home now to be with us, or were he and the others oblivious to the situation? And what exactly is the situation?*

"Look, the Azulays are all in *that* room," Yael was looking out the window and pointing to our next door neighbor's house.

I silently blessed my helpful seven-year-old and ran to open the window. "Zehava! Zehava!" I shouted over to my Moroccan Israeli neighbor, whose large round face I could see through her half-open window. "Do you have any idea what's going on?" I called out in Hebrew.

Zehava pushed the window all the way open to talk to me. "Didn't you see the soldiers outside, in front of our houses?" Zehava called back.

I nearly stopped breathing. "No, I didn't! Why are they there?"

"The Arabs must be starting up. Maybe they tried to get into the *yishuv*." Ironically, Zehava, who was normally fiery and passionate, was now almost casually assuming what I'd feared might happen one day.

Our neighborhood was on the edge of the town, with a miniature field separating us and the Arab village on the other side. Before the second intifada uprising began ten days ago, there'd always seemed to be an "understanding" about not crossing over to our side or into our community.

"I can't believe this—another intifada!"

"Shelly, is that you?" I recognized Efrat's voice suddenly calling out from the row of houses above us.

"Yes, it's me! Do you know what that loud noise was?"

"I can see from my upstairs window that the soldiers are trying to get control of the Arabs rioting across the way. Looks like a group of them were crossing the field and heading towards our neighborhood. What we heard was probably the soldiers shooting tear gas to push them back. My brother's an officer in the army and he once told me that tear gas makes a very loud noise."

I hoped Efrat was right. But who knew for sure.

"What is it, Ema? What did they tell you?" I was confronted by my daughters' young, questioning faces as I pulled my head in from the window.

"I don't know," I told them. Tear gas... soldiers in front of our house... Arabs heading towards us. I felt myself getting a little panicky. "I don't know!" My attempts to keep the atmosphere light and under control seemed to be fading. "Just stay here and play with Eitan," I instructed. "And someone ask Zehava or Efrat to pass along the message that the Cohen girls are with us. I'm going back to the other window to check on things in the front of the house."

"I want to come with you," Michal said.

"No! You have to stay here." I gently sat Michal down on the bed and then quickly bounded down the hall for the second time.

I had to see for myself what Zehava had described. I poked my head out the window where only minutes before I'd witnessed frenzied action on the street below. This time, the street was empty and quiet. Not a mother or child anywhere. Suddenly, I noticed a slight movement near our car.

There they are! Two soldiers wearing helmets and bulletproof vests over their uniforms were crouched down, one hiding behind our family station wagon and one behind the Azulay's car. They were aiming their M-16s at some invisible target. Two more soldiers were positioned at each end of the street, poised and ready for whatever or whoever might come their way.

"Oh my G-d!" I gasped. One of the soldiers by the cars looked up and motioned for me to stick my head back inside and close the window.

Could my worst fear be coming true? I envisioned terrorists heading towards us from both sides. And I was on my own with six young children! My chest tightened and my head began to pound as I closed the window, careful not to make too much noise. My fear kept me from returning to the kids in my bedroom. I really wasn't feeling like I had it together, and it wouldn't do for them to see me like this.

Running from one window to the other, I continued to check on the situation in front of the house and at the street corners. *Are the Arabs coming? Was it really only tear gas? How will I be able to protect the kids?*

The kids! I really needed to get back into that room and be there for them. All my anxious racing around had caused me to lose focus. I hurried back down the hall to my bedroom, trying to emotionally prepare myself for the role I needed to assume as the stable adult who would quiet the children's nerves. *Everything will be okay,* I told myself. *The soldiers have things under control.*

"Okay, everyone," I said, whirling into the bedroom.

"Shhh!" Yael placed her finger to her lips in a gesture to quiet her overly stimulated mother. I stopped short.

Standing with my mouth open, I suddenly felt foolish. I had expected to have to soothe the baby and help calm the girls. But instead, they were all sitting peacefully on the soft, mint green carpet, quietly reciting passages from a book of Psalms. The melodious sounds of the children's prayers filled the room, as baby Eitan, happily snuggled in Hadas' lap, bounced lightly and clapped his little hands.

Exhausted and overwhelmed, I stood still and absorbed the serene atmosphere in my room. *These kids don't need me... I need **them**.*

Awed by the small group of Israeli children, whose faith helped them understand better than I did what they should do in this time of crisis, I took a deep breath and eased my weary body down to join them on the carpet. *Things are going to be okay*, I told myself again. *Everything's going to be all right.*

This time I really believed it.

❧ CHAPTER 13 ❧

"So, was it just tear gas that caused all that commotion in the end?" Mrs. Weissberg asked with concern.

"Yeah, thank G-d it was tear gas that made that huge boom we heard," I said. "Apparently a group of Arabs were crossing the field shouting 'Allah Akbar!' That's Arabic for 'G-d, or Allah, is great' and is also used as a kind of battle cry. Since they were on their way over to our neighborhood, our soldiers had to shoot tear gas at them to get them to turn back. I guess the soldiers also positioned themselves on my street in case the tear gas wouldn't be enough of a deterrence. Thank G-d, it was."

"Man oh man," Fran muttered, shaking her head from side to side. "And, how long did this second intifada last for?"

"It was a part of our lives for about five years," I said. "But, the next story is mostly about Jerusalem."

"Great," Mrs. Weissberg said with a smile. "I've read some and heard quite a bit about Jerusalem. It's such a special place." Her eyes were twinkling as she spoke.

"That's true," I agreed. "And that's why everyone wants part or even all of it for themselves."

"But they wouldn't give away part of Jerusalem, would they?" Fran asked. "Isn't it the capital city?"

"That it is," I answered.

"So let me guess," Carol said. "We're going to hear about maybe giving away Jerusalem, right?"

"Right." I nodded. "To give or not to give. *That* was the question."

JERUSALEM IS NOT FOR SALE
(January 2001)

"This is amazing!" I cried, as we slowly made our way closer to the center of the action near Jaffa Gate. By the time Ilana and I arrived at the edge of the huge protest, nearly three hundred thousand people were already demonstrating. We weren't about to let any part of Jerusalem be given away—not for *any* kind of peace offering.

The crowds were literally covering the streets and sidewalks all around the Old City walls. Religious men and women with their children and all types of hats and yarmulkes were intermingled with bareheaded non-observant protesters of all ages and sizes. Youth from every background and every area of the country also came in droves to show their loyalty to Jerusalem.

"It looks like it's not just us usual right-wingers out here this time," Ilana pointed out. Standing on the curb in her fleece-lined coat and boots, she stretched her neck to see what was up ahead. "It's even more packed further on," she reported.

"It's a great turn out," I said, as we continued up the closed-off Jaffa Road. "The question is whether our prime minister will understand from this that the majority of the country is against dividing up Jerusalem."

"He'll get the message," Ilana said, optimistically.

"Giving away neighborhoods in Jerusalem would just be another sign of weakness on our part. And it won't bring peace."

"Everyone here is probably wondering the same thing: how could Ehud Barak or any other leader in Israel consider giving away part of Jerusalem?" I nearly bumped into an older woman, as I squeezed past a group of teenage girls and around a baby carriage. "We'd be committing suicide if the Arabs got control of any part of this city."

"Yeah, we've already got suicide bombers trying to get rid of us with this second intifada," Ilana said, following me around the carriage. "We don't need to help them along with that."

Continuing on through the crowds, we approached one of the giant video screens showing the speakers on the stage near Jaffa Gate. We stopped to watch as a man, whose family had lived in Jerusalem for many generations, began speaking emotionally into the microphone. "I came to say that no one, no one in the world—not even Mr. Barak—will give this [city] to someone else. We're saying no! We're saying that these walls belong to all the Jews of the world."

Ilana and I pressed forward with even greater difficulty, as the streets became increasingly more congested. Finally, we reached the platform by Jaffa Gate. Politicians and long-time Jerusalemites were sitting on the podium waiting to deliver their speeches. Images of Jerusalem's history were beamed onto the Old City walls. The words "Jerusalem, I pledge" were displayed on large banner signs and projected onto the huge stones. People were holding up homemade posters expressing the importance of keeping Israel and Jerusalem undivided:

"The country is not for sale."

"Jerusalem = Jewish; Mecca = Arab."

We arrived in time to watch Jerusalem Mayor Ehud

Olmert walk over to the microphone and address the ocean of people that came to show their support for a united city.

> I have never been so deeply moved as I am now to see all of you so crowded together here in the streets of Jerusalem, so excited and enthusiastic. ... This is the expression of the deep emotional link of the people of Israel to our everlasting and undivided capital. You have come from all corners of the land and even from abroad, to say, "We are here and we will remain here," because this city is the basis of our very existence in this land.

The mayor's voice reverberated throughout the streets, as well as on radios and televisions as he continued with an appeal to US President Bill Clinton:

> For the sake of the Jewish people and for the sake of the city of Jerusalem, do not be the first president in the history of America who has proposed dividing the ancient and eternal capital of the Jewish people.

The hand-clapping, flag-waving masses responded to each speaker and each impassioned speech with loud whistles and wild cheers. Then, caught up with the energized atmosphere, Ilana and I joined the three hundred thousand voices that rose up to sing the well-known Jewish psalm, "If I Forget Thee O Jerusalem."

> If I forget thee, O Jerusalem, may my right hand forget its skill.
> May my tongue cling to the roof of my mouth, if I don't remember you
> —If I don't raise Jerusalem above my greatest joy.

The song and the music flowing from the loud speakers throughout the blocks and blocks of protestors was a reminder to us and to Jews everywhere—Jerusalem isn't just another place. It's the center of Israel, the Middle East and the whole world. It's the holy city where Jews have always lived and where the two great Jewish Temples once stood on the Temple Mount. The center of Jewish faith, hope and longing, Jerusalem is where the exiled Jewish people, scattered among the nations, yearned to return to for nearly three-thousand years.

And now, standing on the same streets where our ancient Jewish ancestors once stood, we were singing our promise to always remember and to always cherish our holy city. We were pledging our permanent and lasting bond to Jerusalem, the pulsating heart of the Jewish nation.

As the demonstration came to an end and Ilana and I followed the current of people slowly moving away from the Old City walls, there was no question in my mind that no part of Israel should ever be used as a bargaining chip or be divided up for others to take—especially not Jerusalem.

❧ CHAPTER 14 ❧

"The prime minister didn't end up giving away any of Jerusalem, did he?" Fran asked with a hopeful look.

"No. Thank G-d Jerusalem was saved," I answered. "And now," I glanced at Carol and then at Fran and Mrs. Weissberg, "you're going to find out how some of our soldiers were "saved"... by four young children."

SAVING THE SOLDIERS
(April 2001)

"This one doesn't have any rice," Yael pointed to the small aluminum tray in her hand.

"I've got the pot," Hadas said. "I'll stick some rice in that one," she volunteered. The girls were helping me fill disposable food trays that we'd soon be bringing to the soldiers Or Tzion had "adopted" a few weeks ago.

It was a cold and rainy Shabbat night during the week of Passover, when hundreds of soldiers were transported to the small army base on the border of Or Tzion. The second intifada had already been going on for several months and the IDF[85] was operating at full capacity,

---

[85] Israel Defense Forces, Israel's army.

attempting to uproot and destroy terrorist cells in nearby Arab villages and self-governed towns.

Most of the families in Or Tzion had already finished their evening Shabbat meal and were preparing for sleep when scores of soldiers arrived. The army base was swamped and unequipped for such an onslaught of additional troops. Lacking sufficient accommodations and provisions on their base, herds of tired, cold and wet soldiers flocked into Or Tzion.

Residents living closest to the edge of the army base were accustomed to soldiers visiting the town's grocery store and pizza shop. But the sudden late night military infiltration into their neighborhoods took them by surprise. It wasn't clear whether it was a bureaucratic mix-up or some overwhelming emergency situation that had caused a shortage of supplies for the soldiers. Nevertheless, the bewildered Or Tzion families instantly sprang into action. Like concerned mothers, they began fussing over their unexpected "guests."

The women lost no time organizing food to be distributed among the hungry troops. They donated pillows, blankets and some of their husbands' dry clothes to replace drenched uniforms for the night. Some families invited soldiers into their homes to shower or to warm up. Though the boy's yeshivah dormitories were closed for the Passover holiday, the mayor opened it up for the soldiers to use as temporary lodging.

By morning, word got out to the rest of Or Tzion and the townspeople began walking portions of their Shabbat meals over to the "visiting" troops. With many of their own sons or brothers in the army, everyone understood how important it was to aid these young men who were far from home and serving their country. Coming throughout the day and into the next night, the families warmed the soldiers' hearts, as well as their bodies, with smiles and comforting words, winter provisions and portions of their Shabbat meals.

Within a short period of time, the army managed to provide tents for shelter, as well as other basic necessities. But, for a few weeks there remained a shortage of some food supplies.

Or Tzion's municipality continued to help in any way possible. The men's yeshivah and the girls' high school sent their extra hot lunches over to the soldiers, and the grocery stores donated cooking ingredients and various other food items. Many families drove around the army base handing out tasty home-cooked meals or freshly baked goods to any soldiers they met. Gladly giving their rations of canned and dried food a rest, the soldiers gobbled down the delicious delicacies.

"Okay. Bring the aluminum foil over here," I said to Yael, "so we can start covering up all these trays of food."

"We finished putting in the chicken and everything else," Hadas told me, "but there's still some salad left." She lifted the big bowl for me to see.

"And what about this extra gravy? Maybe we could pour it over the rice and green beans," Yael suggested.

Michal peeked into the kitchen. "How many trays are we bringing this time?"

"About twenty," I answered. As I ripped off square pieces of aluminum foil, I regarded my three daughters. Mature Hadas, now almost ten, had light skin, soft wavy hair and a jovial laugh. Always ready to join a fun activity or important mission, Hadas put her heart into everything she did. Feisty Yael, with her little dimples and cute pug nose was a charmer at the age of seven and a half. Though it frustrated her when things didn't go right, Yael was not one to give up easily. Michal, a couple months shy of six, had darker hair than her two sisters and a small round beauty mark on one side of her face. Both friendly and good-natured, Michal attracted all kinds of playmates. All three girls were now standing with me, eager to contribute to the community's most recent goodwill campaign: helping hungry soldiers.

"Let's go," I said, packing the last trays we had prepared into the trunk of the car.

"Are we bringing anyone else's food with us this time?" Hadas asked as she helped chubby-cheeked Eitan into his toddler car seat.

"On the way, we're picking up Tova Epstein, her son Noam, and her soup," I answered. Tova, who was known for her charitable deeds, lived on the next block over. Hadas beamed at the thought of Tova and Noam joining us with more good food for our beloved soldiers.

The soup sloshed around in the giant stainless steel pot as we slowly drove the two-minute ride to the army shooting range. Soldiers were often there, happy to receive whatever people brought over for them to eat while they waited for their turn at target practice.

"It's good we're bringing everything close to supper-time," Tova told all of us in the car. "The last time we came with food, the soldiers said that they hadn't eaten a proper meal all day."

"I heard that they don't have enough fresh fruits and vegetables to go around either," I added.

"Ema, we should have put fruit in with the food we're giving them," Yael said. "There's salad, but no fruit!"

"I ate the last apple in the 'frigerator," Hadas admitted, "but there are some pears and oranges left. We could have brought those."

I sighed. I also wished we could have brought more, made more... done more.

"*Chayalim!*"[86] Eitan exclaimed, as I slowly and carefully

---

[86] Soldiers!

drove the short distance down the dirt road to the back of the open shooting range. Or Tzion residents didn't normally have any reason to come to that area of the base. But we were on a mission. We were feeding hungry souls!

Tova and I each grabbed one handle of the heavy soup pot and walked it over to the clusters of uniforms waiting to hit the target. The kids followed close behind, their arms laden with containers and aluminum trays of food. Little Eitan marched along with us, carrying the soup ladle.

One soldier sitting on a large rock caught sight of the approaching "kitchen crew" and shouted to the others, "Hey, *chevreh!*[87] Over here."

Standing up, he waved his friends over to where Tova and I had set down the huge pot and were already pulling disposable bowls and silverware out of a plastic bag. All at once the soldiers were at our sides, showering us with greetings of "*Shalom!*" and "*Erev tov!*"[88] A soldier with a strong, solid build squatted down to Eitan's level and greeted him with a smile and a friendly handshake.

Yael, Michal and eight-year-old Noam began handing out the food trays filled with chicken, rice, green beans and salad. Tova ladled out the vegetable soup, while Hadas and I carefully handed the steaming bowls over to the waiting soldiers. A hearty thank you accompanied each eager pair of hands that received a bowl. "*Todah! Todah rabbah!*"[89] Just as fast as the soup and trays went out, the gratitude came in.

After we finished distributing the food, Hadas told me that she had purposely left some of the aluminum trays in the car. "I thought it would be a good idea to give them out to others on the base too," she explained. I watched the

---

[87] Guys!
[88] Good evening!
[89] Thank you very much! Thanks a lot!

soldiers energetically devouring their meals and decided that it was a good time to implement Hadas' plan.

"Let's leave the pot here for now and let these guys finish taking for themselves, while we hand out the rest of the food inside the base," I suggested. Tova and the kids agreed, ready to move on to others. We said a temporary goodbye to the group near the firing range and ran back to the car.

"*Kol hakavod*, Way to go!" one soldier called after us, waving his plastic soup spoon in the air.

"See you later!" others joined him.

"See you later!" the kids called back from the car as I slowly pulled away and began driving on through the back entrance of the army base. Almost immediately, we spotted a small uniformed group climbing aboard a tarp-covered army truck.

"Are you leaving the base now?" Tova called out the car window to a soldier with wire-rimmed glasses who was about to climb onto the truck. The light-haired young man came over to the car and explained that his group was going to the Arab town of Ramallah to help clamp down on terrorist activity in the area.

"Have you eaten supper?" I asked the soldier who carried himself with confidence, but looked young enough to still be in high school.

"No, we'll have something when we get back," he replied, "later tonight." Then he was gone, loading himself onto the back of the army truck along with the others.

My maternal instincts suddenly overwhelmed me. They'll miss supper! "Let's get those trays out of the trunk," I ordered.

"But they're already starting to go!" Yael's head was hanging out the window.

"C'mon! Fast!" I was determined. "We can't let those soldiers leave the base without food in their stomachs." *How can they function without eating properly? How can they be expected to defend the country like that?*

Tova and I whisked the trays of food out of the trunk. Within seconds, Noam and my girls were running with them after the olive green truck that was already on its way to the exit of the army base.

"Wait! Wait!" they pleaded with the soldiers riding in the vehicle's open back. I bit my lip as I watched the kids making a monumental effort to reach them before it was too late. The truck slowed, allowing the children to catch up. And then, it stopped.

"We have food for you," Noam panted, handing two foil-covered trays up to one of the soldiers in the truck.

"So you won't be hungry in Ramallah." Yael followed Noam's example.

Hadas and Michal gave over their trays too. The food was immediately passed around to everyone in the truck. Incredibly, it was the perfect number—eight trays for eight soldiers!

Starting on their way again, the soldiers waved goodbye and called out their thanks to the smiling children they were leaving behind. I watched as the army truck slowly disappeared down the road. My emotions were divided. I was worried about the boys who were driving off, but I was also thrilled that our own mission had just been successfully completed.

The elated children ran back to the car. "They would have starved if we hadn't given them all that food!" Yael exclaimed, climbing into the backseat.

"Yeah," Michal chimed in. "Now they'll be okay!"

"We saved them from who knows what," added Hadas.

Bouncing in his car seat, Eitan parroted his oldest sister. "We saved them!"

"We sure did." I slid behind the steering wheel. "And now," I glanced sideways at Tova, "they're going out there... to save us."

·❖· *CHAPTER 15* ·❖·

I THINK I CAN

(October 2002)

"G-d created the Arabs too," Michal informed Chanie, her freckle-faced friend sitting across from her at the kitchen table. "Not all of them are bad."

"But they shoot at us from across the road," Chanie reminded her.

"Right. They're not acting nicely," Michal agreed. "That's sad."

From the couch in the living room where I was sorting and folding laundry, I could hear my second-grader trying to express what I had repeatedly told my children: Not all the Arabs in Israel are against us. Many of them just want to live in peace, like we do. The problem, I had always cautioned my kids, was that one couldn't be sure who was who. "Unfortunately, we don't know who is dangerous and who isn't," I had explained. "So we need to be careful of all of them."

I found it remarkable that at the height of the fierce second intifada, Michal was able to have any positive ideas at all involving the Arabs. This uprising turned many more Arab adults, teens and even children into terrorists. In Judea, Samaria and the Gush Katif area, near Gaza, they threw rocks or shot at Jewish cars driving on the roads.

They also managed to penetrate into a kibbutz and into some settlement towns, where they took lives before escaping or losing their own lives. They'd shoot from their villages into the Jewish towns or into city neighborhoods. Blowing themselves up on buses, in restaurants, stores, event halls and public arenas, they considered themselves great martyrs of Islam and Allah.

These days, fear and anger often overwhelmed us, and yet, here was my kindhearted seven-year-old daughter trying to weed through the devastation and hold on to the idea that some Arabs weren't out to get us.

"Some of them can be our friends," Michal was saying.

"Which ones?" Chanie asked.

"The good ones. Not the ones shooting at us."

"Which ones are those?" Michal's friend sounded confused.

"Let's go play with my new dolls," Michal suggested, abruptly changing the subject.

"Okay." Chanie was just as eager to move on to other things.

I could hear the girls' chairs scraping against the floor, as they pushed themselves away from the table. Leaving the kitchen behind, they marched up the stairs to Michal's bedroom, little bounces cushioning each step.

Watching them, I thought about how my kids, in general, seemed to be less emotionally affected than I was by this second intifada. They were upset that they had to keep the special rock-proof car windows closed when going to or from Or Tzion, and that we didn't allow them to play outside after dark, until things returned to normal. They were also tired of running into the house whenever they heard shots fired from across the field. But for the most part, they were adjusting fairly well to the changes in their lives.

Yehuda was a bit more uptight than the kids, but I was

the worst. At one point during the first year and a half of the terrorism, I felt like I might lose my sanity. I had even secretly considered the idea of leaving Or Tzion and temporarily moving to Jerusalem. But I knew that would mean worrying about the possibility of a suicide bomber blowing up the bus I was riding on or the store I was shopping in somewhere in the center of the city.

I knew my friends and neighbors were also feeling stressed and nervous, but I hadn't heard of anyone talking about leaving. I had wondered if I was the only one thinking of relocating to a different area in the country.

Maybe I'm just not Israeli enough. I'd had the thought many times during the past couple of years. *Maybe I just don't have enough faith that everything will be okay.* Yehuda didn't consider leaving Or Tzion as an option either. *Maybe I'm not made of the right stuff to deal with all of this.*

But to my family in the States, I showed a different, more confident side. The side that was still completely sure about what I was doing in Israel, and why I was living in a settlement town. For them, I still had solid answers.

To my sister, who had asked, "Do you ever think about coming back, with all that's going on?" I replied, "No. This is the only place I want to live."

When my cousin had very nicely offered to have our family stay in her new beach house for a while, "just to get away from everything," I sent her an e-mail thanking her for her offer. Then, I went on to explain how important it was to remain in Israel, and especially in Or Tzion, especially during difficult times.

Slowly, as the months passed, I grew more used to the unsettling circumstances in which we were living. The second intifada was still going strong and I was still on edge, but somehow even I was managing to get through each day more calmly. When my mother warned, "Don't go to any public places," I explained to her that, of course we would be careful and would take all necessary precautions, but that there was no way we would stay home all the time and live like prisoners.

Now I looked up from the laundry when a sudden loud whirring noise came blasting through the open sliding-glass porch doors, just off the living room.

"Helicopter!" Little Eitan came scurrying toward me with his pudgy arm held high and his finger pointing up to the ceiling. A real boy in every sense, Eitan would normally have been excited to have a helicopter whirring high over our backyard. But helicopters, often searching for terrorists or terrorist activity, had become a fairly common phenomenon in our area. We heard them during the day and sometimes in the middle of the night, along with the low-flying military airplanes and periodic cannon-like booms in the distance. I knew my sweet three-year-old boy sensed correctly that the helicopters were a sign that something was wrong.

The children in the private nursery school Ilana and I had set up also reacted to the noisy helicopters. Our group of toddlers instantly stopped playing when a chopper flew over the play yard a few days ago. "Helicopter! Helicopter!" they had shouted, as they sat frozen in the sandbox with their little faces turned up to the sky. Ilana and I had quickly reassured them that everything was okay, despite our own concerns about yet another helicopter monitoring the vicinity. When the whirring grew more distant, the laughter and playing quickly resumed.

Now, Eitan also relaxed, as the helicopter went on its way. Michal and Chanie came down the stairs, each carrying a doll. "We want to play outside," Michal announced.

"Okay, but stay in the backyard," I said. In my mind, the back of the house was safer than the front, because it was bordered on three sides by other houses and was fenced in by tall, thick bushes.

My "safe behind the bushes" theory came up for the first time when my friend Penina, who was now married and living in Be'er Sheva, came for Shabbat during the summer with her husband and two children. Penina and I were drinking cold pineapple juice in the shady yard when we heard the *ra-ta-ta-ta* of gunshots in the distance.

"Is that shooting?" Penina asked, cocking her head to the side, as if it would help her hear better.

I nonchalantly took a sip of my juice before responding. "Yeah, it's shooting."

In the past, I might have been quick to react to the sound of distant gunfire, but over time, unless it was right near our house, I had come to barely notice it. It had become an almost daily event in our lives, and was just background noise to us. Anyway, this time the shots were further off.

"Well, shouldn't we go inside with the others?" Penina's eyes narrowed.

"No, it's okay. It's not close." I felt more relaxed than I had been two years ago. "And some of it might be from our own soldiers shooting back in retaliation, or from the Arabs shooting at each other. Besides," I added, "we're behind the bushes."

"Behind the bushes?" Penina raised her eyebrows at me.

I assumed Penina was wondering if I had lost my mind a little. I realized that most of us in the settlement communities were living in a different reality. It wasn't that we didn't understand the dangers involved. It was just that hiding behind parked cars while walking down the street started to become absurd. Riding in bulletproof buses, instead of in our own rock-proof cars was inconvenient and time consuming. And it just wasn't healthy to jump at every bang or boom, get hysterical everytime somebody didn't come home on time, or run into the house for cover whenever a shot from afar rang out. After a while, our need to live life as normally as possible began to take over.

I had come to realize that the most important thing was to be strong, for my kids' sakes, as well as for my own. Slowly, I was beginning to understand that I couldn't let this intifada "war," with both its physical and psychological effects, overwhelm me. I had to numb myself to some of it, which meant unconsciously becoming selective about which things I would or would not react to. After eighteen years of living in the country, I was discovering even more clearly what Israelis had already known for decades to be imperative: keep on going and keep living your life—no matter what.

I finally understood how they did just that.

"Read me a story, Ema." Eitan dropped his favorite book on my lap, *The Little Engine that Could*.

I eyed the book. It had also been one of my favorites when I was young. The little blue engine in the story wanted to help a much larger, heavier train, filled with lots of toys and food, which had broken down and needed to be pulled over the mountain. As it struggled up the steep incline, the little blue engine's positive attitude and great determination gave it the strength it needed to pull the bigger one along. Chugging and puffing as it climbed, it repeated over and over: "I think I can. I think I can. I think I can. I think I can..." Cheers and cries of joy rang out from the dolls and toys as the little blue engine made it all the way to the top of the mountain and then began pulling the other train with it over to the other side.

I added the undershirt in my hand to the piles of folded laundry spread out on the couch. Then I made some space for Eitan next to me. "Come sit over here," I told him, tousling his sandy blond hair as he scrambled up onto the couch.

Eitan sat expectantly at my side as I picked up *The Little Engine That Could* from my lap and opened it to the first page. "I'll read this to you," I told my cherub-faced boy, "for both of us."

CHAPTER 16

"Wow." Fran said quietly.

"It was a crazy time, wasn't it?" Carol's eyes were fixed on me.

"It was for a while," I said. "But along with the second intifada and other internal problems, there were always lots of good things happening too."

"I'm sure there were." Mrs. Weissberg smiled at me.

"But you know," I said, smiling back at Mrs. Weissberg, "I remember a conversation I had back then with someone who was having a hard time seeing the good around him."

Mrs. Weissberg looked sideways at me. "Did you help him with that, set him straight a bit?"

"Well, not really. But I set myself pretty straight."

Fran laughed. "Oh, go on—tell us about it. You *know* we want to hear."

SORRY, MR. SHOEMAN
(December 2002)

"Israelis are cold."

What? I couldn't believe what I was hearing. If there was one thing I hated, it was when people who lived in other parts of the world criticized Israel or Israelis. It annoyed me when they negatively compared Israel to their home culture, or looked down on the "Israeli way." For years, I'd been hearing, "Whad'ja expect? We're in Israel," or "Typical Israeli!" The belittling, holier-than-thou attitude got under my skin. I especially hated when the degrading and disparaging remarks were flippantly tossed around with no respect for all our young country had accomplished in its short existence. *Especially with all the hardships and challenges everyone's been through here.*

But now the condemnation I had just heard while shopping in the new Jerusalem mall was different. This time, the guilty party was no outsider or newcomer. He was a full-fledged, true blue-and-white Israeli denouncing his own people!

I was about to pay for a pair of shoes when I overheard the shoe salesman conversing with the cashier girl behind the counter. Since he had spoken in a voice loud enough for others to hear, I felt he'd be okay with me responding to his comment.

"I don't agree," I said quietly, pulling my credit card out of my wallet.

The young salesman turned to me in his blue jeans and grey V-neck sweater. "It's true," he insisted.

I handed my credit card to the cashier then looked back at the salesman. "One of the reasons I made *aliyah* and came to live here many years ago was because I felt exactly the opposite of what you just said."

Maybe he's become bitter or disappointed, but I haven't. Yes, there were plenty of Israelis who needed to learn how to behave better, nicer, more politely. But there were people all over the world who didn't act appropriately or even behaved downright badly. And besides, there was no doubt in my mind that in all the years I'd been living in Israel, the good experiences I'd had with Israelis outweighed the bad by far.

"Yeah, well I don't know when you came here, but

things are different now," the young man said, putting my shoes into a bag.

"Maybe so," I answered, "but I still see a lot of kindness and a lot of people helping each other."

"Well, the people you hang around with must be the only ones left who are like that."

"I don't think so," I said. Then, taking the bag with my new shoes from the counter, I shrugged at the salesman and left the store. *He's not right.* I couldn't believe as he did, that with the exception of a small minority, the general goodness of the people was disappearing or had already vanished.

As I walked through the mall, I thought about the many extraordinary people I'd met, even recently, who had contributed to my love for the country. *They definitely weren't cold or unfeeling.*

Riding up the escalator, I admitted to myself that it was true that things had changed in Israel over time, some things for the better and others for the worse. But I was feeling a little unnerved by the idea that the merit and virtue of the people I had a deep connection with for so many years were in question. I felt a sudden need to defend them.

There are so many amazing people here, I began convincing myself as I got in line at the Burger King, where Yehuda and the kids would be meeting me in a few minutes. I remembered Yehuda telling me how just recently he was in a store that didn't take credit cards. He had wanted to run to the bank and take out money, but the storekeeper was in a hurry to close up shop.

"After you withdraw the money from the bank, just slip whatever you owe me under the door," he had instructed Yehuda.

And how about when I had been clothes shopping with my girls last week and the store's computerized cash register suddenly stopped working. The fashionably dressed cashier wrote down my name and phone number, then told me I could take the new clothes home and pay the bill another day!

Moving ahead in line, my mind filled with other memories.

Last summer, Yehuda had purchased two yarmulkes at the *Kippah*[90] Man store and then accidently left them in the falafel shop down the street, where he went on his lunch break from work. He was confused when he got home that night and couldn't find them in his briefcase. About a month later, I was passing that same *kippah* store and decided to stop in to see if, by some chance, Yehuda had accidently forgotten the two yarmulkes there. I knew that even if he had, the odds were small I'd be able to get them back after all this time. Even so, I took my chances and walked into the store.

"*Shalom!*" the bald store owner said. "I've been waiting for you!" he exclaimed with a wide grin. Reaching behind him, he pulled a small, brown paper bag off the shelf and handed it to me. Two crocheted yarmulkes were inside—Yehuda's yarmulkes!

"I've been saving them up there, thinking that just maybe one day you or your husband or somebody would come by and ask me for them!" the man gushed.

I thanked the *kippah* man for holding onto Yehuda's yarmulkes, and was about to leave the store when he leaned over the counter and motioned for me to come closer.

"Do you want to know what happened with these yarmulkes?" he asked. Then, without waiting for me to respond, he began to tell the story. "Your husband apparently went to get a falafel after he left my shop. While

---

[90] Yarmulke, skullcap.

he was eating, he must have put the bag with his yarmulkes on the table and forgot it there when he left to go home.

"Well," the owner rubbed his shiny head, "another man came in after him and noticed your husband's bag, which by the way, looks just like a falafel bag. Anyway, after he finished eating, this man was about to throw your husband's bag away along with his own. And then he felt the *kippas* inside. Right away he recognized that they must have come from my store, because, as I said before, my bags are similar to falafel bags. So when the man left the shop, he turned right instead of left, and came two blocks out of his way to return these yarmulkes to me, so that I could return them to their owner! I remembered right away that it was your husband who'd bought them. So I put them on this shelf, right over here, and waited every day for someone to come by and claim them. But nobody did."

"Until now," I said, moved by the story.

"Until now!" the excited store owner's eyes were sparkling.

"Wow. Thank you so much!" I smiled at him with real appreciation.

"Don't thank me," the *kippah* man said. "Thank the falafel guy."

I smiled as I watched the girl in the royal blue Burger King shirt behind the counter throw some ketchup packets on a tray for the man at the front of the line. *Just last week, Hadas and I were waiting at a red light when the driver in the car next to us stuck his head out the window to give Hadas advice.* "You really should buckle yourself up with the shoulder belt as well as the waist belt," the man told her, rolling his r's Israeli-style each time he said *chagurah*, the Hebrew word for "belt." "It's safer that way, sweetie!" he called out as the light turned green and he drove away.

Hadas gave me a look as if to say, "What was *that* all about?"

"He's right, you know," I said, turning the corner.

"Yeah, but why should *he* care?" Hadas flicked her wrist towards her open window where the stranger had just given her safety instructions.

"He should," I answered. "And I'm glad he does."

I watched a mother and her two small children slide into a booth with their burgers and fries. *And what about that nice bus driver who helped me out when I was in such a rush? He also cared.*

I had spent my last shekels on a Jerusalem taxi that was taking me and another passenger from the center of town to the Central Bus Station. My bus back to Or Tzion was scheduled to leave in ten minutes. The taxi driver was hurrying through the traffic, trying to get me to my stop on time. Suddenly, all traffic stopped.

"No! Not a suspicious object now!" I cried. "We're almost there!"

While the mechanical robot was checking out the situation, the taxi driver said he was going to turn around and take a different, but longer route. I was afraid I wouldn't get to the bus station fast enough, especially if there was heavy traffic. *It doesn't usually take more than a few minutes for the robot to do its job.* I decided to pay the driver and get out of the cab. I planned to run like anything the remaining three blocks to the bus station, as soon as the soldiers allowed everyone to continue on their way again.

The minutes ticked on and I began to feel anxious. The sun would be setting soon and I had wanted to get back to Or Tzion while it was still daylight. With the second intifada going strong, those of us living in towns in largely Arab-populated areas, felt safer traveling to and from home before dark. But it had started to look like I would actually miss the bus that would get me home by sunset. Unless...

Tap, tap, tap. I rapped lightly on the closed, transparent door of the bus that was waiting right next to me on the street. The bus driver opened the door.

"*Shalom,*" I looked up at him. "I just spent the last of my cash on a taxi that got stopped here, turned around and then went a different way," I explained, feeling desperate. "Could I come on anyway? I have to catch a bus that's leaving the Central Bus Station in just a few minutes."

I held my breath as I waited in anticipation for an answer. The nice-looking, slightly overweight driver looked at me briefly and then nodded for me to come aboard. Breathing again, I said "*todah,*"[91] then hurried up the stairs and took the empty seat directly behind him.

Just as the door closed behind me, the robot completed its mission, determining that the suspicious object on the sidewalk ahead of us wasn't dangerous. The bus lurched forward as traffic began to move again.

"Which bus do you need to catch?" the driver asked me. Relieved to be once again heading towards my destination, I sat on the edge of my seat and leaned forward to answer him.

"The bus to Or Tzion."

"Or Tzion? We'd better hurry up and get you to the Central Bus Station!" The driver sat up straighter and gripped the huge steering wheel harder, as if he was determined to get us there faster.

As the second intifada was still affecting our lives, many people became more helpful and sympathetic towards those of us living in the settlement communities. We were often given special privileges, such as reduced fares or free admission to museums or shows and the like. There were still anti-right-wing sentiments, especially among some of

---

[91] Thank you.

the more extreme left-wing organizations, which was calling for dismantling the settlement towns altogether. But for the first time since Prime Minister Rabin's assassination, it seemed like many more Israelis were genuinely concerned for their brothers and sisters who lived "out there" on the "front lines."

"And how will you pay for *that* bus?" the bus driver asked me.

I had planned to take a minute to withdraw cash from one of the bank machines at the Central Bus Station. But now, there really was no time.

"Well..." Getting home before dark wasn't looking so realistic anymore. "I'm going to take out some money when I get to the bus station. I guess... I'll miss my bus."

"So how will you get home?"

"I'll have to take the next bus. It comes in another hour," I said. "It will be dark already, but it looks like I have no choice."

I had considered taking a city bus to the hitchhiking post and waiting there for a ride to Or Tzion. But I figured it would most likely be dark by the time I got there and caught a ride. Anyway, if I didn't have the convenience of driving in my own car, I preferred to be on a bullet-proof bus than in someone else's rock-proof car.

The driver was silent for the remaining minute it took us to reach the Central Bus Station. When the doors swung open for people to get off and others to come on, I stood to leave.

"*Todah rabbah*," I said, taking a step towards the front door.

"Wait," the driver said, reaching into his shirt pocket. "Take this." He held out his hand. "For your bus."

I looked at the coins he was offering me, but didn't take them.

"*Todah*. It's okay, I'll be fine."

"It's okay, take it." The driver reached his hand out further towards me.

People were waiting at the doorway to get on the bus. For a second I stood on the stairs, blocking the entrance and debating with myself what to do. Through the huge windshield, I could see the last person about to get on the Or Tzion bus across the street. I knew it was ready to drive off.

"Okay." I let him drop the money into my palm. *"Todah!"* I said, rushing down the stairs. *"Todah rabbah!* I won't forget this!"

Brushing past the people at the bottom, I dashed over to the other side of the street.

I reached the Or Tzion bus just as it was about to pull away from the curb. Breathing heavily, I opened my clenched fist and handed over the fare I had just accepted from the last bus driver. Inwardly, I thanked him once more. Now I would make it home in time!

The girl behind the Burger King counter was placing drinks on a tray for the family standing in front of me. *You just aren't seeing how the Israeli heart is still warm and beating.* In my mind, I was still arguing with the negative shoe salesman. *Its pulse is still there, and its blood is still flowing.*

I did agree that not everything was as it had been when I first came to the country. Outside influences, as well as inner turmoil, had affected things over the years. The close-knit unit of the Israeli population did need patching up in some areas. But no matter how hard the circumstances pulled at its strings, it was far from being unraveled. Despite our many differences, people still cared about each other and helped one another.

I turned around again and spotted my family on their way over, just in time to order.

"We're coming, Ema!" Michal and Yael were running towards me, followed by Hadas and Yehuda, who was carrying Eitan on his shoulders. Michal reached me first.

"Can I have french fries with my hamburger?" she asked, her shining eyes matching her dark, shimmery hair.

"You can have this crown." A girl not much older than Michal, who'd just gotten her tray of food in front of us, was handing Michal a colorful cardboard Burger King crown. "Or give it to your little brother. We got an extra one," she explained.

Watching Michal take the crown from the little girl, I smiled to myself. "Sorry, Mr. Shoeman."

But I wasn't, really.

CHAPTER 17

"Sorry, Mr. Shoeman," Fran clapped her hands together. "I love it!"

"That was really nice, dear," Mrs. Weissberg said, her bright red cheeks all aglow."

Carol helped me back into the bed. "I think we'll have to end now," she said, handing me my blanket. "I've got another patient to go to."

"Really?" Mrs. Weissberg's smile vanished from her face. "That's too bad." The disappointment in her usually upbeat voice wasn't lost on Carol.

"Well," Carol rested her finger on her chin, "I *could* go see if she's ready for me or not. Maybe she's not available for our session yet."

Fran, Mrs. Weissberg and I spoke among ourselves for a minute, while Carol went to check on the woman in Room 12.

"We're lucky!" Carol told us when she returned. "My next patient is sleeping. I'll give her fifteen more minutes and then I'll have to wake her up. So that's how much time we have now."

"Great!" Mrs. Weissberg clapped her hands together.

"Okay," Fran turned to me, "we're with you."

ROAD MAP AND GROWING PAINS
(June 2003)

The kids quickly put their clothes on over their bathing suits. I gathered towels, water bottles and snacks to bring with us to the swimming pool. Eitan was putting on his new blue sandals, carefully pulling the fat Velcro straps over each chubby little foot. When he finished, he jumped up. "Yay! We're going to the pool!"

It was my first time going with the kids to Or Tzion's outdoor pool that summer. The girls usually went together with friends, and Yehuda would take Eitan on Friday afternoons during men's swimming hours, after his Torah learning session. Today I decided the best way to get relief from the heat was to be around lots of cool water.

Hadas, Yael and Michal wasted no time plunging into the big pool, while I went with Eitan over to the smaller kiddie pool.

"Hi Shelly! Nice to see you here." My neighbor, Tova, gave me a cheery smile, as she waded over to me in the knee high water with her four-year-old son.

"Hi!" I was happy to see Tova. Now Eitan had a friend to play with and I had company while I watched him splash around.

Dangling our feet in the water, Tova and I sat on the edge of the pool and talked about our kids, summer vacation and the Road Map. The Road Map was the newest proposal for peace in the Middle East, promoted by the US, the UN, Russia and the European Union.

"So now we have the Quartet mapping out for us yet another way to have love and peace with our suicide-bombing cousins," I said.

"Deep down inside they're just *dying* to be doves," Tova laughed at her play on words. "All we have to do is give them major parts of our land so they can make their own country. And then we all live side by side in everlasting harmony."

I glanced at Eitan, who was waving his arms around in the water, pretending to swim. "I'll never get how other countries think they have the right to split up *our* country."

"Ema, can you come to the big pool and watch me swim?" Michal, who had come to find us, was now dripping over me in her fluorescent pink-and-turquoise-flowered bathing suit.

"Okay," I said. "I'll get Eitan and we'll be there soon."

"I can keep an eye on him for a few minutes, if you want," Tova offered.

Leaving Eitan with Tova, I followed Michal into the semi-enclosed pool area, where we were met by the strong smell of chlorine and the happy sounds of laughter and splashing. I watched from above as Michal took a deep breath and began swimming across the width of the shallow end, stopping only once to bat away the big beach ball that had landed in her path.

"Did you see?" Michal looked up at me when she reached the wall on the other side. "How was I?"

"That was great!" I bent over the water so I wouldn't have to shout too loudly above the noise. "You've really improved."

"Thanks." Michal's face broke into a big smile. "Okay, I'm going back to my friends now."

"Okay. Just remember to stay here in the shallow part of the pool," I reminded Michal. Spotting Hadas and Yael swimming and diving with their friends near the deep end, I waved to them before leaving.

As I strode past the grassy picnic area, I thought about how there was pain and sorrow in Israel but, at the same time, there was always so much fun and happiness.

At the edge of the kiddie pool, I saw Tova slowly

pulling Eitan and her son through the water with a big yellow inner tube. The boys were holding on tightly as they glided along. I stepped into the water and joined them for a few minutes. Then Tova and I returned to our perch on the side.

"So, do you think we'll survive the pressure to Road Map our way to peace?" I asked Tova.

"We've survived everything else, haven't we?" Tova swished the water around with her foot. "Look how far we've come, despite all the challenges we have here. It's actually pretty amazing."

I had to agree. Even with the never-ending complications and obstacles that Israel was constantly facing, the tough little country always persevered and pushed forward. "It's a country of struggles and also of successes," I said, helping Eitan out of the pool.

"It's a country of *miracles*," Tova replied.

I wrapped Eitan in a towel while Tova pulled a T-shirt over her son's wet bathing suit. Then, slipping the yellow inner tube onto her arm like a gigantic bracelet, Tova asked, "Do you want to join us on the grass for a picnic?"

"I've got some fruit and snacks with me," I told her. "I'll see if the girls want to come. Pick a spot and we'll meet you there."

Eitan ran a few steps ahead on our way to finding his sisters in the big pool. Stopping suddenly, he turned around and looked up at me. "Ema, what's a miracle?"

I looked back at Eitan's questioning face. "A miracle," I said, cupping his little chin in my hand, "is what we're all living—every day."

CHAPTER 18

DEAR PRESIDENT BUSH

(July 2003)

Dear President Bush,

My name is Yael. I'm a girl in the fifth grade and I live in Israel. I don't want to be rude, but I feel like you don't think about us. This peace that you are planning is not really peace for us. And if you had attacks in your country, would you be quiet and not fight back? And would you give parts of your land away to the terrorists? Would you give them the city you live in or maybe some of your towns?

Our prime minister now thinks he has to start giving away places that are next to where I live. Then there might be even more attacks here.

I really don't mean to be rude, but I know you are asking him to do this. You think that you are trying to help us. But I'm sorry, this Map plan is not help for us.

I know that you probably won't read this letter, but I really hope that whoever does will think about me and will give this to you.

Sincerely,

Yael Kaplan
From Or Tzion in Israel

·❧· CHAPTER *19* ·❧·

THE CAVE
(October 2003)

I stood staring at the first set of wide stone steps leading up to the Cave of the Patriarchs. Two Arab men were standing on the left side of the staircase smoking cigarettes. Several others were hanging around lazily passing the time.

Since it was the week long Sukkot holiday, when Jewish festivities are planned at the site of the Cave, I had expected to see other Jews in the vicinity. But no organized event or special gathering was taking place this afternoon.

"C'mon," I told Michal and Eitan, who were standing at my side, "let's catch up to Abba and the girls." Yael, Hadas and Yehuda were already going up the second set of stairs towards the massive building that towered over the small city of Hevron.

Hevron, settled in the Judean Hills just south of Jerusalem, was once the oldest thriving Jewish community, dating back to biblical times. But now, only about 600 Jews lived there amongst more than 100,000 Arabs.

I felt a little tense once we left our parked car across the street and headed for the stairs. As I was climbing them with Michal and Eitan, the bloody 1929 pogrom that had destroyed Hevron's flourishing Jewish neighborhoods flashed through my mind. It was a devastating uprising. Rioting Arabs had massacred the city's Jewish men, women and children, razed their synagogues and burned their Torah scrolls. The ruling British government at the time eventually evacuated the remaining Jews and relocated them to Jerusalem. It was only during the Six Day War in 1967 that Israel was finally able to free Hevron from Arab control.

And now we're able to come here again to this ancient burial place of our forefathers and mothers. "Do you know who's buried in this huge cave?" I asked Michal and Eitan, as we walked up the steps.

"Who?" Eitan asked.

"Adam and Eve. And Abraham, Isaac and Jacob, and their wive's Sarah, Rebecca and Leah."

"Really?" Michal was impressed.

"Uh huh. This is the second holiest place for the Jewish people, after the Temple Mount in Jerusalem. Every year, hundreds of thousands of people from all over the world come to visit here."

"Have *we* ever been here?" Eitan was curiously eyeing the massive stone structure looming above us.

"Abba and I have been to the cave a few times," I told him. "But that was many years ago, which is one of the reasons we decided to come again and bring all of you. And I think Hadas came here once on a class trip."

"I remember walking up all these stairs," Eitan said.

"You've never been here before," Michal informed her younger brother. "I don't remember any of this, and I'm eight. You're only four. So there's no way you were here if I wasn't."

"I have *too* been here before."

"No you haven't."

"Have too!"

"Have not."

I blocked out my arguing children as we reached the top, where the rest of the family was waiting near the building's entrance. "You know," I told Yehuda, out of breath, "I think the last time I was here was before we were married. I came with Liz and some others to celebrate a friend's wedding. The *chuppah*[92] was somewhere around here," I waved my hand in the air to indicate the general area. "Things looked a little different back then. But I remember that while we were all waiting for the bride to show up, some of us went inside to see the tombs."

"A wedding, here? That's pretty cool," Yael gave her approval.

"Was that the first time you'd ever been to Hevron?" Hadas asked.

"No. The first time I came to Hevron was about nineteen years ago. I was learning in Machon Ora and Malka brought us to visit one of our teachers who was living here with his wife and kids."

"There were even fewer Jews in Hevron then," Yehuda said.

"Yeah, in the neighborhood where my teacher lived, there was only a small group of Jewish families living in caravans among all the Arabs. Our soldiers had to watch over them." I paused for a second as I thought about that visit. "I remember our teacher telling us that it was an odd situation. On the one hand, the Jews needed the soldiers to protect them, but on the other hand, many of the Jews and Arabs were actually on friendly terms with each other. He said that he and his Arab neighbor used to help fix each other's cars, and that their kids played together. And his wife told us that she went on her own to buy fruits and vegetables from the Arab *shuk*."

---

[92] Wedding canopy.

"Wasn't she afraid?" Yael asked.

"I don't know," I answered truthfully. "But if she was, she obviously felt it was still very important to live here." I had a lot of respect for the Jews who had made their homes in Hevron. I knew that in recent years they'd had to take more precautions than usual because of the ongoing second intifada. But they were courageous and didn't allow themselves to give in to fear.

"Neither terrorism, nor any government policies that have made things difficult for these Jewish families over the years, have kept them away from Hevron," I told the girls.

"Right." Yehuda nodded. "And Jews keep on coming to this Cave of the Patriarchs. But did you know that Christians and Arabs throughout the centuries also claimed it as a holy place for themselves?" Yehuda was recalling what he'd learned years ago in a Jewish history class he'd taken in college. "The Byzantines and the Crusaders even made it into a church."

"Whoever *they* are," Yael made a funny face.

"And when the Muslim Mamelukes took over Hevron in the 1200s," Yehuda went on, "they made our Cave into a mosque. They banned Jews from passing the seventh step of the staircase leading to what was the main entrance at the time."

"Really?" Hadas looked surprised.

"We weren't allowed to go inside?" Michal's voice was disbelieving.

"Why the seventh step?" Yael asked.

"I don't know," Yehuda said, "but any Jew who tried to come up even one step closer was abused and beaten. Only after the 1967 war, when Israel freed Hevron from the Jordanians, could Jews go inside the Cave again to pray near the tombs of our forefathers."

Eitan tugged at my arm. "Can we go in already?"

"C'mon, let's go see how Abraham and the rest of our biblical patriarchs and matriarchs are doing," Yehuda joked, ushering everyone into the enormous building.

"Hey, what kind of cave is this?" Michal asked, taking in the painted ceilings and walls, the smooth stone-tiled floors, and the electric lights and chandeliers.

"You were probably expecting a dark, spooky place with slimy walls and bats, weren't you?" Hadas asked, wrapping her arms around herself and pretending to shudder with fear.

"This is called a cave," I told the kids, "but actually, it's the building that covers the ancient burial caves below. Obviously this isn't how it looked way back when. It's been renovated and fixed up over the years."

"Right," Yehuda said to the kids. "But don't worry. I'll protect you from any bears or lions we may find," he teased.

I noticed how quiet it was, as we walked through the wide open foyer near the entrance. I remembered other times when the place was packed. People were everywhere, praying and trying to get through the jammed passageways to reach the different rooms and ancient burial chambers. "There's hardly anyone here today," I acknowledged. "Usually lots of people come to visit during Sukkot."

"I guess everyone came on the days when there were events going on," Yehuda said. "I'm glad it's not so crowded."

We walked through the high arched corridors, stopping in each room to view the different large tombs protruding from the floor like enormous hunchbacks. Each one was covered by a thick decorative tapestry or velvet cloth. Some were housed behind walls with window-like openings.

In the first room, a mound-like tomb served as a memorial to the underground burial spot of the forefather

Abraham. Michal stood facing the structure with her sisters. "I wish Abraham and everyone else buried in this cave were still alive," she said with sincerity.

"You know how old they'd be if they were still alive?" Yael rolled her eyes at her younger sister.

"Yeah, but then they could be with all of us and could help *Am Yisrael*."[93] Michal answered.

Yehuda, who was standing behind his three daughters, jumped into the conversation. "Even though they're not alive, it's good we're able to come here and feel some kind of spiritual connection to them," he said, giving the prayer book in his hand a tap.

Yehuda and the three girls lingered for a while by Abraham's room, while I went after Eitan, who'd run ahead to the next mausoleum.

"What's that?" Eitan asked, looking through the grated opening in one of the walls surrounding Sarah's tomb.

"That's where Sarah is buried." I told him.

"Why's she in there?" Eitan asked.

"Because when a person dies they're buried. This is the spot where Abraham buried his wife, Sarah."

"When'd she die?" Eitan grabbed hold of the grate with both hands and pressed his forehead against it, trying to see further inside.

"She didn't die just now. She died many, many years ago, before any of us were born."

Eitan didn't say anything right away. Then, turning away from the tomb, he looked up at me. "How do we know her?"

"From the Torah. Sarah was married to Abraham. You learned a little bit about Abraham in pre-school right?" Eitan thought for a moment and then nodded. "Abraham

---

[93] The people of Israel.

and Sarah were the first people to believe in G-d," I explained. "Nobody else knew about G-d, except them. Everyone else prayed to idols—statues that people made out of wood or clay."

I saw Eitan was listening, so I went on. "It says in the Torah that when Sarah died, Abraham paid a lot of money to buy this cave so that he would have a good and safe place to bury her. And later on, Abraham himself was buried here. His son, Isaac, and his grandson, Jacob, were too, and so were their wives Rebecca and Leah."

"Did Abraham and Sarah tell other people about G-d?" Eitan interrupted.

"That's exactly what they did, all the time. They went from place to place telling people to get rid of their idols and to pray instead to G-d. And sometimes G-d would talk to Abraham and Sarah by putting ideas and pictures in their minds, which would help them teach others about Him."

"Really?"

"Uh huh."

Eitan looked back through the opening in the wall. "Can we talk to Sarah too?"

"That's why we're here." I squatted down closer to Eitan and looked together with him at the giant covered hump protruding up from the floor in front of us. "You know, even though Sarah died a long, long time ago," I began, "her soul is still alive. That's the part of her that thinks and feels and is close to G-d."

"Really?" Eitan said in a squeaky voice. "Where is it?"

"With G-d, and also right here."

"Here?" Eitan turned his gaze away from the tomb behind the grated opening and looked at me.

"Uh huh. But we can't see it, just like we can't see G-d."

"So, is Sarah still close to G-d?"

"Very close. And since her soul is all around us now,

we can actually ask her to help our prayers reach G-d better so they'll hopefully be answered quicker."

"Let's do it." Eitan's face lit up.

"Okay." I felt like giving him a huge bear hug. "You can go first. Close your eyes, if you want, and without talking—just by thinking and feeling with your heart, you can ask her to help you with whatever you want."

Eitan shut his eyes tightly. I waited only a moment before he opened them again. "I asked her if she could help me get a big truck and another one of those cars with a siren and a light, like the one I already have."

"Hmmm," I said. "Okay. Now it's my turn."

"Close your eyes, Ema," Eitan instructed.

Still squatting, I laid my forehead against the metal grating and obeyed. My prayers took longer to complete. I concentrated mostly on health and welfare for my family, and of course, peace for Israel. When I opened my eyes, I found Eitan staring at me.

"Did you ask Sarah to help with something?"

"I did." I stood up.

"Is she going to talk to G-d for you?"

"I hope so."

"Good!" Eitan was satisfied.

We left Sarah's room and walked back down the main corridor towards the hall where the tombs of Isaac and Rebecca were located. Hadas, Yael and Michal were sitting on a bench near the opening of the chamber waiting for Yehuda.

"Abba's inside the room there praying with some other men," Hadas told us.

"Why are they praying in there and not with these other people over here?" Michal asked me.

"Probably because this is one of the days Jews are allowed to go into the hall where Isaac and Rebecca are buried. So it's extra special to pray in there now."

"What do you mean *allowed* to go in there?" Yael asked.

"Jews are permitted to come here inside the Cave, but the Waqf still controls most of it."

"The Waqf? What's that?" Hadas asked.

"Well, a religious Muslim organization called the Waqf controls most of this building and they've made restrictions for Jews who come here. We're only allowed to go into Isaac and Rebecca's section on certain days of the year."

Yael jumped up from the bench. "You mean we're not allowed to go in there whenever we want?"

"Unfortunately, we're not. There are disagreements about if and when Jews should be able to come here to hold events or pray," I explained. We have the same kind of problems with some of our other holy places that have been overtaken too."

"Like where?" Yael asked.

"Like the Temple Mount and also Joseph's tomb. Our visiting rights are limited at those places too."

"We should do something to change that," Hadas said.

I took Yael's spot on the bench next to Hadas. "The disagreements and tensions between the Arabs and the Jews over the years have made the fight for our rights to these places very difficult," I told the girls. "And after the Oslo Accords were signed and also now, with this latest intifada, things have gotten even more heated up over this cave. So, security's been made tighter, which is good. But, unfortunately, there have also been more restrictions put on the Jews who come to visit."

"Dumb Oslo," Hadas muttered under her breath.

"Yeah," Yael said, "and dumb intifada." She gave the bench a little kick. "When's this intifada going to end already?"

"Only G-d knows," I sighed.

Yehuda came out of Isaac's Hall and walked over to us. His gait was slow and his expression looked distant, as if he was far away or lost in deep thought.

"Yay!" Eitan cheered. "Abba's here!"

"That was really something," Yehuda said quietly to me. "The atmosphere by Isaac's tomb is so intense. I haven't prayed like that in a long time. I really felt something special in there."

I was also feeling moved by our surroundings. We were so close, physically and spiritually, to the roots of our people and our heritage.

"Can we go into Jacob and Leah's room next?" Michal asked.

"Yes," Yehuda answered, switching his focus to the children. "Let's go there now."

With Eitan running ahead, we visited the rest of the chambers before leaving the building. Back outside, Yehuda and I held Eitan's hands as he jumped, one at a time, down the many steps. "Bye-bye Sarah," he said, stopping after the third step to look back and wave at the Cave behind us.

Hadas looked at her two sisters. "Race you to the bottom." Wasting no time, she quickly began running down the stairs.

Taking the challenge seriously, Yael chased after Hadas, jumping over steps on her way down. "Watch out!" she shouted, "I'm going to beat you. Remember, I just won first place in the school marathon!"

"Wait for me!" Michal cried. She was much slower than her older sisters and was already far behind them.

Yehuda, Eitan and I watched from above as the three girls whizzed down the steps in their colorful tops, jean skirts and tennis shoes, passing Arab lingerers on the way. We could hear Hadas' jovial laugh as she reached the bottom first, followed closely by Yael and then by Michal.

Descending at a slower pace, Eitan happily continued jumping down with Yehuda and me at his side. We reached an Arab man with patchy skin and bushy eyebrows sitting on a step, staring into the distance.

"*Shalom!*" Eitan said cheerily as his little blue sandals landed next to the gazing figure.

The man slowly turned his head towards our perky little boy. "*Shalom*," he replied passively, before returning to his daydreaming.

Without pausing, we continued on our way down the stairs. An army jeep was parked at the bottom towards the side. A couple of soldiers were leaning against it, casually chatting among themselves.

I turned around once more to take a last glimpse of the ancient giant building at the top of the stairs. I hoped it wouldn't be long before we came to visit again. I knew Jews would continue to celebrate weddings and other special occasions in Hevron, and especially at the Cave of the Patriarchs. *One day, we'll be free to go into every room there and every other place in our country, without being restricted or afraid.*

Waving at the soldiers, Eitan jumped off the last step. "I hope we get what we prayed for," he said, both his feet hitting the pavement at the same time.

I gave his hand a little squeeze. "So do I."

PART FIVE

June 2004—May 2006

·✤· *CHAPTER 1* ·✤·

Fran waited by my bed, as Carol helped me use the walker to make my way to the hallway and back. We passed Mrs. Weissberg, who was sleeping behind her curtain.

"She must be tired," Carol said. "She'll be sad to miss out today."

"Maybe she'll wake up at some point," I said, as we walked back slowly.

Fran had raised my bed into a sitting position. Taking a few deep breaths, I slowly positioned myself under my blanket.

"Phew." I was feeling happy that I'd actually managed to use my foot and my leg a bit.

"Congratulations!" Fran said, smiling at me.

"Keep up the good work and you'll be out of here in no time!" Carol added, setting the walker aside.

"I really hope so." I reached over and poured myself a cup of juice. My ribs were much better these days and I had been able to use the walker. Things were definitely beginning to look up.

"So what's on the agenda for us this time?" Carol asked me.

"Something that affected the whole country and will probably take a while to explain in detail," I answered.

"Sounds serious," Fran said.

"Yeah, it was. So, instead of lots of short stories,

we'll be getting into a longer, continuous story that'll probably take a few sessions."

"Okay," Carol replied. "What will we be hearing about?"

"Gush Katif and the Disengagement Plan."

"Was that something good or something bad?" Fran noticed my grim expression.

Setting my juice down, I turned to her. "That would depend on whether you were wearing orange at the time or not."

"Orange?" Carol pulled the blanket back from my leg so we could continue working.

"Yes," I answered. "Orange."

THE ORANGE CRUSADE
(June 2004-May 2005)

I never particularly liked the color orange. It always seemed so loud and ostentatious. But that was probably the very reason Gush Katif supporters chose orange to represent the campaign against Prime Minister Sharon's Disengagement Plan.

The Disengagement Plan was designed to evict nine thousand Jewish residents who were living in the southern towns of Gush Katif, near Gaza. The bloc of Jewish settlements, which shared their strip of land off the Mediterranean Sea with the Arabs of Gaza City, would be the first area Sharon would evacuate, or "disengage," from the rest of the country. Jew-free, Gush Katif would then be turned over to the Arabs as a goodwill gesture towards peace.

Ariel Sharon had spent years vigorously pushing to

build and develop the twenty-one communities in Gush Katif, as well as the many settlement towns of Judea and Samaria. Sharon had believed it crucial to have a Jewish presence in those more Arab-populated areas of the country. But now, as Israel's prime minister, the very same man who had put the Jews there, wanted to evict them.

Nobody was sure why Sharon had such a sudden change of heart. Some believed he orchestrated his famous Disengagement Plan to take the focus off the charges of corruption and illegal financial dealings that he and his two sons were facing. Others thought the stress and pressure of the times were negatively affecting Sharon's judgment. Many didn't care what the reason was for the prime minister's drastic switch in ideology. They were just hoping it would bring peace.

Both Ariel Sharon and the Disengagement Plan received great international support. The Israeli Left and some middle-of-the-roaders who believed that giving away land would help bring peace, also found Sharon's plan encouraging. But the right-wing Zionists were horrified.

"The people of Gush Katif have been suffering from daily rocket and mortar shell attacks from Gaza since the beginning of the second intifada." Nechama, my tall lawyer friend from across the street, was talking outside with some of the other women in our neighborhood. "For years, they've been living with rocks thrown at their cars and roadside shootings. Mortar shells and Kassam rockets have been landing all around them. And now, instead of getting the Arabs to stop all of that, Sharon's solution is to kick out the Jews!"

"It's crazy." Tova was shaking her head. "Gaza is the center for many terrorist organizations and those towns in the Gush are like a safety shield for the rest of the country. If the Jewish communities are evacuated, terrorists will just take over the area. They'll be even closer to

everyone in the rest of the country and will have a farther
missile-striking range. We'll be flooded with rockets,
maybe even as far north as Tel Aviv."

I was also upset about the Disengagement Plan. "Those
families in Gush Katif spent so many years settling that hot,
desolate area," I said. "They kept it in Jewish hands and
even got it to bloom."

"It won't be so simple for Sharon to expel them,"
Zehava, my heavy-set Israeli neighbor from next door told
us in Hebrew. "Even though they've been living a tough
life in the Gush, those families won't leave so easily," she
assured us. "They have a real love for the Land and a
strong resolve not to given in to terror. And their loyalty
isn't only to their communities. It's to the whole country."

"We'll have to do our best to help them now," Nechama
said, speaking for all of us.

We all joined the nationwide Orange network of Gush
Katif supporters, who did as much as possible to heighten
the people's awareness of the risks and dangers involved
in disengaging Gush Katif. In an all-out Zionist effort to
save the Gush and to stop Prime Minister Sharon's
destructive plan, they tied bright-orange ribbons to their
car mirrors and antennas, backpacks, baby carriages and
anything else visible to the public eye. They put orange
bumper stickers on their cars and held up orange banners
next to the roads or stretched them across highways with
slogans such as, "The People Are with Gush Katif" or "Jews
Don't Expel Jews!" Wearing orange bracelets, orange
T-shirts and orange caps, they stood on street corners and
in parking lots, handing out leaflets, pamphlets and CDs
explaining the arguments for saving Gush Katif. Setting up
orange information booths at fairs or by malls, they spoke
to anyone who would listen about the importance of
stopping the Disengagement... before it was too late.

As the anti-Disengagement crusade got underway, I

began to feel a strong connection to the color orange. It was no longer just another color of the rainbow. It became the voice of the Gush Katif residents, shouting out for them: "We are here! We belong here! We will not be removed!" Orange became the symbol of a heroic Zionistic struggle to stop the destruction of Jewish towns and to keep the enemy at a distance. It represented the fight for the Jewish citizens' rights to their homes, their lives and the Land. It became part of a great attempt to prevent Jews from committing a shameful crime, which had previously been carried out against the nation only by non-Jews... expulsion.

"I hope all the protests and demonstrations we're going to, and the faxes and e-mails we're sending to the politicians will make a difference," Zehava said.

"Looks like the Panim el Panim, Face to Face campaign is going strong," Tova informed us. "Lots of us are out there knocking on strangers' doors and talking about the problems of Disengagement with them. That's got to be doing something."

"Anybody planning on participating in that gigantic human chain that's being organized for next week?" Nechama asked. "It's supposed to be ninety kilometers[94] long. People are going to stand side-by-side holding hands, starting from Gush Katif in the south and reaching all the way up to the Kotel[95] in Jerusalem."

At exactly seven o'clock on the evening designated for the formation of the human chain, more than one hundred thousand people, wearing bright orange T-shirts, ribbons, bracelets and caps, joined hands across the country and sang Israel's national anthem, *Hatikvah,* in unison.

---

[94] Fifty-five miles.
[95] Western Wall—remnant of the ancient wall that surrounded the Second Temple's courtyard.

Helicopters carrying news reporters and camera crews circled overhead, photographing and filming the endless line of human orange links dotting the streets and roadsides below.

Some Israelis were moved by the many pro-Gush Katif efforts we were all making to put an end to the Disengagement Plan. But much of the population was still leading their day-to-day lives as if nothing out of the ordinary was on the verge of happening. That's when some of the "Orange populace" decided to take drastic action to shake up the apathetic public. They believed it was time for everyone to realize that a tragedy was about to occur, and that not just some, but all of the people were responsible for preventing it.

Dressed in orange and singing songs of unity, groups of teenagers and some adults gathered together in passive resistance and formed sit-ins at various intersections across the country. Traffic on the roads slowed and, in some places, even came to a halt. The Orange protesters hope was that the backed up streets and highways would force travelers to think about Gush Katif and realize that the people are not independent of each other. "Disengaging some of the nation would affect all of us, no matter who we are, or where we are," they explained, "just as blocking one intersection affects all the roads and junctions even remotely connected to it."

The road blocking technique did wake up some people to the Disengagement crisis, but it also created a lot of resentment and anger towards the Orange movement. Those late for appointments, work, school and other scheduled events were furious and frustrated over the traffic jams and standstills.

Not all Gush Katif supporters agreed with blocking intersections. But those who did were not deterred by the strong negative reactions they received. Their mission was to get a response, any response, from those who were being passive or uninterested in what was happening.

Droves of police and soldiers were sent to clear the intersections and restore normalcy for drivers. As they did their job, they indiscriminately arrested people who were anywhere in the vicinity of a road being blocked.

"They're grabbing anyone who's wearing orange, looks religious or seems like a right winger," Nechama told me on the phone. "They're even taking minors and throwing them in jail. You don't have to be a lawyer, like me, to know that that's not okay. Even innocent bystanders are fair game. My friend's son was just passing by with his bicycle and they arrested him."

Zehava's teenage son, Aryeh, was also arrested. Zehava was beside herself. "He was participating in a road block sit-in at an intersection in Jerusalem," she told me when I came over to borrow a couple of eggs. "He's only fifteen, but the police took him and many other young protesters and put them all in jail! He can get out if we pay thousands of shekels for bail and if he signs an agreement saying that he won't go anywhere near Gush Katif or to any future demonstrations or protests."

"One of Efrat's daughters is also in jail," I told Zehava. "Efrat told me that the younger prisoners are bonding and keeping up their morale. They're singing, telling each other stories, learning and praying together in their cells."

"They're idealists, these kids. Their spirit won't be broken so easily," Zehava said, handing me two large eggs. "But none of us are very happy about all of this," she admitted. "The Honenu organization's pro bono lawyers are overloaded with calls for assistance. They're working day and night trying to help all of us parents with the legal aspects involved."

Many came out against the demonstrators, with the media taking its usual anti-right wing stance and striking out against the Zionist pro-Gush Katif population. This time, some of the Orange communities even became split about the road-blocking approach. Yehuda and I also wondered if all the negative reactions and massive police arrests weren't detrimental to the cause.

"Maybe it's just backfiring," Yehuda said.

"Something major needed to be done, but this could just be bringing on more problems," I agreed.

Fourteen-year-old Hadas, on the other hand, felt we were being lukewarm about a burning issue. "It's the only thing we're doing that shows everyone that we're serious and that we won't back down about stopping the Disengagement." She looked me in the eye. "Let them be mad. We're also mad! Why don't they care about Gush Katif?"

Hadas wanted to do whatever she could for the families in the Gush, and for her country's safety. She and her friends didn't care if other people were unhappy about it. What mattered was that they were trying to accomplish something vital for the greater good.

At the next scheduled Jerusalem sit-in, Hadas put on her bright orange Gush Katif cap and T-shirt, tied orange ribbons to her backpack and joined the others on the sun-baked asphalt. Neither the threat of being arrested, nor our concerns for her well-being, kept her away. It seemed that most of the orange Zionist youth felt the same. Dedicated to their country and devoted to what they believed was best for their people, they were determined to do whatever it took to make things right.

Thinking about Hadas and her friends in orange rushing to catch the bus to Jerusalem that morning, I sighed. *How could anyone fight that?*

"Somewhere in the middle of all of our Orange anti-Disengagement efforts, something happened that's worth noting," I told Fran and Carol.

"What happened?" Carol asked.

"Someone left our world," I answered vaguely.

"Someone left your world?" Fran looked puzzled. "Who?"

GOODBYE, ARAFAT

(November 2004)

"Arafat is dead!" Yael burst into the house. "Ema!" Yael called out, dropping her backpack on the floor. I quickly emerged from the laundry room with a basket of clean clothes to be folded. "Ema! Did you hear? Yasser Arafat is dead!" Yael didn't give me a chance to respond. "Everyone in school is talking about it! Someone's parents heard on the news in the morning, and then our teacher told us it was true!"

"H-e-l-l-o!" Hadas came in through the still open front door. "Ema, do you know already?" She dropped her backpack on the floor next to Yael's. "Arafat is *dead!* Isn't that great?" Hadas' face was beaming and her cheeks were rosier than usual.

I'd heard the news, but wasn't quite as enthusiastic as

my girls. The former PLO chief had been sick for a while and many had speculated that he would probably die soon. Now the new concern for Israelis was the possibility that whoever took his place might be even more evil. The sadistic Hamas terrorist group was ready to put up a bloody fight with Arafat's PLO Fatah organization for control over the terrorist regime in the country. *Worse than Arafat.* I shuddered at the idea.

Nonetheless, I shared my girls' excitement over his death. Normally, I wouldn't rejoice about someone dying, but during the past forty years, Yasser Arafat was responsible for orchestrating thousands of malicious, fatal attacks in Israel and other parts of the world.

"Arafat was evil." Yael wrinkled her nose in disgust.

"Yeah. And can you imagine, he actually won a prize for *peace*?" Hadas practically spat out the last three words.

"The Nobel Peace Prize," I said.

"He won a peace prize?" Yael's eyes were nearly popping out.

I recalled having the same reaction back in 1994 when I'd heard about the Nobel Peace Prize going to Yasser Arafat, along with Israeli Prime Minister Yitzhak Rabin and Foreign Minister Shimon Peres for their role in the Oslo peace agreements.

"Tell me it isn't true, Ema!" eleven-year-old Yael was standing next to me in her light blue windbreaker with a disturbed look on her face.

As far as I was concerned, Yael's shock and dismay were justified. "It's true," I admitted, putting down the basket of clothes.

The front door was pushed open wider as Michal walked in holding Eitan's hand. "Hi! Hey, Ema, did you know that..."

"She knows," Yael informed her sister.

Michal closed the door, dropped her backpack on the

floor and walked over to me. "You know about Yasser Arafat?" she asked.

"Who's Yassa Airfat?" Being only five, Eitan hadn't heard anything about the death in his kindergarten.

"A really terrible person who..."

I shot Yael a look that said be careful what you say around your little brother.

"...won the Nobel Peace Prize," Yael tactfully finished her sentence.

Eitan looked confused.

"Really?" Michal knitted her brow. "Arafat won a peace prize, Ema?"

I frowned and nodded my head.

"I don't understand," Michal said.

"Yeah. It's crazy," Yael interjected. "And by the way," she added, putting her hands on her hips, "*where's* the peace?"

I stood before my children and shrugged helplessly. I didn't know how to explain to them what I, myself, couldn't even begin to understand. "The world is pretty mixed up these days."

"Pretty mixed up?" Hadas' voice rose in pitch. "I'd say *really* mixed up! And look what might happen with Gush Katif if Sharon gets his way with the Disengagement Plan."

"You're right," I agreed with Hadas.

"But it's good that Yasser Arafat is dead," Yael reassured us.

"Does that mean there won't be an engagement?" Eitan was playing with the Orange ribbon attached to the strap of his little backpack.

"Hmmm." I could feel the girls looking intently at me, waiting for an answer. "I don't know what will be with the Disengagement," I admitted. "We'll just have to see what happens."

"So could we have lunch now?" Michal asked.

"Yeah, let's eat lunch!" Eitan twirled around with his backpack, the Orange ribbon streaming out behind him.

"Put away your things and wash your hands first," I instructed, leaving the unfolded laundry and heading into the kitchen.

"If Airfat's dead, that means *he* won't be eating lunch today, right?" From the kitchen I could hear Eitan talking as he hung his backpack on the low hook in the closet.

"Right," Hadas, who was closest to him, answered. "No more lunches for Arafat."

"No more breakfasts, no more suppers—no more nothing for Arafat." Yael grabbed her backpack off the floor and threw it into the closet with the others, slamming the door shut afterwards. "Goodbye, Arafat."

Setting the lunch makings on the counter, I gazed out the kitchen window and echoed Yael's sentiments. "Goodbye Arafat. And good riddance."

·❖· CHAPTER 3 ·❖·

"Goodbye, Arafat? What happened, I missed some stories?" Mrs. Weissberg woke up.

Fran went over to her bed. "Yasser Arafat died," she said, pulling Mrs. Weissberg's curtain all the way open. "We had to start without you. We only have a limited amount of time each day."

"Shelly's started telling us about the Disengagement Plan and Gush Katif," Carol informed her. "Arafat died around that time too."

"Sorry, Mrs. Weissberg." I felt badly that she missed the first part.

"But at least you woke up now." Fran smiled at the elderly woman, as she helped her into her bathrobe.

"This is a good time for a short break," Carol announced. "While Fran helps Mrs. Weissberg get ready and brings her over here, I'll help Shelly move over to the chair."

"I read something in the news about Gush Katif some years back," Mrs. Weissberg told me when we were all settled in our places. "But I don't remember so well what it was all about. My daughter, Diana, would know. She's more up on the news in Israel. She's supposed to come visit me again tomorrow. If it's around this time, maybe she'll be interested in joining us for a little while."

"No problem." I let Carol prop my leg up on the therapy bench.

"Okay. So is it back to the Disengagement or on to something else?" Fran asked.

"The plan to disengage Gush Katif and some settlement towns in northern Samaria occupied our lives for a while," I said. "It even haunted us in our sleep."

NIGHTMARE AND TEETH
(July 2005)

"Ema! The bulldozers are breaking up everything! I can see them from my bedroom window. It looks like they're ripping apart the whole town! *Ema, Hurry!* Our house is next!" Rolling over onto my side, I unconsciously smashed my pillow over my head.

"Ema, hurry!" Yael was knocking on the half-opened door, waking me out of my nightmare. "Your alarm didn't go off and it's so late!"

Slowly opening my eyes, the bulldozers and my bad dream faded away.

"Eeema."

"What?" I bolted up in bed.

"Abba told me to wake you up." Yael, now almost twelve, was watching me from the doorway. "We have to get going," she persisted.

"We have to stop all of this!" I cried, still half asleep.

"What are you talking about? We don't have to stop anything, Ema. We have to get started. We have to get going! We all woke up late and it will take us a long time to get there." Yael glanced at my rigid form sitting straight up and was satisfied that I was now fully awake. "I'm going to get dressed," she announced, turning from the doorway.

"Oh my G-d," I groaned, sliding back down under my blanket. I couldn't shake my sleepiness or my nightmare. *Everything was so real.* Closing my eyes again, I tried to blot out the terrible feelings that were still lingering.

In my dream, Or Tzion was being destroyed. The people were being forced to leave, while the Israeli bulldozer drivers tore apart the community in a frenzy. The eager terrorists, who would soon be inheriting the abandoned area, could no longer wait on the sidelines. They swarmed into the settlement town and began taking over. But as I drifted back into reality, it was the dark, sinister smiles plastered on the faces of the Jewish bulldozer drivers that remained clear in my mind.

"Hi, Ema. Are you up?" Now Hadas was leaning her head into the bedroom.

"Yes," I managed to reply weakly, "I'm up." But really, I felt down. The despair and sorrow that had accompanied me before I was jolted out of my sleep crept into every part of my body, refusing to leave. My mind was still filled with images of devastation and ruin, and my heart felt crushed.

In the twenty years that I had lived in Israel, I had never imagined the country would be faced with such a threatening and worrisome situation as I had just dreamed. I knew my nightmare, riddled with fears of expulsion and submission to terrorism, reflected the reality of the day. *How did things get so out of hand?*

I glanced at the clock on the nightstand. It was already after eight o'clock. We were driving south that morning to Gush Katif. There were only a few weeks left before Sharon's Disengagement Plan was to be implemented, and we wanted to spend some time there before its possible destruction.

I wished we could have joined the thousands of others from around the country who temporarily moved to the Gush to support the residents and to protest the Disengagement. But I had given birth to our fifth child, Ronit, several months earlier, and Yehuda couldn't leave his job for any length of time. So we settled for showing our solidarity by renting a guest apartment for the weekend in Neve Dekalim, the largest of the twenty-one Gush Katif settlement towns.

Staring up at the white ceiling in my room, I remembered driving down to the Gush with Yehuda and the girls years ago. Hadas and Yael were very young, and Michal was just a baby at the time. We had gone to a secluded part of the beach, where we spent the day enjoying the sun, the sand and the shallow part of the sea near the shore. *It was so clean and beautiful and peaceful.* I couldn't believe anyone would want to give it up.

Yael peeked once more into my room and realized that I had barely moved. "Ema, c'mon," she pleaded. "We want to get there already." Dressed and wearing dangling silver earrings, Yael remained standing in the doorway.

"Okay," I said. "I'm getting up."

It was Friday. Yael was right. If I continued to lie around in bed like a zombie, we would get to Gush Katif too late to do much of anything before Shabbat came in at nightfall. Slowly, I pulled myself out of bed. Satisfied that I was really up this time, Yael left me to finish getting ready.

As I washed and dressed, I thought about how the settlement towns of Judea and Samaria might be next on the chopping block if Sharon succeeded in evacuating Gush Katif. Or Tzion would be no exception.

What kind of peace could this unilateral Disengagement Plan bring? Adding a small-rimmed white hat to my cool summer top and light-weight skirt, I couldn't fathom how erasing Gush Katif from the map and allowing it to become another terrorist breeding ground would bring about anything good. *It's even been in the news that the army has warned against giving away the Gush because it would compromise the country's security.*

"What should we put in the sandwiches, peanut butter and jelly or cheese?" Yehuda asked me.

I'd been so engrossed in my thoughts I hadn't heard him come into the room. "Oh." I turned to face Yehuda. "Peanut butter and jelly's good. And there are some cucumber and carrot sticks that I cut up last night in the fridge."

Yehuda stroked his trimmed, slightly greying beard for a moment and then changed the topic. "I was just listening to the radio. The Arabs are growing more ecstatic all the time about the possibility of getting their hands on Gush Katif. They're dying to take over the whole Gaza Strip. And they're calling Sharon's plan a victory for themselves."

I grimaced.

Yehuda shifted his gaze downward. "This whole thing doesn't make sense," he said. "But," he looked up, before turning to leave, "there's still hope."

I sat down on the edge of the bed. As I stared at the carpet, voices of the many people over the years who had tried to warn me away from living in Israel danced around in my head. I knew some people probably thought I was a little crazy for making *aliyah*. But I believed in the vision—the dream and the hope of a strong, healthy, thriving and secure Jewish country that successfully countered the anti-Semitism of the world, without fear of condemnation from outsiders. I knew that despite its many problems, Israel was a solution to the hate that was out there for the Jewish people.

Still, so many times I'd been asked, "Wouldn't it be better for you to live somewhere safer or less troubled?" I didn't believe there was somewhere safer. The world was a mess. Every place had its own dangers and risks. Terrorism and anti-Semitism were on the rise everywhere. And I knew that even during wars or intifadas, G-d was always watching over Israel.

Five-month-old Ronit's sudden cries from her crib got me moving. Heading down the hall towards her bedroom, I thought about how many times over the years I'd been requested to "consider coming back home, or at least back to the United States where you belong." But I'd always stood my ground and insisted that there was no better place for me or my family. Israel was where we, as Jews, were meant to be. Israel was where we belonged. And for me, there was no "coming back home," because in Israel, I *was* home.

"What cutie?" I smiled at my daughter's angelic, tear-stained face staring up at me from behind her crib bars. "You want to come out? You don't need to cry. Ema's here."

Ronit's pout immediately transformed into a giggle as she excitedly rolled her pudgy little body around on the pink kitty cat sheet. "We need to get you dressed," I said, picking my curly-topped baby up out of the bed. "Today we're going for a long ride in the car down to Gush Katif." Ronit squirmed as I set her down on the pad and began changing her diaper. Then, slipping a pink, one-piece outfit over her chubby legs, I continued my one-sided conversation. "We'll be spending the next couple of days in that beautiful place, helping give the people who live there some support. And you, little girl," I gave Ronit's tummy a gentle poke, "are coming along with us."

"Hi Ema," Eitan, came into the room wearing a pair of shorts and his race car pajama top.

"Hi, sweetie," I answered, glancing his way. "I see you've managed to get yourself half-ready. You need some help with the rest of your clothes?"

"No thanks. I'm going to be six. I don't need help getting dressed." Eitan quickly whisked the pajama top off his head.

"Glad to see it." I brushed Ronit's little curls. "Better hurry and finish up. It's going to take us a while to get there and we have to leave very soon.

"Ema?" Eitan came closer.

I looked at him from the corner of my eye.

"Do the people in Gush Katif have Arabs that don't like them too?"

I stopped brushing Ronit's hair and turned to face my wide-eyed little boy. Although he was young, he understood a lot about the world in which we lived. The second intifada had been a part of Eitan's life in one way or another since he was himself a baby.

"Yes," I answered Eitan, "these days there are Arabs that don't like the Jews in Gush Katif either."

"Oh," Eitan said. "And they want them to go someplace else?"

"It looks that way." I hesitated to say more to my curious son, who had already overheard lots of talk about the Disengagement.

"Will they want us to go away from here too?"

I put Ronit down on the carpet with a toy and then hugged Eitan. "Don't worry. We're not going anywhere." I hoped that was really true.

Putting on his T-shirt with the green turtle decal, Eitan slapped a little green and blue yarmulke on his head. "*Our* Arabs like to have loud prayers and loud wedding music in the middle of the night. But I don't wake up from that anymore."

"That's good." I put some diapers and other baby paraphernalia into an overnight bag and zipped it shut before turning back to Eitan. He was now kneeling down on the carpet, tickling his baby sister under her chin. I smiled as I watched my two youngest having fun laughing together. Then, I wondered about the Gush Katif children. *How much longer would **they** be laughing?* There were only a few weeks to go before they might be evicted from their homes.

I hoped that the thousands of Orange teens and Orange families that had moved in solidarity down to the Gush for the summer would be able to give the people there encouragement and help prevent the expulsion. Sacrificing their vacation months, they volunteered to live in cramped conditions among the residents. They camped out in tents or in sleeping bags on the beaches and public lawns, backyards and crowded houses. Their goal was to temporarily settle as many people as possible in Gush Katif in order to make it more difficult for the evacuation forces to carry out their orders.

Hadas begged Yehuda and me to let her join the others. "It will only be for a short time," she said. "I want to be there too. A lot of my friends are going, and some are already there. I don't care if there are Kassams. Nothing's going to happen to any of us."

Though we wouldn't allow Hadas to go to Gush Katif on her own and we hadn't temporarily moved there, Yehuda and I thought it was important to at least visit whenever possible during this crucial time. We knew a mortar shell or Kassam rocket might be shot over from Gaza while we were there, but that wouldn't keep us or the thousands of other supporters away. Besides, we were already used to facing dangers in our own area.

Eitan stopped tickling Ronit. Now he was squeaking a rubber mouse for her.

"Okay." I slipped the wide strap of the red canvas overnight bag onto my shoulder and picked up Ronit. "Let's go downstairs and see how we can help the others get things ready, so we can be on our way."

"Yay!" Eitan threw the mouse down hard, causing it to squeak one last time.

"Oh, but first," I told Eitan, "you need to go wash up and brush your teeth."

"Oof! Do I have to?" Eitan followed me to the shiny wooden staircase. "I don't want to brush my teeth. Can I not do that, just for today?"

I turned around with Ronit on my hip. "You know, you're really lucky," I told my begging first grader. "Do you know why?"

Eitan shook his head. "Why?"

"Because G-d gave you beautiful, healthy and strong teeth. And you may not realize it, but when He gives you something valuable, it's a gift to be cherished." I bent down a little to get closer to Eitan. "So it's your job to make sure that you do your very best to take good care of that gift. You don't want to treat your teeth badly. And you certainly don't want them to be pulled out of your mouth."

Eitan wrinkled his forehead in confusion.

"You can't forget about them or act like you don't have to be responsible for them. You need them. They are an important part of you." I paused to let things sink into Eitan's young brain. "So you know what *that* means, don't you?"

"What?"

"You have to go brush your teeth."

"A-l-l-l right," Eitan moaned. "But do I have to do it right now?"

"Of course, right now."

"Okay." Eitan turned around and ran back down the hallway towards the bathroom.

I started down the steps with Ronit and the canvas bag.

"Ema?" I could hear the water running hard from the bathroom faucet above us.

"Yes, Eitan?" I stopped at the landing and tilted my head back.

"When I'm done, should I pack my toothbrush so I can brush my teeth while we're there?"

I smiled to myself. "Yes, cutie," I called up the stairs. "And the toothpaste too."

If only everyone learned so quickly.

·❧· CHAPTER 4 ·❧·

OUT OF SORTS

(July 2005)

I stuck the kids' sunhats that I'd grabbed from the closet into a plastic bag and hung them on the handle of the front door. Then spotting Michal still eating her breakfast in the kitchen, I went in to hurry her along.

Are you almost done?" I asked her. "We need to leave now."

"That's what *we've* been saying." Yael bounced down the wooden staircase. "C'mon Michal," she signaled to her younger sister. "Everyone's waiting outside."

"You know what I was thinking, Ema?" Michal said, getting up to throw her banana peel in the garbage. "I was thinking that we need more Jews to come and live in Israel. Then there'd be more people trying to help keep Gush Katif."

"You're right. The more of us that are here, the better it is for all of us."

"Good thing *we're* here, right?" Michal gave me a smile and then went to join the family by the car.

Right, I said to myself, as I began filling up the water bottles we were taking with us. Although I sometimes got upset or angry about what went on in the country, I loved

Israel. And despite the difficult and frustrating times we were in, I knew that the best thing that had ever happened to me was that I'd made *aliyah. Good thing.*

"Okay." Yehuda came back into the house. He was dressed in a short-sleeved shirt and khaki pants. "The trunk's pretty much packed up and I just strapped Ronit into her car seat. Are you ready?"

"Yep, I'm coming." I picked up my purse, the water bottles and Ronit's diaper bag and then set them back down again. "We didn't lock up the house."

Yehuda went to the staircase. "I'll do the upstairs and you can start down here."

I made an annoyed face as I began locking up windows. It had never been necessary to close up the house so tightly until the second intifada. In fact, during the day we usually left the windows open and the doors unlocked, even when we went out for a short while. There was little reason to worry about break-ins or burglaries from the few thousand Jewish residents in our town.

But the second intifada had changed that. With the possibility of terrorist infiltrations, many communities began taking safety measures they hadn't previously needed. Security officials also advised residents to lock their houses as long as the second intifada was still going on.

When we finished locking up, I followed Yehuda out of the house. Turning the key in the front door, I wondered again how things would turn out. Would the second intifada ever come to an end? Would they expel the people in Gush Katif?

I walked slowly down our cobblestone pathway towards the street and then stood quietly next to the car for a moment. I wished we were going to Gush Katif for enjoyment and not because it might be the last chance for us to ever step foot on the soil there again.

"What's wrong with Ema today?" I heard Yael ask her siblings who were in the car with her.

"Who knows," Hadas shrugged. "Lately she gets like this after she listens to the news."

"Well she didn't listen to any news this morning, and look how long it took her to get ready," Yael replied.

"Ema?" Hadas was leaning over Eitan and calling out the window. "Are you coming?"

Without a word, I opened the car door and slid into the front passenger's seat. Pulling the seat belt over my shoulder, I buckled myself in. "Yep," I said, looking straight ahead out the front windshield. "Let's go."

"Okay. We're off," Yehuda maneuvered the silver station wagon out of its parking space.

"Can you turn on the radio so we can hear music?" Michal asked.

"No, I want a story tape," Eitan said.

"If you put anything on now, keep it low. I want to listen to my Discman," Hadas said, the thin, miniature earphone cords dangling from her ears.

"Why don't we all just sing and tell stories," Yehuda joked.

"No way! I think I'll get out now," Yael cried.

I looked back at the children just in time to see Ronit's lips pucker and then open wide, emitting a loud wail.

"What's she crying about?" Michal called over the wails from her seat in the far back.

Hadas pacified her baby sister with a bottle I handed her. "She fell asleep while we were waiting for Ema, and you guys just woke her up with your arguing. Maybe if you'd all be quieter, she'd go back to sleep and I could hear my CDs."

"Well, you're not the only one in the car, you know," Yael reminded her older sister.

"We brought tapes so we could hear stories," Eitan

chimed in. "I want to hear one now."

"No! No stories now. They're boring," Michal interjected. I asked for the radio first."

Still looking forward, I inhaled deeply. We hadn't even gotten out of Or Tzion and the Kaplan family dynamics were already in full play. As we drove out onto the main road, I knew that, for many reasons, this trip to Gush Katif would be unforgettable.

"I can picture that last scene with the kids in the car," Carol said. I only have two, not five, but when they were younger, they would also argue and fight with each other."

"My daughter, Diana, has three little ones," Mrs. Weissberg got into the conversation. "They can be a handful. But I can understand kids getting impatient or restless, especially on long car trips," she said in an affectionate, grandmotherly way.

"And it sounds like you guys were going on a pretty long drive." Fran nodded towards me.

"Down to Gush Katif," Carol said, patting my leg to remind me to continue with my exercises and to get back into the story.

"Right," I began both activities again. "Down to Gush Katif..."

GUSH KATIF
(July 2005)

My eyes opened just as we were approaching the Kissufim junction checkpoint, a short distance from Gush Katif.

"I can't believe it," I said groggily. "I slept so long!"

"You did," Yehuda agreed. "We're almost there," he

announced loudly for the sake of anyone else who might have dozed off along the way.

"Yay!" Eitan exclaimed.

"Finally," Hadas said, stretching her arms.

It wasn't just the glorious beaches or magnificent synagogues. It wasn't just the beautiful homes and gardens or meticulously landscaped public grounds that made us fall in love with Gush Katif. It was the fantastic playgrounds and the incredible zoo. It was the way the flowers, trees, bushes, grass and vegetables grew up right out of the sand. It was the warmth and openness of the people who lived there. It was the courage and unrelenting faith that filled the air. It was how the residents bravely continued to live their everyday lives, despite the daily mortar shells and Kassam rocket attacks... and despite the imminent threat of expulsion.

"Why don't all of you leave your things by the car and come in the house for a cold drink," Tzippy suggested to Yehuda when he knocked on the door to say we had arrived. We were renting the small upstairs apartment from Tzippy and her husband, Eli, for our short visit in Neve Dekalim. We hadn't any idea just how hot the midday southern sun would be, and we were already perspiring just from unloading the car.

The kids and I eagerly followed Yehuda into Tzippy and Eli's air-conditioned home. The Yemenite-Israeli couple had built their red-roofed, two-story house in Neve Dekalim twenty five years ago. As we all gathered around the large elegant dining room table, Tzippy's teenage son set down a pitcher of cold apple juice. His younger sister brought some plastic cups.

"*B'vakashah*, please, help yourselves," Tzippy said in a gentle voice, as she poured juice for us, their latest guests.

I watched Tzippy as she spoke. "My husband and my two older daughters are upstairs right now getting the apartment ready for you." Her smooth, golden-brown face glowed, but her eyes looked tired. "There's a separate staircase and entrance around the side of the house, so you'll have privacy," she went on. "After you go up and look around the place, let us know if there's anything special you need."

Yehuda asked Tzippy about Neve Dekalim and the neighboring communities all around it. We remembered that the settlement Ganei Tal was where Tova's married daughter lived with her husband and baby. And we knew that a couple of families from our neighborhood in Or Tzion had temporarily moved to one of the smaller towns, called Shirat Hayam. Tzippy told us how each one of the twenty-one Gush Katif communities was unique in some way. She spoke pleasantly, but I sensed a tension beneath her hospitable manner.

While Yehuda asked Tzippy a few more questions, I let my eyes roam around the house. It was large and roomy. Everything seemed to be orderly and in its place. I wondered if Tzippy and her family had already finished their pre-Shabbat cleanup or if they were just immaculate by nature.

From my chair, I could see part of the shiny beige Formica cupboards and matching patterned wall tiles in the kitchen. To our right was the polished wooden staircase that complemented the glossy wooden dining room furniture. Knick knacks filled small shelves, and pictures of all sizes hung on the walls.

A large brightly-colored painting depicting the ancient, gilded Temple in Jerusalem, surrounded by all the traditional fruits of Israel, caught my attention. A special prayer in Hebrew, calling for Jews to come and settle the Land of Israel, was inscribed on it. The irony wasn't lost on me.

I turned away from the painting as Tzippy's husband Eli

and the rest of their children came to join us. Eli was of medium height, had a dark complexion and wore a crocheted yarmulke and silver-framed glasses. Shaking hands with Yehuda, he welcomed all of us to Neve Dekalim.

We spoke with Eli and Tzippy for a few more minutes. Nobody brought up the topic of what the near future might bring. We all knew how hard the Gush Katif families were praying and hoping that it would be the Disengagement Plan that would somehow be destroyed and not their homes and their lives.

As we carried Ronit and our belongings upstairs to the small apartment, I wished we had more than two days to spend in the Gush. Though we'd come to show our support, we also wanted to bring the place back with us in our hearts and in our memories, just in case. We wanted to take in everything, to internalize whatever we saw, whoever we spoke to and wherever we went.

At the beach, with Ronit playing next to me in her carriage, I dug my toes into the golden granules of sand and watched my girls jumping the clear blue waves. Yehuda and Eitan were further down the shore, swimming and making sand castles in the area set aside for the men and boys. I knew that not too far away, somewhere along the beach, tents were set up as temporary housing for some of the thousands of people who had spontaneously added themselves to the already existing population. The old abandoned beach hotel was now also filled with volunteers who would be staying there as long as there was still the danger of evacuation.

The once quiet, almost neglected cluster of Gush Katif settlements had suddenly turned into a dynamic center of activity. Even the media, both Israeli and international, had planted themselves in the various towns to report on the day-to-day developments, and to wait for the event that Sharon had promised.

"Why didn't we move here for the summer too?" the kids asked more than once since we'd arrived.

"They need us here, don't they?" Michal asked again that night as we sat around the Shabbat table on the balcony outside the small apartment.

"Yes, they do," Hadas quickly answered before Yehuda or I had the chance. "We *should* move here, at least to help... if the day comes."

"Maybe there won't be *the* day," Yael was hopeful.

"Let's move here, PLEASE," Michal begged.

"It's just not possible for us to stay here now," Yehuda answered. "But we're doing our best to help fight the Disengagement from the outside."

"C'mon, let's finish eating and go walk around," Yael said, changing the subject. "I want to see as much as possible while we're here."

Strolling through the streets of Neve Dekalim that calm Friday night, we wondered about all the townspeople, especially the teenagers who were out mingling with their friends. How were they managing with the idea of this possibly being one of the last Shabbat evenings they'd be spending in the neighborhood where they grew up, on the street where they hung out, in the houses that had always been their homes? Were they discussing among themselves how badly they would feel if it was all taken away from them and destroyed, or were they just focusing on the here and now—treasuring every moment of what might be their last days together?

"Look at that slide!" Eitan's whole body was electrified as he pointed to the gigantic contraption that reached high up to the sky in the middle of the park just up ahead. "It's huge!"

The girls ran after their little brother, who was already climbing up the many rungs of the enormous red and yellow tube slide. They were almost as excited about it as he was.

After sliding a few times, two local boys showed the kids how to whiz down faster. "You'll fly like anything on these." They handed Yael and Michal two flattened plastic soda bottles.

Yehuda and I sat with Ronit on a park bench and watched while Eitan and his sisters repeatedly climbed up the many levels of the jungle gym and then took turns speeding down like lightening on the crushed soda bottles. I tried not to think about how dirty their Shabbat clothes were probably getting.

"We have to come back to this playground again before we go," Hadas said, out of breath, when it was time to leave the park.

"Yeah, we have to!" Yael and Michal said in unison.

"This is the best!" Eitan shouted.

"But it might not be here for much longer," Michal reminded her little brother.

"What? They're going to wreck this too?" Eitan ran over to Yehuda in disbelief.

"Maybe not," Yehuda said, trying to be positive.

"Well, we have to come back here tomorrow," Eitan insisted.

Everyone agreed.

The next morning, we sat outside on the balcony again and leisurely ate the Shabbat meal we had brought with us. Then, later in the afternoon when the sun was less strong, we went looking for the Yamit synagogue that was built in the shape of a huge Star of David. Inside the synagogue was a glass and ceramic artistic portrayal of the evacuation and destruction of Yamit and the other Sinai settlements back in 1982.

"Is it true that some of the people who were kicked out of Yamit moved here to Gush Katif?" Hadas asked.

"It's true," Yehuda said. "Many of them resettled themselves in this area."

"And now, they might be kicked out of their homes again?" Yael couldn't believe it.

"That's so sad," Michal lamented.

"C'mon," I said, "let's go to the zoo." I didn't feel like being depressed again.

"It's great we don't have to pay to get in 'cause it's Shabbat," Hadas said, walking right through the zoo's entrance.

"Wow, this is amazing!" Yael was impressed as we strolled past zebras, ostriches, monkeys, snakes and all kinds of exotic-looking birds. Goats, deer, sheep, donkeys and other animals were lounging in spacious open areas that resembled their natural habitat. "This isn't just some little petting zoo with cute bunnies and ducks," Yael said with amazement. "This is a real, normal zoo!"

"How could this place have such a great zoo?" Hadas asked.

"They've been successful with just about everything they've done down here," Yehuda answered, as we passed a camel sitting like a statue in the sun.

Yael turned away from the animals to face Yehuda. "Even the greenhouses?"

"Especially the greenhouses," Yehuda replied. "A large amount of the country's vegetables are grown in the Gush Katif greenhouses. And the Katif farmers' flowers are exported all over the world."

On our way back to the apartment, Yael noticed the kids playing ball on the sprawling green lawn to our right and younger children running up and down a small sand dune just ahead of us. Her eyes swept past the rows of red-roofed houses, manicured bushes and tall sturdy trees lining the streets and sidewalks. Suddenly, she stopped. "I can't believe Sharon wants to destroy this place!" She raised both arms up in the air and then let them fall back down to her sides. "Has he ever even been here? Maybe he should come live here for a while. Then he wouldn't even be able to think of getting rid of all of this!"

I held Yael's hand as we walked slowly back to the apartment.

"Do we have to go home right after Shabbat?" Michal asked as she helped set the table for our last meal on the balcony.

"We're not leaving until we go back to that playground with the giant slide one more time, right?" Eitan was just making sure.

"Right." I placed a pitcher of cold water on the table beside the small bowls of tuna fish and avocado salad. "But then we'll have to leave."

The sun was setting as we sat down to eat. We had a scenic view of Neve Dekalim and its surrounding towns and fields. Shabbat singing drifted up to us from Tzippy and Eli's house below. We were all feeling relaxed in the serene atmosphere when, suddenly an explosive boom sounded in the distance.

"That must have been a mortar shell!" Hadas gasped.

"You're right," Yehuda said, as we watched the birds from afar fluttering frantically over the area that was just attacked. "It was either a mortar shell or maybe a Kassam rocket."

We could faintly hear mad screeching and squawking as the birds flapped about.

"Great," I said forlornly. We had made it through Friday and all of Shabbat without incident. Apparently, two days of quiet was too much to expect.

"Should we be worried?" Yael looked over the rail towards the smoky area. "It seems pretty far away."

"It's good for us that it's far away," Hadas said. "But what about the people over there?"

We were all concerned about whether somebody had gotten hurt this time. I knew the residents were used to the regular attacks and had adjusted as best as possible, but I imagined it was still difficult for them to live life normally.

Two louder blasts got me up from the table. "I'll go downstairs and ask what we should do," I announced.

I wasn't panicked. None of us were. After all, back home we had been living through our own booms and bangs, helicopters, tear gas, roadside rock attacks and more, courtesy of the second intifada. This was just another thing to add to the list, I reassured myself as I knocked lightly on Tzippy and Eli's front door.

"*Ken*," came the reply for me to let myself into the house.

"*Shabbat shalom*,"[96] I began, walking into the dining room where the family and some guests were calmly eating their meal. "We're sitting outside and wondering about those booms," I told them.

"Mortar shells," Eli said matter-of-factly.

"You probably should go inside," Tzippy advised.

"But it was far from us, wasn't it?" I asked.

"Yes. But six months ago one landed right out here," Tzippy nodded towards the sliding glass doors that led out to their backyard.

"Oh," I replied, with raised eyebrows. "Okay. Well, I'll just go back upstairs and get everyone inside now," I said, quickly heading back towards the front door.

"*Shabbat shalom*." Eli smiled at me as he spread hummus on a piece of challah.

"*Shabbat shalom*." I stepped backwards out the door and then ran back up the stairs. Just as I reached the family, still eating their meal, another boom greeted us. Then a voice

---

96 Have a peaceful Sabbath.

came on the loudspeaker system announcing that everyone should go into their houses and stay there until things calmed down.

"Okay," I said, whisking baby Ronit up from her play blanket on the balcony floor, "everyone inside."

"Let's go," Yehuda hurried the kids away from the table and into the apartment.

"This is just like Or Tzion, with loudspeakers even on Shabbat telling us when we should stay inside because of the intifada," Michal said.

"No. They have it worse here," Hadas said. "They have this all the time."

"It's been going on for many years," I added, placing Ronit in her carriage.

"Really?" Eitan asked.

"Uh huh," Yehuda said, closing the door behind us. "These people have been attacked by mortar shells and Kassam rockets more than five thousand times."

"Really? Five thousand?" Eitan couldn't believe it.

"That's right," Yehuda said.

"Wow!" Eitan was amazed. "G-d's saved them five thousand times."

I nodded my head in silent awe, as I rocked Ronit's carriage back and forth. The miraculous reality that, over the years, not more than two Gush Katif residents had been killed and only a small number had been injured from rocket attacks reminded me that the people there were most certainly being protected from Above.

"Will we still be able to go to the big slide before we go home?" Looking up at me, Eitan was now wondering how the security crisis at hand would affect the end of our visit.

I looked sorrowfully into my son's eyes. They were almost as green as the avocado stain on his white Shabbat shirt. "It doesn't look like it, cutie."

About two hours after we dashed into the apartment,

we emerged with all our things packed and ready to load up the car. Shabbat was over and it was already dark outside. We had to start on our trip back home.

"That was such a waste of time, being cooped up inside like that," Yael complained as she stomped down the stairs with her overnight bag.

"There wasn't even any announcement saying it was okay to go out again," Michal pointed out.

"That's because here they probably never know what will be from one minute to the next," Hadas said.

"Yeah, what're they supposed to do—stay inside their houses all day?" Yael threw her bag into the trunk of the car.

I listened to my kids with a heavy heart. I knew that they weren't only angry about all the hardships the people in Gush Katif suffered every day, they were also upset about the way they were forced to spend their last hours in Neve Dekalim. They had all been a little nervous about the possible Kassams or mortar shells outside. But mostly they had been bored and disappointed that we weren't able to go back out and bid the town a proper farewell.

"We have to say goodbye to Tzippy and Eli and their family," Hadas said.

"But not goodbye forever," Michal made sure to add.

"Hey! Let's come back here again next Shabbat!" Eitan suggested.

"We're lucky we got to be here these past couple of days," I said, taking his bundle and adding it to the trunk load.

"So in a few more Shabbats?"

"This place may not be here then," Yael said.

"Oh." Eitan was quiet for a few seconds. "So where will all the people go?"

"Nobody really knows," Hadas told Eitan. "There aren't any new homes set up for them yet."

I was trying not to think about it. "You know what," I said. "How 'bout if we say goodbye just for now and hope for the best?"

Yehuda slammed the trunk door closed and started walking back to the house. "C'mon," he said, motioning for the rest of us to follow.

Tzippy, Eli and their two youngest were standing at the doorway. I gave Tzippy a warm hug. "We'll be back next year and then we'll see you all again," I told her with confidence. Tzippy smiled, but didn't reply. Again, her brave front was betrayed by the uneasiness in her eyes.

Yehuda handed Eli the key to the guest apartment. "Take care of yourselves." He gave Eli an encouraging pat on the back. "G-d is with you."

"We know," Eli replied. "He's with all of us."

The kids said thank you and everyone went back to the car. Eitan and Michal waved goodbye from their windows.

I knew the family was still watching as we drove away from the house. "I can't look back at them," I whispered to Yehuda.

The car was quiet as we left Neve Dekalim and the rest of Gush Katif behind. Then Eitan said it for all of us. "I hope we come back here again."

"We will," Yehuda answered.

"We have to," Yael insisted.

"No matter what, we have to come back here," agreed Hadas.

Michal leaned forward in her seat. "I want to help work in a greenhouse."

They were all trying to be optimistic.

My feelings were mixed-up inside of me. It had been an amazing visit. I was energized and hopeful. Yet, the dread of a possible expulsion hung over the place like a thick black cloud. Leaning my head out the window, I took one last glance back at the starlit beach, the shadowy palm trees and the "Welcome to Gush Katif" road sign. I could still feel the warm sea air on my face and see Eli's encouraging smile as he, Tzippy, and their children bid us a safe journey home. I realized our family needed to be more like the people of Gush Katif, who were holding onto their faith with every morsel of strength they had left.

"Don't worry," I told the kids. "We'll be back."

"For sure?" Michal asked, a little skeptical.

I wasn't sure about anything at that point. But I knew that even if the Disengagement did happen, and even if terrorists did take over the area, somehow in the future, with G-d's help, Jews would return to Gush Katif to reclaim and resettle the land.

"Yes," I answered my hopeful daughter. "For sure."

The doctor was just leaving when Fran came in to do her routine checks. "Goood morning. Everything all right in here with you two?" She opened Mrs. Weissberg's curtain and handed her a thermometer to put in her mouth. "You didn't give the doctor any problems, did you?" she asked Mrs. Weissberg, who could only reply with a shake of her head after putting in the thermometer. "And what about you?" Fran looked at me with a smile.

"Nope." I closed the book I'd been reading and put it on the stand next to my bed. "I just told him that the pretty Japanese nurse on our shift is looking for a nice, handsome, eligible prince like him."

"You didn't!" Fran left Mrs. Weissberg with the thermometer in her mouth and came over to my bed.

"Right. I didn't," I said truthfully. "But if you're interested, I know he's not married because I overheard two of the nurses talking about him last week."

"Hi everyone," Carol said, waving to Mrs. Weissberg on her way over to me.

"We're not quite ready yet." Fran said, wagging her finger at me and then returning to Mrs. Weissberg.

"That's fine," Carol said, bringing my walker closer. "We'll go for a short walk and maybe try a few stairs in the meantime."

"Don't forget about us waiting here," Fran said, opening Mrs. Weissberg's chart. "I've still got to check Shelly and she promised that today we'd hear about what happened with those Gush Katif towns."

"I tried to get some of that out of her last night," Mrs. Weissberg said, the thermometer no longer in her mouth. "But she was so loyal to the both of you, she wouldn't tell me even half a story in advance!"

"Aren't you the sneaky one!" Carol laughed as she walked with me slowly towards the door.

"I'm surprised at you, Mrs. Weissberg," Fran teased.

"I know. I should have been more patient," Mrs. Weissberg admitted. "But it was bothering me that the prime minister wanted to give away all those settlement towns. Gush Katif sounds like such a special and beautiful place."

"You're right about that," I told Mrs. Weissberg. "Just hang on for a few more minutes. I'll be right back and we can begin while Fran is checking me and even before I start my exercises with Carol, if that will make everyone happy."

"That will be perfect!" Mrs. Weissberg replied.

After we returned, I settled into my chair, ready to begin right away, when a slim woman with shoulder-length chestnut-colored hair walked into the room. She was wearing a soft pink sweater, designer jeans and light pink lipstick. "Oh, there you are, Mother!" she said, walking over to Mrs. Weissberg. "I didn't see you at first because you're not in your bed."

Mrs. Weissberg's daughter came over to our small gathering. "Hello," she nodded to the rest of us. "What's happening over here? Oh, wait. This must be what you told me you've been doing lately,

Mother—listening to all kinds of stories about Israel."

"This is my daughter," Mrs. Weissberg told us. "Diana, let me introduce you to Fran and Carol. Shelly you've met briefly during some of your visits." Mrs. Weissberg gestured towards each of us as she spoke.

Diana smiled. "My mother's told me about your get-togethers. They sound interesting."

"We wanted to hear about Israel, and Shelly was willing to tell us her experiences during her physical therapy sessions," Fran explained.

"She's been living there for many years," Mrs. Weissberg informed her daughter. Then she turned to me. "My Diana's been to Israel quite a few times," she said proudly.

"Those were great trips," Diana admitted. "I'd love to go back again."

Carol was anxious to move along. "Shelly's been telling us about Gush Katif and the Disengagement Plan."

"It's not one of the brighter or more positive periods of time in the country," I told Diana, "but if you want, you're welcome to listen too."

"What do you say, dear?" Mrs. Weissberg looked up at her daughter.

"Hmmm." Pursing her pink lips for a moment, Diana took in the three of us and then returned to her mother. "Sure, I'm up for it. I remember that evacuation plan with those settlement towns in Gush Katif." Turning away from Mrs. Weissberg, she looked at me. "It was terrible, wasn't it?"

Before I could answer, Mrs. Weisberg spoke again. "Shelly lives in a settlement town in Samaria." She informed Diana.

"So you must have been pretty upset back then."

Diana looked at me with sympathy in her eyes.

"Just don't tell us what happened," Carol said. "Shelly's in the middle of explaining everything."

Hanging her purse on the back of the chair Fran had quickly brought in for her, Diana sat down and crossed her legs. "Okay, I'm not saying a word," she promised. "I don't know that much about it anyway. I'm just going to sit here, like the rest of you, and listen."

"So," Fran looked at me, "were you able to save any of that Gush Katif?"

"We made great efforts," I told her. "But so far, none of the anti-Disengagement activities had managed to get Sharon's decree canceled. Even a massive three-day march to the Gush, with thousands of adults, teens and families, failed when it was forced to end in a place called Kfar Maimon, not far from the Kissufim checkpoint."

"That must have been disappointing," Mrs. Weissberg said.

"It was. But many of us still had hope. And with only a few days left, a gigantic prayer rally was organized at the Western Wall in Jerusalem. Thousands of cars and hundreds of buses brought people to the Old City to pray for Divine intervention. Unbelievable crowds, including some from secular and black-hat religious communities, united for the cause, with the hope and belief that crying out to Heaven would make the difference.

"And, I must say," I tilted my head towards the ladies, "seeing all the powerful and passionate prayers and the overwhelming masses of people filling up every inch of the Old City, all for the sake of saving Gush Katif, I was sure G-d would intervene

to straighten things out. I was confident that nothing
would be given away."

SOLDIER & CIVILIAN REFUSENIKS
(August 2005)

More than fifty thousand specially-trained police and
soldiers were standing by to "help" the Gush Katif
residents pack up their lives and disappear. Years ago,
when they first came to settle the area, the government had
supported and helped the families. Now, in less than
twenty hours it would be forcing them to abandon their
cherished homes, flourishing greenhouses, beautiful
neighborhoods and shores, long-time friends, and the part
of the country they'd spent decades building and
protecting. I couldn't believe that after all we had done to
prevent this tragedy, it was about to happen anyway.

Sharon had blocked off Gush Katif, making it a closed
military zone in order to prevent a massive infiltration of
anti-Disengagement supporters. For weeks only actual
Gush Katif residents and some select visitors were
permitted to enter the area. But thousands had already
come into the settlement towns before they were closed off
to outsiders. And many more had managed to sneak in
through unconventional routes, even after the ban went
into effect.

Now, multitudes from near and far were expected to
come to the Kissufim junction to help prevent the
evacuation forces from breaking into Gush Katif in the
morning. Prepared to be stopped along the way by soldiers
or the police, they would abandon their vehicles and walk
through the fields to reach their destination, if need be. The

hope was that the vast numbers of people, both inside and outside the Gush, would be too great a force for Sharon's special "Disengagement army" to expel.

"Sharon's expecting full cooperation from both the police and the soldiers tomorrow," Yehuda said, as he packed up some things to take with him on his trip back down to the Gush.

Most of the soldiers were ready to comply with the evacuation orders they were given. But some were strongly against evicting their fellow Jews. It went against their principles, morals and all they believed in and lived for as Jews in the Land of Israel. As soldiers, they had been trained that their duty was to protect the people, not hurt them. They were supposed to be defending their country, not surrendering it. The idea of forcing their brothers off the Land repulsed them. They were tormented by the absurdity of a strategy that would allow and encourage the enemy to take over.

These soldiers signed petitions stating that they refused to play a part in the devastation of Jewish homes and lives. And they refused to help bring about the possible breakdown of the army's fundamental essence and spirit. The country was divided about whether or not the "refusenik" soldiers were acting appropriately. Even leading rabbis couldn't agree on what was the right thing for them to do, or where their primary obligations lay—to the Israel Defense Forces or to the residents of Gush Katif, Samaria and ultimately all the Jews in the country.

The prime minister had fired cabinet ministers who didn't agree with his plans for Gush Katif and threatened members of his own Likud party with the same treatment if they went against him. Now he was making it clear that he would not let some conscientious soldiers spoil things for him. Those who refused orders would receive harsh punishments for their disobedience, including jail and possibly suspension. And, just for good measure, he arranged for specially-trained riot control police to join the soldiers in their new eviction duties.

Ariel Sharon's message was loud and clear: Gush Katif *will* be evacuated as planned.

"Ema, I know you probably don't want me to, but I'm going with Abba to try to help stop them from getting into Gush Katif tomorrow morning," Hadas insisted.

I felt torn. I was proud of Hadas' convictions and determination to help. At the same time, I didn't want any harm to come to her if things got too heated up or out of control.

Yehuda and I had educated our children to believe in, and to stand up for their country. We instilled in them the belief that although G-d is always watching over us, it is also our duty to watch over ourselves—as individuals and as a nation. We taught them that the ideals and principles of the Torah not only tie Jews to their heritage, but also to their people and to their Land. So a threat to any one of those essential values called for some kind of a response.

Now, my precocious eldest daughter, at the age of fourteen, was resolutely looking me in the eyes and saying, "I'm not going to just sit at home and do nothing! I want to try to help stop this from happening, Ema." Later that afternoon, I watched her walk out the front door with Yehuda, their sleeping bags, overnight supplies and backpacks filled with food and water. They would be joining the anticipated masses who'd be attempting to reach the Kissufim junction before morning, when the evacuation was set to begin.

I knew most of the people heading down there would be teenagers and young adults. The Orange youth had incredibly taken the lead throughout the anti-Disengagement battle. Again and again, they proved to have unwavering drive, steadfast courage and irrevocable commitment to holding onto their Land and protecting their people. They unexpectedly put themselves in the front lines, with equally committed adults backing them up as much as possible. They were determined to stand strong. But who could know what would happen when they'd all be met head on by the evacuation forces?

"You make sure you stay with Abba at all times," I reminded Hadas for the millionth time.

Hadas placed her gear in the trunk of the car. "I will, Ema. Don't worry."

I *was* worried. *What if the two of them got split up or lost? What would happen if they managed to somehow get past the Kissufim checkpoint and into Gush Katif? Would they be involved in a violent confrontation with the police or soldiers once the evacuation began? Would they get caught on their way down there, arrested and put in jail? How would I be able to communicate with them if their cell phones were taken away?*

Don't let her out of your sight," I warned Yehuda. "And please don't forget to let me know what's happening all the time."

Putting the key into the ignition, Yehuda promised to keep me informed and to watch out for Hadas.

"We have to leave now, Ema. We have a long way to go and we want to get there already." Hadas was itching to get on the road.

I hugged my brave daughter through the window and then watched them drive off with only a few hours to go until nightfall. *Would they make it all the way there? Would we actually be able to stop this crazy thing? Would everyone be all right when all this was over?*

I knew all there was left to do was to pray, and to wait and see. Turning away from the street, I walked slowly back to the house. Soon enough, we would all find out.

CHAPTER 7

LAST DITCH EFFORTS

(August 2005)

I spoke to Yehuda and Hadas on the telephone before going to sleep that night. "Soldiers stopped us a few kilometers away from the Kissufim checkpoint," Yehuda told me. "Sharon ordered the army and police to arrest anybody who tried to get close to the Kissufim junction, so soldiers told us we had to turn around and go back," he explained. "We decided to try to go forward anyway. We saw that other cars were heading towards the fields, trying to get there that way. So we joined their convoy."

"Do any of you know the way, since you're off the main road now?" I asked Yehuda.

"We're planning to drive as far as we can through the fields, sleep for a while in the car and then at sunrise start walking. We'll figure it out." Yehuda sounded optimistic.

I lay in bed and wondered how many others, at that very moment, were attempting to reach Gush Katif. *Were there really so many people trying to get there, regardless of the road blocks? Would they all manage?* I was glad Yehuda and Hadas weren't attempting to go through the fields by themselves. Closing my eyes, I finally fell into an uneasy sleep.

A few hours later, I woke to join some of the neighborhood women who'd been gathering just before dawn every morning at Nechama's house to recite special prayers and psalms. "My friend in Gush Katif told me that the women there have been getting together to say pre-dawn psalms for a while," Nechama explained. "I feel like we should be doing that here too. It's the least we can do."

My alarm went off at half past four. Quietly creeping down the stairs, I was surprised to see a light shining from the playroom. I couldn't imagine who would be up at such an hour, or why. As I walked towards the lit room, Yael appeared in the doorway, fully dressed.

"Ema, I'm going with you," she announced. "I can't sleep. How could anybody sleep on a night like tonight? Think what might be happening in a few hours!"

"C'mon," I said, putting my arm around Yael's waist. Silently we walked together in the dark to Nechama's house.

An hour later, when I left Nechama and the other women, the sun's first rays were already lighting up the sky. Yael had nodded off more than once and had decided to go home early. Everyone was still sleeping when I walked into the quiet house. Flopping down on my bed, I picked up the phone and began pressing numbers. *Where are Yehuda and Hadas now?* I lay down with my clothes on and listened to the buzz of the phone ringing on the other end. *What did they do all night?*

"Hi Shelly," Yehuda answered.

Thank G-d he still has his cell phone! "Hi. Where are you two?"

"We're on a bus."

"What? What do you mean you're on a bus?"

"We were with a whole group of people in the fields. As soon as the sun began to rise, we left our cars and started walking. After a while, somebody found a path leading back to the road. We debated whether we should leave the fields or not. It looked like nobody was anywhere near the opening, so we went out. But," Yehuda continued, "the police were there, waiting for us. They were hiding. They arrested all of us, I guess for civil disobedience, and put us on one of the buses that was standing by for people they rounded up."

"Where are they taking you?"

"A policeman just announced on the bus microphone that we're all being taken to the Be'er Sheva jail.

I quickly sat up, flinging my legs over the side of the bed. "Oh, great!" *What would happen now?* "You're both on the bus? They didn't separate you, did they? Are they going to put *both* of you in jail?"

Yehuda answered only some of my questions. "So far we're still together and none of us are giving over any information about our identities. We all left any form of identification at home or in our cars, in case we got arrested."

I knew there was no way the police could know who was who on that bus. But I also knew they wouldn't hesitate to use pressure to get the information they wanted.

"Can you put Hadas on the phone?" I asked Yehuda. "Hadas! How are you?"

"I'm fine, Ema. Just a little tired. We didn't sleep much and we walked a lot.

"Hadas, listen." I was trying to remain calm. "If they ask your name, you tell them what it is. I want you to cooperate with them. Do you hear me?"

Hadas wasn't as concerned as I was about the police or the soldiers. She was just angry at them. "Ema, we didn't do anything wrong!"

"Hadas, listen to me." I tried again. "You're right. But it will probably be better for you if you cooperate. So, if they ask you, just tell them your name," I pleaded.

"I'm not telling anybody my name," Hadas wasn't budging. "I don't care what they do."

I closed my eyes and pressed the phone receiver harder against my ear.

Hadas understood my silence. "I'm sorry, Ema."

Yehuda got back on the phone. "Don't worry, I'll watch out for her," he reassured me.

I changed the subject. "Are there tons of people out there now?" I asked.

"Not really," Yehuda said. "We expected to see a lot more. Even when we drove past Kissufim on the bus, we didn't really see anybody—mostly just lots of police and soldiers. There aren't many people on the roads either."

I was shocked. Where was everybody? Where were the masses that were supposed to come to the aid of all those people who were about to have their lives ruined? Where were the impassioned hordes that only about a month earlier had gathered at Kfar Maimon, ready to make an all-out effort to get into Gush Katif before they were held back by the police and the army?

"What do you mean hardly anybody is out there? What happened?"

"I don't know." Yehuda sounded "down." "It seems like everybody who tried to get here was either blocked, arrested or turned back. Could be there are still some people in the fields."

I couldn't respond.

"Maybe all of this was just too much for everyone," Yehuda admitted. "Maybe people just got tired of fighting, or maybe they just don't want to take the chance that they'll be hurt or thrown in jail." He didn't have any answers either. "I have to hang up now. They're threatening to take away our cell phones. I'll call you as soon as I know what's happening."

I told Yehuda once more to be careful, pressed the OFF

button on the phone and threw myself back down onto the bed. *Yehuda and Hadas are on their way to jail. Jews are on the verge of yanking other Jews from their homes. And there's practically nobody out there doing anything about it.*

I rubbed the temples of my aching head for a minute. Then I leaned over the bed and switched on the radio. Lying on my back with my arm draped over my closed eyes, I listened to the beginning of one of the country's worst tragedies ever.

It was happening.

"I haven't stopped thinking about Gush Katif since I left here yesterday," Carol told us the next day."

Fran wrote something on my chart and then looked up at me. "I'd never even heard about that Disengagement plan *or* Gush Katif before. And now that you're telling us about them, I have to say that I don't get how the Disengagement would be good for Israel."

I met Fran's eyes. "It wasn't. But a lot of people thought that some of the terrorism would end if we gave the Arabs what they wanted."

"Shelly, can you wait a few more minutes before you begin?" Mrs. Weissberg was peering at us from the opening in the curtain around her bed. "Diana said she'd try to make it here about this time again today."

"What do you say?" I looked from Fran to Carol.

"You and I can get started while we're waiting," Carol pointed to the walker.

Soon Carol and I were back in the room and I was in my chair facing the others with my leg up on the bench. Diana had just arrived and was hanging her purse on the back of her chair like she had done the day before.

"Thanks for waiting for me," Diana said. Today she was dressed in various shades of blue with a touch of light blue eye shadow. "I would have been here on time, but I caught my mother's doctor in the hallway on the way over." she looked at Mrs. Weissberg. "I'll tell you about our conversation afterwards." Then, turning to me, she said, "Are we going to hear more about the Disengagement today?"

"We are." I looked apologetically at Diana. "I'm sorry." I was feeling badly that she wasn't also hearing some of the more positive stories.

"It's not your fault, dear," Mrs. Weissberg told me. "You're just relaying what went on."

"Don't worry," Diana reassured me, "I know there's a lot more to Israel than what happened with Gush Katif."

"I think we all do," Mrs. Weissberg said. Then, folding her hands in her lap, she turned to me. "Go ahead dear. We're ready."

I closed my eyes for a moment and then began where I had left off.

THE DEVASTATION BEGINS
(August 2005)

Radios and televisions were blaring all over the country. The media was having a heyday over the Disengagement. It was what they had been waiting for. Two days earlier, soldiers had gone from house to house, handing out eviction notices. Now, all of Israel was listening and watching as the expulsion got under way. Would it succeed or would it be terminated in the middle? Would there be cooperation or would it turn violent?

"Ema, can I come in?" Eitan was knocking on my

bedroom door. I had been listening to the play-by-play news reports of the evacuation proceedings for at least an hour. "Ema, I want to ask you something." Eitan sounded impatient.

I turned off the radio and opened the door for my anxious little boy.

"Yes, Eitan?" I motioned for him to come in.

"Ema, when I woke up, I heard neighbors talking on the street outside my window. Someone said that the Gush Katif people were being taken out of their houses and that some of them were crying. Is that true Ema?" Eitan didn't wait for an answer. "Are they making the kids go out too?"

"What did Eitan just say?" Now Yael was standing in her pajamas at my door with her hands on her hips. She was up early, despite going back to bed just before dawn. Taking notice of my melancholy look, she dropped her hands from their rigid position and softened her tone.

"Ema, are they doing it? Are they making them leave?"

I looked up at my daughter's questioning face. Then, with a frown, I slowly nodded my head.

"That's just great!" Yael turned and marched back down the hallway. Eitan and I stood together in silence as her bedroom door banged shut.

❦ ❦ ❦ ❦

Endless chains of buses brought tens of thousands of soldiers and policemen to Gush Katif. They broke through barriers of people, fences and burning tires that had been set up to keep them out. The first communities slated for evacuation were shocked as the eviction forces solemnly and stiffly filed into their neighborhoods. Their dark uniforms and black billy clubs were a sharp contrast to the golden sand, green lawns and rainbow gardens all around them.

"Look at them coming in like that!" I said while watching the television broadcast that morning at Zehava's house.

Tova had also come to watch, as Zehava's was one of the few households in the community who had hooked up a television, basically for news and educational shows. "I'm not sure I'm ready to see this," Tova said, speaking in Hebrew for Zehava's sake.

Zehava was sitting between us on the couch in a house dress that camouflaged her large figure. "I don't think anybody is," she admitted.

We watched the scene on the television periodically switch locations, as the news showed different aspects of the Disengagement in the various towns of Gush Katif. The black-clad policemen on the screen suddenly changed to soldiers packing up the houses of the many families who'd refused to do so beforehand. The residents' faith that the Disengagement would be stopped was so unyielding that some had even continued to work in their greenhouses up to the last day. Others, still hoping they wouldn't be evicted in the end, had watered their lawns and kept their refrigerators stocked until the very last moment.

Now that moment was upon them.

The soldiers were instructed to throw into boxes everything that wasn't attached to the walls as quickly as possible—a task most of them took seriously, despite the families' fervent pleas for them to stop. They also shared the responsibility with the police for physically removing anyone who didn't willingly leave their house.

We watched people being dragged out of their homes, screaming or sobbing. Many soldiers, both male and female, were distressed by their new duties. Facing the desperate and grief-stricken residents was hard to bear. A few broke down. They couldn't find it within themselves to follow the orders they were given and refused to carry them out on the spot. Some did the job with tears running down their cheeks.

But mostly, the police and the soldiers performed their tasks without hesitation. Expelling the families from their communities, they loaded them as quickly as possible onto a long line of buses waiting to take them away.

"I can't stand to watch this," Zehava said, quickly changing the channel with the remote control. Now we were watching policemen entering the Neve Dekalim synagogue, where some of the community members and supporters had gathered to spend their last hours and moments. The residents had slept, ate, sang, prayed and cried together, clinging to whatever hope they could keep alive. But the solemn-faced soldiers and the unyielding police had now come to clear everyone out.

There was no mercy for the men, the weeping teenage boys and girls, the elderly, the mothers with their young children, or the babies. Everyone shared the same fate. They would all be shipped off—away from their towns, their homes, their work, their schools... their lives. Anyone who didn't willingly comply was removed.

The television cameraman focused on one tear-drenched teenage girl in the synagogue who was begging the policemen to stop. "Don't do this! Please. Please, don't do this to us!"

My two neighbors and I watched as the crying, beseeching girl was guided out the door.

The only thing more uncompromising than the evacuation that was taking place was the people's endless fervent prayers in the Neve Dekalim synagogue. With each person taken, the prayers grew more zealous and more intense. The families understood that G-d, who created everything, was greater than Prime Minister Ariel Sharon. He was greater than President George Bush and all the politicians and leaders in the world put together. They knew He was greater than the determined task force that was at that moment expelling them.

"They have such extraordinary faith, even now." Tova was in awe.

"Yeah." I nodded my head slowly, my eyes fixed to the screen.

Suddenly, the scene on the television changed again.

"Which *yishuv*[97] are we seeing now?" Zehava asked.

"I don't know, but whichever one it is, things aren't looking good there either," I said.

We watched the townspeople and many of the volunteer residents standing outside debating and pleading with the unrelenting soldiers and policemen. "Do you understand what you're doing?" A man with a full beard and a large crocheted yarmulke was trying desperately to explain the seriousness of the situation to a group of soldiers. "This is all going to end up disastrously. Don't you see that?"

The soldiers appeared to be listening, but didn't respond.

"Don't you care about us?" A young woman, her hair loosely pulled back, was now being filmed. "Don't you care about our Land or our country... or our people? And what about our homes?" Her eyes grew larger as she gestured excitedly around her. "These are our *homes!*"

The camera turned away from the emotional woman and rested on a young couple being escorted out of their red-roofed, two-story house, along with their two small children. The mother was holding their baby and crying quietly into his little blanket, while a teary-eyed female soldier gently nudged her forward. Two male soldiers were more aggressively moving the father along. He was

---

[97] Settlement town.

holding their toddler daughter's hand as they walked. The doll the little girl was clutching close to her chest appeared to be the only possession the family was taking with them.

"We'll be back!" the young father declared, his tense face tightening. "You won't win! You can destroy all that we've built, but you can't destroy us."

"*Kadimah!*"[98] A tall policeman, who appeared to be in charge, punched the air with his club as he barked orders at the other officers and soldiers. "Stop listening to the lawbreakers and get them all on the buses already!"

I felt like I was in a daze as I watched four policemen carrying a kicking and screaming teenage boy out of his house by his arms and legs, then forcing him onto one of the buses. "This is Israel," I said quietly. "Not Russia or Germany."

"That's right!" Zehava exclaimed, jumping up from her seat on the couch. "And *they* aren't the Russians *or* the Nazis!" She pointed her index finger accusingly at the television. "That's *us* out there..."

"Doing it to ourselves," I finished Zehava's sentence. "We've become our own worst enemy."

Tova also stood up. Slowly and methodically, she folded her arms over her chest and shook her head in bewilderment at the screen. "It's so unbelievable," she whispered.

I thought about the people we had just seen in the Neve Dekalim synagogue, praying with all their hearts, even as they were being removed. We had also prayed hard for them. I had learned that all prayers had special meaning—not just for individuals, but for the world as a whole. *No prayers ever go unanswered. Even if one doesn't see immediate results, they are never lost.* I knew that even if

---

98 Let's go! Move forward!

every single person was expelled from Gush Katif and the whole Gaza Strip was taken over by terrorists, all our praying would still make a difference in one way or another—if not now, then later. If not for the expellees, then for their children. If not for those living in Israel, then for the Jewish nation as a whole. *Somehow, at some point in time, the effect of those prayers will show up.*

I held that thought in my mind for a few seconds. It was all true and even a little consoling. But as I sat in Zehava's living room and viewed the reality of the moment being recorded in front of me, I felt anything but comforted.

·❖· *CHAPTER* 9 ·❖·

DIFFICULT DAY

(August 2005)

Back at the house I gave the kids lunch, put Ronit down for a nap, then picked up the phone and punched in Yehuda's number one more time. Yehuda answered after many rings. "Yehuda, where are you now? Is Hadas still with you? What's going on with you guys?"

"Everyone on the bus was supposed to be arrested and brought to the Be'er Sheva jail down here. But the police said that the jails were all overcrowded. Apparently, they're filled with pro–Gush Katif 'criminals' like us," Yehuda explained. "So they took us all the way up to Tel Aviv and then kicked all of us off the bus."

I let out a sigh of relief.

"Now we're on a regular bus going back down to the Gush area," Yehuda said.

"Back down to the Gush! Why are you doing *that*?" I was nearly shouting into the phone.

"We left the car down there in the fields. We have to go back now and get it."

"Oh." I forgot about the car. "How are you going to get through all those soldier and police blockades along the way?" I was concerned all over again. "It's probably even more difficult to get there now than it was earlier."

"I don't know. There are a bunch of us in the same predicament. We'll have to figure something out," Yehuda sounded frustrated. "I've got a migraine headache now. I'm going to try to sleep on this bus for a while. Hadas is already sleeping. I'll call you later, hopefully after we get the car back."

I reminded Yehuda to be careful again and then hung up.

"Ema, what's happening with Abba and Hadas?" Michal, who was sitting with me in the living room, had heard my side of the conversation. "Are they coming home now?"

I tapped my foot nervously. "Not yet," I said. "I'll let you know what's happening with them when I know more."

Michal followed me into the kitchen. "What about Gush Katif?"

I wanted to turn on the radio for an update on the Disengagement, while I washed the neglected pile of dirty dishes in the sink. Now, with Michal in the room, I thought twice about exposing my ten-year-old to the news. *Do I want her to know what's going on there right now?* Turning away from the radio, I sat down at the kitchen table. Michal joined me.

"Unfortunately," I told my questioning daughter, "things aren't looking very good."

"Really?" Michal looked at me.

"Yes," I said softly.

"Oh." Michal lowered her eyes.

For a moment, we sat together in silence. Then, I got up and went over to the sink.

Michal stared at the white Formica table top for a few more seconds. Slowly, without a word, she too stood up. Out of the corner of my eye, I watched her quietly slip out of the room.

Anger boiled up inside of me. I pumped green liquid soap onto a wet sponge and began vigorously scrubbing the cups and dishes that were anyway about to be washed in the dishwasher. Setting a cup I was holding back down in the sink, I sighed as I glanced over to where Michal had just been sitting with such sadness in her heart. I could see her young face looking so dejected. *Why is G-d letting this happen?*

Half an hour later, Yael and Michal went to their friends' houses, while Ronit napped and Eitan ran down the block to play with a friend at the playground. I went up to my room to listen to the moment-by-moment news broadcasts. Previous reports told of a few families who'd set their houses on fire before leaving them behind. They had preferred to burn their homes down themselves, rather than let them be destroyed, or worse yet, let terrorists occupy them.

Now I was hearing that the evacuation was going quickly. There were some clashes, but the expellees were acting in an "acceptable manner," not causing the evacuators "too much trouble." Most were leaving passively. Some were simply numb. Others felt they had fought their battle the best they could. Now that it was coming to an end, they had no desire to create traumatic scenes that their children would relive in their minds for years to come. If they couldn't take their jobs, their homes or their possessions with them now, at least they could leave with a little dignity and self-respect.

I was startled by the loud ring of the telephone. Jumping up, I answered it quickly.

"Hi, Ema." It was Hadas. "We got the car and now we're on our way home."

Thank G-d. "How did you manage that?"

Hadas explained that the bus they'd taken from Tel Aviv, after the police kicked them off the first bus, brought them only part of the way back to the car near Gush Katif. They had no choice but to continue the rest of the way by foot. Yehuda used his migraine as an excuse to get the police and soldiers to let them pass through the roadblocks.

"Abba told them he wasn't feeling well and he convinced them that he just wanted to get our car and go home," Hadas explained. "Everyone let us through until we got near Kissufim. The guy in charge there said Abba could only go on to the car if I stayed behind with the soldiers."

"So you stayed with the soldiers and Abba went on ahead?"

"Yeah. I guess they were afraid Abba wasn't telling the truth and that we'd try to get into Gush Katif again. Ema, it was really interesting with the soldiers." Hadas' voice was more animated now. "They kept asking me if I was hungry and offering me their food all the time. I kept refusing and telling them, '*Lo, todah.*'[99] But they didn't want to accept my answer. They were acting like real Jewish mothers trying to get me to eat!"

I tried to picture it.

"When I finally convinced them that I wasn't hungry, they insisted on pouring me water to drink. The whole time I was with them they asked me lots of questions and talked with me while I waited for Abba to come back. I think they wanted me to feel comfortable." Hadas paused and then added, "It wasn't what I had expected from them."

I listened to Hadas' story with mixed feelings. I understood why my daughter thought it was "interesting" to be with those soldiers. Like Hadas and so many others, I was struggling with the image of our "beloved" soldiers who, until now, had always defended and protected us. *Are the boys out there today these same soldiers? Are they the same*

---

[99] No, thank you.

sons, brothers, uncles, cousins, neighbors and friends who everyone is always so proud of? Are they the same young men who the people worry about during times of war, take care of in times of need and pray for—all the time?

Many of us were wondering: Just who *were* these soldiers who sacrificed years of their lives to fight for their people's safety, and were now suddenly turning on a whole segment of our population? Who *were* these soldiers who seemed to genuinely care about the welfare of the citizens, as they did just now with Hadas, yet for the past months aided in aggressively sending our children off to jail? Who were these soldiers who ferociously fought intifada uprisings and unsolicited wars for their country, but were now giving in to the terrorists who were responsible for those battles?

I didn't really know how to respond to Hadas. "We're living in complicated times." It was the best I could do.

After we finished our conversation, I returned the phone to its stand. Sitting on the light green carpet, I leaned back against the side of the bed. The room was quiet. I glanced at the radio. It was beckoning to me. I turned away. It would have to wait.

I wasn't ready to hear more.

"Phew, this is pretty intense," Fran said in a low voice. "Do you want to stop and take a break for a few minutes, Shelly?"

"I could use a drink of water," I answered, eyeing the pitcher that was on the stand next to my bed.

Fran brought glasses from the kitchen down the hall and poured us all some water. I drank mine and went back to my muscle-strengthening exercise, with Carol at my side.

"So," Mrs. Weissberg tapped the side of her half-emptied glass, "do you want to tell us what happened with Yehuda and Hadas?"

"I hope they got home all right." Diana said.

"Oh, sorry. I left you guys up in the air, didn't I?" I realized that while everyone was drinking their water and watching me work with Carol, they were also patiently waiting for me to go on with the story. So, I plunged back into it.

THIS WAS MY HOUSE
(August 2005)

Yehuda and Hadas returned home at ten o'clock that night. Exhausted on every level, they showered and immediately fell asleep. I, however, tossed and turned throughout the night. One by one, the twenty-one towns were being cleared out. It was difficult for me to ignore all I had seen and heard during the day. I rolled over onto my side. As soon as all of Gush Katif was empty and abandoned, the government's plan was to promptly evacuate four of the northern towns of Samaria. There seemed to be no stopping Sharon now.

"You live in a settlement town, right?" an acquaintance I was sitting next to at a wedding had asked me a couple of weeks ago. "Have you thought about where you'll go to live?"

I was a little surprised by the question. None of us in Or Tzion were planning on going anywhere. "Not at all," I answered the stylishly dressed woman with assuredness. "We're not even considering leaving our home *or* our *yishuv*."

"Maybe you should start thinking of a place to move to," she said in a gentle tone. Then carefully setting her fork down, she looked at me with concern. "You might be next."

I kicked off the blanket. Despite the cool air coming out of the air conditioning vents, I was hot and perspiring. *Would we also be expelled, like in that horrible nightmare I'd dreamt before? Would the day come when bulldozers would destroy a relinquished Or Tzion too?* "Have you thought about where you'll go to live?" The woman's sympathetic eyes came back to me as her words now echoed in my head: "You might be next."

ॐ ॐ ॐ ॐ

The second day of the Disengagement was just as harrowing as the first had been. Some of the Gush Katif citizens displayed their outrage, while others were in despair, as they were removed from their homes and led onto the buses. Their tears, entreating pleas and angry words didn't help any of them. Those clinging to one another, to Torah scrolls and benches in the synagogues, or to objects and fixtures in their homes were pried away, some gently, others more forcefully.

Although most of the townspeople continued to resist passively, in some communities friction between the residents and their evictors escalated to violence. Many of the inhabitants of the town of Kfar Darom, which had been captured once before by the Egyptians in 1948, were determined not to lose their community again. Some barricaded themselves inside the synagogue, while others took to its rooftop, stretching a large banner across it which read: "Kfar Darom won't fall twice!"

After hours of clashing and skirmishes with the evacuation forces, the Orange youth and adults who'd been resolved to hold their ground, were eventually dragged away and thrown onto buses. With Kfar Darom joining the other defeated towns, the number of arrested Orange Gush Katif supporters soared, as did those in need of medical attention.

"I don't want to hear or know about what's going on over there for a little while," I told Yehuda, as I watched him stuff his dirty, dust-covered clothes and sleeping bag from the day before into the washing machine. "It's too upsetting."

Walking up the stairs, all I wanted to do was go to sleep. It had been another difficult day. I had just returned from one of the cheap "refugee hotels" in Jerusalem where buses were dumping many of the families. Supporters and sympathizers were greeting them as they arrived. Emotions of the expellees in the lobby ran the gamut—from dazed and in shock to crying hysterically.

Before they were evacuated, some of these families had painted signs on the outside walls and front doors of their houses expressing their pain and anguish:

"WHY?"

"Soldier! Policeman! The minute you remove us, you are directly responsible for the destruction of our home and our family."

"This was my house. Now it belongs to those who murdered my father!"

"My mother was expelled by the Germans, and me, by the Jews!"

"We will return!"

"We don't have anybody to depend on, except for our Father in Heaven."

"Bulldozer driver D9, please don't leave anything."

"Dear soldier, what will you tell your children? 'I was just following orders?'"

Yehuda laid his head on his pillow and watched the long, wide blades of the ceiling fan whirl around. "I can't imagine what it would be like to be forced out of my home."

Sitting up in my bathrobe, I thought about whole families squeezed into small, second-rate hotel rooms, or worse, into a huge army-style tent, for an indefinite period of time. I couldn't imagine it either.

·❧· *CHAPTER 11* ·❧·

MALKA'S PHONE CALL

(August 2005)

I chopped two freshly peeled onions and threw the tiny pieces into the pot on the stove. It was early Friday afternoon and the residents of Gadid, one of the last remaining settlement towns, were being evicted. I couldn't believe they were being kicked out right before Shabbat. For a few seconds I watched the onions sizzle in the hot olive oil. I felt like I was on an emotional roller coaster these days—much of the time mournful, and other times so angry I was burning, boiling or... *sizzling, like these onions.*

The ring of the telephone disrupted my thoughts. "Shelly? Oh, I'm so glad you're there." I immediately recognized Malka's voice. "I am so upset about what's going on."

"I know," I said, turning to my multicolored vegetables lined up on the counter, ready to be made into soup for Shabbat. "We are too."

"You know they just finished getting everyone out of Gadid—on Erev Shabbat?" Malka said. "Now there are only six towns left."

"At least those communities are being allowed to stay until Sunday morning, on condition that they'll leave without any problems." I added some carrots to the soup pot. "I don't understand," I told Malka. "Why didn't G-d answer all our prayers, all our cries... all our efforts?" I was looking for answers.

"Maybe He did," Malka said. "It looks like He said... 'No.' He's the only One Who really knows what needs to happen in this world, and when it should happen. We can't begin to understand these things that are beyond our realm of comprehension. Apparently, for some reason, it was necessary for this horrible Disengagement to happen now."

It was still distressing. But I knew that what Malka said was true.

"Do you remember when I introduced you to Ariel Sharon a few years ago?" Malka's question steered the conversation in a slightly different direction. "It was at the annual Or Tzion luncheon that Yedidya and I have been going to every year since we got married. Sharon was a minister in the government back then, and very pro-settlement. He came to Or Tzion that day to show his support for the settlement towns. Do you remember that?"

"Yes, I do." I remembered it clearly. I also remembered a speech Sharon had given about ten years ago at the funeral of a young woman who was from one of the Jewish towns in Judea and Samaria. Sharon was upset with the government at the time for planning to give away parts of the country and was defending the settlement establishment. I'd just recently read excerpts from that speech in an Israel National News article on the internet.

> The government is hoping that the settlers' spirit will fall, that their faith will break, that they will want to leave. ... I know them for more than twenty years, and I know: Their spirit will not fall, and their faith will not break. Governments will fall and will arise, but the settlers will remain here forever, and will continue to build beautiful communities ...

> I see the next generation ... and I see that they are
> no less [strong] than their parents! ... They lead in the
> settlement enterprise, they lead in the army, they lead in
> love of the Land and in self-sacrifice! For them, Zionism
> is not yet over, and they still have a long way to go. For
> them, the hills of Samaria, the mountains of Judea, and
> the sands of Katif and Netzarim, are not just a historic
> right, but also a true home.

"He was very different in those days," Malka said. "Back when he ran against Prime Minister Barak, we hoped and prayed so much that Sharon would win the elections because Barak was about to give away parts of Jerusalem. We were so sure that if Sharon won, he would get things back on the right track for all of us, weren't we?"

I nodded in agreement. "We were sure," I repeated Malka's words.

"Well," Malka sighed into the phone, "try to have a good Shabbat."

"I will, Malka," I said, before hanging up. *I'll try.*

•‹›• CHAPTER 12 •‹›•

"So that was the end of Gush Katif," I told Carol and the others, letting my leg lie still.

Everyone was quiet.

Then Diana spoke. "Everything gone, just like that." She snapped her fingers.

"Wow," Carol said in a low voice.

"If I'm not mistaken, there were more evictions afterwards, weren't there?" Diana looked at me.

"Yes. There were," I answered, getting my leg going again.

"One of my friends has a young daughter and son-in-law who lived somewhere that also got evacuated, but I don't remember the name of the place." Diana touched her finger to her lips, trying to jog her memory.

"It must have been one of the Jewish towns that were evacuated in northern Samaria," I told Diana. "It was a tough time." I pulled my sweater tighter around me. "I think you've all probably heard enough for now."

"What happened to the towns in northern Samaria?" Mrs. Weissberg asked, sidestepping my idea to stop for now. "I don't think you ever told me anything about this, Diana," she said, turning to her daughter.

Sharing Mrs. Weissberg's curiosity, Fran got to the point. "We want to hear whatever you want to tell us, Shelly— good, bad or otherwise. Am I right, ladies?"

"Right," Carol answered. "Remember, I'm the daughter of a Holocaust survivor. I've heard about some pretty horrible happenings in my life. And I didn't expect that everything would be rosy when we started this whole thing. So, I'm fine with continuing."

Seeing Diana nodding her head in approval, Mrs. Weissberg looked at me with a comforting smile. "Whenever you're ready."

SA NUR
(August 2005)

"Are they coming on buses?" Eitan was scraping the pavement with a long, knobby stick.

"Yeah, they'll be on buses," I said, pouring mango juice into plastic cups that were lined up on the table.

Four settlement towns in northern Samaria were also scheduled for evacuation. Weeks ago, the residents from two of them, Kadim and Ganim, had reluctantly left their homes. But now, one day after Gush Katif was turned into a ghost town, police and soldiers were already making their way into the towns of Sa Nur and Homesh.

Just as had been with Gush Katif, some of the families left mournfully and without resistance, while others put up a struggle. Those who had nowhere to go after they were kicked out of their homes found themselves on the doorsteps of relatives, friends and even complete strangers.

Or Tzion opened its high school dormitory apartments for some of the refugees from Sa Nur. The municipality quickly set up committees to organize and coordinate their temporary absorption. Or Tzion's citizens, equipped with handmade welcome signs, gathered at the town's entrance to await the arrival of the latest expellees. Yehuda and the kids stood next to one of the refreshment tables I was helping set up while we waited.

"When will they be here?" Eitan was now swinging one of his legs back and forth, repeatedly bumping the front of his sandal against the wheel of Ronit's stroller.

"Pretty soon," Yehuda answered this time.

Fifteen minutes later, the buses arrived. As they came closer, some of us held up signs of encouragement for the passengers to see through the windows:

"We're here for you, Sa Nur."

"Don't Despair."

"The Sun *Will* Shine Again."

As the dazed Sa Nur families slowly got off the bus, we clapped for them out of respect for all they'd been through and offered them refreshments. The mayor of Or Tzion then made a short speech to welcome them. "We are honored to be your hosts and we will do our best to provide you with whatever you need for as long as you are here with us in Or Tzion."

"How long will they be with us?' Yael asked, after the welcoming ceremony ended and the Sa Nur families got back on the buses for the short ride to the dormitories.

"Summer vacation is almost over, so they can't stay in the school's dormitory apartments for too long," Hadas reasoned.

"Are we going to have to kick them out too?" Michal was concerned.

I had been wondering the same thing.

Yehuda offered whatever information he had on the topic. "I heard that we're postponing the beginning of the school year, to give the families more time to find somewhere else to live."

"They'll have to find places fast," Yael pointed out. "Anyway, who would want to live out of suitcases in dormitories for a long time?"

"You're right." I said, as we walked to our car. "They'll have to figure things out pretty quickly. Their kids also have to start school at some point—somewhere."

"Which is better, hotel rooms or dormitory apartments?" Michal asked.

"It was fun when we went to Eilat and stayed in a hotel," Eitan was hanging onto Yehuda's sturdy arm and skipping along with the others. "Remember?"

"You wouldn't like it if you had no place to live and that hotel suddenly became your home," Hadas informed her brother, as we reached the car. "And where they're staying isn't anything like a nice hotel in Eilat," she added.

"After this, none of them will probably ever want to go to a hotel again." Yael said. "I wouldn't."

"Neither one is better," Yehuda said. He freed his arm from Eitan and packed the poster board sign the girls and I had made into the car. On the way back to the house Yehuda informed us that more buses from Sa Nur were due to arrive at night. We agreed that some of the family would go to welcome them as well.

That evening, Yehuda put Eitan and Ronit to bed, while Hadas, Yael and Michal came with me to greet the next set of Sa Nur families that had been forced out of their homes. At nine o'clock we were waiting with other Or Tzion residents in the dormitory parking lot for the second group of buses that were on their way. New refreshment tables were set up and organizers were trying to quickly coordinate last minute details. Bruria, a tall business-like woman in charge of arranging basic necessities for each arriving family, was standing in the middle of the small parking lot with a group of people gathered around her.

"We're short one electric hot water kettle," Bruria said.

"Can anybody donate that?"

"They can use ours," one woman offered. Pen in hand, Bruria began marking her list and checking what else was still needed.

"How about a baby bathtub?" she asked.

I raised my hand. "I have one." Ronit had already outgrown her blue plastic tub. *What better use could it be put to?*

Other hands were raised in response to different requests for specific items, or to volunteer for some type of project or activity. I accepted the job of cooking meals for three families who had special diets and couldn't eat the regular cafeteria food that would be provided.

After a few minutes, we heard the roar of the buses as they neared the parking lot. Bruria and the group around her dispersed. The girls and I stood with the others on the side and watched the noisy vehicles approaching. They stopped right next to us.

One at a time, bewildered Sa Nur families stepped down off the parked buses and onto the asphalt. I felt like we were viewing a replay of the scene that took place earlier in the day. *Only, these people look even more exhausted than the ones who came earlier this afternoon.* Some of the younger children were sleeping in their parent's arms or resting their heads on their shoulders. I looked at my watch. It was already after ten o'clock.

"It's the end of a really long and stressful day for them," I told the girls.

Taking my cue from the others who were already rushing to help the weary travelers with their small children and meager belongings, I asked a thin, pale woman carrying her little boy if we could be of assistance. A blue canvas bag was hanging from her shoulder and a smaller plastic bag was dangling from one of her wrists. She had a blank expression on her face and her eyes looked tired.

"*Todah*,"[100] the woman whispered, letting both bags slip to the ground.

I took the heavier bag, handed Hadas the plastic one and motioned for the weary woman to come along with us over to the nearest refreshment table. Michal poured drinks for her and her son. Yael twisted her face into all kinds of funny expressions in a fruitless effort to cheer up the whining boy, who was now squirming in his mother's arms.

"Does this juice have sugar in it?" the woman asked me, raising her voice a bit. "He's not allowed sugar," she nodded towards her son.

I immediately realized that this must be one of the families I would be cooking for. Handing her a cup of mineral water, I explained that there was no need to worry about their special diet. "I'll be bringing food that you can both eat while you're here."

"*Todah*." The woman managed a faint smile that vanished quicker than it had appeared. "I'm Rena," she quietly introduced herself.

"I'm Shelly, Rena. We want to help in any way we can."

"Where's her husband?" Michal whispered to me when Rena turned to shift her son onto her other hip.

"Will anybody else be joining you here?" I was also curious.

"My husband is in the army. He's doing *miluim*[101] and couldn't be with us when we were kicked out. He's getting a few days leave, but he won't arrive here until tomorrow morning." Neither Rena's voice nor her face registered any signs of emotion. It seemed like she was running on automatic.

---

[100] Thank you.
[101] Army reserve duty.

"She's going through this by herself!" Hadas gasped, turning away so only her sisters and I could hear.

After we walked Rena to the dormitory apartment where she and her son would be staying, I asked if there was anything else we could do for them that night. Rena glanced around the small, sparsely furnished and unfamiliar dwelling that was to be their new temporary home.

"I really don't know," she said.

I felt helpless and uncomfortable. *How can we give her more support? Is there anything any of us can do that would make this woman and her little boy feel less miserable?* "I could bring you something to eat now, if you want," I offered.

Rena shook her head lethargically and said that it would be best if they just tried to get some sleep. I squeezed her arm compassionately, gestured for my daughters that it was time to leave, and then followed the girls out of the apartment. Hadas stopped at the door and turned back for one last glance.

"She's not moving," she reported to us, once we were all outside. "She's just standing there hugging her son."

"Poor thing!" Michal cried.

"Let's go home, Ema." Yael took my arm and was pulling me towards our parked car. "I don't want to be here anymore."

"More people are coming," Hadas said, noticing two cars pulling into the parking lot. As we passed the cars, I heard one of the volunteer drivers talking to Bruria, who was standing nearby with her list.

"The mother of the family in this car has a newborn baby," he pointed to one of the vehicles. "And one of the kids in the other car is sick," he said. "They didn't want to come by bus and didn't have any way to get here, so we drove them. They're going to need some kind of baby carriage and maybe some medicine," the man explained.

I glanced again at my watch and noted the late hour. It was almost midnight! *Those people must barely be coping.*

Pushing my emotions aside for the moment, I focused on more practical things. "Tomorrow we can bring the bathtub and the food," I said.

"And also find out what else is needed," Hadas added.

"I'm not coming back here," Yael said. "It's too depressing."

Looking straight ahead as we walked, I winced. I knew I'd be coming back many times, but I agreed with Yael completely. It *was* too depressing.

Carol had to leave, but nobody wanted me to stop talking. "I'll fill you in," Fran told her.

"Please don't leave out any details." Carol turned and looked back at us from the doorway. "I have to admit, it's not going to be as easy for me to concentrate on my work the rest of the day." Then, giving us a little wave, she left.

Fran, Mrs. Weissberg and Diana turned back to me. Mrs. Weissberg sighed, but nobody else said anything. I took that as my cue to continue.

VICTORY AND DEFEAT
(October 2005)

It was a joyous time for millions of ecstatic Arabs. In less than a week, the entire bloc of Gush Katif communities, built up over a period of thirty-five years, was demolished. Then, in a blink, Sharon also disposed of the four settlement towns in the northern part of Samaria that had been designated for demolition.

Tractors and bulldozers immediately began tearing down the houses and buildings in the evacuated communities. Some of the residents who returned to Gush Katif for things they had left behind were crushed as they watched their once vibrant neighborhoods being turned into rubble. Only some greenhouses, various public buildings and the synagogues, which the government decided at the last minute not to destroy, were left standing.

Three weeks later, the Israeli Army completed its withdrawal from the Gush Katif area. The land where the settlement towns once bloomed was officially handed over, concluding the last stage of Sharon's unilateral Disengagement.

"*Allah akbar! Allah akbar!*"[102] Fierce bellows of triumph echoed throughout Israel as the Arabs celebrated their victory by lighting firecrackers, setting off fireworks and firing gunshots in the air. Rushing to burn down the Gush Katif synagogues with blazing flames that licked the sky, their elated, chanting voices replaced the Jewish cries to Heaven that only weeks before had filled the now melting structures. And within minutes, Palestinian flags were rippling in the air at full mast from the rooftops of other remaining buildings, calling out their message loud and clear: "We won! You lost!"

"The whole Gaza Strip is being taken over by gangs and terrorists, now that there's no more Gush Katif." I was pacing back and forth in my living room while talking on the phone with my mother overseas. "And now they can fire their missiles from an even closer range, so they're Kassam rockets are reaching farther into the country! It's not just the town of Sderot or the kibbutzim in the south that are being targeted. Now cities further up the coast, like Ashkelon, and further inland, like Be'er Sheva, are also being hit." I stopped pacing. "You see the peace the Disengagement brought us?"

---

[102] Allah is great!

"I hope where you're living will be safe," my mother responded.

I probably should have been more careful about what I was saying to my mother, who might become worried. I normally avoided discussing any topics or events in my life that I thought might bother or upset her. But at the moment, it was hard for me to keep my emotions from spilling out.

"And you know what else upsets me about this whole Disengagement thing?" I went on without waiting for a reply. "Homes have been arranged for the zoo animals that had to be relocated and for the pets that the families weren't able to take with them. "But the *people*—they don't have any real homes!"

"It sounds terrible," my mother empathized.

"Well, it is terrible. Do you know," I went on, "that all these people's belongings are being stored in big metal containers in some huge storage place somewhere. Nothing will be accessible to them until they have more permanent living arrangements, whenever *that* will be." My words poured out like a raging river. "*And,*" I continued, "if they do want to get some of the things they need in the meantime, they'll have to pay for going into the storage containers! Can you believe it?"

I was barely stopping to take a breath. "My friend Tova has a daughter who was expelled with her husband and baby from the town that was called Ganei Tal. They got special permission to get some clothes and other everyday things from their storage container. But the metal container had been sitting in the broiling desert sun for weeks before it was brought to the storage houses. So when they opened it up, they found that the heat had ruined their furniture and destroyed all their electrical appliances!"

"That's terrible," my mother repeated herself.

I sat down on the couch and then jumped to my feet

again. "Plus... now get this, many of the houses, which have already been, or are now being bulldozed to the ground, still have mortgages on them. These evicted families are going to have to pay the banks those monthly mortgages—for flattened houses that they didn't want to leave and that no longer even exist!"

"Really?" Now my mother's tone changed. "I haven't heard or read anything about any of that in the papers."

"Well," I answered, "it's true. And even though the government is supposed to eventually give some money to compensate the families, it won't be what their houses or businesses were worth and it won't be nearly enough to cover all of their expenses. Just where do people think they are going to get extra money to pay for everything? They've been left without a home, without a community, without a known future, and without a means to support themselves and their families. And besides putting food on their tables, that is, when they finally have someplace to *put* their tables, they'll probably also have to spend huge amounts on psychological help for themselves and their traumatized kids."

I knew my mother wasn't getting any of this from the news.

"Those kids don't know where they'll be going to school now, and they don't have any idea when they'll begin to have a normal life again." I was waving my hands around as I spoke. "The little kids are going crazy with boredom. And most of the older kids aren't in any shape to begin facing the world again, especially when it's populated with people who don't understand their feelings or what they're going through. You try explaining to depressed and angry, displaced teenagers that society isn't against them."

My mother was quiet as I went on. There was really nothing she could say that would make me feel better. I realized it was difficult for others to understand what so many of us in Israel were feeling now. They couldn't fully comprehend the tragedy the country was going through. I wondered how many people in the world knew or even cared about what was going on here. The words "Gush Katif" and "Disengagement" weren't part of most people's lives and might never enter their vocabularies. *Even in Israel, some are behaving as if there's "no need to cry over spilt milk."*

"I hope things get better soon," my mother said, as we concluded our conversation.

"Yeah, me too."

We said goodbye and I pressed the OFF button on the phone. *G-d must have a way to fix all this.* I was trying to make myself feel better. I knew He had a Divine plan and that one day it would unfold. In the meantime, we'd just have to be patient... and hold on for the ride.

We waited while Diana helped Mrs. Weissberg shift a bit in her wheelchair. "I can't sit too long in one position," she told the rest of us apologetically. After she was all settled, Mrs. Weissberg got us right back to where we were. "I imagine those evacuated people from Gush Katif needed plenty of help," she said, looking at me with concern on her face.

"You're right. They did," I told her. "And they still do, even today."

"So did anyone help them?" Fran asked.

Diana looked at her watch and then at me. "I'm going to have to leave soon, but maybe you could just tell us a little bit about how the families managed after they were evacuated."

"Fine," I agreed. "And then that will be it for today."

NOT EVEN A DENT
(November 2005)

My friends and I joined forces, along with many others around the country, to assist the ex-Gush Katifers. "We're trying to help them pick up the pieces of their lives," I told my kids, who were contributing their energies to Or Tzion's house-to-house collection, gathering basic necessities and financial aid for the families. Professionals around the country were also trying to help the expellees. They offered free or reduced rates for therapy, counseling, legal services and other forms of support. Many concerned citizens donated winter clothes, coats and accessories to the families, who weren't accustomed to the colder climates where they were suddenly forced to live.

Women around the Jerusalem area also organized public bridal showers for young Gush Katif couples. The showers would help relieve the couples and their parents of the financial strain involved with making a wedding and starting a new home. I helped Efrat and Nechama arrange such a bridal shower in Or Tzion. To protect their privacy, the brides themselves did not attend. But plenty of other women came with presents and monetary gifts.

A few days after the successful event, Efrat, Nechama and I divided up the money and presents and then drove to the four brides' families to make the drop-offs. Nechama and I brought the first batch of gifts to two families who'd recently moved to Nitzan, just north of Ashkelon, where a small community of prefab houses was partially set up for the expellees. Hadas and Nechama's fifteen-year-old daughter, Tamar, joined us in Nechama's packed minivan.

"*Shalom*,[103] come in." Vered, our first bride's mother, greeted us at the door when we arrived in Nitzan. After making introductions, we unloaded the car and brought the many boxes of wedding gifts inside the small prefab house. Vered's pretty daughter, Galit, who was getting married in a few weeks, smiled meekly and then sat down with us at the kitchen table.

"Thank you for what you've done for Galit and for our family," Vered said in a shaky voice. "I worked for many

_____

[103] Hello.

years in Neve Dekalim's offices and I know just about
everybody who lived there personally. It's so terrible what
happened to all of us."

Vered, unable to hold back her grief, suddenly began to
cry. Covering her face, she sobbed quietly into the palms
of her hands. Galit brought her mother tissues. I glanced
across the compact kitchen table at Hadas and Tamar, who
were both wearing orange tops and rubber orange Gush
Katif bracelets. Neither noticed me looking at them. They
were both focused on the distraught woman sitting next to
me.

Vered wiped her tears and then returned to her role as
hostess. "We got some money to buy things we needed for
living here," she explained. "But it wasn't enough. And we
aren't able to get our things from storage yet. And even if
we could have our own furniture and belongings, we
couldn't fit even half of it in here, this place is so tiny."
Vered sighed and then dabbed at her eyes with the tissue
again.

I felt my face growing hot as I struggled to keep my
own tears from escaping. We talked a bit more, asking each
other questions and gently discussing the dismal aftermath
of the Disengagement. When it was time to move on to the
next home, Vered and Galit walked us outside.

"*Todah rabbah*,"[104] Vered said as we reached Nechama's
minivan. I didn't miss the tense look in her eyes or the
tightness of her jaw as we wished her and Galit good luck
and *mazel tov*[105] on the wedding.

At the second house in Nitzan, Miriam and her young
bride-to-be daughter, Shira, were also overwhelmed with
emotion. Once again we stacked up the gifts, nearly filling

---

[104] Thank you very much.
[105] Congratulations.

the miniature living room area. I then handed Miriam an envelope with a check inside. Peeking into the envelope, Miriam put her hand over her heart and gasped.

"This is so nice of all of you," she whispered.

We all took seats in the small living room. *"Todah,"* Shira said on behalf of her whole family. She went on to explain that her mother was thankful, but was also embarrassed because "so many people have had to help us since we left Gush Katif."

"I'm so grateful to everyone, but we are not used to taking charity." Miriam was staring guiltily at all the boxes of wedding presents spread out on the floor next to her. "We don't want to be in this position of receiving from everyone all the time. We want to be independent, like we always have been. We want to have our lives back."

The soft-spoken woman clutched the sides of her armchair and heaved a heavy sigh. "My husband is so depressed. Every day he goes out and looks for a job, and comes back with no luck. He was a successful farmer and now he feels like he's..." she paused to find the right words, "like he's nothing."

Miriam sat quietly for a moment, rubbing her hands back and forth over the arms of her chair. Then she began again. "Look at this tiny place we're living in," she swept her hand through the air. "All the families waiting to move here from those cramped hotel rooms will be shocked, like we were, when they realize the amazing "caravilla" we've all been promised is nothing more than a flimsy, cardboard house."

A younger, red-headed girl entered the room and smiled awkwardly at the scene before her. Without pausing, Miriam acknowledged her second daughter's presence and motioned for her to sit with us.

Knocking on the hollow wall next to her chair, she went on. "It's not even built well. The quality is so poor that the rain, wind and cold air come right through the seams of the walls and the window panes. Our youngest son hears the wind howling through the house at night and runs to us scared. It's bad enough that he's traumatized from everything else that's happened. He doesn't need this too."

I watched Miriam nervously twisting the ring on her finger as she spoke. "I know we have to be thankful that at least we have something. But this is also only a temporary solution. We'll have to eventually build or buy our own place at some point. But, I don't know how we'll ever be able to do that. The government still owes us compensation money. If we ever do manage to get it, it won't be enough. We've lost so much and we need that money to live on too."

I wanted so badly to tell Miriam something that would help her get through this time. It was painful seeing her devastated. "We're very sorry for all of you," I said softly. "And we're praying for you."

Nechama cleared her throat nervously. "We know it's a difficult time." she said with sympathy. "Despite the apathy that's out there, so many of us care and are trying to help in whatever way we can."

Miriam smiled weakly and then repeated her thanks for everything we had already done. Nechama, the girls and I took turns hugging her and her two daughters. "Stay strong," I said with a heavy heart as we left the house.

"I hope things will start to get easier for all of you soon," Nechama added.

"It's going to take a lot more than hope," Miriam said, walking with us outside. "But we know G-d is with us—wherever we are."

Only the hum of the motor under the hood of the minivan could be heard as Nechama drove us away from Nitzan. Back on the main road, I turned to the girls. "What we did today was a nice thing," I began. "And what others are doing for all of these people is helpful too.

Unfortunately, it barely makes a dent in easing their suffering."

Nechama sucked in her breath. "It will take a long time for them to recover."

"It will," Tamar agreed.

Hadas nodded in the back seat, her voice barely audible. "A long time."

❖ CHAPTER 15 ❖

"I see your mother's been here to visit you again," Fran said as she entered the room. "I met her on her way to the elevator and told her that your ribs were basically healed and that you were doing really well with the physical therapy." She smiled at both me and Carol in recognition of our teamwork on my leg. Then, noticing the empty bed across the way, Fran quickly changed the subject. "Where's Mrs. Weissberg?"

"I think they took her for some tests," Carol said, helping me out of bed and over to my chair. "She probably won't be back for a while."

"And apparently, Diana won't be coming until sometime this evening." I volunteered the information. "I'm actually kind of glad they're not here. I think it might have been a little hard for Mrs. Weissberg to hear some of what I've been describing lately."

"It *has* been a little distressing these past couple of days," Carol admitted.

"Heartbreaking," Fran added.

"I know." It's still difficult for me too. "And now we've gotten to the part where Ariel Sharon also suffers after the Disengagement."

"The prime minister?" Fran looked at me.

"Yeah. Bad things happened to many of our leaders who pushed for the Disengagement, especially Sharon."

OUT OF COMMISSION
(January 2006)

"Ariel Sharon's in a coma!"

"What?" My friend Beth waved me inside her Jerusalem apartment. "He had a massive stroke." My adrenalin was pumping. "I just heard it on the radio in the car. He's in Hadassah Ein Kerem hospital."

"Unbelievable!" Beth closed the door and led me into her kitchen, waiting to hear more.

"Apparently he had to have two brain surgeries, one right after the other," I explained. "According to the news, they put him in an induced coma. The doctors say he's in stable, but critical condition." I plopped my purse down on the kitchen table and hung my coat and scarf over one of the chairs.

"Wow." Beth stood for a moment with her mouth open.

"Yeah, who would have figured something like this would happen?"

"Wow," Beth repeated. Then becoming active again, she went over to the oven to pull out a tray of Nile perch. Setting it on the granite countertop, she looked at me. "You know, it's interesting."

"What is?"

"Well, Sharon messed around with *Eretz Yisrael*."[106]

"That, he did."

"And President Bush has also been sticking his hands in the cookie jar a lot lately. First, he tried to divide up Israel with that Road Map plan of his. Then he backed Sharon, pushing for the Disengagement. And look what happened

---

[106] The Land of Israel.

in the US just days after everyone was evicted from Gush Katif: Hurricane Katrina, which also left tons of people homeless."

"Yeah, that was pretty horrible too," I said, nodding.

"I wonder how long Sharon will be out of commission." Beth sprinkled some olive oil and lemon juice on a fresh salad and began tossing it.

"They said on the news that it doesn't look good for him." I answered. "Actually, it doesn't look so good for us either. Ehud Olmert will be taking Sharon's place as acting prime minister, and from what I hear, he's apparently ready to pick up where Sharon left off." I poured water into the two glasses on the table. "He wants to evacuate us in Judea and Samaria, starting with the demolition of nine new houses that were just built in Amona."

Beth stopped tossing the salad and looked at me. "Really? Where's Amona?"

"Amona's a small community between Jerusalem and where I live, in Or Tzion. It was built about ten years ago on the hill just above the settlement town of Ofra."

"Wow."

"Wow is right." I sat down at my place by the kitchen table. "Okay," I said suddenly, "how 'bout if we don't think or talk about all this stuff right now. I know Sharon's in bad shape and Amona's at risk, but I could use an easy-going afternoon, if you know what I mean. I want to enjoy this great lunch you made for us and not spend the little time we have together dwelling on troubles, politicians or anything else. We can think about all that later."

"No problem," Beth agreed. Then, taking the seat across from me, Beth lifted her glass of water in the air. "To us and our good fortune—to living in *Eretz Yisrael*. May it always remain whole, and may Jews never expel Jews again."

I lifted my glass. "Amen!"

Beth continued. "May we have leaders who know how to get rid of our enemies..."

"Amen!"

"...and not get mixed up about who the enemy is."

"Ahhh, that's a good one," I nodded. "Amen."

"And now," Beth cleared her throat in mock seriousness, "may we let nothing keep us from this delicious meal that is awaiting our immediate consumption." Spooning some brown rice onto her plate, Beth gestured for me to help myself to the rest of the food.

As I reached for the salad bowl, I banished all concerns from my mind. This was going to be a relaxing and enjoyable afternoon.

Amen.

"Sharon in a coma, so soon after the Disengagement..." Carol began working on the area around my knee. "That was so unexpected."

"What was the other one who took his place as prime minister like?" Fran asked.

"Ehud Olmert? He was like a continuation of Ariel Sharon." I answered. "Remember those nine new houses in Amona? Well, an organization that's against the building of Jewish communities in Judea and Samaria claimed that those nine houses were built on private Arab property. So, it filed a petition demanding that the houses be torn down. It was yet another gesture towards the Arabs."

"What about the families who were supposed to live in those houses?" Fran asked. "It sounds like that petition would be a problem for them."

"That's right." I nodded. "Especially since the community of Amona argued that *they* actually owned the land those houses were built on. Their claim was that they'd bought it from an Arab, who wouldn't reveal his identity, most likely because he feared for his life."

"What do you mean?" Carol asked.

"Well, many Arabs consider it disloyal to sell property to Jews. Any Arab who does sell to a Jew is considered a traitor who deserves to be punished severely, even by death."

Carol clucked her tongue. "That's crazy."

"Anyway," I went on, "the case got held up in the Supreme Court, which prevented the families from moving into the nine houses. Eventually, the defense minister and the attorney general accepted a legal compromise to move the buildings, rather than destroy them."

"That's good," Fran said with satisfaction.

"But," I went on, "Prime Minister Olmert refused."

Fran leaned closer to me. "So the houses were torn down?"

"Wait! Did anybody try to stop that, like they did with Gush Katif?" Carol asked.

"Well, Yes. But what happened with Amona wasn't the same as what happened with Gush Katif. Actually, what happened at Amona wasn't like anything we'd ever imagined would happen. And hopefully, it will *never* happen again.

Fran sat up tall. "What exactly *happened* at Amona?"

Carol stopped working on my knee and was now looking at me, waiting for my answer.

"Well..." I paused. "Fine. I guess we could go there," I said, trying to make up my mind. "But, you know that life is a mixture of good and bad. And Israel's got so many amazing, incredible, good and special things about it, even with the bad stuff that happens."

"Yeah, we know all of that," Carol assured me. "What are you nervous about, Shelly?"

"I guess I'm projecting a little, 'cause I know it's easy to get all caught up in the painful or negative parts of life and to lose focus on all the positive that's there too. I know I had a hard time with that at one point."

"Listen, whatever it is you're about to tell us, you don't have to worry," Fran said. "Every country in the world has some inner turmoil, conflicts or controversies that can cause a crisis of one kind or another. It's only realistic to expect that Israel would too."

Carol jumped in. "The hardships and painful happenings just give me more reason to want to get to know Israel and the Israeli people on a deeper level," she added. Some of what you've told us *is* hard to hear. But I'm in awe of the strength, courage and faith that carries all of you through everything that goes on over there. And even with all its stresses and pressures, there always seems to be plenty to laugh and be happy about in Israel. *I* think it's a fascinating place!"

"So," Fran clasped her hands together. "Now that you have our approval, lay it on us. What was it that you were saying you had a hard time with and *what* happened in Amona?"

AMONA
(February 2006)

I rushed to meet my friends at the intersection between Or Tzion and Ofra. We'd come to help stop the police and soldiers from blocking the way to the hilltop community of Amona. A passive-resistance demonstration was about to be held there to help prevent the nine newly-built Jewish houses from being demolished. With Gush Katif fresh in our minds and possibly more evacuations on the agenda, many of us wanted to do whatever we could to help

Amona and its residents. Anyone who couldn't attend the demonstration was to gather at intersections and help keep the roads open for those trying to reach the community.

I was ready to do my part to prevent more destruction and to avert what might soon be a smaller version of the Gush Katif and Samaria disasters. Our failure to prevent the Disengagement was still so painful. I couldn't believe something similar was about to happen again—and so soon! *This isn't just about more people losing their homes.* I told myself. *This is also about giving away our country, bit by bit. It's about jeopardizing the security of all who live here.* I was convinced we were left with no choice but to get out there and try to stop the law enforcers from making another devastating mistake.

The group of men, women and youth who arrived at our intersection spoke to the police, trying to explain and practically begging them not to lower the concrete road barriers off the waiting trucks. When that failed, we lowered *ourselves* onto the road next to the barriers and began reciting psalms in prayer and in protest. If they weren't going to allow us to pass, then nobody else should be able to either.

Only a few hours after I had left the intersection between Or Tzion and Ofra, I discovered how little our efforts on the road had affected events in Amona that afternoon. Sitting halfway off my chair, I listened intently to the reporter on the radio who was describing, with surprise and disbelief, how police and soldiers were using excessive force on those who'd gathered to defend the houses that were slated for destruction.

"Aggression like this against demonstrators is unprecedented here!" he announced excitedly.

I couldn't imagine what was causing the police to be violent. *It was just a passive sit-in type demonstration.* Nobody had planned or expected anything else. The broadcaster revealed enough to make me very concerned. *Hadas and her friends are there!*

After a few attempts I finally reached Hadas on her cell phone and told her to "leave right away!" When she finally walked through the front door a few hours later, I could see right away that a different girl had come home from the optimistic, bright-eyed Hadas who'd left the house in the morning. Now her face was drawn and her eyes looked pained. She was dusty and dirty, and her hair, nearly all pulled out of its ponytail, was a mess. I hugged Hadas tightly and then listened as my anguished daughter quietly explained what had happened.

"We were all just sitting or standing inside or near the houses that were to be destroyed. The rabbis and other adults kept announcing to everyone over and over that the protest was to be passive and nonviolent. Suddenly soldiers and tons of policemen with shields and billy clubs came and began beating everyone. It was so horrible. Some were on horseback and their horses were kicking, and a few even rode over people. There was a lot of screaming." Hadas squeezed her eyes closed for a moment. "I can't even think about some of those people who got hurt."

I waited while Hadas took a deep breath and then went on. "It was chaotic. I tried to escape, but I tripped and fell down and then I felt myself being dragged on the ground. That's when my head banged against a metal pole." Hadas' voice cracked and her face became twisted as she worked hard to hold back her tears. "I was crying. I just wanted to get out of there."

Though it was difficult for Hadas to rehash the ordeal, she went on to explain that she eventually managed to slip away. "As I was running away down the hill, someone told me I should go get checked up at the emergency medical tent that volunteers set up when everything got out of control."

Like Hadas, scores of others had also been examined or treated by the volunteer medics before leaving the area. For some, the emotional trauma they were experiencing was even more damaging than the physical blows they'd absorbed. But many were in need of more serious medical attention, with nearly three hundred people rushed to the hospital.

Bit by bit, as the days passed, the facts about what happened at Amona gradually surfaced. "The reports say that the police who were at Amona were riot police from special units, not from the ordinary police forces," Yehuda told me. "And apparently, many of them were actually non-Jews who'd immigrated to Israel with a Jewish spouse or parent."

I felt a touch of relief that at least they weren't all Jews bashing other Jews. But it didn't erase the darkness that had begun to spread through me.

"How could such a thing happen?" I asked Yehuda, sitting down on the blue plastic slide in our yard and resting my feet on its wide steps.

Yehuda sat down on the grass next to the slide. "The controversy about keeping or giving away this part of the country has become more intense over the years," he said, absentmindedly pulling out a few blades of grass as he spoke. "And these days, our right-wing camp has more political pull and influence concerning what goes on in the country. Many of our boys and men hold high positions in the army too. Even our Zionist radio station was doing well before it was refused a permit and shut down."

"I guess we're like a threat," I said weakly.

"Yeah, and the media's turned us into ruthless 'settler occupiers.'" Yehuda frowned. "Apparently to some, we're just pesky troublemaking mosquitoes that have to be squashed before we do anything worthwhile or before we make enough waves to change some things that might need to be changed." Yehuda looked up at me. "It looks like they wanted to suppress us, punish us, teach us a lesson we wouldn't be able to forget."

Leaning forward, I rested my elbows on my knees and my chin in the palms of my hands. What had happened on the hilltop of Amona, only months after Gush Katif, was like pouring salt into our open wounds. I couldn't imagine how we would ever recover.

"In a way, they got what they wanted." I glanced down at Yehuda. "This is definitely something we will never be able to forget."

·❧· *CHAPTER 17* ·❧·

THE FADING LIGHT

(March 2006)

"Did you see this?" Yehuda waved a piece of paper at me. "I printed it out from the computer last night." He set the page on the table where I was sitting down to breakfast after getting the kids off to school. "A few weeks ago Yehoram Gaon spoke about what happened at Amona on his radio show. I saw parts of it translated into English on the Israel National News site."

I glanced at the printout Yehuda put next to me. I was intrigued. I knew that it wasn't only the right-wing population that had been shocked and devastated by what had happened a month ago in Amona. Middle-of-the-roaders and many left-wingers were also taken aback by the unwarranted violence. Now, Yehoram Gaon, the Israeli singer, actor, television host and radio commentator had also expressed his distress about it on his popular radio program.

"This is some of what he said." Yehuda tapped the paper on the table. "It's worth looking at."

I glanced at Ronit, who was sitting next to me in her highchair eating lumpy oatmeal with her hands. Pouring milk into my bowl of cornflakes, I began reading while Yehuda finished getting ready for work.

As my eyes moved slowly across the page, I discovered that, unlike many of the famous public figures, Yehoram Gaon had spoken up for the right wing and religious families living in settlement towns:

> I know it's not popular today to say nice things about the settlers. All my colleagues in radio and television are very, very angry at them—but what can I do? Only one who fights for his land, cities and fields, and for every caravan and every clump of earth, acquires it by virtue of his love and dedication...
>
> Hand on heart: how many of us would leave our warm house, our dreams of getting rich, our cafés and nightclubs... to be with the Land of Israel, that it should not remain alone? How many of us, out of our own free will, would spend time on a barren, wind-swept hill in a caravan?

Reading on, I discovered that Yehoram Gaon had also spoken positively about the Zionist youth, whose response to expulsion and destruction was to build new communities on the hilltops of Judea and Samaria, rushing to protect each one, as they did in Gush Katif, Northern Samaria and Amona:

> Can you actually think that these, the very best of our sons, would disengage themselves? When it comes to Eretz Yisrael... they will run to fulfill every mission to defend it—even from the roofs of Amona and amidst the hoofs of the attacking horses...
>
> It would be a good idea to think long and hard about this: When the regime fights the people of Amona, who is it actually fighting? Are these youth the State of Israel's real enemy?

I continued on to the end of the page, then clutching the paper in my hand, I silently thanked Yehoram Gaon. I hoped that at least some of his many listeners around the country would hear what he had to say and come to have a better understanding.

Though I felt a bit uplifted by what I'd just read, I still couldn't free myself of the overwhelming grief that made me feel as if I'd just buried a loved one. More than six months had passed since Gush Katif and one month since Amona. Bucking horses, billy clubs and wounded pro-testers remained in my mind. And with the passing days and weeks, we saw the effects the Amona disaster had on Hadas. Suffering from headaches, back pains and a damaged soul, Hadas was also struggling in school. We'd sought appropriate help for her, but we knew that what she'd witnessed and experienced would remain with her for a while.

Wanting to do her part to help, Hadas was in touch with the Honenu staff, who was working around the clock providing free legal aid to anyone who'd been unjustly arrested or hurt. Surfing the Internet, Hadas looked again and again at photos and videos that were taken at Amona. She was trying to identify any police she might recognize in order to help Honenu gather evidence that would bring the offenders to justice. "There were so many of them and they weren't wearing name tags," she told us.

I knew it was difficult for Hadas to relive the atrocity. I begged her to stop looking. But every day I found her in front of the computer, examining the same scenes over and over.

For more than twenty years, my unconditional love for Israel had been like a radiant light that glowed inside me. No situation, no problem, no crisis, personal or national, could cause it to dim. As my connection to the country, the people and our heritage grew more intense over the years, so did the light. But now, despite the sparks I'd just felt after reading parts of Yehoram Gaon's radio speech, that bright, vibrant inner flame had become so faint, it was almost completely extinguished.

"What are we doing here?" I asked Yehuda when he returned to the kitchen, ready to leave for work.

Yehuda sighed, but didn't answer right away. He knew I was referring to living in Israel and all that had recently happened in the country.

"Is this what we came here for?" I walked into the playroom and slowly tidied up Ronit's toys.

Yehuda followed me. "We're trying," he said solemnly.

I thought he sounded as depressed as I felt. If our strong attachment to Israel and everything we've loved so much about it was compromised, then what was the point in remaining?

I left some soft blocks on the floor and sat down on the kids' miniature Winnie-the-Pooh couch. "Maybe," I said soft enough to be a whisper, "maybe we should leave."

Yehuda looked at me for a moment, then said, "Leave? You mean, go back to the States?"

"I don't know. Maybe."

I couldn't believe I was actually talking about leaving. In all the years I had lived in the country, I never, ever, considered severing the unwavering bond I had with the Land and the people. I understood that G-d had designated Israel the homeland for all Jews of all times. I knew it was where we were meant to be. And for so many years it was the only place I *wanted* to be.

But now, I wasn't sure that was true anymore. "We turned against ourselves," I said.

"We did." Yehuda sat down next to me, halfway off the kiddie couch.

"And we've sent a message to the world that it's okay—that it's right—to beat or suppress any Jew who is not of the 'correct' opinion."

"Yeah," Yehuda's voice was low. "Now we'll have to somehow find a way to make things better."

"Somehow?" I looked at Yehuda. "How?"

"I don't know," Yehuda sighed again. "But we have to remember Israel is our home. And look at what's going on in the rest of the world. We need Israel."

I thought about the hatred and attacks on Jewish lives in other countries. Terrorism was escalating everywhere and anti-Semitism was getting worse all the time.

"It's true we aren't the only ones with troubles," I admitted. "Every place has its share of problems and difficult situations that need to be solved. But I can't fathom how we would even *begin* to turn things around here. It seems so hopeless." We'd been fighting against solid walls that refused to budge for a long time. There didn't seem to be enough of us who understood the importance of holding on to all the Land and of establishing a Jewish presence in *every* part of the country. And at that moment, I didn't believe that would ever change.

"Maybe it's just too hard," I said.

"It's hard," Yehuda agreed. He inhaled deeply, then slowly let the air out of his puffed up cheeks. "But we have to keep trying."

I wanted to grab hold of the thin thread of optimism Yehuda was holding out to me. But it didn't seem within my reach anymore.

It was getting late and Yehuda had to leave for work. Back in the kitchen, I gave Ronit a bottle to drink with her oatmeal. Then I sat back down at the table and stared at my uneaten soggy bowl of cornflakes. *Jews should never beat other Jews. Jews should never trample other Jews with horses. Jews should never expel other Jews from their homes.* This wasn't my blue and white Israel. Somehow, it had turned black. Everything now seemed very black. *How could I continue to live here?*

I pushed the bowl away.

Maybe I couldn't.

❖ CHAPTER 18 ❖

I spent the first part of my physical therapy session going up and down the hallway with Carol and the walker. When we returned to the room, Diana, Mrs. Weissberg and Fran were sitting in a semicircle, facing my chair and waiting for us.

"It wasn't easy for me, "Fran said after I sat down, "but I gave these two a short summary about what they missed yesterday."

"We got the limited detail version," Diana told us. "Fran said it would be less difficult to digest that way."

I nodded in agreement. Years later, it was still hard for *me* to digest it all. The horrible feelings started coming back to me these past few days. It was like I had been reliving that period of time all over again.

Mrs. Weissberg leaned forward in her wheelchair and looked at me with concern in her eyes. "Did you really have thoughts about leaving Israel, Shelly?"

Turning my lips inward, I nodded sadly at Mrs. Weissberg.

"But you didn't," Diana said.

"No. Thank G-d, I didn't."

Diana pulled her chair a little closer to mine. "Why not? What happened with you after Amona?"

RABBI OREN'S CLASS
(April 2006)

I loved Monday mornings when I joined a group of women in Or Tzion to learn the teachings of Rav Kook, Israel's first Ashkenazi chief rabbi back in the 1920s. Rabbi Oren had a special way of explaining Rav Kook's remarkable insights and exceptional foresight regarding the Torah, the Land and the people in Israel. I was glad that lately the focus of the class was on how to cope with what had been going on in the country during the past eight months.

"Our people should always strive to be united." Rabbi Oren was handing out photocopies of the text he was reviewing with us that morning. "The importance of keeping the Jewish nation together is paramount, even under extreme circumstances."

Wearing black slacks, a burgundy cardigan sweater and a large crocheted yarmulke, the fifty-five-year-old rabbi opened the book in front of him and began reading aloud. I sat with the others around the long table and followed along with the Hebrew.

"According to Rav Kook," Rabbi Oren said, after reading a few passages, "there's nothing worse than a civil war among our nation. Even in our immediate reality, with the conflicts and divisions between the people here in Israel, we should work on ourselves to love our fellow Jews and to try to bring everyone together. Anger and hatred have always brought us, and will always bring us, to a terrible place.

"In other words," the charismatic rabbi went on, "if we aren't unified, we aren't much of a people. We are therefore at risk of falling apart and, eventually, disappearing. Then, what value would the Land of Israel have, the vessel that was created to hold the children of Israel? Without the people, what good will this Land we are fighting so hard to keep in our hands, be to us? We need not only our Land, but also our people to be whole."

One of the women in the class raised her hand to speak. "But it's suicidal to go along with those who are so willing to give parts of the Land away. They're sacrificing our homes and everyone's security."

A woman sitting two seats away from me in a camel-colored sweater raised her hand. "We should love those who beat us and our children, and who throw us into jail for defending our country?" She spoke softly, but I could tell she was straining to control her emotions. The knuckles on her closed hands were white, and one of her eyes was twitching. I sensed her pain and felt her frustration.

"Some of them obviously despise us," interjected a third woman from the other side of the room. "How can we love them?"

Rabbi Oren nodded his head before responding. "It's difficult. But if we are in the right place within ourselves, then the disdain we feel from some of our brothers and sisters should push us to do more to change the situation so we'll all be closer. We should work for that closeness, rather than pull ourselves away."

"Some are evil," announced an older woman with a raspy voice.

The room grew noisy as the women, bursting with strong emotions, suddenly began speaking all at once.

"After all they've done to us, why should we be nice to them?"

"I find it hard to believe anymore that we're all the same people."

"Now we must worry about how to help ourselves."

Rabbi Oren cleared his throat and began speaking in a calm and even manner. "We *should* keep our distance from those who are truly evil," he began. Slowly the room quieted down. "But who could really be considered evil amongst our people here? We all want peace and harmony among ourselves and with others. It's true that there are some who think that using violence is the way to solve the problems we have with each other. But that does not make them evil. They are misguided, misinformed, or simply don't perceive things correctly."

"Still, they intentionally hurt us in many ways," the soft-spoken woman sitting two seats away from me challenged Rabbi Oren.

The rabbi stroked his thin, dark beard. "That doesn't make them evil."

Would Sharon, Olmert and the other masterminds behind expulsions and beatings be considered evil? I tried sorting things out in my mind.

"Only the truly evil," Rabbi Oren went on, "are the people from whom we should distance ourselves. Those who don't feel any connection to their Jewish roots and want to wipe out the Jewish nation; those who denounce the nation's existence or seek to destroy the Jewish people are the ones from whom we should separate. But the others, though they might have gone down a crooked road, they are still part of our "family." It is, therefore, forbidden to cut ourselves off from them—or them from us."

I felt my jaw loosen and the tension in my back and shoulders lessening a bit. Rabbi Oren had just put something into perspective for me.

"What Rav Kook is saying here," Rabbi Oren continued, "is that it is our duty to find a way to bring closer those who are confused about what's good or right for our people and our country, or who have strayed from the correct path. We shouldn't relate positively only to those we agree with, and discard those with whom we don't see eye to eye. We are all Jews and we are all G-d's children. We're in this together, for better and for worse.

I clicked my pen open and began taking notes. Rabbi Oren turned back to his book.

"When a person doesn't see reality properly or behaves wrongly, it's not only bad for that individual; it's bad for all of us. We are all affected. Therefore, it's the responsibility of every one of us to fix the problem—for all our sakes. There's no such thing as, 'I'm only concerned for myself and that's enough.'"

The rabbi read a few more lines out loud and then, folding his hands on his book, faced our skeptical group. "Think of *Am Yisrael*[107] as a body. The arms and legs represent the different groups among us that are all attached together at the trunk. If one of those arms or legs was diseased or broken, you wouldn't just cut it off and say, 'Oh, I don't need that part anymore.' Unless that limb was in such bad shape that it put the rest of the body at risk of dying, you would do your best to try to save it. You would try to heal it in order to keep the body whole and functioning properly."

We were all quiet, but I felt the restlessness around me. What we were hearing was true. But our pain and our anger were still overwhelming.

Rabbi Oren adjusted his thin wire-frame glasses and read more. The women and I followed along with our photocopies. Then the rabbi looked up. "Rav Kook is saying we need to understand that despite all the confusion, corruption and scandal in the world, there is still a lot of light, spirituality and good. Man's nature is inherently good. G-d created us with moral, upright and

---

[107] The Jewish people.

respectable souls. We need to believe this. We need to find the good within every person—even within those who don't show it. We can't despair and cast aside anyone who is not *truly* evil, who still has some good in him, somewhere.

"We are on trial here and now." The rabbi let his fist fall to the table like a gavel. "We are on trial to see this goodness within our own people—to find the sparks of holiness that exists within each and every one of us."

A woman in lavender sitting across from me shifted in her chair. Her friend next to her stopped taking notes and looked up at Rabbi Oren. Everyone else sat very still as he continued speaking.

"We can also relate to the Jewish nation as we would to rebellious youths going through that difficult teenage stage of life," he said, adding his own metaphor. "Many teenagers do all kinds of unacceptable things. At times, they act recklessly and irresponsibly, often going in wrong directions, and almost always driving their parents crazy."

Some chuckles from our group punctuated the rabbi's last words. He smiled, and then became serious again.

"Would you, as the mother of one of these teenagers, wipe your hands clean of your own child and his problems by simply kicking him out of the house? Or would you try to work with him to improve his behavior and guide him so he will come to understand you and himself better?"

I would try to work with him. I had no doubt about that one.

"It may be difficult, but we shouldn't cut ourselves off from rebellious teenagers who act inappropriately," the rabbi answered for everyone. "And we shouldn't cut them out of our lives. Nothing productive or good will come from such an act of despair. There will only be more pain, and less understanding. We should help our teenagers and stay with them until they grow and learn and change. They have a lot of good in them, only they are in their 'anti'-phase and don't always behave well. We need to believe that with understanding, guidance and lots of love they will improve and mature in the right way. The good is still inside them and it will come out again."

All eyes in the room were focused intently on Rabbi Oren as he spoke. "We have to believe in our teenagers. And we *must* believe in our people. Even if there is friction or resistance, we must work hard and also pray for all who are a part of our nation. We may not see immediate results from our efforts, but we need to have faith that things *will* get better."

"And if they don't?" I had to ask the question.

"We should continue to fight for that outcome," Rabbi Oren answered matter-of-factly. "If it doesn't come right away, it will come later—with the next generation, or the one after that. Remember, the potential is there.

"Rav Kook teaches us that it's not just our obligation to see the good that is in all of us, but to actually help bring that good out with our actions. We must fight the separation and the splitting of our people. G-d is not leaving us, and we can't leave each other."

Tapping on his arm, he continued, "We need to work on healing that arm, for the sake of the whole body. When we are completely healthy, we will thrive together in the Land G-d gave us. And *together,*" Rabbi Oren intertwined his fingers in front of him, "we will be able to face whatever comes our way."

Gently closing his book, he signified the end of the class for that day. "Until next time," he said, rising from his chair.

We all rose with Rabbi Oren and then, as everyone began filing out of the room, I sat back down to reflect for a moment. My heart still ached, but my body felt more relaxed than it had in a long time. Most of what we had learned that morning made sense to me. I even felt a flutter of hope. Still, there were many more questions to be addressed and bad feelings to be purged. I knew it was going to take a lot to help me and the others feel better. *Maybe next week's class will give me more answers.*

Gathering up my pen and spiral notebook, I followed the women out the door. Suddenly, next Monday seemed a long way off.

CHAPTER 19

MISSION

(May 2006)

"It's three o'clock in the morning. What are you doing up?" Yehuda awakened from a deep sleep to find me sitting in my bathrobe and slippers on the carpet in the hallway near our bedroom.

"I couldn't sleep," I said, looking up from the notebook I was reading.

Yehuda sat down next to me. "What's all this?" he glanced at my notebook. "My notes—from Rabbi Oren's class."

"It must be an interesting class if it's keeping you going at this hour."

"Actually, it is." I leaned back against the wall.

Yehuda yawned. "That's good."

"Rabbi Oren's been explaining that we can't just blame others for everything that's happening these days. The religious and right wingers may also have a part to play in what goes on between everyone here." I looked at Yehuda. "I've come to the conclusion that I think he's right.

"What's that supposed to mean?" Yehuda wasn't sure he liked what he was hearing.

"Well," smoothing the page of my notebook with the

palm of my hand, I tried explaining what I had just read from my notes: "If there are people that don't understand us and aren't happy with us, then maybe we need to stop and think about what might have caused those bad feelings. Was there some unfriendliness on our part too? Were some of our thoughts or actions questionable? Maybe we also weren't understanding enough or tolerant enough. Maybe we didn't show those who clash with us enough reasons why they should love and respect us and what we believe in."

"Well, nobody's perfect," Yehuda said.

"Right," I went on. "Sometimes we slip and even fall. Sometimes we may not be as honest, respectful or good as we should be or try to be."

"Yeah, so..."

"So, we should look into ourselves to fix our flaws and improve our ways. It's not just for our own good, but for the good of all of us, that we work on ourselves—our faith, our ethics and morals, etc."

Yehuda stretched his legs out in front of him. I could see that he was tired, but also trying to concentrate. "So let me get this straight," he interrupted. "Rabbi Oren taught that, according to Rav Kook, we should also accept some of the blame for the way we've been treated? If that's true, then I feel worse than I did before. Didn't you say these classes were making you feel better about things?"

"Yep." I stuck my nose into my notebook and began reading out loud. "Once we begin improving ourselves, we can stand up better to all the trials and tribulations we're given. And eventually, we'll be able to help others get to the place where they'll also ask how they can better themselves and help change things."

"And how are we going to do all that?" Yehuda asked.

"Good question." I began flipping through the pages. "Rav Kook believed that even when there are big conflicts and even when we're hurting, we should always make efforts to connect with others in positive ways. It's not good to be only with people who are similar to us. We should get out there and be involved with *everyone*, and show who we are and what we stand for in a way that speaks to others—with love and respect." I looked up. "In other words, we should all try harder to get along and to work *together*, rather than against each other." Now I looked at Yehuda. "You get it?"

"I get it. We're supposed to keep our faith and continue to do all that G-d expects of us while striving to live harmoniously with all our brothers and sisters, even those who disagree with us and our ways." Yehuda summarized in one breath.

"Good for you!" I smiled at him. "That's how we can start to change things for the better."

"Except," Yehuda interrupted, "it's easier said than done."

"Right. It's our challenge and our work."

"And what about things like the security of our country?" Yehuda yawned again. "And preserving its Jewish essence?"

"Well, loving and respecting each other doesn't mean accepting wrong or objectionable behavior." My eyes were following my finger as it moved along the page. "Just like with the rebellious teenager, we should fight the bad conduct, not the child himself."

"Okaaay." Yehuda nodded his head with approval.

"Slowly, slowly, as we all grow closer to each other, we'll begin to share with one another whatever good is in us and in our beliefs. And then, eventually, the layers of negativity and anger on both sides will start to peel off."

Yehuda folded his arms over his chest. "So, things aren't as bleak as they seem. We have the ability to make things better between all of us."

"We have the *obligation* to make them better." Resting the spiral notebook on my lap, I turned to Yehuda. "You see? We have a mission."

"I see." Yehuda nodded.

"Very good," I said standing up. "You were paying attention, even at this late hour. So," I covered my mouth with my hand to stifle a yawn, "I think now would be a good time to go to sleep."

"Thank G-d for that." Yehuda lifted himself up from the carpet more slowly.

Placing my notes next to the clock on my nightstand, I crawled into bed. I thought about how Rav Kook's wisdom seemed almost prophetic. He'd understood what *Am Yisrael* would be going through long before the events of our time occurred. He'd even known what would be necessary for us to do in the situation we were in today. And he understood with clarity just what G-d expected of all of us.

I was beginning to realize how crucial it was to fight for unity and to continue to strive for positive results, even if it was a slow process and even if it was, at times, an upward battle. Suddenly there seemed to be so much to do.

Resting my head on my pillow, one last realization came to me: *This* was why I made *aliyah*. *This* was why I was living in Israel. I wasn't here just for all the wonder, beauty and spirituality. I was here to give of myself, to try to help my people in times of hardship and struggle, to do my part in bringing us all to a place of love and light.

Like Yehuda said, it wasn't going to be easy. But I felt the need and the desire to help all of us heal.

Now, turning off the small reading lamp over my bed, the dark didn't seem as threatening anymore. My own light, the brightness inside me, was beginning to glow again.

And in just a few hours, a new day would begin.

PART SIX

June 2006—July 2009

·❧· CHAPTER 1 ·❧·

Two days went by without any stories. Carol and Fran each had their day off and Diana's brother came instead of her to visit Mrs. Weissberg. Mrs. Weissberg wasn't thrilled about us taking a break.

"Every time I've been able to sit with all of you and listen to the stories, the next day there always seems to be some reason or another that prevents me from hearing more," she told me. "I look forward to all of us sitting together for that 'story hour.' It always gives me something to think about afterwards too."

"Don't worry," I told Mrs. Weissberg. "I'm pretty sure tomorrow we'll be back on schedule."

❦ ❦ ❦ ❦

The doctor checked in on me just before Fran and Carol arrived the next morning. He looked at my chart and then turned to me. "You're doing very well. You'll probably be leaving us soon."

"Really?" I was all smiles. "That's great!" I was ecstatic just thinking about getting back home.

"You might be happy, but I don't think the people around here are so eager for you to leave," the young doctor told me, hanging my chart back on the foot of my bed. "I hear you've been keeping every-one entertained around here." He let a little smile escape.

"She certainly has," Mrs. Weissberg called over to the doctor from her bed. "Don't let her go until she finishes telling us her story!" she joked, pointing her finger in my direction.

The doctor laughed and then left us. Fran, Carol and Diana walked in at the same time.

"We met down the hall on the way over," Fran told me while taking my temperature. "And we decided that we should get right down to things now and not waste any time."

"She means," Carol took over, "that we know you'll be going home soon, and we want to hear as much as possible before that happens."

As soon as Fran took the thermometer out of my mouth, Carol helped me out of the bed for our walking exercise. "When we get back," she turned to the others, "be ready to begin."

As we left the room, I heard Mrs. Weissberg giving her daughter instructions. "Hurry Diana, help me get closer to Shelly's chair!"

AMAZING THINGS
(June 2006)

Dear Mom,

I know you're not an e-mail person, but since I wasn't home when you called the other day, I thought I'd send you an e-mail to update you a bit.

We're doing all right. Summer vacation is nearly here, which means the kids will all be home and I'll have a break from working in my nursery school for a couple of months. One thing I plan to do is go power walking more often.

My friend Yaffa and I like to whiz around Or Tzion at night when it's cooler outside. We walk fast past the archeaological ruins near our house and then all the way over to the cell phone towers with their huge antenaes reaching up to the sky on the other side of town. It's amazing having the ancient world and the modern world all in one place, like in Jerusalem and just about everywhere else in Israel.

Speaking of Jerusalem, yesterday I met my friend Navah there and we went to the latest "Free Jonathan Pollard" rally near the center of town. Do you know who Jonathan Pollard is? He's an American Jew who handed important information over to the Israeli government in the '80s. He gave Israel a head's up about the latest security threats other countries were planning against it. And because of that, he's been locked up in an American prison for the past twenty-one years. What's strange about his case is that any other person charged with similar crimes in the US served three to five or maybe, at the most, seven years in prison. But Jonathan Pollard was sentenced to life.

Everyone here in Israel is upset because Pollard didn't do something to hurt another country. He gave Israel a chance for self-defense and helped it continue to exist. And besides that, the US and Israel have always been allies. They even had an official agreement that they would share security intelligence with each other. So actually, Israel had a legitimate right to know that information Pollard passed on.

Anyway, for all these years, people in both Israel and in the US have been holding rallies and lobbying for him to be granted clemency, or at least given a shorter sentence. At the rally yesterday, his wife spoke. She thanked us for all of our efforts and asked that we keep trying to help Pollard gain his freedom so he can finally come join her here in Israel. It would be really amazing if he'd be able to do that some day.

And now I'm going to tell you about something else amazing that actually happened here in Or Tzion. Last week our friends, the Feldmans, invited us to a wedding in their backyard. It's a great story. The bride and groom met after they'd both made *aliyah*. They each had only a few friends and no relatives living in the country. Their parents couldn't afford to make them a wedding or come to Israel, so they were going to get married without a celebration. But the Feldmans, who'd gotten to know the couple a bit, decided to make a wedding for them in their backyard!

They set up the *chuppah* on their lawn and some of their son's musician friends got together and formed the band. The photographer and video guy were both from Or Tzion, so they gave discounted prices. All the women who came to the celebration pitched in with the food. And while we women danced and whirled around with the bride on the patio, the men whooped it up with the groom on the lawn near the *chuppah*. It was a real exciting and down to earth celebration!

But what was the most amazing thing about it? Except for the Feldmans and a handful of the couple's friends, the bride and groom didn't know any of us there! We were all strangers who, in an instant, had become the friends and family who made their wedding special. Pretty neat, huh?

Okay, that's it for now. Hope everything is going well with you. Please let me know when you're planning to call again, so I can make sure to be home.

Love, Shelly

"So, is that Pollard guy still in prison for helping Israel?" Fran wanted to know.

"He's been locked up now for thirty years and his health has deteriorated," I told her.

"I've heard quite a lot about him," Diana said. "It's sad that nobody's been able to get him out yet."

"At least that incredible backyard wedding had a happy ending," Carol acknowledged.

"And that power walking sounds like fun," Mrs. Weissberg said. "That's the trend these days for keeping fit, isn't it?"

"It's healthier than going to the gym," Diana informed her mother. "The air is fresher outside."

"Any kind of exercise is better than just sitting around all day," Fran said. "So if any of you want to join me at the fitness center for one of my classes, you're certainly welcome. You too, Mrs. Weissberg and Shelly," she said, smiling affectionately at the two of us, "after we get you both out of this place and back on your feet."

"I'd love to jump around and do a million situps with you," Carol said. "I still have a little bit of extra weight that I never got rid of from fifteen years ago when I was pregnant with my twins." Carol pinched her waistline through her white uniform. "But since none of us are going anywhere at this point, I think we should probably get on with it. What are we up to, Shelly?"

"Hmmm. We've covered a lot. I think we've reached the next two wars."

"The next *two* wars?" Fran laughed. "Only two?" she crossed her arms in front of her. "Why not three or maybe four?"

"It's like jumping from the frying pan into the fire," Carol said.

"Believe me, we weren't too thrilled about it either." I stretched my leg out on the therapy bench. "But really, I'm trying my best to keep all of you from getting bored."

"Ha!"Carol snickered. "That's a good one."

"Don't worry about us," Mrs. Weissberg said, missing my little joke.

"There's certainly no need to worry about Shelly either," Fran assured everyone. "If there's one thing I've learned about life over there in Israel, there's no being bored for too long."

"Yeah, something's always keeping us on our toes," I agreed.

"Like two wars." Diana smiled at me.

"Yeah." I returned her smile. "Like two wars."

DOUBLE WAR, TRIPLE KIDNAPPINGS
(July 2006)

"They took one of our soldiers!" Hadas ran into the kitchen where I was clearing the supper dishes from the kitchen table. Yehuda was loading up the dishwasher.

"What are you talking about?" I dropped a handful of dirty silverware into the sink and turned to face Hadas.

"I just read it on the Internet. Hamas snuck through

underground tunnels and got to our army posts. They attacked our soldiers and kidnapped one of them!"

Yehuda and I looked at each other and then quickly followed Hadas over to the computer to see the report. It was true. Ever since Gush Katif was handed over, Hamas terrorists, who were elected by the residents of Gaza to rule the area, had been increasing their rocket fire on southern Israel. And now they'd attacked some IDF soldiers and captured nineteen-year-old Corporal Gilad Shalit!

The news about the kidnapping and about the young soldiers Hamas had just murdered in its attack swiftly spread throughout the country. While Israelis mourned for their slain boys, they were especially worried about Gilad Shalit.

"He's only a kid!"

"We've got to get him back fast!"

"We have to retaliate against Hamas and bring Gilad home!"

In an attempt to prevent the kidnappers from moving their young captor deeper into hiding, Israel launched air strikes on Gaza's bridges and main power plant. Then the army began an all-out effort to put a stop to Hamas' Kassam rockets and mortar shells, and to search for Gilad Shalit.

The IDF[108] dropped thousands of leaflets from helicopters into Gaza, warning civilians to leave the area before it began its military operation. Despite this act, Israel was still condemned from all sides of the globe.

"We're always the bad guys," I said at the restaurant in Jerusalem where Benny, Yaffa, Yehuda and I had just placed our orders. "It doesn't matter how humanitarian we are."

---

[108] Israel Defense Forces.

"That's right," Benny agreed. "Lies and negative media coverage will do that. Remember that saying, 'Damned if you do and damned if you don't?' That's us." Benny took a warm roll from the basket on the table. "They'll probably find a way to blame us for the kidnapping of our own soldier too."

"Have you ever heard of any other army, *anywhere*, sending out warnings to civilians before attacking?" I leaned forward with my elbows on the table.

"Nope," Yehuda answered. "We're the only ones who do that. Too bad it didn't help the people in Gaza. Hamas won't allow their own citizens to evacuate the war zones. They actually want their people to be killed so everyone will accuse *us* of being vicious murderers."

"That's how it is these days." Benny was now putting butter on his knife. "They can be as violent and ruthless as they want, but we're not allowed to defend ourselves, no matter how careful we are to protect lives."

"Well, if we're going to be condemned for defending ourselves then maybe we should just ask Hamas to *please* keep their mortars and Kassams to themselves," Yaffa joined in. "And, while we're at it, let's ask them to *please* give back Gilad Shalit," she went on. "Then, when they fully cooperate, which we all know they will *of course do*, there will be nothing to fight about and all will be well."

"Uh, I think you might want to come up with a different plan," I joked with Yaffa from across the table, "just for safe measure."

"You think?" Yaffa winked at me. "Okay. So, maybe we won't say 'please.'"

❧ ❧ ❧ ❧

It wasn't enough that Hamas had captured Gilad Shalit and was firing Kassam rockets at us in the South. Only a few weeks later, grief and worry gripped the nation doubly hard as Hizbullah terrorists in Lebanon attacked Israel with Katyusha rockets in the North. Like Hamas, Hizbullah also struck Israeli soldiers guarding the border. But, unlike Hamas, they didn't kidnap only one of the soldiers. They kidnapped two.

Things are going from bad to worse, I groaned to myself as I handed Ronit a banana to eat in her highchair. Hamas was still hiding Gilad Shalit somewhere in Gaza, and now Hizbullah had Ehud Goldwasser and Eldad Regev up north in Lebanon or possibly in Syria.

"We're targeting Hizbullah's military positions with air strikes," Yehuda informed me after listening to the news.

"I wonder if that will be enough." I was concerned. "Hizbullah's Katyushas are hitting us like crazy in the North. Everyone in Kiryat Shemona, Tzfat, Haifa and the other towns and cities up there are hiding out in bomb shelters."

"Well, it looks like we'll be sending our ground troops into Lebanon," Yehuda replied.

"Here we go again." I'd felt, as many had after the First Lebanon War ended in 1985, that it was just a matter of time before our soldiers would be crossing back over the Lebanese border again. The IDF[109] had kept a certain number of soldiers in southern Lebanon for security purposes. But when the Israeli government agreed to pull those soldiers out of the security zone in 2000, Hizbullah terrorists rushed in and took over the area.

"Our boys will have to go back over there," Yehuda

---

[109] Israel Defense Forces.

said, "since we're being sucked into a second war with Hizbullah."

In many ways, the Second Lebanon War with Hizbullah was similar to the war in Gaza with Hamas. In both wars, Israel was bombarded with daily rocket attacks aimed at the country's civilian centers. Both Hamas' leaders and Hizbullah's leader, Hassan Nasrallah, pushed for prisoner exchanges for the Israeli soldiers they'd kidnapped. In both cases, the Israeli government was considering trading as many as a thousand convicted Arab terrorists to get its soldiers back.

"Hizbullah doesn't care about the people in Lebanon any more than Hamas cares about its citizens in Gaza," I said, washing banana off Ronit's hands and face. "They do the same kinds of things Hamas does to raise their civilian death toll, like hiding themselves among the people."

"Yeah," Yehuda replied, "and when the number of casualties goes up, the world once again screams about 'those brutal Israelis.'"

I took Ronit up to her room and arranged her stuffed animals along the side of her crib, making space for her to lie down. One after the other, like little soldiers, I lined up the long-eared bunny rabbit and the white kitty cat, the fluffy teddy bear and the smiling lion. "Now you can take your nap, cutie." I covered Ronit's curled-up body with her sunny yellow blanket. Then I watched her eyes close as she sucked on her pudgy little thumb. Standing next to her crib, I thought about our three soldiers who had fallen into enemy hands. *Their mothers probably also watched them fall asleep when they were babies.*

The two wars were softening the anger and bitterness many of us felt towards the soldiers after Gush Katif and Amona. We were once again concerned for our men and boys who were now risking their lives to defend our country.

Some soldiers, who were still emotionally and morally struggling with the painful expulsions, found it difficult to rid themselves of their recent anti-IDF sentiments. But most of the boys called up to serve did so without any doubt as to where their duty lay, and without looking backwards.

Ronit's breathing grew heavy and her thumb gradually slipped out of her mouth. I was happy she could fall asleep so quickly, with no cares in the world.

"Ema? Where are you?" Michal was calling me from the hallway outside Ronit's bedroom. "Ema?" she peeked her head through the half open door. "Oh, there you are."

"Shhh," I said softly, pointing to sleeping Ronit. "Let's go somewhere else," I whispered, taking Michal by the elbow and leading her out of the room.

"Ema," Michal began again once I closed Ronit's door, "I don't get why there are two wars going on here now. The second intifada ended last year, so now the terrorists in other countries think it's a good to time for *them* to start up against us?"

I followed Michal across the narrow carpeted hallway into her pink and blue bedroom. "Many would have liked the second intifada to go on forever," I told her. "But thank G-d it's over. And don't worry, these wars will end too."

Michal, who had just turned eleven, sat cross-legged on her blue carpet. "I heard that some people are leaving the South to go to safer places in the country and that most of the people in the North are living in bomb shelters."

"Right. It's been really hard on those living in the South, and now the North is also being hit like mad." I lowered myself onto Michal's pink bean bag chair.

"It must be crowded and stuffy in those bomb shelters."

"I'm sure it is." I was very thankful that we lived in the middle of the country and weren't personally experiencing such things.

"It's probably horrible for them," Michal went on.

"What if some of the women are pregnant or if there are families with little babies or hysterical kids?" She was concerned. "They have to sleep and eat in there too, right?"

"I assume many of them do." I sunk deeper into the cushiony chair. "A lot of Northerners will probably also move to other areas until the war up there ends."

Michal reached up and plucked a small pink heart pillow off her bed. "Do you think any of the people will come here, or to the other *yishuvim*,[110] like the Sa Nur people did after the Disengagement?"

"Could be."

"I'm glad we live in Or Tzion," Michal said. "We don't have to worry about missiles, bomb shelters or running to live somewhere else."

I smiled inwardly at the irony of it all, considering all we'd been through over the years, sandwiched between Arab villages that didn't want us around any more than Hamas or Hizbullah did. "Right," I agreed. "Now, *we're* the lucky ones. But we still have to worry about those suffering in the other parts of the country."

"And we have to worry about our soldiers," Michal hugged the soft pillow to her chest, "especially the kidnapped ones."

"You're right about that too," I said. My heart ached, just thinking about them. "No matter what," I looked at Michal, "We still have to worry about our soldiers."

---

[110] Settlement towns.

·❖· CHAPTER 3 ·❖·

AIDING THE WAR REFUGEES
(July 2006)

Eitan was struggling to maneuver a purple bicycle out of the shed.

"You're pretty strong for a seven-year-old." Yehuda walked across the backyard lawn and stood next to Eitan. "Need some help with that?"

Stepping back, Eitan let Yehuda take over. "Ema said we don't need these two bikes anymore," he motioned to the purple bicycle next to him and the little red tricycle he'd already pulled out of the shed. "So we're going to bring them to the families who came to live here last week because of the war with Lebanon."

"That's a good idea," Yehuda said. "The children who came from the North to escape the war are probably getting bored without their friends from home or any of their own toys and games."

"Right," Eitan said with a nod. "That's what I told Ema too."

Yehuda put the bicycles in the back of our station wagon. I added a bag of games, dolls and small toys that our kids were willing to give away. Opening the screen door, I called into the house, "Okay, who's going with me to bring these things to the families from the North?"

While the Gaza War with Hamas continued in the South, the Lebanon War with Hizbullah was progressing with intensity in the North. More than a million people were seeking refuge in bomb shelters and hundreds of thousands had already fled the Kassams and Katyushas for the calmer middle areas of the country.

Hadas and Eitan drove with me to the two rows of students' caravans that were supposed to be vacant for the summer, but were filled with refugees from cities and towns in the North. Hadas helped me take the bicycles out of the car when we arrived at the caravans with our gifts. "Where did the people staying here come from?" she asked, as we walked towards the first caravan.

"Abba told me a lot of them are from Tzfat," Eitan answered, carrying the plastic bag with dolls and stuffed animals.

"That's right." Katyusha missiles were landing in and around Tzfat all the time. I was concerned about my friend Rachel, who'd become a special education teacher and was now living in the northern city of Tiberias, not far from Tzfat. And of course, I wondered how everyone from the Livnot program was managing. I'd heard that Arnon and Meira were organizing volunteers to help the elderly and the sick, and to bring food and provisions to those in shelters.

"I want to go up north to volunteer in the bomb shelters," Hadas said, as if she had just read my thoughts. "I could play with the kids and keep them occupied. Or help give out food."

I held my breath. *Of course. I should have figured she'd want to do that.* "There's a war going on there, Hadas. I know people are going up there to help out, but I'm sorry, I can't let you go."

Before Hadas could reply, I knocked on the sun-faded wooden door of the first caravan. "We're dropping off the bicycles and the bags here," I said, quickly changing the subject.

A short woman flanked by two young children on either side of her opened the door. "Shalom." She didn't look surprised to see us. Many other Or Tzion residents had already come to visit the refugee families from the North, bringing basic supplies and offering their assistance and moral support.

"Shalom. Welcome to Or Tzion," I said. "We brought some things for your children to share with the rest of the neighbors who are staying here now." As soon as I finished speaking, the little boy and girl left their mother's side and rushed over to examine what was in the bag Hadas was holding out to them. Another young boy who was standing outside spotted the red tricycle and ran over to it.

"You can ride it," Hadas told him. The boy immediately sat on the crooked seat, and with excitement in his eyes, began pedaling up and down the asphalt path in front of the caravans.

An older daughter came to see who was at the door and offered to distribute the toys and games between some of the other families. "*Todah rabbah,*"[111] the mother said with a faint smile, her tired eyes watching her children enthusiastically sifting through the bag.

I felt the woman's stress overshadowing her appreciation. I imagined that the affects of war and living in a cramped two-bedroom caravan without any of the possessions or luxuries of home was wearing.

We drank some water the woman offered us and then went to knock on a few more doors. On the way to the next caravan, we ran into a young man wearing a black yarmulke and a white shirt with his sleeves rolled up. He

---

[111] Thank you very much.

and his wife were on their way back from doing laundry. "There are only a couple of washing machines for all of the families to use," he said setting down the bundle of clean clothes. "We always have to wait a long time to do just one load, so we've been hand washing whatever we need for the next day, hoping everything will dry in time on the line outside."

"I can do a couple of loads for you." I was eager for the chance to help in a more concrete way.

Hadas, Eitan and I ended up collecting laundry from four families. "It's hard being away from home," one of the men told us, as he threw a pair of dirty socks into the plastic bag he was filling. "If it weren't for the war," he tied the bag shut with its yellow pull string, "I would *never* have come to a settlement town like this—with Arab villages all around it. But after being here these past few days," he smiled as he handed me the bag, "I'm very glad we did. It's more peaceful than I expected and I'm already connecting a bit to the people in the community."

The woman in the last caravan helped us bring the bags of dirty laundry to the car. "To be honest, I would never have believed I'd be living in Or Tzion or in any other *yishuv* in Judea and Samaria, even temporarily," she admitted. "But now we're all feeling very lucky that we're able to be here."

"It's so funny," Hadas said after the woman left. "If it weren't for the wars, probably *none* of these families would have ever come here."

"Right." I agreed. "Who would have thought we'd be one of the safest places in the country for people to stay? It just goes to show you..." I started the car and began backing away from the caravans.

"What does it show us?" Eitan asked.

"We should never take things for granted, and never assume that everything will always stay the same," I said.

"Things can change at any time, when you least expect it—for better, as is in our case, or for worse, like what's happening in other parts of the country."

When we arrived back home, Yehuda was waiting for us in front of the house with more stuffed bags. We were now going to different families who were staying at the other end of the *yishuv*, in the girls' high school dormitory apartments.

"Abba!" Eitan called through his open window.

"I packed up the things you told me we're bringing to our 'adopted family,'" Yehuda told me. "But maybe you'd better double-check that everything's here."

"What do you mean, 'adopted family'?" Eitan asked.

"We agreed to be in charge of helping one of the families, the Greenbergs, who just came from Haifa," Yehuda said. "They'll be staying in one of the dormitory apartments until the war ends."

"Until which war ends?" Eitan cocked his head to the side.

"We're hoping both wars will be over soon," Yehuda said. "But these people came here because of the war in the North."

"Oh," Eitan said. "They were *also* too scared to stay in their own houses."

"What are we bringing them?" Hadas wanted to know.

"We're bringing a couple of pots, mixing bowls and some cooking utensils," I said, making a quick check of the contents in the bags before putting them in the car next to the laundry bags. "And a few fun things for their kids too."

"We met the Greenbergs last night, a few hours after they arrived," Yehuda told Hadas and Eitan. "They're very nice."

"Do they have any kids my age?" Eitan asked, hopping back into the car.

"Are they happy to be here?" Hadas asked.

"Yes, and yes," I answered, getting in on the passenger's side. "They have three young children. They tried to stay in Haifa, but it was too hard for them. None of them could sleep. The sirens, the explosions and their shaky nerves kept them up all night and on edge during the day."

"Those poor kids," Hadas said. 'They were probably really afraid."

"Their mother told us it wasn't easy for any of them," I continued. "Any loud noise made them jump. And she said that it was a nightmare every time there was a siren and they had to run to the shelter."

"We're here," Eitan said, as we pulled into the small parking lot. "Why are people coming to live here every summer?" He remembered that we came to the same dormitory buildings a year ago when we visited the expelled Sa Nur families.

It's not every summer," Hadas said. "It's only when they need a place to be."

"There are different families here this time," Yehuda explained, taking the bags of toys and kitchen supplies out of the trunk.

"Let's hope next summer will be quiet and uneventful," I said.

"It better be," Hadas grabbed one of the bags. "Last summer was ruined by the Disengagement and this summer by the wars."

"Yeah, we didn't get to go camping last year like we always do," Eitan moaned.

I understood the children's disappointment. I wasn't thrilled with how our summer vacation was turning out either. But I knew that, if nothing else, we were all once again learning valuable lessons about giving, sharing, working together and helping our extended family—*Am Yisrael*.

"Can we go camping this year?" Eitan asked.

"We'll see what happens," I answered vaguely. I couldn't try to figure out what we might or might not be doing, if and when things quieted down some time in the future.

"We're taking things one day at a time," Yehuda spoke my thoughts out loud.

"All right," Eitan quickly dropped the subject. "So can I be the one who gives them the dinosaur we brought?"

"Yes, you can," I said.

We each took a bag and began walking towards the dormitory apartments. Eitan swung his arms enthusiastically as he walked. I could tell he was excited about meeting our "adopted family." Happy that he was able to change his focus so easily, I wished I could also feel less tension and be more relaxed. *Who knows*, I thought as we entered the building, *maybe they'll find our kidnapped soldiers soon. Maybe the fighting will end quickly.* I glanced at Eitan, who was now skipping up the stairs. *Maybe we'll get to go camping this summer, after all.*

CHAPTER 4

ALL QUIET ON NORTHERN FRONT

(August 2006)

The tents were up and the sleeping bags were spread out on their mats. Yehuda prepared the barbecue grill, while the kids and I ventured off to the creek that was flowing through our campgrounds.

A week ago, the Second Lebanon War ended with a UN-imposed ceasefire. Nobody was sure how long the quiet in the North would last, but our family and many others decided to take advantage of it. With only two weeks left of summer vacation, we gathered our camping gear and headed up to the Galilee and the Golan Heights for a few days of nature, adventure and much needed relaxation.

"I'm really happy we got to come here now," Yael was hopping from one smooth stepping stone to another, as we walked through the creek's cool streaming water. I was also relieved to be finally doing something fun and more restful. Plus, I felt good knowing that, just by being in the North, we were helping bring the area back to life.

Hadas took off her sandals and sat down in her clothes on a low rock in the water. "Ahhh, that feels great," she said, immersing herself up to her waist. "I want to stay right here forever!"

We took it easy for most of the day, staying near the water as much as possible. At night, it took a while for the family to unwind. The kids complained about the heat, and argued about who would be sleeping where and which sleeping bag they would each have. After everyone finally settled down, I lay in the tent listening to the crickets. The night air was quiet and still. I could hear the low voices of the croaking frogs and the rushing water in the distance.

Only a few days before, deadly Katyusha rockets were crashing into the very area where we were now sleeping under the peaceful moon and starlit sky. More than four hundred thousand Israelis living in the North had left their homes, jobs and schools to escape the fear and stress of war. *And now*, I thought ironically, *the first chance we had, so many of us jumped to leave **our** homes to come up here!*

The Galilee and the Golan Heights were favorite Israeli vacation spots during the summer months. Northerners geared up all winter for the barrage of campers and tourists who jammed into their hotels, cabins and campsites each year. This summer, the Second Lebanon War changed everything. Only volunteers and charity organizations bringing food and provisions to the bomb shelters came to the area.

When the Katyushas stopped coming, many of us grabbed the opportunity to spend our last remaining vacation days in the beauty and fresh air of the Galilee and the Golan Heights. Massive crowds didn't show up as in previous years, but the trails, shops, tourist sites and restaurants were all open again.

Although we were helping boost the war-devastated economy for the people in the North, I felt a twinge of guilt about relaxing and enjoying ourselves while Hamas was still shooting Kassam rockets and mortar shells into the South. *This is a complex country we live in.* Closing my eyes,

I turned onto my side. *So much always happening, yet life still goes on.*

We had a light breakfast at the campsite in the morning before beginning our day's excursions. On the way to our first hiking trail, we passed through the quaint city of Kiryat Shemona, near the Lebanese border.

"Look at the big hole in that house!" Eitan was pointing out the car window. Yehuda stopped the car at the side of the road, allowing us to gaze for a minute at the small stucco house with the gaping hole in its side.

"Was it hit by a Kassam?" Michal asked. She'd been blowing bubbles with her gum, but now, licking her sticky lips, she stopped to look out her open window.

"I'm not really sure what the difference is between all the rockets and missiles sent our way," Yehuda answered. "All I know is that Hamas is shooting off Kassams down south into the Negev and Hizbullah was firing Katyushas into the towns and cities up here in the North," he explained. "That house must have been one of Hizbullah's successful hits."

For over a month, Hizbullah had fired more than four thousand Katyushas into northern Israel—nearly a hundred and fifty rockets each day. Miraculously, they missed the majority of their targets. Nonetheless, physical and emotional damage was widespread and Israelis living in the North were still trying to get their nerves in check. As they slowly returned to their normal lives, some were literally picking up the pieces of their destroyed homes or other buildings around them.

"Wow!" Hadas couldn't take her eyes off the enormous opening. "Their house is ruined."

"Hopefully nobody was hurt," I said.

"Are there people inside?" Eitan unbuckled his seatbelt to get a better look.

"I'm sure there aren't," I said, staring at the war-torn

house. "The inside must also be a wreck."

As we drove through Kiryat Shemona, there was nothing to indicate that most of the residents had either left the area or had been stuck in bomb shelters for most of the summer. The city appeared to be functioning normally. Everyone seemed to be going about their everyday lives as if nothing had occurred to change that. I noticed a boy walking his dog and a young woman with a baby carriage crossing the street. Cars and buses were running as usual, and children were in the playgrounds or riding their bicycles.

"It's hard to believe that Katyushas were exploding all over the place here," Yehuda said.

But then, turning the corner, we spotted an apartment building with part of its roof blown off. It stood out above the lower, adjacent buildings, adding more evidence that a nasty war had, in fact, stormed the city.

Yehuda stopped the car again when we came to a demolished stone wall further on. This time, everyone except for Ronit, who had fallen asleep in her car seat, got out and walked over to look at the ruins.

"That must be where the rocket actually landed," I said, indicating the blackened ground near some of the crumbled stone.

"I thought there were a lot of miracles in this war," Yael looked at me. "What about all these places that have been destroyed?"

"Just think how much worse it could have been," Yehuda said. "Thousands of missiles were fired. There were plenty of direct hits, but a lot of them didn't strike anything significant, or anything at all."

"Right," I said, nodding. "I spoke with Arnon in Tzfat and he said that most of them landed in nearby fields but not in the city itself.

"And remember when the war ended and we drove the

Greenbergs back to their home in Haifa?" Yehuda asked. "Well, when we got there one of the neighbors told us that a Katyusha had landed in the open area between the Greenberg's apartment building and the one directly behind it. What are the odds of it missing both buildings like that?"

Hadas jumped in. "I heard about people who were inside their houses or other buildings that got hit, but nothing happened to them. They'd left the room seconds before the rocket came through the ceiling or wall."

"There are a lot of near-miss stories," Yehuda said. "In many of the incidents, everything caved in all around the people inside the building, but not in the spot where they had been sitting or sleeping."

"Wow," Michal said, as we all got back into the car.

"But some people *were* hurt, and even killed," Yael pointed out.

"Even with lots of miracles, war is always terrible," I told her.

Yael settled herself in the far back seat and then changed the topic. "When are we going to help the farmers pick their fruit?"

"Which farmers?" Eitan asked. "Why do the farmers need help?"

Yehuda started the car. "They couldn't be in their fields to harvest their crops or pick the fruit in their orchards on time because of the war," he told Eitan. "So people are coming now from other parts of the country to help them do that fast, before it's too late and everything gets spoiled."

"We're going to help them too, right?" Hadas was hopeful.

"We were going to," I said, "but every place I called said that they don't need us because so many other people have already come to help out."

"I wanted to pick fruit," Michal moaned.

"Don't worry," Yehuda said, "I heard that some blueberries are still left on the bushes, even though blueberry season's basically over. I don't know how great they are now, but tomorrow we're going blueberry picking just for fun, like we do every year."

"Yay!" Eitan cheered.

"The best part," Yael said, rubbing her hands together, "is eating the berries while we're picking them."

We spent the rest of the day hiking on trails through nature reserves. Ronit, with her little white sunhat, bounced along in the baby carrier on Yehuda's back, as we walked on dusty mountain paths and waded through cool waters.

"This is the life," Yehuda said when we reached a large natural pool with a rushing waterfall plunging down from the cliff above.

"We didn't bring any clothes to change into," Yael said, after coming out of the water with her clothes dripping.

"It's so hot, we'll dry off fast on the hike back," Yehuda told her.

The heat wave continued the following day. I grabbed the sunscreen and reminded the kids to bring their sunhats and water bottles before we left the campsite that morning to go blueberry picking. By afternoon, everyone agreed that being in the water was the only way we'd survive the sweltering heat for the rest of the day.

We drove a while to Nahal HaKibbutzim riverbed to seek refuge from the heat. The kids ran straight to the elevated bank where people were taking turns swinging from a thick twined rope attached to a large tree. One at a time, they pushed off the bank with their bare feet and swung through the air before dropping into the water below.

"Eitan, wait!" Yehuda called, as Eitan stepped forward

to take his turn. "Let me get closer in case you need me to help you after you jump in."

"Look over here, Eitan!" I waved to my energetic son, who was all smiles as I snapped a picture of him in his shorts and Spiderman T-shirt, tightly gripping the rope with his little hands.

Over and over again, the kids jumped from the edge, swinging like Tarzan, then plummeting into the water beneath them. Even Yehuda had kicked off his sandals and joined in the fun a couple of times. Too scared to even *consider* flinging myself like that into a body of water, I waded around in the more shallow part, smearing sunscreen on my face and arms, and taking pictures of everyone.

It took a little convincing, but I did join in on the next adventurous activity, which involved two enormous concrete pipes sticking out of the water. The kids lost no time climbing into the tunnel-like-pipes and riding the rushing stream that was gushing out, shooting them like cannon balls back into the reservoir.

"C'mon, Ema," Michal urged me. "You can do this!"

"I'll do it together with you the first time," Hadas said, her light skin already taking on a slightly sunburned shade of pink. "You can sit behind me."

I sat down and held onto my brave eldest daughter, tightly clutching her wet T-shirt in my nervous hands. As the water whisked us through the pipe, I shut my eyes tightly and shrieked, "W-a-i-t! I'-m n-o-t r-e-a-d-y!!"

Yehuda and the kids were in the water on the other end, waiting to give me a hand after Hadas and I torpedoed out.

"How'd you like it, Ema?" Yael asked, still laughing at my initial reaction.

"It was a little scary," I admitted. Then, looking at Yael I said, "C'mon, let's do it again!"

At the end of the third day of our camping trip,

everyone helped pack up for the ride back home. Yehuda and Hadas took down the tents. Yael and Michal stuffed the sleeping bags into their sacks. Eitan kept Ronit occupied, while I gathered items that were strewn about the campsite and collected the clothes that had been drying on tree branches.

"Why do I have to take care of the sleeping bags?" Michal complained.

"Yeah," Yael said, smashing the last bit of a dark green sleeping bag into its matching sack, "we have the hardest job."

"I'm the one who has the hardest job," Eitan said with pride. "I have to make sure Ronit doesn't wander off."

"*Selichah*?[112] You guys think you've got it hard?" Hadas was on her knees inside one of the emptied tents. "Who wants to help me get all these leaves and pebbles out of here?"

I was only half listening to the children's grumblings. Although I was feeling much more relaxed than when we had left Or Tzion a few days earlier, my mind slowly began to shift back to reality as we got ready for our trip home. The Second Lebanon War was over, but as far as many of us were concerned, it had ended badly. In general, the people weren't happy with how it had been conducted either. Unfortunate mistakes and bad judgment calls had caused over one hundred and twenty soldiers and more than forty civilians to lose their lives. Plus, we hadn't been able to rescue Ehud Goldwasser and Eldad Regev, who Hizbullah was still holding hostage.

According to the treaty signed to end the war, the IDF had to withdraw and international troops were to move into southern Lebanon to try to provide security for Israel.

---

[112] Excuse me!

Hizbullah was to be disarmed and was to allow the Lebanese government to have control over its own country. It was forbidden for any foreign powers, including Iran and Syria, to rearm Hizbullah or any other terrorist groups in Lebanon.

These ceasefires don't usually last very long. We'll see what happens this time. I threw some empty water bottles into the nearby garbage container.

"*Yallah ya*[113] Nasrallah." Walking back towards the rest of the family, I could hear Michal singing. "*We'll get you good, Hizbullah!*" The popular song that poked fun at the Hizbullah leader, Hassan Nasrallah, could still be heard playing on most radio stations. The kids knew the words by heart.

"That's not how it goes," Yael reproached her sister, as they rolled up two more sleeping bags. "You're not singing it right."

"Well, that's how *I* sing it." Michal retorted.

"It doesn't matter what the exact words are," Yehuda said, folding up the first tent. "It's a catchy tune and that's all that matters. Now can everybody argue a little less and work a little more?"

"*Yallah ya*, Nasrallah," Eitan began singing from under the wooden picnic table where he and Ronit were investigating bugs in the shade.

"*Yallah* Nas ah ah," Ronit sang, poking a black beetle with a little twig.

An hour later, after stopping for ice cream and the bathroom, we were enjoying a quieter ride home. The kids had piled into the car, fighting over who would get to sit next to little Ronit, and then, one at a time, they all eventually fell asleep.

---

[113] Come on.

Yehuda and I were discussing which part of the trip we had enjoyed the best. We both agreed it was just what we all had needed.

"But it ended too quickly," I said.

"Yeah," Yehuda said, switching the radio on softly, "it always does."

The loud monotonic beeps that announce each hourly news report sounded. Then the radio announcer's voice came on. We listened to the news of the day, including the update on the situation in the South. It wasn't looking good. Hamas was still acting relentless against both the Israelis and its own citizens in Gaza, not caring how many people they killed on either side. Israel was continuing with air and ground strikes in Gaza, and still searching for Gilad Shalit.

The newscaster reported that another siren had just gone off in the town of Sderot, which was getting the brunt of the Kassam and mortar shell attacks, now that there was no more Gush Katif to absorb them.

"Well, the Second Lebanon War is over," Yehuda spoke over the newscaster, "but it looks like things aren't quieting down so fast in the South."

Before I could respond, familiar music filled the car.

"It's the Nasrallah song!" Yehuda turned up the radio, forgetting about the sleeping children in the back.

"Hey, it's the *Yallah* song!" Eitan woke up with a start, accidently jabbing his elbow into Michal, who was sleeping next to him.

"Ow! Watch it!" Michal reprimanded her brother. Stretching, she too awakened to the words she had been singing only a few hours earlier.

"*Yallah ya* Nasrallah," Yehuda and Eitan sang along with the radio.

Ronit yawned, then giggled and clapped her pudgy hands as Michal and I joined in.

Hadas and Yael opened their eyes at the same time, just as the next stanza was about to begin. Yehuda made the radio louder and our two older girls quickly got into the act, singing the rhyming Hebrew words into their fist "microphones."

> Even if you shower us with rockets that you send,
> Or threaten the Galilee with your Syrian and Iranian friends,
> Even if you make more Katyushas fall,
> Know that there's no despair here at all.
> For, together we'll overcome the trouble that you cause.

Turning around in my seat, I lifted my hands in the air like a conductor, just in time to lead everyone in the chorus. "Okay. All together now!" I called out.

With my hands rhythmically waving back and forth and Yehuda tapping the steering wheel like a drum to the beat of the music, we left the North behind us—the whole family, now wide awake, whizzing down the highway, bellowing out in unison: *"Yallah ya* Nasrallah. We'll get you good, *Inshallah*[114]... with all the Hizbullah!"

There was no doubt in any of our minds—we'd be returning again next year.

---

[114] G-d willing; lit., Allah willing.

"Yallah ya... and whatever the rest of the words are!" Mrs. Weissberg was enjoying herself, trying to mimic the way our family sang the Nasrallah song. "I can't get over how there always seems to be so much happening over there." Mrs. Weissberg's eyes widened as she spoke.

Diana smiled. "It's true. There weren't any wars going on any of the times I went there, but there were always plenty of interesting things happening or some fun holiday being celebrated, like Purim or Sukkot, or..."

"What's that?" Fran interrupted.

"What?" Diana looked at Fran.

"What you said, Soocoat."

"Sukkot? It's a Jewish holiday that lasts for a week," Diana answered. "Anyone who celebrates Sukkot builds a wooden hut-like structure called a sukkah, which basically takes the place of the house throughout the holiday. Shelly would know better than me, but I think it's supposed to resemble or remind us of the fragile dwellings our ancestors lived in when they were wandering in the desert and G-d protected them and provided them with everything they needed."

"You explained that well," I praised Diana.

"I only know what I remember from being in Israel during Sukkot," Diana admitted. "In Israel," she told the others, "sukkahs are everywhere—in people's yards and on porches. Even restaurants have sukkahs for people to eat in!"

"There aren't too many sukkahs where I live," Carol said. "But the family across the street from us builds one every year. When my boys were little, they would peek inside to see how it was decorated."

Mrs. Weissberg turned to Diana. "Remember when you and your brother were young and we'd sometimes join the Schwartzes in their sukkah next door?"

"Okay," I said in a clear voice. "I've decided. Our next story is going to include something about the holiday of Sukkot, among other things."

"Sooocoat it is," Fran said.

Carol laughed goodnaturedly at Fran's funny pronounciation of the holiday. "Sukkot," she said, looking affectionately at Fran, "and 'other things.'"

TRANSFORMATIONS
(September 2007)

"I want our *sukkah* to be really beautiful this year." Yael was pulling out a colorful paper chain from one of the bags of decorations.

"I think we always have a beautiful *sukkah*," I said, emptying the contents of a second bag onto the cobblestone "floor."

It was the afternoon before the holiday of Sukkot. The kids, with the exception of napping Ronit, were helping me put up the *sukkah* decorations. For the next seven days, the *sukkah* would serve as our outdoor home. We'd be experiencing a less materialistic and more spiritual side of life as we ate our meals, played, learned and entertained guests in the wooden hut. Some of us would even be sleeping in the *sukkah*. Feeling closer to both nature and G-d, we'd be sharing the night with the moon and the stars, awakening to the birds singing and the sun's rays shining through the palm branch-covered roof. There'd be no heavy locks or bolts on the thin wooden door, for the Divine protection all around us would be our safeguard, just as it was when the nation was in the desert.

"I want to go visit my friends' *sukkahs* after the meal tomorrow night," Eitan said, picking up a picture of a *lulav*[115] and *etrog*[116] from the pile of decorations. He was eager to follow in the footsteps of his older sisters, who traditionally went "*sukkah* hopping" with their friends every year. "And after I go to their *sukkahs*," Eitan went on, "me and my friends will be coming here to visit ours." He looked at me for approval.

"Ema, did you buy enough snacks for when my friends come over?" Michal was concerned there wouldn't be enough for her guests as well.

I told Eitan that he and his friends could visit our *sukkah* and others that were close by in the neighborhood. Then I told pre-teen social butterfly Michal not to worry, "There will plenty of snacks for everyone who comes."

We were all looking forward to spending time in the *sukkah*, as well as having a week of vacation to rest and go on *tiyulim*[117] around the country. Now, hammering, drilling, music and laughter permeated our *sukkah*'s walls and echoed throughout the neighborhood, as families

---

[115] A closed palm branch used on the holiday of Sukkot.
[116] A yellow citron used on the holiday of Sukkot.
[117] Hikes, trips, excursions or outings.

prepared for the holiday.

"Thank G-d we celebrate Sukkot in Israel." Yehuda was standing on a plastic chair in his rumpled around-the-house work clothes, hanging a desk lamp from one of the narrow beams of the makeshift roof. "In other parts of the world it can be freezing this time of the year, and sometimes it even snows."

"I wouldn't want to be anywhere but here for the holiday," I said, admiring a bright "Welcome to Our Sukkah" sign that Eitan had just made in his third grade class.

"You're both glad you came to live in Israel, even with all the stuff that's been happening here, aren't you?" Michal looked from me to Yehuda.

"Yep," I answered without hesitation.

"We're very glad," Yehuda agreed.

"But weren't things different when you first came?" Michal was curious.

"Some things were different." I opened a little box of thumbtacks and placed it on one of the plastic chairs for everyone to use.

"Right." Hadas took a few thumbtacks out of the box. "There were still Jews living in Gush Katif then." She began tacking up a picture of a dove with the words "Sukkat Shalom"[118] written on it.

Sometimes I still felt the same bitterness Hadas was now displaying two years after the Disengagement. But I knew that, although in some ways things seemed worse, many things were actually better. And as time went on, I felt even more strongly that we in Israel and the Jews on those planes making *aliyah* every year had an important role to play. We could all make a positive impact on the

---

[118] Sukkah of peace.

country. But how to relay all that to my children?

"Well..." opening a flower-patterned bed sheet to hang as a wall covering, I paused to collect my thoughts. "It's true some of the problems we're faced with today didn't exist before, or maybe not to the extent they do now. But lots of good things have been happening too." I attached a corner of the sheet to one side of the wall.

"Look at the glass half-full, not half-empty," Yehuda said. "The people *are* split about certain things, but we come together when we need each other most, like, for instance, if there's an accident or difficult weather conditions, or a war. And despite our many troubles, we've come a long way in a very short time and we're still progressing—a lot."

"Abba's right," I said. If we look closely, we can find something good or positive in everything that happens." Rav Kook was popping up again.

"What about the Holocaust?" Yael was skeptical. "That was worse than bad. What good or positive thing came out of that?"

"I'll answer that," Yehuda said, aiming the light from the lamp he was setting up towards the middle of the *sukkah*. "It's hard to express how terrible the Holocaust was. It was so shocking that it caused many Jews to understand that we need to have a place for ourselves in the world. So we fought to have our own country back and, thank G-d, we succeeded."

"Thank G-d," I agreed, as I finished putting up the flowered sheet. "The Nazis did a lot of evil and murdered millions of innocent people, but they failed in their mission." I caught Yael's eye. "We didn't disappear like those monsters wanted. There are still Jews all over the world, and look how many of us are here in Israel these days. Our little country is growing and developing at an amazing rate. And we're becoming important to the world as time goes on."

"Mmmm," Yael pursed her lips. "I guess all that's true."

"Things will be even better for all of us here, hopefully soon," I wanted to share some of the optimism I had begun to feel again. "As we start doing what's needed to turn everything around, we'll see a real improvement. And you know, sometimes things need to break down a bit in order for them to be rebuilt in a stronger and better way." I hoped I was making sense.

"Why should things have to get bad first?" Michal wasn't happy about that.

"They don't have to," I placed a glittery picture on the wall opposite the hanging sheet. "Often, it works out that way in order for a big change to take place. Sometimes it takes getting so low down in the pits that there's nowhere left to go but up!"

"So we have to climb out of the pit." Eitan had been paying attention.

I smiled at Eitan. "It's what we did after the Holocaust. The Jews who came to Israel from the concentration camps of Europe after the Second World War were nearly broken. They had no army or sophisticated weaponry to use when the Arabs fought them after Israel became a state in 1948. Yet they won the war. And their children and grand-children won just about every war afterwards, even when the country was attacked by more than one enemy or when there was a surprise attack."

"That's right." Yehuda had finished with the lamp and was now straightening the *sukkah d*oor. "Once we were displaced wandering Jews. And now we have our own state again with our own army, our own solid air force and our own navy to defend and protect us, and to fight for our freedom and safety. Now we're able to stand up to all who are against us."

"And," I continued with my point, "these same Holocaust survivors who came to Israel went on to farm the land like nobody else could. They and the generations after them made the deserts bloom again. And since then, despite terrorism, war and all the other problems our country is always facing, we've managed to advance both agriculturally, economically and scientifically in ways nobody expected. Who would have thought so many good things could come out of something so horrific like the Holocaust? But with G-d's help, we managed to make our way up from the most hopeless and desperate state of being."

"We've still got our problems," Yehuda said, picking up his hammer from the ground and taking a nail out of the small tool kit next to the door, "but think how far we've progressed in only fifty-nine years. We've become one of the most medically and technologically advanced countries in the world. Our doctors and scientists win all kinds of international prizes. With our quick growing and developing, we've even been able to send satellites into space!"

"What's a sattel light?" Eitan asked, giving me a string of shiny blue and white Jewish stars to untangle.

"It's like a space rocket," Yael told her brother as she handed a thumbtack to Hadas, who was standing on a chair hanging a plastic pomegranate.

"There's another good thing that's been happening lately," Michal said, stringing her colorful paper chain throughout the *sukkah*, "Look at how many people are making *aliyah* these days. People even come to live here during wars and intifadas."

"Why do they do that?" Eitan wondered out loud.

I looked at Eitan and suddenly remembered the answer my fellow newspaper reporter in the US gave so many years ago when the news staff wanted to know why *I* was going to Israel. "They *do* that," I told Eitan with a feeling of déjà vu, "because they're Jewish."

Except for faint music and the muffled voices of our neighbors, the *sukkah* was quiet for a moment. Everybody was absorbed in their tasks.

Yehuda banged a nail into one of the flat hinges of the sukkah door and then closed it. "We've come a long way and have overcome many troubles throughout our history," he said. "It may take a little time, but with patience and conviction, we'll be able to work out any situations we're having now as well."

"What's convikshen mean?" This time it was Michal struggling with the more sophisticated English word.

Yehuda put the remaining nails back into his tool kit and turned to Michal. "In this conversation it means believing in ourselves and being convinced that we'll be able to do whatever we need to do to make things right, no matter what troubles or difficulties come our way."

The kids had finished putting up the last of the decorations, so I started cleaning up the papers and strings that were strewn all around. Yehuda grabbed the broom from the corner and began sweeping the *sukkah floor*.

"Okay, sounds good," Yael said, dropping her last thumbtack back into the little cardboard box, "especially if more people make aliyah and help us." Opening the door Yehuda had just fixed, she gave me and Yehuda a thumbs-up before turning to leave.

"Yeah, they can help us climb up to the top of the pit," Eitan said, following his sister out of the sukkah.

"And be part of our 'growing and developing,'" Michal called over her shoulder on her way out.

"*And,*" Hadas let a little grin escape, "our rebuilding." Without looking back, she grabbed the empty decoration bags and went to join her siblings in the house.

Turning away from the door, I glanced around at our

work. It wasn't only our family and the country going through transformations. Every year, plain boards and wooden beams were turned into beautiful *sukkahs*.

"It's really nice." Yehuda was also looking over our creation. "And this year, it didn't fall down even once in the process of building it!"

"Hmmm." I pushed a loose thumbtack from the dove picture further into the wall. "I guess that's what happens when we have conviction and don't give up until we get it right."

Carol announced that it was time for me to do more stair climbing. "I know we're in the middle of everything," she apologized to the ladies, "but, we're going to have to take a few minutes break to do that now." Carol tapped me on the shoulder and motioned for me to stand up. "I think you need to have a little more conviction when it comes to those stairs," she told me with a chuckle, "and be sure not to give up until you get them right."

"Hopefully this won't take long." I told everyone. Then, taking hold of the metal-framed walker, I slowly began moving alongside Carol towards the door.

"Take your time, dear. We're not going any-where," Mrs. Weissberg told me.

I worked hard on the stairs for the next fifteen minutes. Then Carol and I made our way back to the room. Diana and Mrs. Weissberg stopped their conversation when they saw us coming in. Fran quickly snapped her cell phone shut, saying goodbye to whoever was on the other end.

"You know," Fran slipped her phone into the front pocket of her white uniform, "in that Sukkah story and also in some of the others, Shelly's mentioned Israel's achievements and contributions to the world. I'm really impressed with how much has progressed over there in such a short period of time. And I'm wondering why what I've seen or heard about Israel in the news over the years has mostly been about the political situation, with Israel usually not portrayed very well. I didn't know that there's a whole beautiful thriving culture and advanced nation of people there. And I'm amazed at how far the country has come, all things considered."

"All things considered, is right," Carol agreed.

"If I were Jewish," Fran looked at all of us, "I'd do whatever I could to help promote all the positive things about the country and denounce the negative way the media reports about it."

"What makes *me* crazy," Diana jumped in, "is that Israel gets yelled at and boycotted for everything while the terrorist organizations barely get slaps on their wrists."

Mrs. Weissberg leaned forward and reached over to pat her daughter's leg. "Israel seems to be a pretty strong little country. I believe it will continue to survive whatever comes its way—be it pressure or condemnation from other countries, internal problems..."

"Rocket attacks," Diana added.

"Hey, whatever happened with the war and all the rocket attacks in the South?" Carol was now gently massaging my leg. "How'd Israel get them to stop all that back then?"

"Eventually there was a ceasefire with Hamas," I answered. "But that only lasted four or five months. Hamas and the other terrorist groups usually break these ceasefires after a while," I explained. "So, every now and then Hamas stops firing their Kassams and mortar shells at us, but then they start up again. That's how it's been for years now."

"Those terrorists—you just can't count on them

to be stable peace partners, can you?" Carol laughed at her own joke.

I laughed with her. "*You've* been listening!"

SDEROT

(December 2007)

Efrat, Ilana and I were sitting in Efrat's living room, about to begin our friendly book writing critique session. But first we chatted about what was going on in our lives, in the world and in Israel, like we did every week.

"I wish we'd get those Kassam rockets that are still crashing into us to stop," I told my writing partners. "Some of them are reaching so far up the coast they may soon be able to hit Tel Aviv."

"Well, Hamas promised to attack more than ever before, so that's what's happening." Efrat, dressed in earthy tones and a bead necklace, placed some homemade muffins and a box of herbal tea on her low coffee table. "It was inevitable," she went on. "We left Gush Katif, Hamas forced the PLO's Fatah out of that area and then Syria and Iran began equipping it with all kinds of financial and military aid. Even our Egyptian "peace partners" have been letting Hamas smuggle all kinds of terrorists and weapons into Gaza through underground tunnels." After pouring steaming water into the last teacup, Efrat looked at me and Ilana. "What could anyone expect would happen when the entire Gaza Strip has been turned into one big terrorist haven?"

"I've been thinking a lot about the people living in Sderot," Ilana said. "Now that there's no more Gush Katif,

Sderot's the closest Jewish town to Gaza and it's been getting hit the hardest."

I grabbed a muffin and then turned to Ilana sitting next to me on the couch, "Did you know that Efrat and I went down to Sderot two weeks ago during Chanukah?"

"No," Ilana looked surprised. "What'd you do there?"

"Well, since the Sderot residents have been running for shelter every day, they're lives have been really turned upside down. So the Judea and Samaria municipalities organized an afternoon of events to give them support and to help raise their spirits. People from our area went down to Sderot in special buses to participate and help out."

"Oh yeah, I heard about that!" Ilana said.

"High school students, youth groups and people like us went door-to-door, passing out Chanukah doughnuts," I explained. "There were activities for the younger Sderot children in one of the rocket-proof buildings. And later on, there was music from a live band with lots of fun Israeli dancing for teenagers and adults in the community center's gymnasium."

"It was a small effort we all made for the town," Efrat added.

"Right." I took a bite of my muffin. "Some people go down to Sderot with convoys of cars to buy things from the shops and grocery stores to help boost the businesses there. Others call up the townspeople to talk with them as part of that moral support campaign that was recently started. And we," I pointed to myself and Efrat, "couldn't pass up the opportunity to go there with jelly doughnuts and smiles to brighten up their lives for a few minutes on Chanukah. We even got Yehuda to drive us there because the buses from Or Tzion were full."

"I'm impressed." Ilana nodded with approval. Then, narrowing her eyes to slits, she looked from me to Efrat. "Weren't you scared to be there?"

Efrat and I exchanged smiles. "Nope," I answered for both of us. "At least not for the first ten minutes."

"Hmmm." Ilana folded her hands over the pages of her story that was resting on her lap. "Would you like to elaborate on that?"

"Well," I began, "after we unloaded the cartons of doughnuts from the car, we split up. Yehuda went off to *daven Minchah*[119] in the synagogue across the street and would meet us afterwards. Efrat and I started walking towards some nearby apartment buildings with the two sixteen-year-old Or Tzion girls who drove down with us. When we got there, a few minutes later, we joined up with other teenage girls from a different town, who'd also come to volunteer."

I paused to take a sip of tea, so Efrat took over telling the story. "We handed the girls some cartons of doughnuts to give out to the residents in the apartments. Just as we were all about to go into one of the buildings to knock on doors, we heard the neighborhood loudspeaker crackle. And then came the alert call: '*Tzeva adom. Tzeva adom.*'"[120]

Putting my teacup down, I picked up where Efrat left off. "For some reason, it didn't register in my brain what was happening until Efrat, the girls and a couple of other kids began rushing towards the entrance of the building. An older girl from Sderot, who was acting as our guide, hurried everyone inside and told us to huddle down on the floor under the concrete stairway. A younger Sderot girl, who was about eleven years old, crouched down next to Efrat and started crying."

"She was very scared," Efrat said. "She was shaking. So I held her shoulders and tried to calm her down a little.

---

[119] Recite the afternoon prayers.
[120] Red alert; lit., "Color red."

She'd probably been through the alert and the siren hundreds of times, but each one is a new traumatic experience for those kids."

"Not just for those kids," I pressed my hand to my chest. "I was also terrified at that moment!"

"I can imagine!" Ilana said.

"When we first got to Sderot," I backtracked a little, "other volunteers stopped our car at the city's entrance to give us instructions about what to do in case there was a Kassam attack. I remember thinking, *Oh my G-d, It's like being in a war zone!* But I'd quickly pushed aside my fears, figuring the chances were slim of something happening in the exact spot where we were going, and during the exact few hours we'd be there."

Efrat stifled a laugh with the palm of her hand.

"For me, the worst part of being hunched down under those dark stairs was waiting those long seconds to hear when and where the Kassam would land," I continued. "I kept thinking, *Is it going to fall here? Is it going to land on top of us?* I started to worry about my head, so I covered it with my arms—as if that would really help."

"I probably would have done the same thing," Ilana said.

"I felt myself becoming stiff and tense," I went on. "It seemed like the longest thirty seconds I had ever lived through. The girl next to Efrat was still sniffling with her head down to the floor. I thought about Yehuda. I remember taking one hand off my bent head and fingering my cell phone, but it was as if I was semi-paralyzed, and anyway, I couldn't really see in the dim light to dial his number. Then, one of the older teenage girls whispered loudly to her friends, 'Maybe we should say the *Shema*.'"[121]

---

[121] Traditional prayer affirming G-d's Oneness, recited daily and often during life-threatening situations.

"That was a good idea," Efrat said.

"Right. My panicked mind also thought so. Right away, I closed my eyes and started whispering the *Shema* to myself. I was concentrating hard on the words and feeling so thankful that we hadn't allowed Hadas to come with us, even though many of her friends did go on the buses.

"And then... we heard it." I held my breath, as if I was reliving the incident. "It was like a huge thunder cracking the sky open. It was so loud, there was no doubt it had struck very close to us. I think my heart stopped beating for a second." As I spoke, my hand automatically covered my heart. "A boy about nine years old, who had run into the building with us, started crying and told us that he wanted to use someone's cell phone to call his father. He said that it was the first time he'd been outside without his parents when there was a rocket attack."

"The teenage girls who had come to volunteer were also pretty shaken up," Efrat said. "They asked the older Sderot girl to take them to a rocket-proof area right away. The younger Sderot girl who'd been crying went with them. The boy stayed behind with the two girls who came in the car with us and waited for his father to come get him."

"So what did both of you do then?" Ilana asked.

"I wanted to see what was going on outside," Efrat said, "to check where the Kassam landed and see if anybody was hurt."

"I was less enthusiastic about going out of the building right away," I admitted. "I was very nervous about being unprotected. But I was also curious about what the Kassam had hit. So after I called and spoke with Yehuda, Efrat and I slowly walked outside and looked around."

"And...," Ilana prompted us, "what did you see?"

Goosebumps flew up and down my arms as I remembered how hard it was for me to take those first steps out of the building. "We saw a stream of water

running down the main road, which we found out was
from a rooftop water heating unit that had exploded when
the Kassam hit. We went down a few stairs and turned the
corner. People were standing in clusters on the street,
talking in tense whispers among themselves in Hebrew and
Russian.

"An ambulance had already arrived and another came
just as we got there. We asked an anxious-looking Russian
Israeli woman for information. She pointed to the building
next to us and told us in her accented Hebrew that a
Kassam rocket had crashed into an old man's apartment on
the fourth floor."

I looked straight at Ilana. "That was only about five
buildings away from where we'd been hiding under those
stairs!"

"Wow," Ilana whispered.

"I couldn't believe how close we had been to the attack
site, and of course that explained why it had sounded so
loud," I told Ilana. "Suddenly I felt even more thankful
than I had before that we'd walked out of that apartment
building in one piece!"

"We were both glad that the old man and the other two
people the paramedics were putting into the ambulances
weren't injured," Efrat said, absentmindedly ruffling the
pages of her story as she spoke. "Someone told us they
were in shock."

"Everyone on that street seemed pretty traumatized," I
admitted. "Television cameras and photographers were
there interviewing people and taking pictures of the
exploded rocket. I saw the Kassam up close when the
rescue team carried it out of the building.

"Remember a Russian man was shouting into one of the
TV cameras?" Efrat reminded me. "He was saying that he
didn't think Prime Minister Olmert was doing enough to
stop the attacks that they were subjected to every day."

I rolled my pen back and forth between my fingers as I thought about all the people we'd seen just after the Kassam had struck. "Efrat and I began walking around the area with the two girls from Or Tzion who, after a while, got up the nerve to leave the building and joined us outside. We spoke to a few more Sderot residents and I remember a big man with a large, veiny nose told us that more than half the people had left town. He said that just about everyone living in third floor apartments or higher had already left Sderot." I looked at Efrat. "And remember we noticed that the buses passing by were practically empty?"

"Yeah," Efrat said, nodding, "and the taxi driver who drove us afterwards to the planned events told us that the people who'd remained in Sderot didn't go far from their homes unless it was absolutely necessary. That's why there was almost nobody on the buses and the taxi companies were practically going out of business," she told Ilana. "We knew what he was saying was true because when we'd invited a mother and her two children to the activities that would be starting soon, the mother told us that she wouldn't take her kids anywhere that wasn't near their house."

"Well, I don't know about you," I told Efrat, "but I breathed easier once we were on the road driving away from Sderot that evening. Nearly the whole time we were there, and especially when we were outdoors, I was feeling very tense."

"You seemed pretty calm," Efrat said.

"Well, I was trying to be, but really I wasn't. I *am* glad we went though, for two reasons." I looked first at Efrat and then at Ilana. "One: because as we stood on that street below the apartment building that was struck, people came and took doughnuts from us. I think eating them might have been a little comforting—maybe took their minds off their troubles for a minute or reminded them it was Chanukah. And two: because whoever we spoke with realized that they weren't alone in their suffering. The fact that we were there showed them that people from other parts of the country cared and were willing to come and be with them, despite the danger."

"It's amazing that you both went," Ilana said, smiling at us.

"Yeah, but I wish we'd do more to stop all the Kassam attacks," Efrat said.

"I wish we'd get Gilad Shalit back from Hamas," I added.

"And Eldad Regev and Ehud Goldwasser from Hizbullah," Ilana reminded us.

With a sigh, Efrat picked up the pages of her story and waved them in the air. "We really should get on with this."

"How do we always manage to get so far off track at these meetings?" Ilana asked, reaching for her pen on the coffee table.

"Okay," I said, straightening up and becoming more business like, "let's get started. We all want to get to sleep at a decent hour tonight, right?"

"Why don't you go first this time, Shelly?" Ilana suggested.

"Fine." I passed out a copy of my story to each friend. Then I cleared my throat and began reading out loud.

As we plunged into the inspiring world of literary creativity, Sderot, Kassams, kidnapped soldiers and life outside the walls of Efrat's living room slowly faded into the background. It was how all of our pre-critiquing conversations ended—until the next time.

Diana and Fran both had to leave. And my session with Carol was basically finished. But everyone wanted one more story.

"Got any more of those man-on-the-street tales?" Carol asked.

"Yes, that would be a wonderful way to end our gathering today," Mrs. Weissberg approved.

BEAUTIFUL FLOWERS
(May 2008)

"*Selichah*, do you have change for a twenty?" Yehuda was waving a twenty shekel bill out the car window. The passenger waiting at a red light in the car next to us quickly checked his wallet then shrugged his shoulders as if to say "sorry" when he didn't find the right amount.

Yehuda and I were in a rush to get to a carpet store that was about to close for the day. "If we have to stop to get change for the parking meter, we'll be late," Yehuda told me. "So let's try to get the change now and not waste any time."

Sticking my head out the window, I waved at a robust man with a large tattoo and a short curly ponytail who was about to cross the street in front of us. "Shalom. Would you have change for a twenty?" I asked him.

The man shoved his hand into his pants pocket and pulled out some coins. "No," he said, shaking his head, "but I've got a few shekels here if you want."

The light turned green. I kindly refused his offer and we drove on.

At the next red light, the woman in the car to our left found the amount we needed in her purse. Leaning over the passenger's seat, she handed the money out the window to Yehuda. "*Todah rabbah*,"[122] Yehuda said, stretching to give her the twenty shekel bill.

"Now we won't be late!" I said, pleased that we'd succeeded in our mission. Although, I still didn't have much faith in the country's leaders, my belief in the people on the street was being renewed all the time.

Ten minutes later, with our car parked and the meter taken care of, we started out for the carpet store. "I thought it was on this street," Yehuda said, stopping at the corner, "but I don't see it. Now I'm not sure where it is."

Pressed for time, I asked directions from the first person who walked by.

"Sure, I know that store. It's one street over." The bushy-haired man, wearing a white T-shirt and a brown suede vest, pointed to the right. "C'mon, I'll show you." Jovially making small talk, he walked with us until we reached the next corner.

"I think we can find it from here," Yehuda assured our friendly "guide."

"Okay," the man said. Then with a big smile, he gave Yehuda a hearty slap on the back. "Tell Tuvia, the owner, that Doron Mizrachi sent you. And tell him that I said you should get a discount!"

Smiling back at Doron, we thanked him for his

---

[122] Thank you very much. Thanks a lot.

assistance and began walking up the street. In the carpet store, I showed Tuvia the carpet sample that interested me. "I like this blue one, but I'm not sure it matches our couch."

The greying store owner peered at me over his glasses. "So why don't you take it home with you and see?"

"Take it home?" I loved the idea, but didn't want Tuvia to lose business because of me. "Don't you need it for other customers?"

"Don't worry about it." He pulled the rectangular piece of carpet off its metal holder and handed it to me. "As long as you return it by the beginning of next week, it should be fine. You can tell me then if you're interested in ordering it or not."

Carpet sample in hand, we started back towards the car. Yehuda pointed towards a fast food stand on the way. "I want to get a quick falafel."

"The parking meter's about to run out," I reminded him, as he took his falafel and placed a fifty shekel bill on the counter.

"I know," Yehuda said. "I'm just getting my change and we'll go."

"Maybe you have the exact amount?" the man behind the counter asked Yehuda. "I just ran out of all my small cash."

"Sorry, I don't," Yehuda apologized.

"Okay, so pay me another time," the man said.

Some things don't change, I thought as we hurried back to the car.

A few days later I felt the same way, when Yael came home from Jerusalem and told me about an adventurous bus experience she just had.

"Ema, you have to hear what happened this afternoon while I was on the bus in Jerusalem!" Yael found me in the playroom making Play-Doh shapes with Ronit.

"We were riding on the bus towards the center of

town," she began, "when all of a sudden, a woman who was just about to take a seat collapsed in the aisle! She was young and didn't look sick or anything. She just sort of fainted."

"That's a little scary."

"Yeah, but Ema, you have to hear what happened then." Yael sat on the edge of one of the plastic kiddie chairs. "Right away, people got up out of their seats and rushed over to help. Two of the passengers picked her up from the floor and set her down across two seats. Then the woman's husband, who had just finished paying the bus driver, suddenly realized something was happening with his wife and hurried over to her."

Yael paused to take a breath before continuing. "The woman woke up right away and everyone started giving the husband advice about what to do to help her. People were shoving their water bottles at him and saying she should drink, maybe she was dehydrated. Others were pulling food out of their bags and backpacks, saying she should eat because it would give her energy." Yael's eyes lit up. "I'm telling you, Ema, it was really wild."

"I can picture it."

"The bus driver heard all the commotion, but he was already driving again and didn't know what was going on. He called out from his seat, 'What's happening? Does somebody need me to take them to the hospital?' Then the husband told everyone around him that his wife would be fine and that there was no need to go to the hospital."

"So, she was okay?"

"Yes. She seemed to be all right, but people kept handing her husband all kinds of things. He was holding so much food and so many water bottles, he didn't have a free hand to do anything. So an older woman, who kept saying 'she needs to eat,' stuck some bread straight into the woman's mouth!"

"Ha!" I laughed.

"Then it was time for me and my friend to get off the bus. I saw that the wife was sitting up and drinking some water on her own. Everyone was going back to their seats, and the husband was thanking them for all their help. I heard the driver say, 'Thank G-d she's all right.' I guess he was glad he didn't have to rush the bus to the hospital."

"What a story!"

Yael was about to reply when the phone rang.

"Shelly?" It was Yehuda calling on his cell phone from the car.

"That's me."

"You want to hear what happened just now, when I went to return the carpet sample and to pay what I owed for that falafel I got last week?"

I smiled at Yael and leaned back in my chair. "Sure. Why not?"

"Well, the falafel owner was about to close up the place for the day when I got there."

I was listening.

"He thanked me for coming back so soon with the money. Then he said he was about to leave, but that he still had a whole bunch of falafel balls left. So guess what?"

I was ready for anything. "What?"

"He packed up everything he had left over and gave it all to me to bring home. Now you don't have to cook supper. Isn't that great?"

I nodded. "That's pretty great!"

I had that familiar warm feeling again as I hung up with Yehuda. Although things weren't as rosy as they could be, and our "garden" did have some thorns in it, I had to admit, beautiful flowers were still blooming everywhere.

"I have some news to tell all of you!" I said, as the ladies brought their chairs close for our next session. I had waited until after my walk with Carol to make my announcement.

"I know what she's going to say," Carol told the others. "But," she looked at me, "I'll let you be the one to tell them."

"Tell us what?" Fran was feeling left out.

"The doctor just told me my last day here will be on Tuesday!" I gushed.

Diana did the calculations. "Tuesday? That's two days from now."

"How long have you known about this?" Fran turned to Carol.

"Well, I met with the doctor this morning and gave him Shelly's progress report," Carol said. "We discussed the option of her going back home to continue with her therapy there. Since she's getting back to herself now, I guess he decided two more days would be enough time for her to finish up here."

From the looks on their faces, I could see that everyone in the room had mixed feelings. I understood them. I was so excited about going back home. But I was also feeling a little emotional about leaving my new friends. Some of us had spent nearly a month together. We'd formed a real connection between us.

Mrs. Weissberg was the first to speak. "Congratulations, dear! We're so happy for you. You'll be going back to your family and friends."

"That's great, Shelly!" Fran came over and gave me a hug. "That's wonderful." Her voice was a little strained, as if she was trying to hide a touch of sadness behind the excitement.

"I'm glad for you too." Diana smiled at me. "I guess that means there'll be no more get-togethers like this when I come to visit my mother." She patted Mrs. Weissberg's arm.

"No more Israel stories." The realization hit Mrs. Weissberg whose smiling face suddenly lost some of its bright color.

"And no more Shelly." Carol didn't even pretend to be all cheerful. "I have to admit," her eyes were fixed on me, "that as happy as I am that you'll be getting out of here and going home, I'm sad you're leaving us."

Fran was looking at me and nodding her head.

"We're going to miss you." Mrs. Weissberg said. "It'll be boring here without you and all of this," she gestured towards our little circle. "I'm actually sorry now that I never made it to Israel."

"I'm thinking it's time to go back there again for another visit," Diana said.

"Make sure you come see me and my family when you do," I told her.

"So, are there any stories left that you can tell us before you leave?" Fran looked hopeful.

"I hope there are, because I've rearranged my schedule so I can stay a little longer today," Carol admitted.

"Of course," I said, reassuring everyone that I wasn't gone yet.

"We're going to have to work extra hard these last two days to get your walking and stair climbing in better shape before you leave us," Carol told me. Then she turned to Fran, Diana and Mrs. Weissberg. "Tomorrow, while I'm finishing up with Shelly, maybe we should have a little goodbye party."

"For sure." Fran nodded her head again.

"But," Mrs. Weissberg raised her eyebrows at me, "in the meantime..."

RAMI LEVI & THE MOTLEY CREW
(March 2009)

With only ten days to go before Passover, it was traditionally one of the busiest times of year at the nearby Rami Levi supermarket. The large store was hopping with activity when I arrived with Hadas and Ronit to do our pre-holiday shopping.

Matzah and all types of festive foods and cleaning materials were stocked to the maximum. The aisles and cashier lines were buzzing with Jews of all backgrounds checking labels, searching for specific items and discussing which product they should purchase. Even the Arab employees were getting in on the action.

"Selichah." A woman in a long-sleeved blouse and a long denim skirt approached one of the Arab workers stocking the shelves. "I'm looking for those sponges that are soft on one side and rough on the other side."

"Here you go." The young mustached man handed her a pink two-sided sponge.

"Actually, I don't think that one will work, because that color would be for my meat dishes and I need a blue one for my milk dishes," the woman said apologetically.

"Oh. So then you should buy one of these." The Arab worker, who'd obviously become acquainted with supermarket items used in a kosher kitchen, plucked a cellophane package off the shelf with both a pink and a blue double-sided sponge. "There's one for milk and one for meat too."

"Yeah, that's good," the woman took the package and dropped it into her shopping cart. "*Todah.*"

I pushed my own cart down the aisle with four-year-old curly-haired Ronit sitting in its fold-out seat and seventeen-year-old Hadas at my side. After getting matzah and some other food supplies, we stopped to pick up a few cleaning products. A heavyset woman wearing a long T-shirt over her stretch pants was examining something on the shelf across the aisle. "Is it kosher for Pesach?" she asked the long-haired young man standing next to her.

"Yeah, Ema, it's *kasher l'Pesach,*"[123] the slouching son with a small, shiny stud glimmering from the side of his nose, answered his mother with strained patience.

"Are you sure? Does it say it is?" the woman flipped a handful of her long hair over her shoulder as she continued to grill him.

"I'm sure. It says so right here." I could see the son pointing to the label on a plastic bottle of green liquid soap.

"But is it a good kind?"

"Oh, that's the best kind." A middle-aged woman wearing thick red lipstick with long, matching painted fingernails and lots of strong perfume, stopped to give her opinion. "We buy it all the time."

"Really? That's great!" the heavyset woman enthused.

"Yeah. And look, it's got a cute swan shape to it." The

---

[123] Kosher for Passover.

woman picked one of the bottles off the shelf and held it up so the big woman could view it better. Placing a can of oven cleaner in my cart, I could see the son rolling his eyes.

"And I see it does say kosher for Pesach on the label. I'll get it. Thanks a lot, you're a lifesaver!"

"You'll be happy you got it, I'm telling you," the heavily made up woman called out as she pushed her cart around the corner.

I chuckled to myself. Then I instructed Hadas to take Ronit to get some chocolate chips and cocoa, while I went to find toilet paper.

"The list of prices on this sign is a little confusing, isn't it?" I turned to the short elderly woman standing next to me, who was also checking out the different brands of toilet paper.

"Forget about that," she told me. "Look at how many types of toilet paper there are to choose from. Here's one that says its pineapple type. Is that pineapple-flavored, pineapple-scented or pineapple-shaped? What's that supposed to mean—pineapple? And who needs pineapple toilet paper anyway?" The hunched over woman and I laughed together before we each grabbed one of the cheapest brands and continued on with the rest of our shopping.

I found Hadas and Ronit in the baking section. They were waiting for me near two couples, one much older than the other, who were standing around a shopping cart. The men of both generations had small crocheted yarmulkes on their heads, and the women were both wearing sweatsuits.

The older woman was talking loudly and waving her hands about. "I'll be baking a lot, but who needs all this sugar? Who put all this in here?" She pointed towards several bags of sugar that were piled up inside the cart. Her husband, who was holding two more sugar packages, quickly handed them to the younger man to put back on the shelf behind him. "And who put all these cans of corn in here? I never buy canned corn. I only buy frozen corn!"

I leaned over and whispered to Hadas, "You know that saying: too many cooks in the kitchen? Well, here," I discreetly pointed with my elbow towards the two couples, "there seem to be too many shoppers around the cart!"

"Watch out!" Hadas warned me.

A man pushing a big floor-polishing machine was coming our way, maneuvering around the shoppers and their carts as he made his way up and down the aisles. "*Shukran*,"[124] he said, as we moved out of his way.

Over in the next aisle we passed a girl in a black skirt and striped top crouched down to the floor, helping her mother pick out soup mixes from the bottom shelf.

"No, not that one," the mother was directing the girl from above. "I want the *pareve*[125] one, not the meaty one. Yes, that one's good." The mother took the soup mix container from her daughter and examined its label. "Oh, but it says it's only for those who eat *kitniyot*[126] on Pesach."

The girl bent back down to replace the soup mix and began checking the others.

"How about that one?" her mother said, pointing. "Or maybe that one."

We left the pair to their soup choices and turned down the toiletries aisle. The hippy son and his heavyset mother in stretch pants were there.

"We'll get the roll-on kind," the mother said, examining the many different deodorants. "It's better than the spray."

With a sigh, the son stuck his hands into the back pockets of his ripped jeans. "They're all fine, Ema."

"But which brand and which fragrance?" His mother

---

[124] "Thank you" in Arabic.
[125] Neither meat nor dairy.
[126] Legumes.

was busily inspecting the variety lined up in front of her.

Reaching for some toothpaste, I heard a familiar sugary voice coming down the aisle. "Sweety, it doesn't really matter. Deodorant is deodorant, you know. Either it works or it doesn't." The strong scent of perfume was filling the air around us. I turned to see the woman with the red lips and fingernails again. "But actually," she told both mother and son, "I've found that the dry ones usually do the job better than the wet ones."

"Oh, you're so right, I'm sure," the mother agreed. "Thanks again! You're amazing!"

Plucking the nearest deodorant off the shelf, her son tossed it into the cart and began briskly walking up the aisle. I watched as his mother hurried after him, eager to find out exactly which brand he'd chosen.

All ten cash registers were in use when we went to stand in line.

"Did you bring coupons with you from the paper?" the cashier asked when it was finally our turn. I shook my head. The girl took a few coupons from the pile next to her register. "Here, take these. They'll be good for some of the things you're buying."

I was impressed. Had she collected all those coupons to help the customers get a discount on their bill?

Out in the parking lot, I looked at Hadas. "Well, that was an interesting shopping experience!"

But it wasn't over yet. As we were setting our bags into the trunk of the car, a van with the words "Rami Levi" written on it in huge bold letters was slowly passing by. Traditional Passover songs were blaring out of the two loudspeakers attached to its roof. A bunch of teenage boys were bobbing their bare crew-cut heads in and out of the open windows while singing and drumming with their hands on the sides of the van to the familiar Seder tune, *"Di-Diyenu! Di-Diyenu! Diyenu, DIYENU!"*

"Hey, that's funny. It's an Arab driver!" Hadas noticed the irony of it all.

I lifted Ronit out of the cart and then turned to get a better glimpse of the animated van. "Yeah," I laughed, "and the guy sitting next to him has long, curly *payot*[127] and a black yarmulke on his head. What a motley crew!"

"A what?" Hadas asked.

"A motley crew. It means an odd collection of different types of people mixed together."

Hadas snickered. "I feel like since we got here, we've been part of one big motley crew."

I buckled Ronit into the car seat, then watched with Hadas as the van continued to the end of the lot and vanished around the bend. "I guess you could say that's true."

Hadas turned to me with a smile. "I like that."

"Yeah," I looked at her and smiled back, "me too."

---

[127] Sidelocks.

CHAPTER 9

HOLDING DOWN THE FORT

(April 2009)

I strolled alongside Malka and her husband Yedidya up the last short stretch of the paved mountain road in Or Tzion. Ronit was holding Malka's hand, as the elderly couple, who were like family to us, slowly made their way from the car we'd parked near the top of the mountain. Yehuda and the older kids had gone on ahead of us with a folding table, plastic chairs and the makings for a barbecue.

"Sounds like they're playing some good, spirited music up here," Yedidya said as we approached Or Tzion's mountaintop Independence Day Happening.

"Look what we have here!" Malka exclaimed. The festivities were spread out over a large leveled area and children of all ages were jumping around on air-blown castle Moon-walks.

"I want to go to the dinosaur." Ronit was watching kids climbing up giant inflated creatures of different shapes and colors and then bouncing back down to the bottom.

"Hey, isn't that Eitan over there?" Yedidya spotted my independent nine-year-old waiting in line to ride the mechanical bucking bull.

Shifting his weight back and forth from one foot to the

other, Eitan was eager for his turn to sit on the brown leathery imitation bull. He would hold on tightly for as long as
possible, before its fast, jerky movements would eventually
throw him down to the thick mats below.

"Boy, he must really like the idea of riding that thing."
Yedidya had stopped walking and was now leaning on his
cane. "He didn't lose any time getting over there, did he?"

"I want to go with Eitan," Ronit begged.

"That's for older kids," I said, catching Eitan's eye and
waving to him before moving on, "not for cute little
four-year-olds, like you."

We paused by the food and drink tables to look around
for Yehuda and the girls among the crowd. "Ema, can I
have popcorn?" Ronit's big eyes were glued to the popping
kernels in the oily popcorn machine.

"I remember that after Gush Katif and Amona, I didn't
feel like celebrating Independence Day," Malka told me. "I
was so down. I felt so bad about everything that had
happened then."

"I know," I said, nodding my head.

"It took some time," Malka admitted, "but, thank G-d, I
feel more into the spirit of the holiday again. We'll never
forget those tragedies. But we also can't forget how
important it is that we're all living here and helping the
country just by being here." Though Malka was getting
older and a bit frail, her blue eyes still sparkled as she
spoke.

"Ema, I'm hungry," Ronit said. "Can I have pizza?"

Still holding Ronit's hand, Malka steered her away from
the food vendors. As we passed the big arts and crafts tent,
we saw Hadas crossing over the open grounds towards us.
"Hi. We're over there," Hadas pointed further away from
the main entertainment area. I could see Yehuda waving
his arms high in the air, trying to catch our attention.
"Abba said we should set everything up more towards the

side, so the smoke from the grill wouldn't bother people."

"Great," I said. "We're heading over there. Can you take Ronit to one of those big jumping things? She's getting antsy."

"Okay. Let's go, cutie." Hadas smiled at her little sister and led her towards the huge inflated giraffe.

"Yay!" I heard my happy preschooler shout, as she walked with Hadas. "And then I want to jump on the dinosaur, okay? And then the..."

I set the bag of hamburger patties and chicken wings I'd brought on top of the portable table and pulled over two plastic chairs for Malka and Yedidya. Yehuda was squatting over the mini grill, dumping coals into it.

"You made it!" He greeted our guests with a big smile.

"Yeah, we made it, slowly but surely," Yedidya said, taking a seat. Wearing casual slacks, a Polo shirt and a mushroom-colored cap over his grey-white hair, Yedidya looked relieved to be sitting down. "This is quite a setup you have here." He gestured towards the scene in front of us.

"We saw Hadas. And Eitan is by the mechanical bull," Malka said. "But where are Michal and Yael?" Malka shaded her eyes with her hand and looked ahead in the distance—past the jumping kids, the music and infor-mation booth, the food stands and the bucking bull. "I don't see them anywhere."

"They might have gone to check out the bungee jumping." I grabbed a chair and sat down next to Malka. "Kids get a thrill from jumping from heights, flying towards the ground and then bouncing back up with just a rope attached to them." I looked at Malka and made a face. "You'd never catch me doing anything scary like that!"

"By the way," Yehuda said, as he fanned the fiery coals with a piece of cardboard, "there's an incredible view from up here. On a clear day, you can see way up north and pretty far down south too."

"Really?" Yedidya was intrigued.

"Uh huh," Yehuda replied. "We can see a lot of area from up here, but not quite the same distances as when Abraham saw the whole country from on top of Mount Ba'al Chatzor three thousand years ago."

"Malka got up to look at the mountains around us. "Ba'al Chatzor should be somewhere around here. Which one is it?" she asked, standing next to Yehuda in her patriotic blue and white cotton dress.

"It's over in that direction," Yehuda pointed to the mountains in the distance. "It has an air force base on it."

"Not exactly what was there thousands of years ago!" Malka laughed.

Eitan suddenly appeared, sweaty and hot. His face was red and the bits of hair poking out from under his sun cap were matted onto his perspiring forehead.

"How was the bull?" I asked, handing him a small bottle of mineral water.

"It was fun! But of course I fell off. Now I want to go on a horse. I just saw Ronit, and she wants to ride together with me. It only costs five shekels for each of us."

"You have horses here too?" Yedidya smiled at Eitan. "I assume they're the real thing and more gentle than the bucking bull you just rode."

Ronit came running over to me in her polka-dotted outfit, followed by Hadas. "Can I go with Eitan on a horse? Please?"

Before I could answer, Malka spotted Yael coming our way and called out to her, "Oh, here's our Yael!" She waved to Yael, who was carrying a slice of pizza in one hand and an open can of Coca Cola in the other."

"Hi, guys!" Yael greeted Malka and Yedidya.

"Hi there," Yedidya said. "How's our bungee jumper

doing? And where's your bungee jumping sister?"

"Michal found some friends," Yael said. "They're hanging out somewhere around here."

"Hey! Can I have pizza too?" Eitan asked.

"I'm thirsty," Ronit was eyeing the can of Coke.

"I bought this with my own money," Yael told Eitan. "Ask Ema and Abba for money to buy your own stuff. And you, sweety," she bent down closer to Ronit, "you have your own little water bottle. Drink your water—it's much healthier." Yael grinned and batted her eyes at me. "Right, Ema?"

I looked at my two youngest. "We're having a barbecue soon, remember?"

"Just let them go on a horse and they'll be happy," Hadas suggested.

Suddenly, the lively music that was being amplified throughout the grounds stopped. An announcement came over the loudspeakers that a magic show would be starting in fifteen minutes.

"Okay." I took Ronit's hand and started walking. "First the horse, then the magic show."

"I know how some magic tricks are done," Eitan told Yedidya.

"Yeah?" Yedidya gave Eitan a pat on the back. "So that makes *you* a magician too."

"C'mon, Eitan," I called over my shoulder, "we have to hurry if we want to get back in time for the show."

Hadas saw a friend and went over to talk with her. Yael agreed to watch the food on the grill while Yehuda took Malka and Yedidya to one of the lookout points.

Yehuda welcomed the opportunity to play tour guide for the elderly couple as they gazed out over the mountainside. "Okay, I'll show you what's around this area," Yehuda began. Now if you look that way," he pointed over the valleys and mountains, "you'll see the settlement town of Shilo, where the Mishkan[128] was located for more than 350 years and the twelve tribes gathered. And further on this way," Yehuda pointed in the other direction, "is the town of Beit El and the mountain where Jacob had his famous prophetic dream with the angels going up and down the ladder to heaven."

Yedidya flipped up his clip-on sunglasses to get a better look. "It's like living through our history."

Malka's eyes shone. "The Torah just comes alive here!"

Yehuda paused so everyone could look on a bit longer. After a moment, he continued. "Now, you see the red-roofed houses on the other side of those Arab villages?"

"That's got to be another Jewish town," Yedidya said.

"Right," Yehuda replied. "That's Ofra."

"Then, if I'm not mistaken, that batch of houses on the hill just above Ofra," Yedidya pointed with his cane, "must be Amona, where all the action took place a few years ago."

"Exactly," Yehuda nodded.

Malka shook her head. "I don't want to even think about what went on over there."

The music stopped once more and the magic show was announced on the loudspeaker again. Yehuda remembered the meat on the grill.

"We'd better get back. But if you want, later on we can look some more from a different spot."

After we watched the magician act, we sat down to eat. "I'm glad you and Yedidya are here with us," Michal told Malka, adding onion to the hamburger in her pita and then smothering it with ketchup.

"And you have no idea how happy I am that we're here

---

[128] The ancient Tabernacle that housed the Ark with the Ten Commandments.

with all of you." Malka's thin hand caressed Michal's smooth, tanned arm. "Especially on top of this wonderful mountain, with the music of *Eretz Yisrael*[129] and all these beautiful people and historical sites. I've been to Or Tzion many times, but I didn't know you had all of this up here."

"Well, we didn't always," I told her. "We had to fight for this mountain. The government didn't want us or our neighborhoods up here. We had lots of trouble getting permits to build what you see now."

"Why didn't they want us here?" Yael asked.

"Because even though it makes sense to include this area in Or Tzion as the town expands, the Arabs didn't want us to have it," Yehuda answered. "Mountains are strategic property. From up here, we can see the area all around us, as well as everything that's going on in our *yishuv*[130] below. And so could the Arabs, if they lived up here." Yehuda wiped a spot of ketchup from the side of his mouth before continuing, "If they were here instead of us, they would know when we came and went, where we were at any given moment, how we lived our daily lives. They'd have a great advantage over us and probably wouldn't hesitate to use their knowledge against us."

I cleared my throat loudly and shifted my eyes sideways towards Ronit, indicating that Yehuda should watch what he said around her. Ronit was oblivious, licking her fingers from the sticky peach she had just eaten.

"What kinds of problems did the government give you about building here?" Yedidya asked.

"Well," Yehuda began, pouring himself some water, "the Arabs started claiming that this mountaintop belonged to them. So, about seven years ago, when we saw that

---

[129] The Land of Israel.
[130] Settlement town.

it was going to either be us up here or them, we set up a small outpost-type encampment. Some of the residents took turns staying in it to make sure the area didn't fall into Arab hands. There were prayer services and classes for adults and teenagers, and special activities for the kids."

Putting a chicken wing on Ronit's plate, I jumped in to continue the story. "More than once, the government had the army evacuate everyone, just like it orders evacuations and demolitions to hilltop communities and outposts today. It was a difficult situation. Some of the female soldiers were crying as they helped force everyone to leave."

"After we got kicked off the mountain, some of the residents came back," Yehuda said.

"Then, one day," I leaned closer to Malka and Yedidya and lowered my voice, "Arabs from one of the nearby villages came up with a PLO flag and started wreaking havoc. They pulled down our Israeli flag and tried to destroy the temporary structures we'd put up. When our security team arrived on the scene, the Arabs ran away."

"After that incident," Yehuda said, "we were banned from coming to the top of the mountain and from building anything up here. But when the Arabs couldn't prove that they had any real claim or ownership to the land, the army started leaving us alone."

"That must have been when they let us build up here." Michal had been listening as she ate her burger.

"Right. There were disagreements with the government about certain things and then some agreements were worked out." I collected the disposable plates and cups, and threw them into a plastic garbage bag. "Eventually we were given official permission to build everything you see here today."

"That's the kind of success story I like to hear," Malka

said, getting up to help me clear the table. "Thank G-d they haven't tried to expel you from Or Tzion like they've been doing with some of the other settlement communities."

"So far, so good," I agreed.

"Actually, the towns in Judea and Samaria are really growing," Yehuda said. Despite the building freeze and the giant concrete wall that was built separating us from the rest of the country, people are coming to live here all the time."

"Even during the intifadas," I added, "and with the troubles we have on the roads because of the Oslo Accords, the Road Map, and all the other political agreements over the years, people still keep moving here. Did you know that the most recent population census shows that our region has the highest and fastest growth rate in the whole country?"

"I didn't know that," Malka said.

Yedidya chuckled. "I guess this is the place to be."

"But it looks like there will be more problems for you," Malka said. "The new American president is supposedly going to be pushing hard for another building freeze that would affect the settlements and parts of Jerusalem."

"He can push all he wants." Hadas, not quite eighteen, had no patience for politicians. "It doesn't matter what the queens, prime ministers or presidents of other countries want. They don't own us."

I tossed the tied up garbage bag to the side. "I think everything's going to be fine. Our towns in Judea and Samaria have been around for thirty years already. There's more than a quarter of a million Jews living here now, and more are coming all the time."

"Right," Yehuda said. "We're not going anywhere."

Malka wiped her hands on a napkin and looked at the children. "Your parents are right. G-d didn't bring us back to our country after so many years of exile for nothing.

Everything's going to work out, you'll see. Israel's here to stay. And that means all of it, including Jerusalem, the Golan Heights, which Syria wants, *and* Judea and Samaria."

"One day we'll be going back to Gush Katif too," Michal added.

I smiled. "That's right." Then turning to Ronit, I changed the subject. "But right now, the only place I'm going is over to the arts and crafts tent with Ronit."

"How' bout if we take a walk and you show me a different view now?" Malka asked Yehuda.

Hadas stuffed her cell phone into the front pocket of her jean skirt. "I'll go with you."

"I'm going to find my friends," Michal announced.

Eitan kicked off his sandals and started running towards the inflated platform with the Rope Pull. "This time, I'm going to pull the rope all the way to the edge!" he shouted to everyone over his shoulder.

"C'mon sweety," Yael took Ronit's hand and started towards the big army-style tents, "I'm going to help you choose which art project to do."

"Wait," Yehuda said. "Somebody should stay here to make sure kids don't wander over and get near the coals. They're still hot."

"Don't worry," Yedidya said, repositioning himself to be more comfortable on his chair. "You all go on to wherever you're going. I'll be just fine sitting here listening to the music and watching the fun."

"Are you sure?" I asked.

"Yeah, I'm sure," Yedidya said. "Somebody's got to be here to hold down the fort."

"That's right," I agreed, turning to follow Yael and Ronit. *Somebody's got to be here to hold down the fort.*

CHAPTER 10

CANDLE STILL BURNING

(June 2009)

"I'm happy we live in Israel." Hadas was setting the supper table.

My heart leaped as I stirred the spaghetti sauce on the stove. "I'm glad to hear you say that." I wondered what was on my daughter's mind.

"Kids here aren't afraid to play outside or go places by themselves."

Now I understood. I knew Hadas had been talking with one of her friends who had just returned from a visit overseas with her family. "Every country has its risks and security problems," I told her. "But you're right. Kids here are pretty independent and have a lot of freedom."

"And we aren't afraid of each other. We can ask for help and take food from each other and feel comfortable going into each other's homes, even if we've never met before..." Taking the forks and knives out of the silverware drawer, Hadas looked at me. "Ema, did I ever tell you what happened when I went to Tel Aviv with the girls from Bnei Akiva[131] last year?"

---

[131] A religious Zionist youth group.

"What happened?" I put the lid back on the pot of sauce and turned around to face Hadas.

"The place where we were staying for the night had beds and bathrooms, but no showers," Hadas began. "One of my friends and I weren't happy about that. We didn't take a shower at home beforehand like the others did, and we really wanted one before Shabbat."

"So what did you do?"

"Well..." Hadas began placing the forks and knives next to the plates on the table. "We went across the street and knocked on doors in one of the apartment buildings."

"Really?"

"Yeah. The people in the first three apartments we went to weren't home. But in the fourth one, a woman, who was about twenty-five or thirty years old, opened the door. She was wearing a training suit and sneakers. And she had a sweatband on each wrist. She looked like she was about to go out jogging or something like that. But she told us she was in the middle of cooking."

"So you asked her if you could take showers?"

"Yeah. We told her we came from the *yishuv* Or Tzion with our group of Bnei Akiva girls to spend Shabbat in Tel Aviv and that we didn't know we were supposed to take showers beforehand. We figured she wouldn't mind letting us shower by her, just like it wouldn't be a problem if a couple of girls came to one of our houses and asked us if they could shower by us," Hadas replied.

"And... what'd she say?"

"She was really nice. She gave us towels and told us that when we were finished, we should come into the kitchen and have a snack. She put out pretzels and potato chips for us. And you know what else? She got a little excited when we told her that our group would soon be going door-to-door, passing out Shabbat candles to anyone who doesn't usually light them, but would like to."

Hadas placed the last fork on the table and turned to me. "She said that even though she wasn't religious, she also lights Shabbat candles. Her mother in Jerusalem always lit them, and since she got married and moved to Tel Aviv, she's been carrying on the tradition."

"Sounds like she was happy about it."

"She was. And we were happy we went to her apartment!"

I was also happy. Hadas seemed to finally be healing after Gush Katif and Amona.

"We're back!" Yael breezed into the house holding Ronit's hand. "That was fun, right Ronitoosh?" She gave her little sister's hand a squeeze. "I took her to the playground and we met some girls from my class there," Yale explained. "They kept saying she's such an adorable sweetie!"

"That's because she is an adorable sweetie." Hadas gave Ronit a big kiss on her cheek then left to get a few things I had asked her to buy from the grocery store before supper.

I looked affectionately at Ronit in her play clothes with her little tanned toes peeking out of her miniature sandals. Then I turned to Yael. "Did you, by any chance, see Michal or Eitan out there? It's almost time for them to come home."

"I saw Eitan riding his bicycle down the block," Yael said, heading for the computer in the other room. Then, as if it was an afterthought, she turned back to me. "Didn't Michal say she was meeting a bunch of her friends at the pool this afternoon?"

"Oh, right." It wasn't easy for me to keep track of everyone's whereabouts. Ronit wasn't a problem. But my active soon-to-be fifth grader and his three teenage sisters were always coming and going, especially Michal, who at fourteen usually had a full social schedule. I gave Ronit some crayons and a coloring book, and then poured a package of whole wheat spaghetti into a pot of boiling water.

"Sha-a-lom," Yehuda walked in. "Mmm, something smells good."

"Abba!" Ronit left the picture she was coloring and ran over to Yehuda.

"Hey, munchkin—Abba's home from work!" Yehuda happily greeted Ronit, who was giving his leg a big bear hug. Then he came over to me. "How's it so quiet here?"

"Well, Yael's on the computer, Hadas went to the store for me, Michal should be walking home from the pool about now and Eitan's outside somewhere with his bike," I updated Yehuda.

Yehuda whisked Ronit up onto his shoulders. "We'll go see if we find Michal and Eitan."

A few minutes later, Hadas was back from the grocery store. "Where is everyone?" She put the plastic shopping bag she was carrying onto the kitchen counter. "I thought we'd be sitting down to eat already. My friend is picking me up soon."

"I found them," Yehuda came in with Michal and Eitan, just as Hadas finished her sentence.

Michal watched me draining the spaghetti in the sink, her wet hair twisted back into a long braid. "Ema, let's eat outside tonight. It's good picnic weather."

"Hmmm, okay." I nodded absentmindedly. While everyone was out, I'd been thinking about my conversation with Hadas. It brought out my patriotic sentiments. I was again feeling very privileged to be living in *Eretz Yisrael*, and in Or Tzion. I was especially glad to hear Hadas say that she was happy to be growing up in Israel.

"Ema, what's for supper?" Eitan ran into the kitchen. He was dirty from playing soccer and from eating a drippy popsicle while riding his bicycle.

We opened up a folding table on the cobblestone patio.

Yael and Michal brought out the table settings that Hadas had already placed on the kitchen table.

"C'mon, you little cutie. I'm going to get you!" Hadas began chasing Ronit around on the lawn, laughing and twirling her in the air. Watching Hadas' free spirit—alive and well—it was clear her emotional scars from a few years ago were fading, and that she'd be all right.

I had hope for the rest of the nation too. As I brought the food outside, a parable I'd heard came to mind: Long ago, a rabbi was walking home at night when he noticed a light coming from the house of the town shoemaker. Although it was late, he knocked on the door. After being invited inside, the rabbi asked the shoemaker why he was still up mending shoes at such a late hour. The old man, bent over his worktable, looked up at the rabbi and replied, "As long as the candle is burning, it's still possible to repair."

"That's right, sweetie..." Hadas was giving Ronit a horsey-back ride to the patio where everyone was already seated around the table. "We're going to have a yummy picnic supper."

"Hey! Save some for the rest of us!" Yael reprimanded Eitan, whose plate was piled high with salad.

"Yeah, I didn't get any yet!" complained Michal.

"Why do they always have to find something to argue about?" Yehuda asked me. "And since when do kids fight over salad?"

"Don't worry," I said, taking the salad bowl Eitan had set down and placing it between Yael and Michal, "the candle is still burning."

"What's she talking about?" Yael looked at Yehuda.

Yehuda made a "don't ask me" face and shrugged.

"Are you feeling all right, Ema?" Hadas gave me a playful pat on the shoulder before sitting down with Ronit.

"Yep," I answered cheerfully. "I'm feeling *just* fine."

•⊰⊱• CHAPTER 11 •⊰⊱•

(November 2014)

I said my goodbyes to everyone in the US, wiping my eyes more than once as they threatened to dampen my cheeks. Then, in a wheelchair, I boarded the airplane. Practically in Heaven, I did emotional cartwheels as we flew high over the blue-green Mediterranean waters and glided down the smooth Israeli runway.

"There she is!" Eitan, lanky but handsome, was pointing in my direction as the airport attendant pushed my wheelchair into the spacious Arrivals area of the new Ben Gurion Airport.

I could see my family's eager faces among the crowd of people who were waiting to welcome their friends and loved ones from behind the designated floor line.

"Ema!" nine-year-old Ronit was standing next to Yehuda, waving her hand at me excitedly.

"Let's go over to her. I don't care if we're not supposed to cross that line," Yael said.

Without a moment's hesitation the whole family came rushing towards me. Eitan reached me first. "Ema, I missed you!" Putting aside his teenage tough guy image for a moment, he bent over and wrapped his arms around my neck.

"We all missed you!" Yehuda said, handing me a bouquet of assorted flowers.

One at a time, Hadas, Yael and Michal gave me a big hug and a kiss.

"Can everyone move out of the way?" Ronit was struggling to get closer so she could also hug me. "Ema, I wish you hadn't gotten hurt. You were gone too long." She pressed her lips hard against my cheek.

I returned everyone's affections the best I could, given my limitations. Showered with love and overcome with excitement, my throat tightened with emotion. "I'm so happy to see all of you!" The words came out strained as I again fought to hold back tears. "And I'm so glad to be back in Israel!" My soul was already soaring with delight, just breathing in the air and soaking up the spirit of the people.

Yehuda took over for the attendant and began wheeling me forward. The kids stuck close as he pushed me along.

"We were worried about you, Ema," Hadas said, walking next to me.

"I know you were. I really missed all of you." I held onto Ronit's hand as she walked on the other side of the wheelchair.

"At least we could talk sometimes on the phone and send e-mails," Michal said.

"It would have been better if we'd skyped each other," Yael pointed out.

"Ema, I'm telling you," Eitan began, moving closer with my luggage cart, "it wasn't the same at home without you."

"We cleaned up the house for your welcome home," Yehuda made sure to let me know.

Michal caught my eye. "It really needed a good cleaning."

"Abba let me have a lot of treats!" Ronit happily

leaked the secret.

Giving Ronit a fake look of shock, Yehuda turned to defend himself. "But I told her to brush her teeth doubly well and I made sure she ate good food too."

"Yeah, since the older girls weren't around much and Abba and I didn't want to cook, Abba took me and Ronit out for falafel and shwarma[132] all the time," Eitan informed me.

"We ordered lots of pizzas too," Ronit added.

"You're such tattletales," Yael rebuked Eitan and Ronit, as we passed through the sliding doors and headed outside towards the parking lot.

"No we're not," Ronit said. "We didn't tell her about the table that broke."

"Or about the paint that spilled on the carpet." Eitan glanced at Yehuda with a guilty look.

I laughed, not sure I wanted to hear more. Closing my eyes to whatever situations I might have to face, I took a deep breath of fresh air. I was back—and it felt wonderful!

⌘ ⌘ ⌘ ⌘

My first couple of months home I was happily working on getting my life in order again. I thought about my family back in the US. And every time I did my physical therapy exercises, I felt like Fran, Carol, Mrs. Weissberg and Diana were in the room with me. On my last day in the rehabilitation center, they brought a farewell cake and, teary-eyed, we all said

---

[132] Middle Eastern pita or flat bread sandwich with meat that was roasted slowly on a rotating spit.

goodbye, promising to keep in touch through e-mails.

Fran and Carol each sent me a couple of hellos through the Internet after I returned to Israel. I replied briefly, asking them to give my best to Mrs. Weissberg and Diana.

Now, basically recovered and settled again in my normal routine, I decided to write the ladies about one more Israel experience. Going back several years, I'd start from where we'd left off. It wouldn't be an ending to my story, as my life in Israel would thankfully be continuing on for many more years. But I thought it would bring things full circle and might even be a bit of an inspiration for them... as it had been for me.

BUILDING OUR DREAM TOGETHER
(July 2009)

I was excited as we walked through the spacious corridor of Terminal One in the old Ben Gurion Airport. Our family had special passes to greet the planeload of new *olim*[133] who were arriving on that morning's chartered Nefesh B'Nefesh flight.

The American nonprofit organization Nefesh B'Nefesh had already helped twenty thousand Jews make *aliyah* from the United States, Canada and England. Its goal was to make immigration to Israel go smoothly. Yehuda and I had friends who worked for Nefesh B'Nefesh in Jerusalem, and

---

[133] Immigrants.

we personally knew many people who moved to Israel with the organization's help and support.

"Things have really changed since Abba and I made *aliyah*," I told the kids on our way towards the Arrivals hall in the old airport, where the Nefesh B'Nefesh welcoming ceremony would begin.

"Israel's gotten more organized over the years," Yehuda said.

"And Nefesh B'Nefesh didn't exist back in our time, in the 'old days,'" I joked.

"They probably didn't have these big welcomes for people coming to live here back then either," Michal added.

"Is this airport open now because all of us are coming here for the ceremony?" Eitan, who was almost ten, noticed the place was mostly empty and quiet.

"I think so," I told Eitan. "With the new airport up the road, this one is only used for special purposes or for events like the one we're going to now."

"I wish we could have gotten up later to be here for this," Yael moaned.

"So do I," Hadas said under her breath.

"Yeah, why does the plane have to land at seven o'clock in the morning?" Michal also complained.

"Don't worry," I reassured my three tired teenagers. "I've been told this is an experience worth losing sleep over."

As we continued on towards the hall, I remembered how nervous and excited I was the first time I flew to Israel, twenty-five years ago. Now I was thrilled that my family and I would be celebrating with many others who were also about to make Israel their new home.

"Do we know anyone who's coming on this plane?" Michal asked.

"Nope," I said. "But I know a family that's coming on the next Nefesh B'Nefesh flight in a couple of weeks. And in a few months, my friend Liz, who moved back to the US about eighteen years ago, is returning to Israel with her family!"

"Really?" Michal said. "That will be fun for you, Ema."

"Yeah, I can't wait to see her again!"

"We have a new kid in our class who just made *aliyah* from France with his family," Eitan said.

"My friend from India has close relatives who are trying to get here," Michal said. "Most of her family came a few years ago and now they're waiting for the rest to come."

"It's the 'ingathering of the exiles,'" Yehuda said.

"Well, I think it's great that Esther's *mother* made *aliyah*," Hadas said, taking hold of Ronit's hand to help her keep up with the rest of us.

"Your friend Esther from Chicago?" Yael asked me.

"Yep. About a half a year ago, Esther's mother made *aliyah*," I told Yael. "She was nearly eighty when she packed up and moved to Jerusalem."

"That's pretty old for someone to move here," Eitan said, as we turned the corner and caught up to another family walking ahead of us.

"People make *aliyah* at all ages," I told him. "Not everyone comes with their family or when they're young and single, like Abba and I did. Many older people want to spend the last part of their lives here."

"And sometimes teenagers come on their own," Yehuda added, "to pave the way for the rest of their family."

"Look!" Ronit pointed ahead to the Arrivals hall.

"Whoa, it's crowded in here!" Yehuda said as we entered the large hall.

Hundreds of people were gathered for the event. Yehuda and Eitan made a beeline for the refreshment tables, while the girls and I ran to find seven seats together among the many rows of chairs.

"It's funny to hear so much English in one place,"

Hadas said, taking in the activity around us.

"Yeah, it's strange," Yael agreed. "Everybody who came here to meet the new *olim* must be either American or American-Israeli, like Ema and Abba."

I smiled. "My Sabra girls."

"I don't think hearing a lot of English is so funny," Michal said. "But, it does seem funny that we came here today even though we don't know anybody on the plane."

"I like that we're here just to welcome new people to Israel," Hadas said.

"Where's Abba?" Ronit squirmed in her seat. "Can I go to Abba now?"

"I'll take Ronit to find Abba," Yael said. "We can get something to eat and drink over there," she added, gesturing with her hand towards the snack tables on the far side of the noisy hall.

Hadas, Michal and I left some of our things on the chairs to save them for when the ceremony would begin. Then we followed Yael and Ronit. We found Yehuda and Eitan munching on cookies and fruit.

After we had our fill of snacks, Hadas and Michal walked with me towards the big glass doors that led outside to the landing tarmac, where everyone would soon be greeting the newcomers. A woman in white slacks and a rose-colored blouse was standing at the guardrail, staring out of one of the large full-length windows on both sides of the glass doors.

Pulling my digital camera out of its case, I tapped the woman lightly on the shoulder. "Would you mind taking a picture of us?"

"Not at all." She took the camera from me. "But you'll have to hold my flag."

Hadas took the woman's medium-size blue and white Israeli flag and held it in front of her as we posed for the picture.

"Now, do you mind taking a picture of me?" The woman asked, holding out her camera and quickly brushing away a stray tear. "I'm waiting for my daughter," she explained. "She's eighteen and she's making *aliyah* today. She's on that plane out there that just landed. I'll be able to meet her now and we'll spend a little time together. But," another tear escaped, "I'm leaving tomorrow. I've been visiting my older daughter, who already lives in Israel. I was supposed to go back to New York already, but I stayed on so I could meet my younger daughter here."

I found a tissue in my purse and handed it to the woman. "Do you have any other children?" I asked her.

"No, it's just my husband and me and our two daughters. I want to live here too. But I'm taking care of my elderly parents." She dabbed her eyes with the tissue. "I'm hoping we'll eventually be able to make some good arrangements for them so we can come join our girls."

"I hope so too," I said.

"I really didn't mean to cry like this," the woman tucked the tissue into her pocket. "Do you mind taking a picture of me now?" Standing with her back against the rail, she held her flag close and smiled for the camera."

"Poor thing!" Michal lamented after we wished the woman good luck and then went to stand a bit further to the side. "She really wants to be here."

"I guess if she really wants to be here," Hadas told her sister, "she'll find a way."

"I've heard these Nefesh B'Nefesh welcoming ceremonies are emotional," I said. "But I didn't expect this—tears even before it begins!"

"It looks like it's about to start now." Michal noticed that everyone was moving closer to the exit doors. "Maybe they're finally letting us go outside."

"Let's hurry up and tell Abba and the others. I want to be one of the first ones out there," Hadas said. "I'm getting excited about greeting the new *olim*."

"Me too," Michal said.

Me too.

A few minutes later, the exit doors swung open and the crowd made its way outside. The new immigrants had already descended from the airplane and buses were now bringing them over to where we were all waiting by the old Arrivals building. Giant loudspeakers blasted out a lively version of the song *"Heveinu Shalom Aleichem"* as the first busload approached. The excited welcomers were instructed to open up a pathway between them so those who were arriving could walk easily to the building.

Nefesh B'Nefesh co-founder Rabbi Yehoshua Fass personally greeted every newcomer stepping off the bus. Soldiers then handed each of them a small plastic Israeli flag before they started on the path toward the building where the ceremony would officially begin.

The enthusiastic assembly that had been waiting to greet everyone could barely be contained. Holding up handmade signs with slogans such as "Welcome Home!" or "Welcome to Eretz Yisrael!" they sang, cheered and clapped their hands to the music, as the brand new Israeli citizens walked slowly past them.

I stood with Hadas, Yael and Michal, clapping and singing. The spirited teenage girls next to us were enthusiastically waving blue and white flags and bopping up and down to the beat of the music. Yehuda and Eitan were standing further behind us on the stairs of the building, so Eitan could have a better view. Ronit, perched on Yehuda's shoulders, was vigorously waving her own little Israeli flag back and forth. The sound of a shofar bellowed out above all the excitement.

Government ministers who would soon be speaking on stage eagerly shook hands with each new immigrant who passed them. Personal video cameras, digital cameras and press cameras were everywhere, recording the momentous occasion. Two teenage girls suddenly shrieked with joy and ran down the middle of the pathway, spraying their friend who had just stepped off the bus with hugs and kisses.

I couldn't stop smiling. I was filled with nostalgic memories of my arrival in the country. The El Al plane I'd traveled on had landed not far from where we were now. I remembered how when it touched the ground, the other passengers and I had also clapped our hands to the song "Heveinu Shalom Aleichem" as it played throughout the airplane."

A lot has happened since that day. I had changed and grown in many ways. Israel had too. We'd been through a lot together.

As I watched the new immigrants approaching, I felt a great appreciation for them. *These people have come here now to help us build our future.* I wanted to personally hug each and every one of them as they walked past me.

"*Mazel tov! Mazel tov!*" Cries of congratulations were aimed at a couple walking with their little girl and pushing their baby stroller forward. The young parents returned the cheerful greetings with smiles that stretched across their faces.

"Hey!" a college student in a T-shirt and knee-length checkered shorts ran wildly over to his buddy who'd just gotten off the bus. "You did it!" he cried. I watched as they gave each other bear hugs and enthusiastic slaps on the back.

A frizzy-haired Israeli woman with a tiny silver nose ring stepped into the middle of the pathway and offered to help an elderly woman carry her bag. "Here, let me take this into the building for you."

The music switched to a different popular upbeat song. Two men suddenly jumped into the walkway from the sidelines. They threw their arms over each other's shoulders and began dancing backwards while facing a man in a business suit who was walking down the path carrying his laptop in its case. Laughing at their antics, the businessman decided to join in on the fun and danced along with the men all the way to the building.

I reached out and touched a woman on the arm who was passing us. She looked a little bewildered from all the excitement as she progressed through the "split sea" of people on both sides of her. "*Mazel tov!* Congratulations!" I called out to her. The woman stopped walking and turned to face me.

"Thank you," she said, with a nod of her head. "*Mazel tov* to you too."

More buses came. More hugs, laughter and singing filled the outside receiving area. The Nefesh B'Nefesh crew tried in vain to keep the walkway clear for those who had just arrived. The overwhelming thrill and dynamics continued until the last busload made it to the building and entered the old Arrivals hall. As I walked behind the escorting crowd up the steps to the big glass doors, I turned and caught a glimpse of the female soldiers near the buses dancing in a circle, whirling each other around on the empty tarmac to the music that was still blaring from the loudspeakers.

Yehuda was waiting for me at the doorway with Yael, Eitan and Ronit. "That was such a moving and exciting welcome, I had tears in my eyes," Yehuda said, a little embarrassed.

"Aaaw, Abba," Yael patted Yehuda on the back. "You're so emotional!"

Michal and Hadas came towards us from inside the hall. "Guess what?" Michal said. "We just saw one of the cameramen interviewing some of the new *olim*. One of the families who came has a little boy named Gilad. They said he was born a week after Gilad Shalit was captured and that's why they named him Gilad. I guess they wanted to be in *solidariut* with him, or however you say it in English."

"Solidarity," I told Michal.

"That's cool!" Eitan said.

"We'd better get back to our seats," Hadas urged everyone. "The man on the stage is saying we should all sit down so the speeches can begin."

Although the place was packed with nearly a thousand people, the seats we had saved were still waiting for us when we got back. "I'm glad nobody took our places," I said, sitting down next to a red-headed Israeli woman who was sipping coffee from a Styrofoam cup.

"Some people looked at your seats and were trying to decide if they could sit here or not," the woman told me in Hebrew. "I told them it looked like they weren't available. So they left."

"*Todah rabbah*," I thanked the woman. "How did you like the welcome we gave out there?"

"It was something else! I had no idea it would be like this," she said, her eyes shining. "We're here to pick up my sister's son who just made *aliyah* with these other people today." She pointed to the teenage boy sitting between her and her husband. "He's only going to be with us for a few weeks, because he decided to go right into the army. He wants to serve Israel and his people."

"Wow!" I leaned forward to talk to the young man. "That's pretty amazing," I told him, switching to English. Despite the baseball cap he was wearing, I thought he looked like he could already be a soldier in the IDF, with his crew cut and strong build. "How's your Hebrew?" I asked.

"Not so good," the boy answered with a shy smile. "But I'll pick it up quickly when I get into the army."

"We live on a kibbutz, but my sister left Israel years ago," the aunt told me. "She and her family live in America.

But he," the woman gave her nephew a little pat on his arm, "he wanted to live in Israel. We're very proud of him!" She was all smiles now. I saw the uncle nod his head in agreement.

Hadas gave me a nudge. "Ema, we're supposed to be quiet now, the guy with the microphone is waiting to speak."

"I can't see anything," Eitan complained. "Can I sit on the floor up in front?"

"Yes," Yehuda said. "But make sure you come back before the end so we don't have to look for you when it's time to leave."

"Ladies and gentlemen, *shalom*," a British-sounding accent came over the loudspeakers. Everyone quieted down. "*Boker tov.* Good morning and welcome! My name is Danny Oberman, executive vice-president of operations for Nefesh B'Nefesh." All eyes and ears turned to the podium in the center of the stage.

"It's my honor and privilege," Mr. Oberman went on, "to welcome the 232 *olim*, including 22 new IDF soldiers and 100 children, who arrived on today's flight. To each and every one of you, allow me to be among the first to welcome you home!"

The hall filled with cheers and applause from the audience. I clapped enthusiastically along with everyone else.

Mr. Oberman said a few words and then introduced Nefesh B'Nefesh co-founder Rabbi Yehoshua Fass. Rabbi Fass' light-brown closely-trimmed beard grazed the microphone as he spoke: "This is the day that G-d created for us to rejoice and be happy in. He kept us alive, and sustained us and enabled us to reach this occasion. *Mazel tov*! To our precious new *olim* —welcome home!"

When the applause died down, the young rabbi continued. "No one's *aliyah* should ever be viewed as a fulfillment of an individual odyssey or journey. When you stepped foot [here], your grandparents and your great-grandparents and your great-great-grandparents who were yearning and praying and dreaming of this moment, were with you... It's humbling to think that [we have] the privilege of living something that we've been dreaming for, for hundreds of years."

After Rabbi Fass finished his speech, Israel's minister of transportation, Yisrael Katz, greeted the *olim*. Then short, balding Natan Sharansky ran up onto the stage. I remembered how, more than two decades ago, Israelis had protested and demonstrated for Sharansky who, was at the time, a Soviet refusenik and Prisoner of Zion. For years, he and other Jewish refuseniks had fought tirelessly and courageously for the right to emigrate from the Soviet Union so they could come to live in Israel.

The Israeli public had been overjoyed when Sharansky was finally released and allowed to be re-united with his wife Avital, who'd made it to Israel some years before him. Euphoric crowds had welcomed him as he landed, a free man, in Israel's Ben Gurion Airport. Together at last with his people, Sharansky had become a hero in the eyes and hearts of Israelis and Jews worldwide.

Now, standing on the stage before us in his tan short-sleeved, button-down shirt, Natan Sharansky, chairman of the Jewish Agency for Israel, was welcoming the newest group of Israeli immigrants. "I'm coming here today, not because I'm a chairman or [because] before that I was a [government] minister," he began in his heavy Russian-accented English. "But I'm coming because I want again and again to enjoy that moment that I enjoyed when I made *aliyah* and I felt that all the people of Israel were with me. I want to feel it again—that all of us are together with you. All of us are so excited and so happy that you came!"

I sat up straight in my seat as I focused on the

remarkable man speaking into the microphone.

"Each of you is finishing a two thousand-year journey [in the Diaspora], and is coming home. Now each of you is going to different places here... You will see that [you have] a tour guide—the Bible. You really did come to those places from which your ancestors were forced to leave two thousand years ago... You will feel yourself a part of the history, but also you will feel that everything you're doing will be building the future for all the Jewish people..."

Sharansky paused for the audiences' loud applause to die down. "Together, with the best of what you are bringing with yourselves, and with the best of what we brought from the former Soviet Union, and with the best that they brought with the Ethiopian *aliyah,* and with the best that the Sabras did while building this land—we together will make our home better and better, and freer, and more and more enjoyable for every newcomer." At the end of his speech, more excited applause and high-pitched whistles filled the hall.

When everyone quieted down, the CEO from El Al Airlines praised the new arrivals and thanked them for making *aliyah.* Then, Nefesh B'Nefesh co-founder Tony Gelbart approached the microphone.

"It's you, the *olim,* who make the difference," Gelbart told the hundreds of pairs of eyes facing him. "There's something like ninety-three kids on this flight. I want you to stand up." Wearing a suit and tie, glasses and a crocheted yarmulke on his head, Tony was gesturing with his arms for all the children to rise from their seats. "Kids—stand up and yell. Scream!" The cameras in the room turned away from the stage and faced the children of all ages and sizes who were now standing and shouting, waving their hands or flags. Ronit decided to join them, raising her arms up in the air and flailing them happily from side to side.

"You know," Tony Gelbart spoke loudly into the microphone to restore calm, "I love the parents and grandparents making *aliyah*. But the kids are the future. Now, there are over twenty young men and women here going right into the army." Tony pointed towards the audience. "Can you guys stand up, wherever you are?" I exchanged smiles with the red-headed aunt sitting next to me, as her nephew stood up proudly with the other young men and women. The hall came to life even more than before with wild whoops and loud clapping for the soon-to-be Israeli soldiers.

"You young children," Gelbart was now nearly shouting, "take a look at these older young children," he instructed. "They're the ones who are going to be protecting you and protecting this country. And I'm sure you'll have your chance to serve this country in many, many ways. Each one of you is a hero of Israel. Each one of you will make the path for the other people who are going to follow you. And believe me, with the help of the minister of immigrations, Sofa Landver, with the help of Natan Sharansky, with the help of all the people in both places, and with El Al—they will come! Believe me. I'm telling you, there's a list... There's twenty thousand more people who are already ready to get on the planes!"

Leaning his thin frame against the dais, Mr. Gelbert spoke more softly now. "We want you to do one favor for us at Nefesh B'Nefesh. When you go out to Israel and the people say, 'What are you doing here? Why did you come here?' just tell them one thing," Gelbart raised his voice again. "That you are living proof that Zionism is alive in the world, and that Israel is your home and that Jews are always coming home!" Loud whistling and cheering rang throughout the room.

As Tony Gelbert left the stage and the audience became calm again, Sofa Landver, originally from Russia and serving as Israel's Minister of Immigrant Absorption, came up to the podium. Wearing a black dress with a white tailored jacket and large dangling earrings, Sofa greeted everyone in her Russian-accented Hebrew. "The Jewish nation's home for Jews who are scattered all over the world is here," she pointed down, "in Israel."

After Sofa finished speaking, Rabbi Fass, Natan Sharansky, Tony Gelbert and the others gathered on the stage with her. They invited one of the new families from the Nefesh B'Nefesh flight to join them as well. Hugs and handshakes went all around as the mother, father and their four children, all wearing Nefesh B'Nefesh sports caps, came up onto the stage. Sofa handed the father his official Israeli immigrant certification booklet. Cameras flashed and clapping and music filled the room as the father opened the thin, pocket-size booklet and, with a huge grin, proudly held it high for everyone in the audience to see.

When the stage cleared, the soldiers who'd given flags to everyone coming off the buses filed to the front of the room and formed two straight rows near the platform. Eitan jumped up from his seat on the floor and ran over to Yehuda. "This is great!" he enthused.

We all stood with the soldiers for the national anthem, "*HaTikvah*."[134] Michal reached behind Hadas and tapped me on the arm. "Ema, will there be another ceremony like this that we can come to again?"

I nodded. "There will be many."

Standing with their hands at their sides, the soldiers began singing "HaTikvah." Everyone in the room, both new and veteran Israelis, quickly joined in. Many stood straight, while others swayed, and some sang with their eyes closed. Leaning forward, I looked down our row of

---

[134] "The Hope," Israel's national anthem.

seats at my family. I could see Yehuda and Eitan holding hands as they sang. Yael had Ronit in her arms and was gently swaying from side to side. Michal and Hadas were watching the soldiers by the stage and singing along with them. The whole room filled with emotion as the words to "HaTikvah—The Hope" resonated throughout the hall.

> As long as deep in the heart,
> The Jewish soul yearns,
> And forward to the East,
> The eye looks towards Zion.
> Then our hope is not lost.
> The hope of two thousand years
> To be a free nation in our land,
> The land of Zion and Jerusalem.

We were Jews of every age and background, singing together. We all loved Israel and we all wanted to be a part of it. I was feeling especially happy, and also thankful, that I belonged to this big, diversified family whose roots were lodged deep in the Land. We all had hope that one day our country would be strong and unified, and that we'd have real and lasting peace. Scanning the room, I was also hopeful that many more like us would come and help make that happen.

"HaTikvah" ended and the music faded. More hugging and energized conversation punctuated the end of the welcoming ceremony. I stood watching the two rows of soldiers slowly disperse, as everyone began leaving the hall.

"I'm glad we did this, Ema," Yael told me.

"Me too!" Ronit bounced in her big sister's arms. "It was fun."

We walked down the wide corridors of the old airport terminal. Filled with tired but happy and excited people, the place felt alive.

"Ema," Hadas said, as she and I followed more slowly behind the others, "Thank you for bringing us."

"You're very welcome." I linked arms with my daughter.

"And something else, Ema." Hadas paused and tilted her head affectionately towards me. "Thank you for coming to live in Israel."

I smiled and kissed Hadas on the cheek. Then, feeling the light inside me growing even brighter, I looked ahead towards the rest of the people, as together we all moved forward.

EPILOGUE

(February 2015)

"Sorry, but it's still my turn to be on it," Eitan said.

"No, it's not!" Ronit, who had just turned ten, was standing impatiently next to her fifteen-year-old brother, ready to occupy the seat she was hoping he'd leave. "You've been on it for a long time already. It's my turn now."

"Both of you are going to have to come back later," Michal told her younger siblings, "because I said a long time ago that I would be needing it now. So actually, it's my turn."

The kids were arguing over the computer, as usual. I decided to put an end to it. "Okay guys, I have to check my e-mail. Everyone please go do something else."

"But, I'm in the middle here," Eitan said, sulking.

"Well, I'm after Ema," Michal said decisively.

"It's not fair! I never get it when I want it," Ronit followed Eitan and Michal out of the room.

With a sigh, I sat down on the padded swivel chair in front of the screen and clicked onto my mailbox. There was one new letter waiting for me. It was from Carol! Settling back in the chair, I began to read.

Hi Shelly,

I hope all is well with you and your family. I just wanted to let you know that the other day I got an e-mail from Diana. She said that she's been thinking a lot about Israel and decided to go for another visit on a special ticket she was able to get right away. She wrote that one of her closest friends just made aliyah and now she's also been discussing with her husband about the possibility of her family moving there. She asked me for your e-mail address so that she could write you and hopefully see you when she's in Jerusalem next week. Mrs. Weissberg is so envious! Diana wrote that her mother would also love to go on the trip, but that she isn't completely back to herself yet. So she'll have to be satisfied with seeing Diana's pictures and videos.

Now, for even more exciting news: After I read Diana's letter, I told Fran about it. And, as you know, Fran and I really want to see Israel too. We've been talking about flying there together for a while. And now it looks like we're actually going to do it! We've already begun looking into flights with El Al airlines and we hope to make the trip in the late spring. I'd love to experience some of the holidays you told us about that are celebrated around that time. Do you think it would be possible to participate in a Passover Seder or maybe join in the flag-dance march to the Wall? I didn't think it would work out for me to go so soon, but now that we're about to book our tickets—I'm getting really excited!

Of course, we want to get together with you, and meet your family and hopefully some of your friends. We're both looking forward to a reunion. One thing will be different though. We won't be sitting and listening to your stories. We'll be having our own Israel experiences and our own stories to relate to others!

So what do you say? Is it a date?

Hope to hear from you soon,

Carol

I twirled once in the chair and then got up to find Yehuda. He was sorting out some papers at the dining room table.

"Guess what?" I sat down next to him.

"What?" His eyes stayed focused on the papers he was shuffling.

"Looks like we'll be having some special visitors soon."

Yehuda let the papers drop and looked at me. "Really?" He knew exactly who I meant. I had told him many times about my "therapy-story friends" and how I hoped to see them in Israel one day.

"Yep," I answered. "And you know what else?"

"No. What?"

"They're not expecting it, but when they get here, I've got a whole slew of new stories for them! I can fill them in on the last bunch of years that we didn't get to and bring them up to date."

"Hey, maybe I could get in on this with you guys," Yehuda said. "I'm a good storyteller."

"Hmmm," Lowering my head, I squinted and pretended to be thinking hard. "Well... okay." I looked up at Yehuda. "But you'll have to come up with your own unique, momentous or captivating Israel stories to tell. You've got some of those, don't you?"

"Of course. Doesn't everyone in this country?" Yehuda grinned.

"Yep." I nodded. "Just look at *me*. I've got so many Israel stories to tell... I could write a book!"

www.ingramcontent.com/pod-product-compliance
Lightning Source LLC
Chambersburg PA
CBHW052345020726
47503CB00001B/116